D0916914

# FEY BLOOD

## An Amarah Rey, Fey Warrior Novel

Harmony A. Haun

ISBN: 978-1-7363432-2-7 Paperback
ISBN: 978-1-7363432-3-4 e-book
ISBN: 978-1-7363432-5-8 Hardback

First edition January 2021
Second edition March 2021
Third edition April 2022

Author Contact: harmonyhaunauthor@gmail.com

## An Amarah Rey, Fey Warrior Books

AWAKEN

FEY BLOOD

DARK TEMPTATIONS

# DEDICATION

This book is dedicated to all of the readers who survive this crazy life by diving into a better one. You're not alone.

# FEY BLOOD

## An Amarah Rey, Fey Warrior Novel

# Word Definitions

All "The Unseen" words are English words translated into Estonian. Click on each hyperlinked (ebook) word to listen to the pronunciation from Google.

Alfa: Alpha
Beeta: Beta
Esimene: First
Kaitsja: Protector
Konsiilium: Council
Libahunt: Werewolf
Maa Family: Earth Fey
Müstik Family: Mystic, First Fey
Õhk Family: Air Fey
Täiskuu: Full Moon
Täitjad: Enforcers
Tulekahju Family: Fire Fey
Ülim: Supreme
Valvur: Guardian
Vanemad: Elders
Vesi Family: Water Fey
Võitleja: Warrior
Võltsimatu: Pure

# Amarah Rey Series Playlist

Listen to the entire series playlist here: Spotify

# Dangerous Love

Dangerously In Love by Beyonce

It's only been two months since my entire life has been turned upside down. Only two short months since I learned about the hidden, magical, mystical preternatural world that exists right in front of my eyes. A world full of beauty and magic, but in the blink of an eye can turn evil and dangerous. My world. Then again, the regular human world isn't so different. The stakes are just a bit higher in The Unseen. If we fail, if we let evil win, we're not the only ones who will perish. Evil won't stop at the human world just because they're oblivious to it. If we fail, no one will survive.

I had been thrown in… no, aggressively pushed, into the deep, turbulent end of the pool. I've barely been able to keep my head above water. I still struggle to believe I have power and am capable of...only God knows what. Literally. I grew up believing I was human, and being human comes with a lot of limitations. I'm still having a hard time getting out of my head and out of my human thoughts. They hold me back and everyone is frustrated, myself included. Even if they don't say anything to my face, they don't have to, I can feel the frustration. I can see it.

I have come a long way in only two months, but demons and betrayal are unrelenting. They don't care that I still need training wheels. They aren't going to take a break and wait until I'm ready for them. Unfortunately, that's just not how the world works. Either of them. So, I work hard. I push hard in all of my training. I'm getting very good at fight training, which is weird because I've never considered myself to be a fighter. Now I'm the official Võitleja, Fey Warrior. Oh, how life throws you curveballs! I'm getting better at accessing my power, but it has so much more potential. *I* have so much more potential. That part of my training is all mental, and well...we've discussed that. So...

Some people have already played on my naivety and ignorance. Someone I let myself get vulnerable with, someone I thought I could trust with no hesitation, is now being held in a cell at Headquarters. Also, someone I thought was trying to befriend me early on, was just trying to alienate me from those that would help me the most. Turns out, she's unhappy with the Queen and wants to be the one calling the shots. Her betrayal led to several attempts on my life and the death of six Fey from the Tulekahju Family, the Fire Fey. Princess Aralyn of the Õhk Family, Air Fey, is still out there, somewhere. She's still scheming and plotting her grab at the throne and who knows what else. Yeah, I've been way too gullible and am beating myself up for it.

In all of the madness, I did manage to finally get one thing right. I've finally accepted the unnatural, magnetic connection I have with Logan instead of running away from it. I still don't understand it, he doesn't either, but it's our reality. It's our normal, and it has been one mind-blowing, glorious month since I finally got out of my head and followed my heart. We all know how foolish and reckless the heart can be, and considering my previous character misreads, my caution was necessary.

Yet with Logan, it's the complete opposite of judging a book by its cover. The connection we have lets me know the whole story, down to his core. He can't hide from me and I can't hide from him. We can literally feel each other's feelings completely.

No guessing.

No wondering.

No BS.

It's honest and pure, but can also be extremely distracting. We both have the power to block the connection when we need to. We still don't know the full possibilities of our connection, but just like everything else in my life, I'm figuring it out as I go.

I'm sitting at the kitchen island, coffee in hand, eyes only for the six-foot, muscular and flawless man standing at the stove, making us breakfast. My little dog, Griffin, also has eyes only for him, but for *very* different reasons. Logan is wearing a pair of basketball shorts, low on his hips, hugging a nice, firm ass. I know what that ass feels like under my hands when his gorgeous, naked body is on top of me. Just thinking about it sends the butterflies flying in my stomach and throbbing between my legs.

Logan turns around and catches my eye. He gives me that half-smile that means he knows exactly how he affects me, and then he slowly walks toward me. A circle birthmark and small scar on his chest, over his heart, are the only things marking his otherwise flawless body. My eyes slide lower, tracing that v until it vanished under the shorts sending my heart into fits. He spins the stool around, places one hand on each armrest, and leans that perfect body into me. His dark brown hair is tousled from sleep, but his green eyes are alert and utterly serious as he looks at me.

"You keep thinking those thoughts and I'll burn breakfast," his voice is deep and seductive and his words caress my skin. He really is perfect.

I place my coffee cup down on the counter and take my time running my hands up his arms, appreciating the muscles he works hard for. "Who needs food for breakfast anyway? I can just have *you*," I bite my lip as I look up at him.

He gently pulls my lip out from under my teeth. "You already did," he chuckles as he leans in closer.

"What about dessert?" I find his soft lips with mine.

He slips his big hands under my thighs and lifts me easily onto the island counter. The feeling of his fingers digging into my skin quickens my breaths. I wrap my legs around his trim waist, run my hands through his hair at the back of his neck, and lose myself in the kiss.

This has been my life over the past month and my only regret is that I fought it for so long. I'm entirely consumed by my feelings for Logan, and not just the physical ones, though they are always a look or word away. When we're together, nothing else matters.

Nothing.

And that's dangerous because the reality is, too much matters. There's too much at stake, too many threats, and a million responsibilities. We can't afford to be distracted. It could be way worse than a burnt breakfast. It could be fatal.

Logan is the one to pull away. He always has way more control and willpower than I do. Then again, he has had *centuries* of practice. How can a girl compete with that?

"As I was saying," he gives me that teasing half-smile and chucks my chin, "breakfast is the most important meal of the day."

He walks back over to the stove, giving me his muscled back for my viewing pleasure, and busies himself with cooking.

"Breakfast isn't the most important meal. If it was, then people wouldn't have success with intermittent fasting. Every meal is important," I sigh. Breakfast is a moot point. I'm just trying to think of anything else besides what I have planned for the day.

Logan senses my mood change, as always. "Are you sure you still want to do this? You don't have to, you know. You don't owe him anything, Amarah."

I sigh again, "I know, but I need to see him. I need to see his face and ask him why. It doesn't make sense to me. I know you don't get it, but I need to understand. I want the truth and I want closure. I can't get that if I don't go see him in person."

Logan walks over to the island with two plates, "c'mon, you need to eat."

I hop off the counter and go back to my seat. "I'm not even hungry," I grumble. I'm feeling grouchy now and it isn't fair to Logan. Then again, life's very rarely fair.

"You need your strength."

He's right. He's usually right, and I hate to admit it. He made us veggie omelets and sweet potato hash browns. It looks and smells delicious. I love that we we're both into fitness and staying healthy, most of the time. The second I take the first bite, my hunger emerges from my grumpy cave. I *am* hungry and my body needs the fuel. Damn the mind for being so stubborn sometimes.

We finish eating breakfast and cleaning up the kitchen and I head to the bedroom to get ready to leave the house. While we're home, I'm usually in a tank top and boy short style underwear. I'd switch to the unattractive, oversized sweats and long-sleeve tees for winter. We'll see how much Logan loves me then. It's late September, and it's still warm. One of the things I love about Albuquerque is that we get all four seasons, very distinctly, and we're still at the tail-end of summer.

I put on a pair of black jean shorts, a black t-shirt with white Harry Potter glasses and lightning scar, black sneakers and I'm good to go. Once upon a time, I thought I wore black to mourn my broken heart, but turns out that's just what I buy more of. As the Fey Warrior, black is the best thing to wear anyway. You can blend in and hide with the shadows at night. I even dyed my hair back to my natural dark brown. The fire red had been fierce, and I miss it, but it isn't practical.

I walk out into the living room and Logan is sitting on the couch with Griffin, waiting for me. He's wearing dark blue jeans, a red v-neck t-shirt, and black and red sneakers. The man makes t-shirts the sexiest damn thing I've ever seen. They hug his chest and arms like a second skin. The red of his shirt is the perfect contrast to his caramel skin but I don't think he could look bad in anything. His hair is combed to messy perfection. It's grown out since I met him and is longer all around. His hair has a natural curl to it and it comes down longer in the front, just above his right eyebrow.

I walk over to the couch, sit down on the arm, and lean into him. I run my fingers through his hair, "I love your hair like this."

"Really? I was thinking it needs a trim."

"No way! It's perfect." I still can't believe this gorgeous man is here with me. And it isn't just that. He *loves* me. I still have to pinch myself sometimes to make sure I'm not dreaming.

"You're perfect," he whispers as he lays a gentle kiss right below my ear. "So perfect I could *eat* you." His teeth graze against my skin causing me to sink further into him. The memory of his face between my legs earlier that morning brings a moan from my throat. Then he pulls away. "Are you ready?"

"Oh, you evil, evil, man. You're going to pay for that later." The gleam in his eyes and his devious smile says he's looking forward to it. I sigh, "I suppose. I just want to get it over with."

Logan usually drives us around, but today, I want to drive. I open the garage door and it's the perfect picture of his and hers. His black Chevy Silverado 1500 and my Black Camaro SS. We complement each other in literally every area of our lives. It's more than just our connection, it's our style, our taste in music, our personalities. It's almost like fate. We are meant to be together. Considering my background, the truth about my conception, perhaps I'm not far off in thinking that we were destined to find each other.

I pull onto I-40 heading West at a quick 70 mph. I signal over to the far-left lane and keep it at a steady 80 mph. I drive a Camaro for a reason. I love the speed but keep it safe. Again...*most* of the time. I'm not in the mood for talking, so I turn up the stereo, and Three Days Grace's song, *Right Left Wrong*, blares through the speakers. It's the perfect song for how I'm feeling about getting close to the wrong person. Music always has the words and the feel. Always.

I finally exit on Rio Grande and head towards Old Town. I find a parking spot easily, which is a miracle, and put the car in park. I'm not looking forward to confronting Andre, but I have to. I shouldn't have even waited this long. The truth is, a part of me feels guilty about using him. I didn't do it intentionally, but I did it nonetheless. I had been running away from Logan and Andre was there to comfort me and give me what I craved at the time. Someone choosing me for me, not because of some crazy connection. It isn't fair to lead Andre on, although, in my defense, I was always upfront about my feelings for Logan. Still, feelings got involved, on both ends. I've definitely come to care for Andre. The *real* Andre, that he never showed to anyone. He hides behind jokes and flirting as a way to keep everyone at arm's length. Why? Why else? He's been hurt badly before and doesn't want it to happen again. Hence, why I'm feeling so damn guilty about being that person, but that's not the only reason why I'm here, and that's not the reason he's locked up.

Andre has been accused of being the one to tell the traitor, Aralyn, about the dragon scales. They're the Fire Fey's...*family heirloom* if you will, and they've been hiding them in secret for generations upon generations. What Andre did is a huge betrayal to his people. He's locked up for working with the traitor. The traitor who tried to have me killed! And I had let him get *very* up close and personal. He violated my trust. Hell, he lost everyone's trust, and the Andre I know, or thought I knew, would never have done that. That's why I need to talk to him. I need to know why.

"Amarah, hey, come back to me," Logan is gently shaking me.

Reality slowly comes back into focus. "Sorry. I was just thinking about everything that's happened. You know, I'm not blameless in all of this. I think that's why it's taken me so long to do this."

"What do you mean?"

"Andre fell for me and I let him. I let things go too far. I knew what he was feeling and I didn't stop it. Hell, I was confused about what I was feeling too, with our connection, Hallana and your past. I just...I wanted something *normal* and simple. I wanted to believe that's what I wanted." I shake my head and finally meet his unwavering, patient gaze, "but...the second I saw you again, I couldn't deny it. I tried," I snort. "Lord knows I *tried* to fight my feelings for you. But the second I saw you again, I turned my back on him and I let him *fall*. That wasn't fair to him."

"Are you regretting your choice to be with me?" His eyes watch my reaction closely.

I know he's asking because of all the complicated emotions he must be feeling from our connection. We're still figuring it out and emotions aren't always easy to decipher. Especially mixed and complicated ones. Still, how can men be so dumb sometimes? So insecure?

I scoff, “you’re joking right? You can’t *seriously* be asking me if I regret being with you.”

“I can feel your regret. No BS, remember?” His eyes are guarded as he waits for my answer.

“My regret is for *hurting* Andre. For leading him on in the first place when I could have, *should* have, stopped it. I may have been confused about our link and your history but...” I lean over and reach for his face, “Logan, there was never any other option. Connection or not, I know I was always meant to be with you. You’re like the sun in my sky, or in your case, the moon,” I smile. “Just one look from you, one smile, and I melt. The way I feel about you, honestly, scares me sometimes. I feel like I’ll never be able to get enough of you, and with all the danger in our lives, the only thing that scares me is the thought of losing you. I love you Logan Lewis, and I need you to know that.”

“You’re not going to lose me.” He brushes my hair out of my face, his gaze heavy and heated, “Amarah Rey Andrews, I am so in love with you.”

We both lean in for the kiss and my heart feels like a stone in my chest. It’s so full of love, and need, and emotion, it’s almost painful. This man is everything to me, and I barely know him. It scares me how much I loved him, need him, want him. I’m scared of not only losing him but also losing myself. Love is a dangerous, dangerous thing, and I’m dangerously in love with him.

I get it, Queen Bey, I get.

# Guilty Conscience

Whose Side Are You On by Tommee Profitt, Ruelle

I plan on speaking to Andre, quickly, getting my answer and closure, and then leaving. So, I hadn't alerted the Queen to our visit but that didn't mean she doesn't know. We entered the underground Headquarters through the San Felipe de Neri Church. No one approached us or stopped us, and it would seem security is lax and that Headquarters is extremely unprotected, but that's so far from the truth.

I've learned that there are cameras on every corner of Old Town, surrounding the Church, at every entrance and several more inside. I'm sure we had been spotted as soon as we entered the streets of Old Town and had been watched as we parked and approached the Church. No doubt the Queen had already been alerted to our presence.

As Võitleja and Kaitsja, we can come and go here as we please. In fact, I have a room here and Logan lives here, although he basically just lives with me now. We went zero to a hundred, real quick! And I'm not complaining. My room here at Headquarters is beautiful, and I would like to use the natural hot spring at some point, but my house is my home. It's mine. It's where I'm most comfortable, and luckily, the Queen doesn't mind. In fact, most Fey have their own places and some even have human jobs. All Fey can use glamour, if needed, to hide their Fey features around humans. Some Fey, like myself and the Queen, don't need to use glamour. Either way, humans are blissfully oblivious to us.

I'm grateful for Logan as we walk down several tunnels and hallways that make up the immense underground tunnel system that runs under the city and into the Sandia Mountains. I've been studying the labyrinth, but it's a lot to learn, and I haven't had the hundreds of years of practice that Logan has. I follow his lead physically but he's following mine in every other way. He's giving me the silence I need to think and stay focused on my task at hand.

We finally come to a stop in front of an opening with a hallway lost to shadows. The dungeon is not lit or marked in any way. No one would have any idea there are cave-like rooms that have been turned into cells at the end of this unremarkable and dark hallway.

"Do you want me to come with you?" Logan asks.

I laugh sarcastically, "yeah, cause that will go over well. Bring the guy I chose with me to confront the guy who wants to be with me. No, but thank you. I need to do this alone."

He nods, "I'll be here when you're done."

"Thank you," I say automatically. No flirting. No games. He knows what this is costing me. He always seems to know when to push and when to pull, and for that, I'm grateful.

I'm distracted as I think of what I want to say to Andre. Will he even want to talk to me after all this time? Tough luck, he *has* to. He needs to explain himself to me. I should have come sooner, but he has to understand how betrayed I feel. If he doesn't, he's about to. I enter the dark hallway, and it's not too far in, before the first turn comes up and I lose what little light streams in from the opening. I access my power and bring a flame to life in the palm of my hand.

I found out I'm a Master of Fire by sheer force last month. While I was training with the Fire Fey, Aralyn had sent a demon attack and we were caught off guard, completely unprepared, and greatly outnumbered. We would have all been slaughtered if I hadn't been able to *finally* break through and use my power. I'm Müstik Fey, the first Fey Bloodline to be created on Earth. We can slightly control all four of the elements, but we're not Masters of anything. I shouldn't be able to be a Master of Fire, causing everyone to be confused. Except for me and the Queen.

My mother, the Queen's sister, died giving birth to me. She gave me her life-force because I was created not conceived the natural way. God sent Archangel Michael to Bless my mother with me, to be used as a weapon against the demons.

Against evil.

But you can't create life out of nothing, so my mother gave her life for mine. A life for a life. Why my mother? Well, it was her mother, my grandmother, who created the rip in the atmosphere that allowed the demons to access Earth. So now it's the Fey's responsibility to control the rip and contain evil on Earth, and because they had slowly been losing the war...ta-da!

They got me.

Only the Queen and I know my secret. No one else, not even Logan, knows that I'm half Angel. I'm the first of my kind and we're in uncharted waters. We have no idea what I'm capable of and how powerful I can become. The Queen and I keep this secret to keep me safe. We don't know what would happen if the truth got out. I'm sure others would want to use me, weaponize me for their benefit, conduct tests on me, use my blood. Who knows? People can be quite creative and imaginative when they want power. So, the secret is being kept from everyone, even though it's really, really hard to deal with the questions and suspicious glances, and even harder to lie to Logan.

My flame lights up the path a couple of feet in front of me. It's enough to guide me down the tunnel with all its twists and turns. I finally see a faint glow up ahead. As I get closer, I turn one last corner and I'm suddenly standing in a fairly large room. It's decently lit, so I close my fist around my flame and pull my power back to extinguish it.

There are three smaller caves carved out on each side with bars installed to enclose them. Six cells made to hold all kinds of preternatural beings. I have no idea who, or what, is being held here, or which cell Andre is in, so I open up to my power and send it searching for his energy. This room has terrible energy.

Anger.

Sadness.

Desperation.

Madness.

It feels like it will drain the happiness right out of me. I don't want to stay here longer than necessary. I find Andre in the last cell to the left. I quickly pull my power back and cut myself off from the room's nasty energy. I sigh and walk to the cell, both determined and apprehensive.

Andre is sitting on the stone bench that has been left purposefully when the cells had been carved out. He looks up as I approach the bars.

My heart sinks in my chest.

The normally, well-groomed and handsome baby-face that I'm used to seeing is lost to overgrown hair. His clothes are the same I had last seen him in and they're covered in dirt from sitting and laying on the ground. It breaks my heart to see him like this, but I have to be strong, and remember why I'm here. Why *he's* here. He betrayed us. He betrayed *me*.

"Amarah?" He asks with suspicion. His voice is hoarse, as if he hasn't used it in a while.

I'm standing about a foot away from the bars. I want to get closer, I want to reach out to him and make sure he's ok, but I somehow maintain my composure.

"Yes, it's me." My voice is empty of emotion. Cold.

"You finally came!" He tries to speak louder but his voice cracks. He clears it and tries again. "I knew you would."

There's such *hope* in his voice. He walks over and places his hands on the bars, as close as he could get. "I was starting to wonder a little but I knew you would come." He has a big, genuine smile that starts to thaw my heart instantly.

I can't see his dimple, but even covered in dirt and hair, there's no denying he's handsome. There's no denying my attraction to him. My attraction that clearly blinded me to his motives. I'm pissed and hurt and want answers, but seeing him again, and seeing him this way, tugs at my heart strings. My memories of him, my perception of him, hurts.

How often do we see what we want to see?

How often do we ignore the red flags in hopes of what *can* be?

How often do we fall in love with the potential?

I've wracked my brain over and over again, trying to replay every word, every memory, and I can't find where I went wrong with him? And it's driving me crazy.

"I'm not here for you, Andre. I'm here for *me*. I need answers. I need to know why," I cross my arms and hold my ground. I have to be strong.

I see the hope and happiness slowly drain from his eyes as he realizes this isn't going to be a pleasant visit. My heart sinks further in my chest, as I'm flooded with the memories of looking into those deep brown eyes. Not the eyes that tease with meaningless flirting, but the ones that had been open and vulnerable. His honest eyes had always taken my breath away, with their unique almond shape, slightly tilting up and outlined with the darkest, longest lashes I'd ever seen on a guy. They way he looked at me with those eyes...

Awe.

Passion.

Love.

I thought we had been healing each other. I'm such a fool.

"I see," he says sadly. "You came to judge me too."

I hate seeing his eyes reflect pain but I make myself look into them. As much as I've always wanted to take his pain away, this pain he's feeling now is his own doing, not mine.

"No, I came for answers and to understand why. I let myself be vulnerable with you. I trusted you! You even said yourself, no lies between us, yet this was the biggest lie of all! You *used* me. You betrayed me, Andre. How do you expect me to forgive you for that?"

"I'm sorry."

"You're sorry? Really? That's all you have to say to me? What was the plan you and Aralyn had, Andre? Were you supposed to try and kill me too?"

"What? No! What lies have they been telling you?" He sounds genuinely shocked.

"Don't start pointing the finger now, Andre. You're the one who lied to me! You're the one who used me! You made me believe in you! You made me care for you!" I'm so hurt I'm practically yelling at him from a foot away. Looking at him now, I hardly recognized him, and it isn't just because of his physical appearance.

"You fooled me into giving you a piece of my heart that I can never get back," I whisper, shocked at my own admission, "and I don't even know who the real Andre is."

"Amarah, I *never* betrayed you. *Never.* Everything I told you, everything I felt...everything I *feel*...is real. Yes, I should have told you about my past with Aralyn, but I would *never* hurt you. How can you believe that?"

I study him His eyes. His words. I let the silence spread between us for a minute. His eyes are pleading and his words are telling.

"What do you mean your *past* with Aralyn?"

"I used to sleep with Aralyn a long time ago. That's ancient history. I thought I loved her once upon a time but turns out it was one-sided and she was the one using me. Amarah, you have to believe me. I never meant for any of this to happen."

This doesn't make sense. "What exactly do you mean a *long* time ago? How long?"

"I dunno, it's been a couple of years. I swear I had no idea that she was plotting to take the crown. I'm telling you, she used *me*, not the other way around."

"So, you didn't know about her plans to kill me?"

"I swear, I didn't know *anything* she was planning. I was with her way before we even knew who you were."

"But you told her about the dragon scales. That part is true, right?"

He sighs, "yes, unfortunately, that part is true. We talked about a lot of things and she was *very* good at distracting me and seeming very innocent. Still, I'm not sure how she got me to tell her everything, even the Fire Fey's most precious, hidden secret, but she did. Amarah, it was like I *couldn't* lie to her. Like I had to tell her the truth when she asked questions. I know it doesn't make any sense but you have to believe me. I didn't just willingly give up the information. I would never betray my family, my *Blood* like that."

"What are you saying? That you were forced to tell her everything?" My mind is racing with his admission and the truth of his words.

"I don't know about... *forced,* because she never did anything like torture to gain information, but..." he shakes his head, "I would have never just blurted out about the scales. I still don't understand it. I don't know how or why I told her everything. It doesn't make sense to me."

"What about a spell? I don't know if this is my human side talking or if it is something that's real, but there are Witches, right? Could she have been working with a Witch and spelled you to tell the truth?"

He seems to think about it for a minute. "I honestly don't know, but that's the best possibility I've heard so far."

I know he's telling the truth, every word. It's hard to explain but part of my power is being like a human lie detector. I can sense energy. I just know, in my gut, when something feels off and not right. It's like a very heightened intuition and I haven't been wrong yet.

There had been attempts on my life, and an attack on the Fire Fey that left six people dead. The Queen, and especially Hallana, wants...no *needs*, someone to blame. It's part of the healing process and feeling like you're making progress in an otherwise fucked up situation with no leads. Andre is paying the price when he might be a victim just as much as the rest of us.

"I'm getting you out of here," I say. "We're going to figure this all out. There are more questions than ever, but why you would be working with Aralyn, is not one of them. You don't deserve to be in here anymore than the rest of us."

"How are you going to get me out? Hallana is hell-bent on blaming someone. I told her everything I told you, but she didn't care. She didn't hear a word I said."

"Have you spoken to the Queen?"

"No, only Hallana."

"There's our answer. Hallana hasn't told the Queen anything that you've said about any of it. She needs you to be the bad guy, Andre. Six of your people are *dead*. She needs someone to punish for that, but the Queen is fair. Once she knows the facts, and that you're innocent, she won't let you stay here and suffer. I won't let that happen either."

"Amarah," he looks at me with such hope and love in his eyes, "thank you."

"Don't thank me yet. Let's get you out of here first. I'll be back."

I can't handle the look in his eyes. He still loves me. I left him here to rot in this cell for a month, and the whole time he's been suffering, I've been living in bliss with Logan.

He's innocent.

I know it in my bones and I had turned my back on him. I claimed to have some sort of feelings for him, to care for him, but I left him to suffer the second it made my life easier. It had been easier to make him out to be the bad guy so I didn't have to be uncomfortable in the middle of him and Logan. In a situation that *I* created and put myself in. I betrayed Andre because I'm a coward and took the easy way out. I feel more guilt than ever. If I had just come to see him right away, none of this would have happened, and maybe we would have found a lead on Aaralyn too.

Fuck.

# A Lead

Just Say When by Walker Montgomery

Logan and I are in the throne room, sitting at the discussion table. I insisted on waiting to make sure Andre is ok. I left him to suffer in a cell for an entire month when he's just as innocent as the rest of us. I will not make the same mistake of leaving him *again*. Not until I know he's going to be ok.

The Queen listened to my story and the idea that Aralyn is working with a Witch. It isn't too hard to believe since she had gone to the Vampires for an alliance as well. Why wouldn't she also go to the Witches? She's desperate to become Queen and turns out, she's been on this mission for a lot longer than we originally thought. Who knows how deep and wide her treachery web is spun? It makes me more anxious and nervous about who I can and can't trust.

Hallana on the other hand is much harder to persuade. She and I had started as rivals, but that was mostly a lot of misunderstanding, and women being catty women. She trusts me with her life now, as I trust her with mine. Still, she's reluctant in agreeing to let Andre go. She needs someone to blame for everything that has happened. I don't blame her, but the rightful person to blame is nowhere to be found, and I refuse to let Andre pay any more of the price for something he didn't do. At least not intentionally.

She finally agreed to let him out and to let him return home. She promised there would be no retaliation, but that he has a lot to make up for. It's fair and it's the best that I can do for him.

Logan and I have been sitting in silence. I have too many thoughts swirling in my head to do much talking. Yet again, he gives me the space I need when I need it. He doesn't get uncomfortable in my silence.

He knows all about my brief relationship with Andre, not a relationship as in boyfriend and girlfriend, but as something more than just friends. I know he isn't one hundred percent comfortable with it, but I'm not one hundred percent comfortable with his past relationships either, so we're even. We've both made out choice.

I chose him.

He chose me.

There's no need to dwell on anything that came before us. Although, that's easier said then done when our pasts are a part of our present. Still, good communication and our connection to each other help keep us from spinning into crazy thoughts.

The door at the back of the room finally opens and the Queen walks in followed by Andre. As they reach us, I can see that Andre has showered. He's wearing clean clothes and his face is back to baby-face perfection. This is the Andre that I'm used to. I can't help it; I stand up as he walks up to me and throw my arms around him. He never hesitates as he wraps his arms around me and pulls me in.

"I'm so sorry this happened to you," I whisper. "I should have been there right away and this wouldn't have happened. I'm so sorry, Andre."

"This is not your fault, Amarah. This is all Aralyn. She is the one to blame. For *everything*."

I pull back from the hug. "I know, it's just…" I shake my head, "I shouldn't have left you there without talking to you first. I was just so shocked and felt so betrayed. I wouldn't have even had to feel that way if I had just let you speak your truth. I caused us both unnecessary pain."

"It was a month, Amarah, not a year or worse. Trust me, I've been through worse. I knew you would come. Thinking of you got me through every minute, and now I'm out, thanks to you," he says, as he gently touches the side of my face.

My heart skips a beat, I can't deny Andre means something special to me, and I also realize that nothing has changed for Andre the entire month he's been in the cell. He still looks at me like he's in love with me. Only, everything has changed for me in the past month. I'm wholehearted, head over heels, in love with Logan. There's no more uncertainty as there had been when I was with Andre before, and this is the reason why I had put off seeing Andre for this long.

I didn't want to face him.

Even though a part of me loves him, it just doesn't compare to what I have with Logan and I don't want to be the person to break Andre's heart. Even more than that, I don't want to be here in person to see it in his eyes. Ugh, I'm such a coward.

"Ahem," Logan clears his throat loudly from his seat behind me and brings me back to reality. No doubt he felt what I felt at that moment and didn't like it. If I were in his shoes, I wouldn't either.

"Let's sit down," I say nervously, and head back to my chair, next to Logan.

The Queen is at the head of the table to my right and Logan is on my left. Andre walks around the table and takes the seat directly opposite of me. He's in a position to clearly see Logan and me, *together*. Although nowhere he chose to sit would hide the fact, and I don't want to hide, it's just that I also don't want to flaunt it either. It is what it is. I chose Logan and I know it's the right choice, hands-down, no questions, but I don't need to make it harder than it has to be on Andre. I just hope Logan will follow my lead and not antagonize Andre like they're known to do to each other.

I have my hands clasped on top of the table as I lean on it, trying to be neutral. Logan leans onto the table too, reaches out, and cups my hands with his. It's a fairly innocent gesture, but I know he's making it clear to Andre that he's won. I'm his and he's claiming me but I also know that he's needing just a bit of reassurance. As gorgeous and perfect as he is, it's still hard for me to believe he gets jealous and insecure sometimes.

I unclasped my hands so I can lace my fingers with his. His large hands enveloping mine easily. I look up into his beautiful green eyes and I send as much reassurance as I can down our link and into my eyes. He gives me a little half-smile and I can't help but smile back.

He has me, completely.

Just this one simple look, this one simple touch, and I'm pulled into him like he's gravity. In an instant, the room around us is gone, it's just Logan and me, and nothing else matters.

So much for not flaunting.

"Amarah," the Queen's voice brings me back to the room. "Thank you for bringing this to my attention. I'm also feeling a little bit guilty that I did't talk to you myself sooner, Andre. I trusted your Princess to handle the situation, and now I see that it was not handled the way it should have been. For my part in it, or lack of my part in it, I am sorry."

"It's quite alright my Queen. As I told Amarah," he looks at me, his eyes slide to Logan, then our hands, and back to me. I can see the hurt in them, but there's nothing I can do. He knew what it was when he got involved. This situation is as much his fault as it is mine. I can't take the entire blame. He looks back at the Queen, "I have been through worse. It was only a month and the important part is, I'm out now. I will do everything in my power to make up for my part in all of this. We will catch Aralyn and make her pay for what she has done to all of us."

"Is there anything at all that you can tell us about Aralyn's plans? Was there anything you heard or saw during the time you spent with her?" The Queen asks.

"Trust me, I've been trying to remember anything that can help us since I was put into the cell, but..." he shakes his head, "it was such a long time ago, and I wasn't visiting her intending to *spy* on her. She was very careful and never said or did a thing to make me suspicious of her. Then again, like I said, I wasn't looking for anything."

"I understand, Andre," the Queen is being very gentle with him. No doubt not wanting to make the situation worse. But gentle won't get us answers.

"No," I interrupt. "I don't believe that. Andre, you are more than you let people believe. Aralyn used you and banked on the fact that you're just a flirt, someone who jokes constantly, and doesn't take anything seriously. I *know* that's not true. I know that's not you. You had to have seen something! Anything!"

"Amarah, I..."

"Think about it, Andre, if you felt like you *had* to tell her the truth, you must have been spelled somehow. Is there something that was always there, always the same, when you were with her? Maybe you drank something? Or ate something? There has to be something that she did to you or got close to you to affect you."

"Well, now that you mention it, there was something." I can see that he's digging deep into his memories, reliving his moments with her. "After we..." he hesitates, "after we had sex, she would always give me this chocolate. She said that a friend of hers made it and that it was like eating a piece of Heaven. She said it was the icing on top. Kind of like the saying that people smoke after sex, well, Aralyn fed me chocolate, and now that I thinking about it, I don't think I ever saw her eat any."

"That's good! That's helpful. There could have been something in the chocolate that made you reveal secrets and answer any question she asked honestly. Was there anything that could identify who made it? A wrapper? A bag or box it came in?" I ask eagerly.

"She always brought it over to me in a small tin. Now that I think about it, she never even touched the chocolate itself. She always handled the tin and I took the chocolate out myself. I do remember a design on the tin. It was like a..." he snaps his fingers, trying to think of the word, "like a...*sigil* or brand of some kind."

"That's good, Andre. Really good! Can you draw it for us?" The Queen asks excitedly.

He shrugs, "I can try."

"Good. I'll go get some paper. I'll be right back," the Queen says, as she hurries off and disappears behind the dais.

"I see some things have changed after all," Andre says coldly, as he sits back in his chair and crosses his arms.

"Andre, I'm sorry, but you knew what it was from the beginning. You knew this was always a possibility. I never lied to you about anything."

"Oh, and I did? Is that it?"

"Well, not a lie exactly, about Aralyn, but that's not what I'm talking about. That doesn't have anything to do with my decision to be with Logan."

"I can't help but think it does. If none of this happened, if I was still in your life over the past month, if you hadn't felt betrayed by me, would you have run into his arms?" He glares at Logan.

Logan lets go of my hand and leans aggressively onto the table in Andre's direction. I put my hand on his arm to pull him back. Not that I could hold him back. He let me.

"Logan, don't," I whisper.

He has a point. If he had still been an option, I may not have fallen quite so quickly into bed with Logan, but it would have happened, eventually. There's no denying the connection I have with Logan is stronger than anything else. No one and nothing can compare to it. Andre's unfortunate situation had just made that clear sooner rather than later.

"I don't know," I say, barely loud enough for anyone to hear.

This is what I was dreading. Being in the middle of these two men in my life. They both mean a lot to me and I don't want to hurt either one. Would I have run to Logan if Andre hadn't been locked up? Would that night have changed everything?

"I'm sorry, I never meant to hurt you. I do care about you, Andre..."

Andre puts his hand up. "Don't, just don't, Amarah. I don't need your pity."

I scoff, "my feelings for you and caring about you is *not* pity. How could you even say that?"

We don't get a chance to resolve any issues because the Queen is heading back with paper and a pen. Once back at the table, she glances at us, no doubt she can feel all the tension, but she doesn't say a word.

"Here, Andre. What symbol did you see on that tin?"

He sighs heavily, "it was such a long time ago, I don't know how accurate it will be but it was like an upside-down triangle, except the lines at the tip of the triangle kept going past each other, and they both ended in hooks. Then there was a *V* in the center of the hooks, at the bottom tip of the triangle. Then, I remember there being an *X* inside the triangle, towards the bottom, and the bottom ends of the x came outside of the triangle, and an *R* right in the middle toward the top."

He stares at it for a long time, then turns the paper around to face towards us. "Does this look familiar to anyone else?"

We all shake our heads. "I've never seen it before, but I'm sure someone has," the Queen says.

She copies the image on a second piece of paper and gives me one. "Amarah, you take one with you. Perhaps Valmont will recognize it, and you can take it with you as you continue your search for a Witch. Valmont may not recognize it but a Witch definitely has to. This looks like Witchcraft to me, although I'm no expert on the subject."

I take the piece of paper and stand up. Logan follows my lead. I don't want to sit here in this awkward tension longer than I have to.

"We'll find whoever this symbol belongs to my Queen, and we will find out what's going on. I'll keep you updated." I turn to Andre. "Andre, thank you. This is very helpful," I say quickly and then turn to walk away.

"Amarah," Andre stands up and I turn back around to look at him.

I know he's hurt, but the hurt is no competition for love. He still loves me and I just don't understand how or why he fell so hard, so quickly. The look in his eyes makes me uncomfortable because there's nothing I can do or say that will make that look ok. I can't give him what he wants. I couldn't before and sure as Hell, not now.

"Thank you, for everything. I owe you for saving me in more ways than one."

I scoff, "you don't owe me for anything, Andre."

"I do, and I will always be here for you." He doesn't even glance at Logan or seem to have any care in the world that he's standing right next to me. He has eyes only for me. "I'll wait for as long as it takes."

I don't know what the Hell to say to that, so all I say is, "I'll be in touch," and walk away from the table as fast as I can. I can feel their eyes on me as Logan and I leave. I cannot get out of this room fast enough.

I keep the speed walking pace out to my car. I don't feel comfortable until I'm safely locked inside. I rest my head on the seat, close my eyes, and let out a sigh that feels like fifty pounds has just been lifted off me.

Logan hasn't said a word, but now he leans over and brushes my hair behind my ear. "Hey, you ok?" He asks softly.

I open my eyes and look at him. I expected to see jealousy and hardness in his eyes, but what I see is genuine concern. I'm not prepared for that.

"You're not angry," it isn't a question, just the truth I see in his eyes.

"Why would I be?"

"You saw the way Andre looks at me, and he flat out said he would wait for me. That's not exactly him letting go."

"You can't control how he feels or what he wants to do. It's his life and he'll live it how he wants to. Why would I be mad at you for what he feels?"

"Because I'm the reason he feels that way. I put him, and you, in this awkward situation." I sigh, "and I know you felt what I felt earlier. I don't know how I would feel if I was in your shoes. Wait, that's a lie. Yes, I do know how I'd feel, and it wouldn't be pretty. I'm sorry you have to deal with all of this mess."

"You chose *me*, Amarah. I'm here with you, not him. I doubt he'll be the last to have feelings for you or be attracted to you. Hell, I think Valmont on some level is... *taken* with you, and I don't blame them. We can't control the outside world. All we can do is control this, us. As long as we have us, and it is honest, nothing and no one else matters."

"I will always choose you, Logan. No hesitation, no second thought, it's always going to be you for me."

"Ditto," he says, as he leans in for a kiss, but stops right before our lips met.

"I'm still eagerly waiting for my punishment from earlier. Perhaps you need reminding," he whispers against my lips, as his finger makes lazy, teasing circles around my nipple, causing them to harden and butterflies to erupt in my stomach. Then he gives one a gentle squeeze, causing me to suck in a breath, before he pulls back, denying me my kiss and his touch.

"Ass," I scowl at him and send all my sexual frustration slamming down our link at him.

He just chuckles and smiles, making me melt into my seat. Yeah, I made the right choice.

4

# Never Take A Moment For Granted

All Or Nothing by Theory of a Deadman

I call Emerson, Valmont's daytime contact, on the drive back home. I originally thought he was one of Valmont's top lieutenant Vampires, but turns out, he's human. He had been a Navy SEAL, and apparently, he's *very* dangerous. I'm not sure how he came to be employed by Valmont, and I don't see how *any* human can match up with Vampires and Werewolves, but hey, what do I know?

"Emerson," his deep voice answers on the first ring.

"Hey, Emerson. It's Amarah."

"Hey, Amarah. I was just getting ready to call you. You first, what's up?"

"I have a new lead, potentially for a Witch. I need to talk to Valmont. Can you have him call me when he, ummmm...wakes up, please?"

"Sure thing," he says nonchalantly, as if we're discussing the weather and not preternatural dealings.

"What did you want to talk to me about?" I ask.

"I finally heard back from the Albuquerque Coven. The Ülim has finally decided to meet with you and Valmont. Valmont will make arrangements and then he'll be in touch with you.

"It's about damn time they finally agree to meet us. It's only been a month! Alright, thank you, Emerson."

"No problem." He hangs up before I can say goodbye or anything else.

I guess that's all we needed to discuss. He must be busy, after all, he is handling the daytime dealings and schedule for one of the most powerful Virtuoso Vampires that exists. Basically, he's a Master Vampire. It's similar to the Fey Mastering their power, only for a Vampire, it takes much longer and the perks are pretty astounding...and terrifying. Good thing he's an ally. I just need to hold up my end of the bargain and find a Witch willing to help us. So far, no luck.

"The Albuquerque Coven is finally going to meet with you?" Logan asks. He has some pretty amazing abilities too, like Werewolf hearing.

"Yes, finally. I hope they will help us, because Valmont is starting to lose his patience, not that I blame him. He's held up his side of the alliance so far and I haven't delivered," I sigh.

"It's not your fault, Amarah. He knows that."

"If he knows it or not, doesn't mean he's willing to just let it be a one-sided alliance forever."

"I know, but it's only been one month and you have both been trying. He is failing to find a Witch right alongside you. Give it time. I know you'll get this done," he reaches over and grabs my hand. His warmth seeps into my skin, calming me.

"I seriously don't know how I would do any of this without you," I quickly glance at him and then back at the road. I can't afford to lose focus while driving, and with Logan, losing focus is as easy as breathing. It just happens.

"I'm not going anywhere," he squeezed my hand reassuringly. "What's the plan for the rest of the day?" He asks as

We're pulling into the driveway.

I sigh, "would you hate me if I just wanted to snuggle up with you on the couch, with some wine, and watch movies for the rest of the day?"

"One, I could never hate you, and two, I'll take any down-time with you that I can get. I know we won't always have this alone time together, you need to continue your training soon, so I'll take advantage of it while I can."

I park the car in the garage and we both get out and walk to the back of the car. Our bodies meet in the perfect, comfortable way they always do, as if our bodies were meant for each other. I wrap my arms around his neck as his large hands circled around my waist and I look up into his handsome face.

"So that's a yes then?"

"Yes. As long as I'm with you, I don't care what we are doing. Well, maybe we can do more than just watch movies all day," he wiggles his eyebrows at me and pulls my waist against his body so I can feel him growing hard between us.

My skin instantly heats with the feel of him against me and I blush, "I would say you're terrible, but it's like you were reading my mind, so what does that make me?"

"Beautiful," he whispers as he comes in for the kiss.

We stumble to the front door, tangled in each other and both laugh when we almost fall. I open the front door and his strong arms picked me up easily as he carries me inside.

He pushes me up against the wall and devours my mouth with his. His tongue is exploring my mouth like it's the first time he's tasting me. I tighten my legs around him and he steps in closer, grinding his hips into me. I can feel him straining against his jeans and I'm throbbing with need. I groan in frustration as my hands struggle to get his shirt off between our pressed bodies. He lowers me to the floor and it's a race to see who could undress who the fastest.

He spins me around and pins me, my cheek flush against the wall. My hips push back, away from the wall, my core desperately searching for contact. His large body looms over me as he leans into me. I can feel his erection pressed hard against my ass and his breath warm on my ear.

"You're mine, Amarah. All mine," he growls as his powerful hands dig into my waist and yank me against him.

His words strike me like a hammer on my chest and sena a hot trail of blazing fire straight down between my legs. I love that he's possessive. I love that he claims me, even in private. I want him to take what's his. More than that...I *need* him to.

I can feel him position himself to enter me but he doesn't. I try to push myself back onto him but his hand on my waist holds me firmly in place. A whimper, a plead, escapes my lips.

He rubs himself across my clit slowly, back and forth. I can feel him getting slick from how wet I already am. My breathing is heavy. My skin is hot and tight. I feel frantic. Desperate for him. He keeps stroking himself against me, agonizingly slow, over and over. I try to fight his hand on my waist again but his strength easily overpowers me. I'm at his mercy. His slow taunting mercy.

"You're mine," he repeats as he continues to tease me with his languid strokes.

All the nerves in my body are firing at once. The sensation of his hands gripping my waist, his massive chest expanding against my back with each breath, the warmth of those breaths tickling my neck, all while he pumps his hips over and over bringing me close to the edge.

"Please," I whimper. "Give me more," I try to move my hips, to increase the pressure on my clit, to move faster against his erection. I feel strung out, close to an orgasm, and my body is begging to feel him inside of me.

"Say it," he demands.

"I'm yours, Logan. I'm all..." but my breath is forced out of my chest as he pushes inside of me and the orgasm slams into me at the same time. My body jerks and clenches around him, soaking his hard length from base to tip. I hear him groan behind me as my body squeezes him, claiming him inside of me as he claims me with his words. My legs are shaking, barely holding me up.

Logan wraps his strong arm around my waist, holding all of my weight, and keeping me from crumbling to pieces on the floor. His hard length pumps inside me, slowly giving me inch after inch, forcing my body to open up for him.

"Fuck, Amarah, you're always so wet and so fucking tight."

The aftershocks of the orgasm subside and I slowly take control of my legs as Logan moves his arm from my waist and up my stomach. In an almost bruising grip, he grabs my breast and crushes my back into his chest, all while never losing his rhythm.

He's finally able to give me all of him and pounds into me in deep, hard thrusts. One hand still gripping my breast as the other moves between my legs. His fingers move skilfully over my clit, using my own wetness as lube as he brings me quickly to another orgasm.

"Oh my God, Logan, I'm close again."

"I'm not going to last if you cum on my cock again, Amarah."

"Cum with me," I gasp as the orgasm hits me hard.

Logan pumps into me one, two, three more times and I feel his cock pulsing inside of me as he releases his pleasure deep inside of me. My body feels like liquid and only Logan's hold on me keeps me upright.

We remain standing, Logan using one hand against the wall to support us and the other to hold me against him. He stays buried in me as we catch our breath. When he finally pulls out of me, the sensation sends a shiver down my spine and my knees begin to buckle.

Logan quickly scoops me into his arms and carries me to the couch where he lays me down and slides in behind me. He lays on his back and pulls me onto his chest, in our favorite after-sex position, holding me close. We cuddle in the afterglow of lovemaking, completely naked and exposed. I'm still uncomfortable with being naked just to be naked. Logan, on the other hand, is comfortable in his skin. He says it's partly because of his Wolf side and being one with nature, and partly because he's lived so long. How can he *not* be comfortable in his skin after three hundred years? I guess he has a point.

Again, being raised as a human gives me yet another disadvantage. I'm just not comfortable walking around naked. However, at the moment, I'm comfortable lying in Logan's arms, letting him aimlessly run his fingertips over my skin. I have my head on his massive chest and my leg thrown on top of his.

I'm in Heaven.

I finally break the silence and prop my head up with my hand so I can look at him. "What are you thinking?" I ask softly.

He looks at me and brushes my hair behind my ear with his free hand. "Absolutely nothing at the moment."

I scoff, "I don't understand how guys can do that. Just not be thinking *anything*. I feel like there's always a million things on my mind."

"I'm just happy. And satisfied," he gives me his teasing half-smile, causing my heart rate to spike again.

"God, why are you so fucking perfect?"

He scoffs, "I'm far from perfect, Amarah, but with you, I want to be. You make me feel...*different*."

My brows furrow, in confusion, "good different or bad different?"

He chuckles as he smooths his thumb over my worried brows, "good different. I'm not used to being this open, this...*vocal*, with anyone. I'm not always good with it, but I'm trying to be. For you, I'm trying to be everything you need."

"I don't want you to change who you are, Logan."

He shakes his head, "you don't understand. You make me feel like the man I've always wanted to be. You bring me peace, and calm. I don't know what it is about you, but for lack of a better word, you've tamed me. My Wolf. My anger."

He's opening up to me and I don't want to interrupt him with silly questions, so I remain silent, eagerly waiting for him to continue, to learn everything there is to learn about Logan and his past.

"I was lost for a long time, after Analise. After losing my Pack. Once Ana became Queen, she took me in and gave me purpose as Kaitsja, but I was still lost. Still angry. I let my anger take control and threw myself into fighting. Killing. Centuries past me by and I couldn't even remember why I was so angry, but it was rooted in me by then, too deep, and I didn't know how to be any other way. I just learned to live with it. To hide it when it needed hiding and to let it out when it demanded to be heard."

"Women came and went. After so long of being alone, I wanted to be with someone. I tried. But I just couldn't feel anything besides the anger."

"What about Hallana?" I can't help but ask. I feel insecure and childish but I need to hear it from *him*. I need to know what it was, from him.

He sighs and runs his hand through his hair, "Hallana is a good person, Amarah, she really is."

"I know that but what is she to *you*, Logan?"

"She's someone who tried, really hard, to be what I needed, but she never even scratched the surface. I thought if I gave it time, maybe I would see her the way she saw me. Maybe she could help me. But she only added to my anger."

"How?"

"Because I wanted to be different and I couldn't. It frustrated me more and more every time I was with her."

"Then why be with her?"

"I'm a man. A man has needs, Amarah, even angry ones."

I nod my head in understanding, "why me?"

"Honestly, I don't know. It happened the second I felt your energy, your power. It's like it called to *me*. To me, not my anger. It pulled me to the surface and I've been here ever since. I don't know how, or why, but I've lived long enough, and been alone long enough, that I don't want to question it." He gently lifts my chin with his fingers and moves his eyes from mine to my lips and back again. "I just want to enjoy it. I just want to enjoy being with you and everything you bring out of me. And kissing you something I enjoy immensely," he says as he leans in and claims my mouth with his.

It's a slow, exploring kiss. His tongue dancing with mine in a slow, seductive tango. I feel the desire starting to pool between my legs again. I'm insatiable for this man.

For his lips.

For his tongue.

For his body.

For his words.

For his mind.

For his heart.

For him.

We finally break the kiss, both of us breathless, both of us on fire and desperate for each other. He gives me one of his big, beautiful smiles and my body melts all over again.

"What kind of spell did you put on me, Logan Lewis," I smile back.

"Hopefully one that will last forever."

"Forever is a long time. Are you sure that's what you want? Only little 'ole me for the rest of your life? And that is a *long* fucking life," I laugh. "C'mon, you'll get bored." I try to deflect and come across as teasing him, but deep down I'm worried that my words are true.

"Amarah, I'm a Werewolf, part *Wolf.* When we mate, and I don't want you to think just sex, but when we pick our mate, truly pick them, we mate for *life*. It's in our nature and part of who I am. I've given you my heart, Amarah, you're my mate, and I will never betray you. My bond with you is stronger than anything else. I will defy the Queen herself if it means putting you first. Do you understand?" His green eyes are very serious as he searches my face.

"It's my turn to play you a song," he smiles and gets up from the couch to get his cell phone from the pile of clothes we left by the front door. He comes back to the couch and sits his phone on the armrest. The speakers start playing, *All or Nothing* by Theory of a Deadman.

"Come here," he pulls me into his arms and holds me tight. I feel so small and so safe wrapped up against his big body.

He starts singing the chorus and I listen closely to the lyrics. My heart feels heavy in my chest, my throat feels tight, and I feel my eyes getting watery. I don't trust my voice, so I just cuddle into his arms, listening to his voice sing with my ear pressed against his chest. I'm so overwhelmed by my feelings, and the feelings I feel through our link, that a tear falls down my cheek followed by a quiet sob.

Logan sits up and brings me with him, "Amarah, what's wrong?"

I shake my head, "nothing bad, it's just...I've never had this before. How do you handle all the dangerous situations? How do you run full-speed into Hell when you have this?"

"When you have what?"

"Everything to lose," I whisper.

"Hey," he gently picks my chin up, "you and I are both warriors. We're both powerful and damn hard to kill. We can't just hide out or run away. Too much is at stake for that. The world is bigger than just us, Amarah, but neither one of us is going anywhere, ok? We do this *together*. We protect each other."

I just nod my head. I don't want to think about anything happening to Logan. I don't know if I would survive. You know, you *can* die from a broken heart. I've experienced that pain before, but I know nothing I've experienced would even come close to what I feel with Logan. What we have is untouchable and incomparable to anything else.

I close my eyes and focus on his strong arms holding me. His arms are a shield and I feel invincible, like nothing bad can ever happen to me, as long as I'm in his arms. If I lost this...I don't even want to think about it.

My cell phone rings and pulls me out of my dark thoughts. "I better get it. It might be something important." I climb over him and off the couch. I have to rifle through the pile of clothes on the floor but I finally find my phone.

"It's my sister, Danelle," I say out loud to Logan. "Hey, sister," I answer quickly before I miss the call.

"Hey, what are you up to?"

"Oh, nothing much," I look over to Logan, both of us still naked, and blush, "just relaxing. What are you up to?" I ask as I head into the bedroom for some clothes.

"Just getting off of work. I wanted to see if you were going to be free this weekend. I have some time off and wanted to come up and visit you."

"Yea, that would be great! I don't have anything planned. Ummmm, you will get to meet my boyfriend too," I say with a smile. It's crazy saying it out loud. Logan is my boyfriend, but it feels like so much more than that.

"Oh, ok. I didn't know you were dating anyone."

"Yeah, it's new, but I think you're going to like him! He's really sweet."

"Ok, well, I can't wait to meet him. So, I'll see you this weekend?"

"Sounds good. Can't wait!"

I put on some underwear and a tank top and walk back out to the living room. Logan had put on his boxer briefs and is in the kitchen pouring us wine.

"So I'm meeting the family," he gives me a teasing smile.

"Just a sister, calm down," I laugh. "I've always been so close to her. How do I even start by telling her the truth? Oh, and by the way, I'm not *actually* your sister or even human. Oh, and my boyfriend, yeah, he's a Werewolf. Surprise!"

Logan hands me my glass of wine, "play it by ear. You don't have to tell her anything if you don't want to. What do you want for dinner? I'm starving."

"I know, I just don't like keeping secrets and lying. Yeah, me too, we did skip lunch, didn't we? Mmmm how about pizza?! Pizza, wine, and movies sound like a great night to me."

Logan steps in close, "I swear you read my mind." He leans in for a quick, soft kiss. I can taste the wine on his lips and I want more. I always want more. My cell phone rings again and we both look at the screen.

Valmont.

"Better answer it," Logan says.

"Hello, Valmont."

"Amarah Rey," his British accent comes over the phone in a smooth, easy tone. "Seems like we finally have some good news for each other."

"Finally. What did the Supreme, what do you guys call her, Ülim, say?" I ask eagerly.

"We have a meeting with her on Thursday, at 8:00 p.m."

"Ok, good. That's in a couple of days and leaves me free for the weekend. That works for me."

"Good, then it's a date. Emerson mentioned you also had a lead?"

I ignore the *date* part. I still can't figure out Valmont. I never know if he's saying things just as words or to insinuate more, and I don't want to know if it's the latter.

"Yeah, turns out Andre was able to draw some sort of symbol that he remembered from his visits with Aralyn. I was hoping maybe you might recognize it. I can send you a picture, hold on," I walk over to the pile still on the floor and find the drawing where we left it when we walked in.

I place it on the counter and send the picture to Valmont and wait for him to get it.

"Hmmmm, this resembles Witchcraft, but I'm afraid I do not recognize it or know what it means. Witches are very private and keep their work to themselves. Perhaps the Ülim will know what it means. We can ask her when we meet with her on Thursday."

I sigh, "ok. I hope she's more help than the smaller out of town Covens we've visited have been. I'm getting awfully tired of being told no."

"That makes two of us, Amarah Rey. I have lived a long time, and consider myself to be a very patient man, but my patience is not without end."

"I know. I'm trying to hold up my end, Valmont, I am."

"Of this, I am certain of. I do not question you or your word. However, my people still need protection and I will get it by any means necessary."

"Give me a little more time. I'll find a Witch willing to help us. No need to start another war. We have too many enemies as it is. Just, give me a little more time."

"The Witches would be an awful enemy indeed, but you are the one I do not wish to have as an enemy, Amarah Rey. I will wait a bit longer. Meet me here, Thursday at 7:30 p.m., and we will go see the Ülim together."

I never understand why Valmont is so intent on not being my enemy. Yes, I can potentially be very powerful, but more powerful than he is? Doubtful. Still, he always makes it known that I intrigue him. Damned if I know why.

"I'll be there. Bye," I hang up.

"Well, hopefully, this time everything works out," Logan says.

"It has to because I don't know what else to do if it doesn't, but that's a problem for Thursday. How 'bout we get that pizza going and finally have our movie night?" I ask with a smile.

"Preheat the oven, I'll go grab the pizza." He heads out to the garage where the extra freezer is. I can never fit everything in my refrigerator freezer. I also look in the pantry and grab a box of brownie mix.

Logan comes back in and I hold up the box with a gigantic smile plastered on my face, “and we’re making brownies!”

If this is all I do for the rest of my life, enjoy the small things with this gorgeous shirtless man, it will be enough. I’ll die happy. However, the chances of that happening as we’re fighting demons, allying with Vampires, and meeting with Witches, all while waiting for the traitor, Aralyn, to strike again, it’s highly unlikely that this will be my life forever. Life is never that easy, in The Unseen or the human world. You’ve gotta learn to dance in the rain, and never take a single moment for granted.

Easier said than done.

# My Guardian Angel

Emerge Part I by Ruelle

The sun is a blinding white light in the crystal-clear blue sky above. It reflects off of the pure white sand that surrounds me as far as I can see. I've seen pictures of White Sands National Park, but this is my first time here, which is strange considering I lived about an hour and a half away my entire life. Seeing it now, the pictures don't even come close to doing it justice, it's absolutely beautiful and breathtaking.

I'm wearing a thin, long red dress with a train that blows in the gentle breeze for what seems like a mile behind me. The sand is cool and soft beneath my bare feet which surprises me. Sand is usually scorching hot when the sun has been burning it all day, but it isn't. Everything is perfect. Absolutely perfect.

I'm content just walking along, alone, with no intent or purpose. A raven screeches up in the sky and I look up. I have to shield my eyes from the sun, but I see the raven, flying like a jet-black sign in the sky. The urge to follow it overwhelms me and don't second guess it. The raven flies low and slow, waiting for me. I walk leisurely through the rolling hills, keeping my eye on the raven. It dips low behind the next hill and I lose sight of it. I stop, wait a few

minutes, but it doesn't fly back up in the sky and I feel a small pang of panic. I pick up my pace and head in the direction the raven had disappeared.

On the crest of the hill, I see a green oasis sitting in the middle of white desert. Just like you would expect to see in a movie. There are a handful of vibrant green trees surrounding a small crystal-clear lake that reflected the clear blue sky, and a tent set up next to it. I hear the raven screech again, but I can't see it. I take that as a sign and continue down the hill towards the oasis.

I approach the lake cautiously, but I'm not scared. It's beautiful, peaceful and so...*colorful*. The air smells crisp and clean, a balm to my soul, and it makes me want to stay here all day. There's a hammock strung between two trees and is the only thing I see that provides a place to sit, other than the ground. The tent drapes are closed, but I can hear someone, or *something*, moving around inside.

"Hello?" I call out.

The raven screeches up above me. I can see it now, perched up stoically in one of the trees. It's looking right at me and seems to be oddly *aware*. As if it's intelligent beyond normal raven abilities.

"Well, hello to you too, raven. Why did you lead me here, huh?" I ask out loud, not expecting an answer.

"Perhaps she was leading you to me," a smooth, relaxed, Scottish voice says from behind me.

I spin around quickly and am instantly left speechless. A guy stands just outside of the tent wearing nothing but some worn khaki shorts. He's about 5'11 with a medium build, but muscular, with a beautiful tan. His stomach is adorned with ripples that bunch and flex when he moves even slightly, and are by far the most defined abs I had *ever* seen. His square jaw is almost *too* defined yet, he pulls it off. His lips are full and a medium shade of pink. They soften his features immensely.

His light brown hair is longer than most guys tend to keep it, but what draws me instantly, are his eyes. They match the crystal blue sky *exactly* and they sparkle with a humorous light that calls to me. I feel like a moth to a flame, being pulled into the light.

I snap my jaw shut. "Oh, ummmm, I'm sorry to bother you. I'm not sure how I even got here," I laugh nervously.

He gives me an amused half-smile, "it's quite alright, really. No apologies necessary, Amarah."

My name sounds so good on his lips, so smooth, in his accent. I feel myself take a step forward and stop. I shake my head trying to clear my thoughts and I realize he said *my* name. My eyes widen and I can't hide the shock on my face.

"How do you know who I am?"

He shrugs nonchalantly, never losing the humor in his gaze. "I know many things. Not only do I know who you are," he walks towards me slowly and whispers in my ear, "I know *what* you are," as he walks past me.

I turn and watched him walk toward the hammock. What? How can he possibly know what I am? No one knows except… no, no way. Couldn't be. Could it?

He sits on the ground with his legs crossed and motions to the hammock, "come, sit with me and we'll talk."

I slowly walk over to the hammock but I don't take my eyes off of this man for a second. I don't know that I can trust him. He doesn't seem to want to hurt me, besides, I'm the one who came to his place, not the other way around. Still, caution is always best, in any situation.

I sit down on the hammock, "how do you know what I am? Only one other person knows the truth. How is it that you do?"

"I believe you already know the answer to your own question but I'll explain nonetheless. I'm not of the Earthly world, Amarah. I see and know quite a bit."

"Are you Michael? The Archangel that Blessed my mother?"

His smile widens, sending my heart into overdrive, and his eyes sparkle with more humor. I want to drop down from this hammock and crawl to him. He's like a magnet tugging at me, daring me to come closer. It's like the connection I have with Logan, only a million times stronger.

Is this what it feels like to be next to Angel?

Next to a Divine being?

Do people feel this way around me?

When my head stops spinning, I can finally speak. "Wow! This is unbelievable," I shake my head. "I have so many questions! I don't even know where to start."

"I have an idea. Why don't I help you with one of your problems, aye?"

"Ok, what problem exactly? I have more than a few," I laugh.

Michael smiles again and it's mesmerizing. I'm usually not one for blued eyed, white boys, but wow, the need to go to him is *strong*. I want to feel his stomach flex as he laughs and looks at me with those hypnotizing eyes.

"I know you have a Witch problem, aye?" He leans back on his hands, and sits there, looking as comfortable as if he's on the lushest piece of furniture.

My eyes eagerly roam his body and I have to concentrate really hard to form words. "Yes. We can't find one that is willing to help us. Can you help?"

"I believe I can." The raven gives a low, *kaaa*, up in the tree. I had forgotten it was there. Michael continues, "you need to find Revna. She is a powerful Witch, and I do believe she will be willing to help you."

"Why? Why would this Witch be willing to help us when all the others have said no?"

"Revna is not like the other Witches. She is a solitary Witch and is not a part of a Coven. This allows her to be more...*flexible*," he gives a very devious half-smile that sends my heart racing again.

I dig my nails into my palms to steady myself. I close my eyes, focusing on the pain, and that helps.

"How do I find her? And what will she want in return? If I've learned anything from dealing with Vampires, help doesn't usually come for free."

"You're quite right. Everything has a price. What her price will be, however, I cannot say. That will be for you and her to discuss, aye? As far as how to find her, the raven will lead you to her as she has led you to me."

"Why are you helping me with this? Why does an Angel care about the Vampires getting protection against fire?"

"So suspicious, Amarah," he chuckles. "Are you questioning the motives of an Angel?" The humorous light seems to dance in his eyes.

I hesitate, "no, I'm just trying to understand. That's all."

His crystal-clear, blue eyes stare at me and I swear he can see into my soul. Then again, I'm sure he actually *can* see my soul. He keeps staring at me, gives me a coy smile, and I finally look away and fidget with my dress. He's so damn attractive, he makes me nervous.

"I could give a damn about the Vampires, Amarah. I'm helping you and only you. And do you seriously have to ask me why? After all, I've been with you from the beginning."

"Yeah, I guess you're right. You're like my guardian Angel then."

Michael throws his head back and laughs heartily sending goosebumps down my arms. "Oh Amarah, I've been called *many* things, but a Guardian Angel? That's a first." His eyes sparkle with humor, then I watch them turn to something...*darker*. He leans his body toward me as if daring me to touch him. "I'm a warrior first and always," he says seriously.

I want to ask more questions. I have so many questions! But all I could think about is *touching* him. I'm on my knees in the sand without even realizing it, slowly crawling toward him. Just then, a Wolf walks up on us out of nowhere and steals our attention. It has chocolate brown fur, piercing amber eyes, and it's larger than any Wolf I've ever seen.

"Amarah," the voice comes from the Wolf but that can't be right. Wolves don't talk. I stare harder and again, I hear the voice in my head, "Amarah, wake up."

"Logan," I jolt upright and almost head-butt Logan in the process.

"Whoa, whoa, I'm here, Amarah. What's wrong?"

"Holy shit!" I place my hand on my chest to try and still my frantic heart. "Nothing. Nothing, I was dreaming and... I think, I think...I was feeling your Wolf."

"Yeah, he's close to the surface. It's a full moon tonight. You know how hard I have to fight to control him on a full moon. Hey, are you sure you're ok?" He brushes the hair out of my face and gives me a worried look.

"Yeah, I know. It's ok. I'm ok, I just wasn't ready for it that's all," I smile. "I promise, I'm fine."

"Alright well, there's coffee. C'mon."

"Ok, I'll be right there."

I head to the bathroom and stare at myself in the mirror. "What the Hell was that?" I ask myself quietly.

I had been *dreaming* of Michael the entire time yet, it felt so *real*. The last time I felt a dream this real, was when I dreamt that I was fighting evil. Even then, that dream had been fuzzy and not as solid and clear as the dream I just had. Michael, the raven, the sand, the dress...all of it, had looked and felt so real!

"It was just a dream, Amarah," I whisper to myself again. I turn on the faucet and splash some cold water on my face. I dry my face off and head into the kitchen.

"Good mornin' good lookin'," I say as I walk over to Logan and give him a quick kiss. I haven't brushed my teeth yet because you don't brush them right before you're going to drink coffee.

"Good morning, beautiful," he hands me a Snoopy coffee mug and holds one of his own.

The first sip hits my soul and I immediately feel better. Grounded. Hazelnut creamer and coffee only, Logan has been staying with me for a month now, and we're slowly learning everything about each other. One of the most important things though, is how I drink my coffee. He drinks his black.

I force my dream into the back of my mind and focus on the present. "How are you feeling? I didn't even realize it was a full moon tonight."

"I'm fine, just a bit on edge. Everything is always extra heightened on full moon days and nights, but I've done this for a long time. I'll be fine," he reassures me. "Now, what about you? You have to meet Valmont tonight and visit the Ülim and I won't be able to go with you."

"Shit! I completely forgot that's tonight. Fuck," I say with feeling. "I don't want to do this without you."

"I know, but it'll be fine. Valmont will make sure that nothing happens to you. Of that, I'm sure of."

"Yeah, great. I know you trust him to keep me safe, but he

still makes me uneasy. And what if something does happen and he has to protect me. What will I owe him then? You know nothing comes for free with that damn Vampire."

"Nothing is going to happen, Amarah. It's just a meeting to see if the Ülim is willing to help, that's all. There is absolutely no reason to believe anything will go wrong."

"I know you're right, but I'm still so new to The Unseen and all the rules. The last thing I want to do is insult the Supreme unknowingly and start something I'm gravely unprepared for."

"Just let Valmont do most of the talking, ok? He knows the Ülim and more importantly, he knows the rules. Just follow his lead and everything will be fine. C'mere."

I snuggle in his embrace and sigh heavily, "ok."

I want to argue that I'm not ready. I want to make a million excuses as to why I shouldn't go to this meeting. I want to stay here, in my home, and hide like I've been doing for a month. I say that I've been enjoying my time with Logan, and that's the reason why I've been hiding in my home like it's Fort Knox, but that's only part of the reason. The other part is, I'm still scared and am in way over my head.

I had made so many mistakes and misjudgements since finding out I'm the Võitleja. I still struggle with believing I'm more than I have been my whole life. A normal human. I'm not a human though, but I do have a lot to learn. I still feel unprepared, uneducated, and insecure, and those are not good characteristic to have as a fierce Warrior, but it's my truth.

The truth is, no one else is going to do this if I don't. I have a responsibility and a duty. I can't hide anymore. Mistakes are only failure if you refuse to learn from them. What matters now is how I move forward. Time to jump back into the action and do better this time around.

# Hiding In Plain Sight

Black Magic Woman by VCTRYS

The valet attendant quickly runs to my door and opens it for me. "Thank you," I smile.

I notice Emerson standing very bodyguard-ish next to a black, stretched Cadillac Escalade. All black everything. The bodyguard outfit, the SUV. I shake my head. Emerson sees me immediately and waves me over.

I walk up to him, "hello, Emerson."

"Nice to see you, Amarah," he subtly nods his head. All business, this one. "We're ready to go."

He walks over to the back door and opens it for me. "Thank you," I say as I climb in and hear the door shut behind me.

Valmont is sitting on one of the back seats that face forward. He fits in perfectly with the luxury of it all. His silver-white hair framing his face like smooth silk. He's wearing an all-black suit, black shoes, and only a turquoise tie and pocket square. He always knows how to dress to bring out those piercing turquoise eyes. He's hauntingly beautiful but in a very masculine way.

I slide into the seat opposite him. The inside of this thing is ridiculous! The seats are oversized, plush black leather that resemble extremely fancy theater seats. There's a huge flat-screen TV mounted behind me, and there's built-in shelves on each side that hold crystal glasses and decanters filled with who knows what kind of expensive alcohol. That's just what I notice right away. If I had to detail out everything this SUV had to offer, we'd be here all night.

"Wow, don't you like to travel in style," I say in awe.

"Do you not like it?" Valmont asks in his British accent that suits him and our surroundings perfectly.

"It's beautiful, but it's just too fancy. I've never really been around fancy, so it makes me a bit nervous."

"It is just a vehicle. You're the beautiful one, Amarah Rey, and should be surrounded by elegance always." I can feel his turquoise gaze taking in my face and body.

Valmont also makes me nervous in ways I don't completely understand. A part of me is attracted to him, his darkness and the threat of danger he poses. Another part of me is utterly terrified of what and who he is.

I shift in my seat, ignoring the compliment, and I glance at him briefly, "thanks, but no thanks. That's just not me."

Valmont studies me for a minute and then changes the subject. "I'm sorry Logan couldn't join us tonight. Full moon, isn't it?" He asks with a devious smile.

"Yes, it is." Looking at that smile on his face I start to wonder if he purposefully planned this. "You picked tonight on purpose, didn't you?"

His smile widens slightly, but he doesn't show his fangs. There's humor in his eyes now, "I'm sure I don't know what you are insinuating, Amarah Rey. Tonight, is when the Ülim agreed to meet with us."

"Uh-huh," I cross my arms. I don't believe him for a second, but nothing I say or do will change anything about tonight. It is what it Is what it is, so I focus on business. "Where exactly are we headed? I have no idea where the Witch Coven...*lives*."

"They have a shop Downtown. Maybe you've heard of it or seen it, Nature's Magical Whispers & More?"

I shake my head, "no, that doesn't ring a bell. I don't go Downtown much. What kind of shop is it?"

"A Witch shop, of course, except the modern day has turned it into something more normal. They sell natural herbs and remedies, crystals and beads, clothes, they even offer tarot readings and some spells."

"That makes sense. People today are really big on stuff like that. So, they're hiding what they really are, but not really. Lucky them."

"Indeed. It's a much different day than it was back in Salem during the Witch Trials."

"I can't even begin to imagine what that must have been like."

"Humans have come a long way since then, but still, they're not ready for our world. I don't think they ever will be."

"I think you're right." I feel the SUV come to a stop, park, and then the engine turns off. "Are we here?"

"I can sense the magic in the air already. Can't you?"

I shake my head, "no, I can't feel anything. I'll have to sense it with my power, not just simply being near it. Or, I'll have to feel the magic in the air physically. I can feel things like glamour when I touch it, but not just being next to it. At least not yet, anyway. I'm still learning how to use my power."

"Of course," he says softly.

He doesn't say anything else and there's nothing on his face to show he's disappointed or that he's judging my lack of skill. I appreciate him for that. The passenger side back door opens and I See Emerson step to the side and hold the door open. I start to get out of my seat, but Valmont stops me.

"Allow me, please."

Valmont exits the SUV first and then stands off to the side and holds out his hand for me. I don't need any help getting out of the vehicle, but Valmont is being a gentleman, and I don't want to seem rude or ungrateful. The last thing I want to do is offend him or hurt his feelings. I need him on my side tonight. I take his hand and it's just another hand in mine. It's still hard to believe that he's...*undead*. He just seems and feels too alive. Too real. Too normal. Nothing about him is normal and I can't let myself forget that.

We're parked on the street in front of a two-story building that looks like any other business or shop I've seen and been inside a million times. There's a sign above the door that read, *Nature's Magical Whispers & More*, and there are decals on the front windows that read, *tarot card readings inside, crystals*, *herbs*, and a flashing neon *open* sign. See? Complete natural and normal for this day and age. Nothing shouted, *dangerous*!

"Emerson, you stay here with the vehicle. Pierce, you come with us," Valmont instructs.

I'm so preoccupied with examining the building that I didn't even notice Pierce is with us. He must have been the one driving. Pierce is also one of Valmont's bodyguards, but unlike Emerson, he's a Vampire. He looks exactly like the first time I met him. He's very, Idris Elba, with his hair buzzed short, matching beard and mustache that always seems to stay the same length. Come to think of it, does your hair still grow as a Vampire? If he shaved his beard, would it be gone forever? I'd have to ask sometime.

"Amarah Rey," Valmont stands in front of me. He's a bit taller than Logan but not nearly as big or muscular. That doesn't stop him from overwhelming me with his presence though. "Are you alright?"

I nod my head and focus on the Vampire in front of me.

"Yeah, sorry, I was just...*thinking*. I'm ok. I'm ready."

"You better be. This is a very important meeting and you need to be fully aware and focused. Do you understand?"

I cross my arms, "yes, I'm not a child. I know what's at stake and I understand. Now let's go."

Pierce leads us up the stairs and opens the door for us. I follow Valmont inside. As soon as I cross the entryway, the hair on the back of my neck and arms stand up and I goosebumps run down my arms.

"Whoa," I whisper. "I feel it now. I feel the magic in the air. It's... *heavy*."

"Yes, a Witch on their own can be very powerful but it's rare. The power comes from being a Coven, a family. This is a very powerful Coven, Amarah Rey, do not insult them or cross them in any way. You do not want them as an enemy."

I remember what Logan said, to follow Valmont's lead. "I don't plan on it, but I also don't know all the rules. I'm following your lead."

"Good," he says plainly and continues towards the back of the shop, I follow, and Pierce brings up the rear.

We come to the end of the shop and there's a doorway that leads to a room beyond however, you can't see into the room because of the hanging bead curtain. The curtain parts and a young lady walks through. She's about my height but curvier. She has thick, dark brown hair that's either naturally wavy or curled, and it hangs just past her shoulders. Her face is very bright and pleasant, with high, round cheekbones and dark brown eyes. She looks to be in her early twenties, but I don't know if Witches age like humans or like other preternatural creatures.

"The Ülim is expecting you," she says in a soft, pleasant voice. "Only Valmont and Amarah from here."

Pierce looks at Valmont for direction and he nods in agreement.

The young girl returns his nod. "Follow me," she instructs, as she disappears behind the bead curtain, leaving behind the click-click of the beads hitting each other. I guess she expects us to follow and doesn't wait around to hold our hands.

Valmont takes the lead again and I follow close behind him. On the other side of the bead curtain is just a normal storage room with extra supplies for the shop. I guess the Witches don't want to chance someone walking through the curtain and stumbling across actual Witchcraft. Can't blame them for being cautious.

I catch sight of the young woman turning a corner before she disappears again. Valmont follows and so do I. We round the corner and we're immediately met with a staircase that heads down to a basement. My heart starts to race a bit. Nothing good ever comes to anyone walking down into a Witches basement, right? Agh! Too many movies, Amarah.

As soon as I start down the stairs, I feel the magic in the air increase. It's more than just heavy, it's hard to breathe. It feels like humidity in the air but thicker and it feels...*alive*. As if it will crawl down my throat and suffocate me.

"I can hear your heart racing, Amarah Rey, and the smell of your blood..." he shudders, "you must calm yourself."

I take a deep breath and blew it out slowly. I can cut off the connection I have to Logan easily now, so I use that familiar feeling and try to cut myself off from the magic in the air. I feel my power rising up inside of me. I concentrate on blocking the outside energy pressing in on me. I imagine my power covering me, my body, and most importantly, my mind. Luckily, it works, kind of. I can still feel it, but it's like a distant buzz now and not so suffocating.

"Thank you," Valmont whispered as we reached the bottom of the staircase.

The basement isn't very big, and it's very well-lit, which I'm grateful for. There are tables to sit at as well as taller ones to stand at. There are supplies, trinkets, bowls, containers, and candles everywhere. I also notice a very small raised dais off to one side but it isn't for a throne. No, it's for their altar. Actually, seeing something like this in person, sends a cold shiver down my spine and creeps me out.

A woman is standing at the altar. She isn't much taller than me from what I can tell. She's wearing a black, flowing dress with gold designs, that I can't quite make out, on it. Her hair is dark brown, like the young girl's hair, but hers is lined with grey, and combed in a loose messy bun on top of her head. She's busying herself at the altar and doesn't seem the least bit concerned that she has company, even though we know she was expecting us.

"Ahem," the young girl clears her throat. "Ülim, Valmont, and Amarah are here."

The woman at the altar stops moving and seems to be praying. Again, she doesn't seem concerned that we're waiting. Valmont and I stand here, patient and silent. Well, Valmont is being patient. I want to respect her space and her prayer, but after what feels like hours of being ignored, I'm getting fed up.

She *finally* turns around, "thank you, Alisha, you may go."

She walks forward to the end of the dais but stops before descending the few steps that would put her directly in front of us. Apparently, she wants the advantage of looking down on us. Her entire demeaner and attitude towards is rude, as if we're nothing more then gum on her shoes, and she's annoyed that she has to deal with it.

Her face is aged but not terribly, and if I had to guess, I'd say she's in her late fifties. However, with magic, she could be a lot older than she appears. Her eyes are dark brown as well, and they look at us shrewdly and annoyed. Besides the air of superiority, I can also feel the power coming off of her, her energy. Surely, she'll be able to help us. I hope.

"Welcome to the home of the Desert Rose Coven. I'm Mae Delaney."

# Mae Delaney

Sweet Dreams (Are Made Of This) by Marilyn Manson

"Ms. Delaney, it is a pleasure to finally meet you," Valmont gives a sweeping bow. "This is Amarah Rey Andrews."

"It's a pleasure, Ms. Delaney," I follow Valmont's lead. "Thank you for meeting with us."

"Amarah," Ms. Delaney studies me. "I've heard quite a bit about you recently. Although, word of mouth and stories are easily exaggerated and therefore, not easily trusted."

"Well, I don't know what you've heard, but I tend to agree with that statement."

"Mhmm," she holds her hands together, fingertips touching, and continues to study me. It's making me extremely uncomfortable. I don't like people staring at me. I think it's rude to stare and it's pissing me off.

"Is there a problem, Ms. Delaney?" I ask as nicely as I can, trying to keep the irritation out of my voice.

"No problem. So, what did you want to discuss?"

I guess we were just going to stand here and get down to

business. No polite, *welcome and make yourself comfortable*, here. Again, rude. Powerful or not, this bitch is grating on my nerves.

I look at Valmont to try and tell him with my eyes, *you take the lead because you're not gonna like it if I do*. Luckily, he understands my intention, or picks up on my irritation, he nods his head slightly and turns his attention to the Ülim.

"Ms. Delaney," Valmont puts on a dazzling smile, but not enough to show fangs. "We are in need of a powerful Witch, such as yourself, to assist us with a spell."

"You can stop the flattery and charm, Valmont, it's wasted on me. What kind of spell exactly?" Mae asks in a bored tone.

Valmont doesn't skip a beat and doesn't change his demeanor in the slightest. He isn't fazed by the Witch's disinterest.

"Thanks to Amarah Rey, and the alliance we now have with the Fey, we are in possession of the very last dragon scales to exist. We were told that they can be used as protection against fire however, they need to be magically infused to work."

"I see. And what benefit would the Witches gain in helping with all of this? From what I gather, we would only be assisting in making you and your people more powerful. Why would I want to do that?" She asks condescendingly.

"Ms. Delaney," Valmont continues calmly. "Surely you see..."

"Are you fucking kidding me?" I interrupt. "Sorry, Valmont, but I just don't understand the need to always ask, *what's in it for me*? Why is it so hard for everyone to help each other? Why is it that it always has to be, give *and* take? Are you and your Witches not a part of this world? Are you somehow *invulnerable* to demons and the war we're in? If the demons continue to get stronger and come through the rip faster than we can send them back, are you somehow safe from it all? Because if you are, please share your secret with us!"

"How dare you come in here, to *my* home, and talk to me like this!" Mae is obviously offended.

In a day and age where everyone is easily offended, I don't care. Besides, this is a serious situation and we should all be on the same side. I'm annoyed with always having to give something back. And this magic on the air is pushing against me, a constant force like someone tap, tap, tapping me, forcing me to pay attention. It's adding to my irritation.

"Amarah Rey," Valmont whispers a warning.

"No. No, I'm trying to understand. Tell me, Ms. Delaney. What exactly are you hiding that makes you and your Witches impervious to defeat? If we lose the war on demons, are you not just as lost as the rest of us? We're all on the same side and yet no one acts like it!"

Valmont begs, "Amarah Rey, please, calm down."

"Don't tell me to...ahhhh," I wince in pain.

Valmont is instantly in front of me, holding my arms. "What is it? What's wrong?"

"I don't know. It's my head. It feels like there is a hot poker stabbing me." I rub my forehead. "Ahhhhh!" I scream in pain, falling to my knees, as I squeeze my eyes shut against the pain. I clutch at my head, rocking back and forth on my knees. "Valmont, what's happening?"

"Amarah," Valmont follows me to the ground but there's nothing he can do to help me.

I feel him stand and hear him address Mae, but his voice is muffled and sounds far away, as if I'm under water. The pain is all I can focus on.

"You're doing this to her. You're trying to get inside her head. That is against the rules without her permission. You are violating Your own code. Stop at once! You can damage her if you force yourself into her mind!"

"She'll be fine, mostly, if she's as strong and powerful as the rumors have been suggesting," Mae continues to try and force her way into my thoughts.

"You must stop. Now! Or I will *make* you," the threat drips like fresh blood from his lips. I've never heard him so angry, and even behind all of the pain, his anger scares me.

"You can try and stop me Vampire, but you won't even get close."

I still can't see, but I hear the footsteps of more Witches coming into the room. I can feel the magic in the air getting thicker, stronger, attacking me.

"This is madness, Mae!" Valmont is yelling, barely controlling his rage.

The pain is unbearable and all I can do is scream. It feels like skin is being torn from my body, peeled back inch by slow inch, as fire tries to burrow in. I feel hands on me as Valmont comes back to kneel on the floor with me.

"You must *fight it*, Amarah Rey. Do not let her in. Force her out. Use your power, Amarah Rey, *fight*!"

I hear his words but the pain is all I can think about. I can't think clearly, but somewhere deep inside of me, my power hears him. My power reacts to his demand. My power *is* me. And he's right, I have to try and fight. I let go of my head and place my hands on the floor.

All I can feel is the Witch's magic. Their magic is everywhere, surrounding me, crawling on me, and trying to get *inside* of me.

Suffocating me.

Squeezing me.

Clawing at me.

I focus on me, my power, as I call on it and send it down into the floor to find the natural Earth below. I know I can use the natural magic from the Earth to strengthen me and ground me.

"Lord, please help me," I manage to whisper through the pain.

I feel the power of the Earth come to me and travel up my arms. The same type of power I had when I killed all the demons that had attacked the Fire Fey's home. Only this time, I know I can't use fire. Even if it is *my* fire, I don't know how Valmont will react to it. I could kill him. I focus on the power and just think one final thought.

OUT!

"Get out of my head!" I yell as I release my power with all I have.

I hear screams and yells all around me, and in the background, the sound of a lot of glass shattering. The pain in my head slowly subsides until it's completely gone. I cautiously open my eyes and lift my head. I had been right, Witches surround us, but they're all on the floor now. They start getting up slowly, one by one, dusting themselves off, and murmuring to each other. The only thing in the room that isn't completely broken or damaged is the altar.

Valmont is kneeling on one knee only a few feet away from me. His normally silky smooth, perfectly placed hair has been windblown, but other than that, he looks unaffected.

I catch sight of Mae, out of the corner of my eye, as she's standing back up. I had knocked her on her ass. Good, she deserved it, but I'm not sure she'll agree. Great, this is going to be fun. There's no way she was helping us now.

I rise unsteadily to my feet. I feel light-headed and my legs are weak. I can feel them wanting to buckle, only pure stubbornness keeps me standing.

Valmont comes to my rescue and wraps his arm around me. I hate being weak and I don't like it when I need help, but I don't protest. Instead, I leaned slightly into him, thankful for his strength and steadiness.

"Thank you," I whisper.

I make eye contact with Mae and tip my chin up in defiance. I'm pissed at what's happened but it's hard to look and feel tough when you can barely stand. Hey, at least I didn't pass out from the exertion this time. Kudos to me.

Mae is studying me again, this time with less disdain, and finally breaks the silence.

"Leave us," She instructs the other Witches. They all look at each other and hesitate.

"Now!" Mae yells.

The Witches don't hesitate a second time. They all hurry out as fast as they can and leave me and Valmont alone with an angry Ülim. Only this time, I'm completely depleted and defenseless if she wants to attack me again. I can only hope her magic is depleted as well.

Mae finally descends the stairs on the dais and stands in front of a knocked over table and chairs. "Valmont, will you help me set this table upright?"

Valmont looks down at me. I steady myself on my own two feet and nod. He slowly moves away from me and helps Mae pick the table and chairs up.

"Please, let's all sit," Mae suggests.

Oh, *now* she wants to be polite? I scoff, and if I had enough energy, I'd roll my eyes too, but I don't say anything. I don't trust myself to take a step on my own. I know that if I try to move without help, I'll fall back down to the floor. Of course, I can't let that happen now. I can't afford to show such weakness after what's just transpired. Luckily, I don't have to.

Valmont, ever my knight in a Tom Ford suit and silver-white

hair, walks back to me and holds me firmly by the elbow. He's insanely strong and can probably throw me across the room with the strength in his pinky. He's supporting me with that hidden strength without it looking like he's helping me too much.

I look at the Vampire and muster a soft smile. I hope he can see my appreciation for what he's doing without me having to say it out loud. He returns the gentle smile, concern clear in his eyes, and I have to look away before I get emotional over it all. We make it the few steps to the table and sit down. I'm instantly relieved but try not to let it show on my face.

"Amarah," her voice is a bit shaky. The look on her face is one of regret. She knows she fucked up. "I am so sorry. I should have never done that to you. I don't know what came over me. Will you forgive me?"

"Forgive you?" I ask incredulously. "You know *I* was worried that I would come in here and do something wrong, something against the rules because I'm still learning the ways of The Unseen." I laugh harshly, "and it was you, the *Supreme*, leader of this Coven, that broke the rules and attacked *me*. For no reason!"

"I am so sorry. The way you spoke to me," she shakes her head. "No one dares speak to me like that. I was offended and wanted to see just how powerful you are. It wasn't right."

"That's Amarah Rey for you. Always speaking her mind, seemingly ignorant to the offense or repercussions," Valmont chuckles. "One of her more frustratingly, yet refreshing, qualities."

I glare at him, "you're not helping."

"Apologies," he says sincerely, but the humor is still dancing in his eyes as he looks at me. "I only speak the truth. Still, what you did Ms. Delaney, Amarah Rey has the right to retaliate."

"Please, call me Mae. Yes, I know the rules, Valmont, no need for a lesson, and I will not argue. Whatever price you require,

Amarah, I will pay it."

"I only want you to *help* us. That's the reason we came here in the first place. That's all I want. That's my price."

Mae lets out a heavy sigh, "Amarah, I only wish I could help you, but I can't."

"You have to! That's my price!"

"I can't help you not because I don't want to, but because I physically *can't*. I know what you need and I'm not powerful enough to do it. Even with the entire Coven behind me, I cannot do what you need. Believe me, Amarah, I would never claim to be less powerful in any situation unless it was the truth. You have to believe me."

"Well shit! If you can't help us then who can? We've already talked to several of the smaller, out of town Covens, and no one will help us."

"It is not because they didn't want to. They probably didn't say so, but it is because they couldn't either. The Desert Rose Coven is the strongest and most powerful Coven in this region. I don't know where you will find a Witch powerful enough to do what you ask."

I sink back in my seat, feeling utterly lost and defeated. If the Ülim can't help us or even think of anyone that can...we're screwed. *I'm* screwed. I'll be forfeiting my end of the alliance with Valmont and the Vampires.

"Perhaps you can help us identify this image then," Valmont pulls his phone out of the inside pocket of his vest and hands it to Mae.

Mae looks at it and nods, "yes, I know what this is. This is Lucifer's sigil, and the *R* belongs to a Witch that has long since been excluded from *any* Coven. Revna."

"Revna? Lucifer?" I ask out loud.

I've heard the name, Revna, before, in my dream with Michael.

Why would Aralyn have this sigil? Who is this Witch, Revna, and why is Aralyn in contact with her? There are suddenly so many questions.

"Why isn't this Witch part of a Coven?" I ask.

"Because she started doing more dark magic than light magic. Most Witches work in both, but very rarely you will have a Witch that only works light magic, and some that only work dark. Either way, it doesn't fit into a Coven when you refuse one or the other. We must be properly balanced."

"So, this Witch, Revna, is not a good Witch?" I ask to confirm.

Why on earth would Michael tell me to seek her out if she is only into dark magic? Maybe that's what I have to deal with in order to get the spell we need? At this point, I'm willing to consider anything, within reason, as long as I complete this alliance.

"Who's to say what's good or bad?" Mae shrugs her shoulders. "It's just the way of the Witches."

"And you don't think Revna is powerful enough to help us either?" Valmont asks.

"I don't think she is, no, but I could be wrong. I don't know what strength she's gained in the darkness. Darkness tends to lend more power, it's true, but the costs are higher. Always higher. I'm sorry I can't be of more help, really, I am, but I *am* in your debt unless you name another price, Amarah."

"I don't have another price," I grumble.

All of this running around only to end up back at square one, plus the attack, and this damn magic in the air, is making me grouchy. My head is starting to hurt again, but this time from my own damn thoughts, and not forced magic.

"Then I will owe you a debt. I will be here, waiting for you to collect, and if for some reason I pass before my debt can be repaid, it will be upheld by the next Ülim. I swear by it."

We walk back out the way we came. The other Witches are busy fixing everything my power has broken. Apparently, this is all the shattered glass and noise I heard. It looks like a tornado came through this little shop and left nothing unbroken. A part of me feels bad and another part of me feels good. They deserve no less for breaking their own code and trying to force their way into my mind. I guess I kind of understand what Mae was talking about now.

Balance.

Good and Bad.

Light and dark.

It makes sense.

We're standing on the sidewalk next to Valmont's fancy SUV. I'm slowly regaining my strength and no longer require Valmont's support. The fresh air feels good on my skin, and I breathe deeply, filling my lungs and expelling all the magic and tense energy.

"There's no magic out here. I feel like I can finally breathe properly. I feel better," I sigh with relief.

"What the Hell happened in there?" Emerson asks. "One minute, all is quiet, and the next thing I know, glass is being sprayed everywhere out here. It felt like the whole damn store shook. It's a miracle it's still standing."

Valmont chuckles, "that would be Amarah Rey's doing."

Before we can discuss anything further, a group of drunken fools, stumbles up to us. There's a mix of seven friends, all out for a night on the town, and all shit faced from what I can see. As they get closer to us, they start to, *ooh and ahh*, over the fancy Escalade. Emerson is trying to keep them at bay and usher them along past us. He's failing, miserably. He may be a dangerous man but he's struggling with a group of drunks. If I was in a better mood, this would be hilarious, but I'm too drained to summon the energy to tease him.

I sigh and cross my arms, “and *this* is why I hate coming Downtown.”

As they stumble around, one of them starts my way. “Hey, sexy, wanna have some fun tonight?” He slurs in my direction.

“Not only no, but Hell no.” I give him my harshest bitch face. He’s so drunk that it doesn’t even faze him.

“Oh c’mon, don’t be a tease,” he says as he reaches out to grab me.

The instant he touches me, my power reacts and I see his true form.

“Demons!” I yell, right before they attack.

# In the Line of Fire

Dead Of Night by Ruelle

The guy that had just tried to hit on me a second ago is now snarling in my face. It's the strangest thing to see a human face look so...*monstrous*. I haven't seen a demon in human form since the club two months ago. I've only been attacked by demons in their natural form. I almost forgot that they can possess humans.

The realization hits me that I'm with two Vampires that can die, well, I mean, we could *all die*, but Vampires are like gasoline to fire, and soldier demons can control fire, which backs me into a corner. My power is fire. Also, General demons can create it. I prayed that there are no General demons tonight. The slightest spark or touch and the Vampires will be immediately consumed by the flames and die.

For good.

Adios.

No coming back a third time.

I don't know what demons can and can't do in human bodies, but I know one thing, we can't kill them this way.

"Don't kill them!" I yell out hoping the others will listen to me. "They're just humans that are possessed, don't kill the humans, just...*hurt* them," I say as I struggle to control my own possessed human.

I'm barely keeping him at bay and then I have the most basic self-defense instinct ever. I kick him between the legs, and sure enough, down he goes. I take the moment to quickly look around and each of us has a possessed human trying to attack us. It's easy enough to control them in this form, considering Valmont and Pierce have Vampire strength, and Emerson is not a small guy and knows how to take care of himself.

I notice the other three humans have backed away and are trying to make sense of what's happening. By the looks on their faces, they're shocked at how their *friends* are acting. The alcohol clouding their judgment isn't helping them piece everything together either. Not a bad thing considering The Unseen is...well, *unseen* by humans.

We have all the human bodies down on the ground when they start gagging.

"Oh great," I say breathlessly. "They're all going to throw up now. Just fucking great." I throw my arms up in frustration.

Oh, how wrong I am. The guy closest to me is on his hands and knees convulsing, but instead of puke, a black mist starts to escape from his mouth. I look around and the same thing is happening to the other three on the ground.

"What in the actual fuck is happening?" I ask no one in particular.

"The demons are vacating the bodies. They'll soon take their true form and then they'll be more dangerous." Valmont looks at me, and I see the slightest bit of fear in his eyes for a split second before it's gone, as he takes control of his emotions.

Just then the door to the Witch's store opens and Alisha came out. "What's going on?" She asks.

"Alisha, right?" I ask.

Alisha nods.

"These humans have been possessed by demons and they're about to take their natural form. Can you hide us with magic? Humans can't see what's about to happen."

The black mist is solidifying on the sidewalk right in front of us. The demons are almost fully materialized.

She gulps visibly but sounds confident, "yes, I can do glamour easily enough."

"Good. Valmont, get these four over with the others out of harm's way. You and Pierce need to stay at a safe distance as well. You're more vulnerable than me and Emerson. We can handle it."

"You're still weak from earlier, Amarah Rey..."

"I said we can handle it and I don't want to be worried about you, now please, go!"

The four demons are solid and as real as ever, their red eyes are all for *me*. My power is a beacon to them and they'll always be drawn to me when I use it. Drawn to kill me. I'm half Angel and good and evil will always try to snuff the other out. 'Tis the way of the world.

One demon is larger than the others and seems to have more intelligence in his eyes. His body is thicker too, he has muscle, and doesn't just look like a skeleton with skin. No, he's definitely stronger. I've never seen a General demon before, but I'd bet all I have, I'm about to fight one right now. All four demons start my way and I realize I don't have my weapons.

"Shit. Emerson, some help please," I say hurriedly as I pull my power out and around me like a shield. It's one of the most basic things I can do with my power, and it doesn't drain me as quickly as actively using it does. Unfortunately, I'm about to use it. I take a deep breath, call fire to the palms of my hands, and pray to God that Valmont and Pierce stay out of the fight.

Emerson has a knife in each hand and slashes two demons in the back. They shriek in pain and turn to face him, but the General demon and one other are still coming for me. Two is better than four, I'll take what I can get. The General demon on my right suddenly sweeps his tail at my feet, I see it coming, and jump back out of its reach just in time.

I re-form the fire in my palms to resemble flaming balls and throw them at the demons. The soldier demon deflects it easily and the General demon absorbs the fire right into its chest where it hit, useless.

"Shit," I say to myself.

I run at the demon on my right. I jump and used its own body to keep my momentum going upward, as I wrap my legs around his neck, and swing my body weight back down to the ground. I tuck my head in and roll on my back bringing the demon down headfirst to the ground.

"Emerson, I need a weapon!" I shout.

He drops to the ground and sweeps the legs of a demon out from under it. He also unsheathes a knife at his ankle in the same smooth motion and throws it up in the air toward me. I catch it, mostly on the handle, but a small part of my pointer finger wraps around the blade. I don't feel the cut, but the blood pouring down my hand, lets me know it's there. My finger is still attached so, no time to stress about it now.

The demon I put on the ground is getting up and the other demon is growling at me. I take two quick steps and used the fallen demon's back to launch myself at the other one. I take the knife in both hands and bring it down as hard as I can in the center of the other demon's head. The demon lets out a piercing cry and falls to its knees. I try to pull the knife free, but it's stuck deep in its skull. I notice a mark on its forehead that I don't remember seeing on other demons. It looks like a crudely drawn upside down cross.

The mark distracts me, I forget about the other demon, and pay the price. I feel claws rip through my back. I let out a painful scream and fall forward just as the demon in front of me starts to burn. The demon behind me, grabs me by the shoulder, and throws me into the air. I'm sent flying and hit the sidewalk, *hard*, before I roll to a stop.

I can feel my energy and power fading. I'm too drained from protecting myself against the Witches earlier. The demon is walking slowly my way and I watch as it creates a fireball and launches it at me. I catch it and suffocate it in my fist. The demon shrieks and sends another one at me. I catch this one too but my power is fading. I close my fist around it and scream in pain as I manage to suffocate it, but not before it burns me.

I'm struggling to get to my feet as the demon is getting ready to send a third fireball at me. This time, I don't think I can stop it. I see the ball of fire flying at me in slow motion, and still, there's nothing I can do. I can't move out of the way fast enough. All I can do is close my eyes and brace myself for what's about to happen.

I feel something hit my body followed by a gush of wind. I wait for the intense pain that only seems to come from fire. Burns are the worst pain I've ever felt. Well, next to heartbreak. When I don't feel the pain, I slowly open my eyes. I'm back over by the SUV and

Emerson is standing over the last demon body that's dissipating back into black mist.

Valmont is kneeling next to me, "Amarah Rey, are you alright? Are you hurt?" His voice is normal and steady but his eyes dart frantically between mine and rake over my body looking for injuries.

I try to stand and my back tightens in pain. I hesitate but push through the pain and stand up. "I'm alive, I'll be fine." Valmont doesn't seem convinced but I don't give him time to argue.

"You came and got me out of the way of that last fireball," I say more to myself. "Valmont, the fire could have *touched* you. One tiny touch of fire and you would have been *dead*. What were you thinking?" I scold him.

"I couldn't sack off and do *nothing*, Amarah Rey. I had to save you. Besides, if you'll recall, I'm extremely fast. It's one of my many strengths," he says arrogantly.

"I would have been ok. It would have hurt like a bitch, but I would have survived. Valmont, you could have died!" I yell, trying to make him understand the gravity of the situation.

"Yes, but I didn't and neither did you, Amarah Rey. So, please, stop with the lecture."

"Why? Why is it so important that *I'm* ok? You were willing to sacrifice yourself to save me. I need to understand *why*."

"Come, let's gather ourselves and get you home and safe." He ignores me and starts to walk away.

I reach out and grab his arm, "No, Valmont. Don't just walk away from me!" I get up close and in his face. I want to look into his eyes and understand why he's willing to die for me. "Why?" I whisper.

Valmont brushes the hair away from my face and I see a tenderness in his eyes I've never seen before. Maybe Logan is right.

Maybe Valmont cared about me in a way I didn't realize. I've always thought he's just playing with me and intrigued because of my power. Maybe that's mostly it, but looking in his eyes now, I know there's something more there. No matter how small. It's there.

Valmont stands up straighter and gives me his devious smile, enough to show his fangs, "because you can look into my eyes when no one else can and that intrigues me. Not to mention, we have an alliance, Amarah Rey. That alliance doesn't work without you. We need to complete this task. If we had protection against fire, this night would have gone *very* differently. I cannot simply let you get hurt or die if I can help it."

"You're lying."

"Am I?" He taunts me.

"Yes," I say defiantly.

Valmont throws his head back and laughs, "Oh, Amarah Rey, just as bold as ever. Calling me a liar to my face." He looks at me and lets all of the humor fade from his face until only, cold, empty eyes are staring at me. "Do not forget what I am and how easily I can kill you if I wish. One day I might not be so tolerant of your... *boldness*."

"I've never forgotten what you are or how dangerous you are, but I'm not afraid of you. Don't get me wrong, you scare the shit out of me, but I'm not afraid of you." I lift my chin as I face him.

He leans into me, his silky hair brushes my cheeks, and I can smell his clean scent with a touch of bergamot and the ever-present, peppermint. He's so close I think he's going to try and kiss me. It sends my heart racing and I still can't decide if I'm attracted to him or if he creeps me out.

"That is your mistake," he whispers against my lips and then slowly pulls away.

He leaves me standing here, alone, and climbs into the back of the SUV. Pierce and Emerson are staring at me. They just witnessed everything that happened and I wonder if they're as confused as I am. I look over at them and they both chuckle.

"Oh, bite me," I say as I walk over to the SUV and follow Valmont inside. "Let's go!" I yell from inside and slam the door shut behind me.

"Not the best choice of words, Amarah Rey." Valmont watches me, as I slide into my seat, his eyes trailing along my neck. "Be careful what you ask for."

He makes a show of running his tongue, slowly, over his fangs. The look in his eyes is...*ravening*, and sends my heart racing, only, I don't know if it's racing in fear or excitement.

"I already told, I'm not afraid of you. You're not going to hurt me."

"You're quite right," in the blink of an eye he's leaning over me, arms braced against the back of the seat, blocking me in. His breath tickles my neck as his next words are whispered in my ear. "My bite will do everything *but* hurt you, Amarah Rey. My fangs sinking deep into your vein will bring you pleasure like you've never felt, and you'll be *begging* me to bite you, again and again."

He trails a sharp fingernail along the vein in my neck, causing me to gasp at the sudden touch. My chest is heaving, and all I can focus on is that one touch along my neck, and his scent invading my space.

"Your heart is pumping your blood rapidly into your veins as we speak. Is it because you're afraid I'll bite you or because you're excited at the thought of me penetrating you?"

I swallow hard and finally find my voice, "you wish." I try to sound disgusted but I only sound breathless.

He grazes my neck with his nose as he inhales deeply, "mmmm, so delicious." He moves back so he can meet my eyes. He takes my chin in his hand and jerks my face up, forcing me to look at him. I clench my jaw in defiance and meet his turquoise eyes.

"The next time you say those words, I *will* comply, Amarah Rey. Do. Not. Tempt. Me. Further," his voice is a cold command as he eases back into his seat across from.

"Whatever," I cross my arms and look out the window, attempting to play off my anxiety, trying to ignore him, *and* my racing heart.

Only I can feel his gaze on me and it makes me shiver and heat up at the same time.

I'm disgusted at his arrogance.

I'm disgusted at the thought of him biting me.

I'm disgusted at the thought of him drinking my blood.

I'm disgusted at the fact that I'm not disgusted at all.

A voice deep, deep inside the darkest part of me begging me to find out if there's truth behind Valmont's claim. Begging me to be let out and follow the Vampire down a new, dangerous and exciting road.

This dark voice is just as terrifying as Valmont is. I shove her back into the darkness, demanding that she stay there and be silent. She goes, reluctantly, but I know she'll be back. I need to complete this alliance and be done with Valmont. I don't like what he does to me.

What he awakens in me.

# Uncomfortable Revelations

Mercy by Shawn Mendes

"We should take you to Headquarters to be healed," Valmont says normally, as if he didn't just threaten to bite me.

"No, I want to go home. I'll call the Queen and she can send a Healer to me."

"As you wish."

We sit in silence for a long time. Instead of going crazy over my own confusing thoughts and feelings, I focus on everything that happened tonight. What a bust. The Witches can't help us or even point us in the direction of anyone who can. Demons are possessing humans more than ever and had been close when I used my power. Too close. I need to continue my training. I've been putting it off, but I can't any longer. I have to become stronger. I'll tell Logan we need to arrange my training when he gets home. I hope he's having a better night than I am.

I finally break the silence, "I think we need to find this Witch, Revna."

"Why? You heard Ms. Delaney. She can't help us."

"Mae doesn't know for sure. Why else would Aralyn be working with her? Aralyn came to you and offered you the scales in the first place, right?"

"Yes," he nods in agreement. "So, you think that she offered this because she was working with a Witch that could do what needed to be done, and that Witch is Revna?"

"Yup. That is my thought *exactly*."

"Yes, I see how that makes sense, but how are we going to find this Witch?"

I think about my dream with Michael. *A raven will lead me to her*, I think to myself. But when and where? I still can't believe that it had all been true. The dream was real. I still haven't told anyone, not even Logan, about the dream. I don't know why, but I feel like it's sacred somehow. Like it's meant just for me. So, I keep my information to myself.

"I don't know, but we will. I know we will, and we will finally complete the alliance and I can stop feeling guilty."

"You have nothing to be guilty of, Amarah Rey. You have come through on your end, already. You found out the truth about the scales and you convinced your Queen to give them to us. I imagine that was not an easy feat. The fact that we are struggling to find a Witch to finish the task is not your fault."

"I still feel bad about it. Your people are not being protected. *You're* not being protected, and being around me is not helping you stay away from demons, obviously," I snort.

"I am not your responsibility, Amarah Rey. I'm very powerful and have been for a very long time. You do not need to concern yourself with my safety. Quite the opposite."

I don't know what else to say, and arguing with the centuries-old Vampire, is pointless and will get us nowhere. We stay quiet and in our thoughts for the rest of the ride back to the casino.

We pull up to the valet close to 10:00 p.m. All of the adrenaline has left my body, leaving me exhausted and aching everywhere, the burn in my right hand is excruciating, but at least it cauterized the knife cut on my finger. Valmont gets out of the SUV first, and offers to help me out, once again. Only this time, I'm grateful for his assistance. I move as little as possible and wince as the wounds on my back pull and stretch.

"Are you going to be able to drive home?" Valmont asks with concern.

"Yes, I can drive. It's not like it takes much to sit there and push a pedal with my foot."

"Bloody Hell, you're stubborn. I won't argue, but at least let me know when you've made it safely home. I know Logan will not be home for some time. Will you at least accept Pierce going with you in case there's another attack?"

"The demons are only drawn to me when I use a lot of my power. Trust me, I don't think I can use it anymore right now even if I wanted to. I'll be fine."

He sighs heavily and I know he isn't happy with my answer.

"But thank you for the offer, Valmont. I'm going home to soak in the tub and wait for the Healer. Thank you for...saving me, earlier. I won't forget it."

He stares at me for a moment and I can't quite read the look in his eyes. He finally nods curtly, "you're welcome. Have a good night."

"You too."

I slowly head to where my car is parked. They left it up front and hadn't take it back to the parking garage and I'm extremely grateful that I don't have to wait. The valet comes running in my direction and opens the door for me. I slide in as gently as I can but it's impossible not to be in pain with the slightest movements. I wince in pain as my back brushes the back of the seat. The valet looks a bit lost and neither one of us know what to do or say.

"Here are your keys, Miss," he says nervously.

I reach for them, which causes my back to stretch, but I keep the wince off my face. "Thank you" I managed a small smile. He nods and quickly closes the door.

"I don't blame you dude. I don't blame you. Awkward," I say to myself in the privacy of my car.

I hit the brake, push the start button and the engine roars to life. I try to put the car in drive, but my right hand is too badly burnt to touch anything. I have to reach over and awkwardly put the car into drive with my left hand. Lucky for me, I hold the steering wheel with my left hand, so driving is fine except for the pain in my back.

I call Ana on my way home and she says she'll send a Healer right away. I finally pull into my driveway and park my car in the garage. Logan's truck is gone, as I knew it would be, but it makes my heart feel heavy nonetheless. After tonight's activities, I want him here with me. Regardless of what I told Valmont, I don't want to be alone.

I turn the engine off and put my head back against the headrest. I close my eyes and just sit as still as I can. I'm not looking forward to climbing out of this low ass car with my back all cut up.

"Stop being a little bitch, Amarah. The sooner you get out, the sooner you can relax and not move anymore," I encourage myself.

I open the door and slide to the edge of the seat. I move both of my legs out first, so I can stand as straight as possible, and not twist my body. I grab a hold of the door frame and pulled myself up and out. I had forgotten my hand is burnt to Hell and send a sharp pain down my arm when I grab the car door. I let out a small cry of pain, but I manage to get myself out of the car.

I'm walking around the back of the car when I see movement in the front yard. My heart starts racing and I still don't have any weapons on me. I need to start carrying at least my daggers. I pull at my power but it's weak. I'm tired and spent. Still, I *will* put up a fight.

"Seriously, can this night just end?" I whisper to myself, waiting to see what's lurking in the shadows.

"Valmont! Jesus! What the Hell are you doing here? You scared the shit out of me." I let my power recede with the last of my adrenaline and I barely keep myself from dropping to the ground in exhaustion.

"I did not feel comfortable leaving you in such a wounded state, *alone*. I knew you wouldn't accept my offer of assistance, so I didn't ask."

"Fine," I sigh. I'm too tired to argue, and besides, I'm relieved someone is here. Valmont wouldn't have been my first choice but hey, beggars can't be choosers, right?

"How in the Hell did you get here before me?" I ask.

Valmont just chuckles, "again, one of my many strengths, and I do have many, *many* strengths," he says teasingly. "Let's get you inside."

I try to ignore him, like always, as I head towards the garage door that leads into the house. Valmont follows me. I hit the garage door closed behind us and open the door to the house.

"Do I need to like, invite you in, or something?"

Valmont laughs heartily, "Oh, Amarah Rey, you do amuse me. You've watched too many movies. I do not need permission to enter. Unless you have some ward or spell to keep me out?"

"Laugh at me all you want. I'm still learning all the rules. I'm still figuring out what's real and what isn't."

"Yes, of course. My apologies," he gives a sweeping bow.

I walk inside and let the door shut on him in the process. Why are men always such a pain in my ass?

Griffin greets me, like he always does, excited and happy beyond belief. It breaks my heart that I can't reach down and lift him up. I walk into the kitchen and turned on the lights, then head over to the couch and gently sit down, as straight as I can, on the edge. Griffin runs over and jumps in my lap to give me kisses. I'm relieved to be home, but I can't relax due to my pain and my company.

Valmont follows me into the living room and sits down on the chair next to the couch. He lounges, if that's what you can call it, as if he's in his own home, completely comfortable and at ease while still looking sophisticated and elegant in his fancy, tailored suit. Only he's lost the jacket, vest and tie.

"What a lovely home."

I scoff, "yeah, sure. Compared to the life of luxury you're used to. This must look so...*inadequate*."

"No, truly. Your home is very warm and cozy. Smells a bit too much like Werewolf for my liking, but cozy."

"Well, I had planned on soaking in the tub, but there's no way I'm doing that now. I won't be able to relax knowing you're out here."

"Why ever not?" He looks offended. "It's not like I'm going to disturb you. I'm only here to make sure you're safe, that's all. I'll stay until close to dawn and then Logan will be here shortly after that." He explains, as if he's giving a presentation, just stating the facts.

"You're already here, no need to try and convince me."

"You know, I don't bite. Not unless you want me to, remember?" He smiles broadly and makes a show of running his tongue over his fangs again. "And I promise I would make it *exceedingly* pleasurable."

I can't help but shudder as I watch his tongue caress his fangs. Would it be pleasurable? Like the movies suggest? How can having your neck pierced be anything but painful? I'm mostly put off by the thought but that small voice inside of me can't help but wonder what it would be like.

Valmont moves forward in the chair, resting his forearms on his thighs and leans further towards me. "Are you imagining what it would feel like? To have my fangs inside you?"

His voice is deep and smooth. I've never heard it sound this way and it glides across my skin. Goosebumps erupted on my arms and I realize I'm still staring at his mouth and his incredible cupid's bow. I blink and move my eyes up to meet his. His turquoise eyes that see and know too much.

"What? No." I swallow and try to gain back my composure. "I'm not into being *fed* on. Thanks."

He smirks and his eyes seems to be laughing at me. "Now who is the liar, Amarah Rey?"

I put all my effort into looking bored and uninterested but I don't say anything. I can't say anything. I hadn't lied when I said I didn't want to be fed on but...I can't help my curiosity. How would it feel?

"We should take a look at your back and at least clean it while we wait for the Healer to arrive."

"I'll be fine." I try to sit back further on the couch and wince in pain.

"Amarah Rey, come on, don't be stubborn." He gets up and heads into the kitchen. He turns on the water and leaves it running as he starts opening up cabinets and drawers.

"What on Earth are you doing?" I try to turn my head around to see in the kitchen and immediately stop. Every movement hurts.

"Where would I find a bowl, cloth, and scissors?"

I sigh, "cloth under the sink, bowl in the bottom island drawer, and scissors in the small drawer to the left on the island."

I hear Valmont shuffling around in my kitchen and just shake my head. Never in a million years would I believe that a Vampire would be in my home, trying to take care of me, while my Werewolf boyfriend s out running under a full moon. Has this really become my life? Just a couple of months ago I was sitting on this couch with my girlfriends after a normal night out. Only, then, I was miserable. Sitting here now, claw marks across my back and in pain, I feel oddly whole and complete.

Valmont comes back into view. He sits the bowl with steaming water down on the side table. "Can you lay on your stomach?" He asks plainly.

"I can try."

I put Griffin on the couch and stand back up. I walk to the front of the chaise side of the couch and kneel on it first. Then I lower myself in a push-up motion, but it's hard to do because I have to use the back of my right hand due to the burn on my palm. I end up falling, more than lowering, until I'm flat on my stomach and I can finally relax. I let out a sigh of relief and I don't ever want to move again.

Valmont moves around the side table to stand beside me. "I'm going to have to cut your shirt off."

"What?" I exclaim.

It isn't so much the fact that he has to cut the shirt as much as it will leave me *without* a shirt on...in front of Valmont. Granted, I'm laying down and he won't be able to see anything...*private*. Still, it makes me nervous.

"How else am I going to be able to clean the wound? The shirt is already destroyed from the claw marks."

"Fine. Do it," I say through gritted teeth.

I feel him kneel next to me and then I feel his hand on my lower back, lifting the shirt. His hands are warm and I don't know why that fact always surprises me. Maybe because he's the undead? My heart starts racing and I know he can hear it. How am I supposed to hide my heartbeat from a damn Vampire?

"Amarah Rey, please, calm down. I'm not going to hurt you." His British accent is calm and soothing and a damn lie.

"I know," I whisper. I try to calm myself but it isn't easy. I'm nervous and uncomfortable. No way to get around that.

I hear the scissors start to cut and Valmont lets out a sigh, "parts of the shirt are stuck to the dried blood. I'm going to have to pull it free."

"Fuck." I try to steady my nerves, but just thinking about it hurts. "Just do it."

He takes me at my word, and I feel the first tug of the shirt, as it pulls the dried blood off with it which causes the wounds to re-open. I can't help it. I cry out in pain. It hurts worse than when the demon made them.

"I'm sorry, Amarah Rey. Almost done. Just one more." He tugs and I cry out, again, tears escaping my eyes.

I'm thankful to be face down so Valmont can't see me crying. There's no hiding the fact that I am but at least I don't have to face him. I don't know why, exactly, but I don't want him to think less of me. To think I'm weak. I don't make another sound and let the tears escape silently.

"Amarah Rey, are you alright?" His voice is low and soft as he's trying to be comforting. I appreciated his care but I'm far from alright.

I just nod my head, not trusting my voice. I hear the water splash and drip as he wrings out the cloth. The warm cloth feels good on my back as he gently wipes the wounds. His touch is gentler than I could have ever imagined. He's being careful not to hurt me more than he has to. It's sweet, but I still don't understand why he's here.

He's Virtuoso. Master Vampire. He could have sent Emerson Pierce, or *anyone else* to keep me safe. He didn't have to come himself, yet here he is. I want to ask why. I want to ask the hard questions, but if you ask the hard questions, you better be ready for the hard answers.

So instead, I ask, "how bad is it?"

"If you had just been human, you would have needed many, many stitches, and you wouldn't have been walking, but the wounds have already started to heal a bit."

"I still don't understand how he was able to cut me. I had my power shielding me. I don't know how he got through it."

"You were already very weak from dealing with the Witches. Perhaps your power wasn't as strong as it normally is."

"Yeah, that's probably what happened," I agree. Although, I can't shake the feeling that there's more to it. What was the mark I saw? Always so many questions and never enough answers. "I've also never fought a General demon before. I'm assuming that's what it was?"

"Indeed, it was. I also have never seen a soldier demon capable of possession. They must be getting stronger."

"Fuck my life. Of course they are."

"Considering you were *exhausted, and* had no weapons, I would consider tonight a massive success."

I scoff, "easy for you to say."

Valmont gently moves the hair off of my upper back so he can clean the last wound. I heard him put the rag back in the bowl of water and sigh with relief that it's done. The tears stopped at some point and I'm beyond exhausted. It's extremely quiet and I can no longer feel or sense Valmont next to me. He's done this once before, where he goes deathly still. It weirded me out then and it's weirding me out now.

I turn my head to the side, and there he is, sitting utterly still next to me, staring at my back. "Valmont, are you ok?"

He inhaled and seemed to come back to life. "Yes, quite alright," he gives a weak smile.

"Ok, I know I don't know you *that* well, but it doesn't take a psychic to know something is wrong. What is it?"

"Honestly?" He asks. "I'm not sure. I feel...*different* when I'm with you. I've lived a very, very long time, Amarah Rey, and I have never experienced these…*feelings*," he spat the word as if it tasted bad just saying it.

And here we go, this is going to be the hard conversation I didn't want to have that seems inevitable. So, I guess I'm asking the hard questions after all.

"What do you mean? What feelings?"

He isn't looking at me now, he's lost, deep in his thoughts. "It's hard to explain. I just feel the need to be...*good*. Better. You have this glow, this energy about you. I *crave* to be near you. It's like your skin begs for me to touch it."

He gently traced his fingertips across the unhurt skin on my back and my heart instantly starts racing, but I can't move so, I just lay here as Valmont continues.

"Your scent," he leans down and puts his face inches away from my neck, his silky hair gliding across my face, "is intoxicating." He closes his eyes and shudders, then slowly pulls away. He gives me eye contact now, "and your eyes...I don't understand how you can look into my eyes, but you do. You *see* me. It's like you can see into the very heart of me and your eyes beckon me to be...*more*."

I try to speak, but my voice fails me. I clear my throat, "Valmont." It comes out as a whisper. I close my eyes and try to steady my heart. I try again, this time with more conviction, "Valmont,

I don't know what you think this means, but I haven't meant to...*attract* you. I'm in love with Logan."

"You say that so confidently, but why does your heart betray your words? I can hear your heart beating out of your chest, Amarah Rey, and yet, I do not sense fear. Why do I affect your heart so, if not by fear?"

Shit. What in the actual Hell is happening? Am I attracted to Valmont?

No!

Ok, maybe a little, but so what? I find a lot of people attractive. It's not like people act on every single attraction. That would be crazy. And how do I explain this to a Vampire that can hear my damn heart beating and sense my emotions?

"The truth? You make me nervous. No, I don't fear you, I don't believe you'll hurt me. I know," I continue before he can say anything, "maybe that's my mistake, but I believe it. And yes, I am... *attracted* to you," I grudgingly admit. "On some *weird* level, but that doesn't mean I'll betray Logan. Do you remember our first conversation?"

"Amarah Rey, I remember *every second* I spend with you."

I ignore that and continue. "We both talked about betrayal and how much we despise it. How can you sit here now, and ask me to betray Logan?"

"I have done no such thing, Amarah Rey." He sounds offended.

"Not with direct words you haven't, that's true, but you *want* me to."

"I..."

There's a knock on the door, and I sigh with relief.

"That must be the Healer. Can you please let them in?" I ask, without trying to sound too relieved.

Valmont answers the door and a young voice carries in. "Oh, hi! I'm the Healer. Queen Anaxo sent me to help Amarah."

I recognize the voice instantly and smile. "Mariah! I didn't know you were a Healer?! I'm so happy it's you. Now get over here and heal my broken ass, please!"

I'm not the only one happy to see Mariah. Griffin is barking and shaking his whole body trying to get her attention. She's the one who watched him when I left for my training. She reaches down and picks him and he's instantly as proud as can be.

She laughs and makes her way over to the couch. She hisses, "Oooo girl, this looks so painful! Don't worry, I'll get you all fixed up and good as new."

Honestly, I'd be happy to keep the damn pain, if it meant I don't have to finish the awkward conversation with Valmont. I glance in his direction, and he's back to being the confident, and slightly always amused and arrogant, Vampire.

Everyone around me has *centuries* of practice controlling their emotions and it pisses me off how easily they act like they don't care. It makes me question the sincerity of what they choose to reveal. Why are the choosing for me to see their emotion or vulnerability? Is it a game? Is it a trick? Is it meant to throw me off guard? Hinder me in some way?

I can't trust anything I see or hear, and yet, here I am, a wide-open book for anyone to read! I need to work on my own emotions and expressions. Add that to the list of endless things I need to accomplish.

# 10

## Healing

Feels Like This by Maisie Peters

"Amarah, I'm so sorry I wasn't there with you last night. This would have never happened," Logan's voice holds such sorrow.

He gently traces the scars on my back, scars I'll carry with me, and always have as a reminder of how close I had come to death. Mariah was able to heal me, but she wasn't able to stop the wounds from leaving scars. She was completely confused and thrown by this fact. That makes two of us. But in the end, I don't really mind the scars. It reminds me of one of my favorite quotes by Khalil Gibran, "*out of suffering have emerged the strongest souls; the most massive characters are seared with scars.*" Yeah, that's fitting.

"It's not your fault. No one could have known the Witches would break the rules of magic or that demons were possessing humans right down the street," I say with my head in his lap, finally able to relax, now that it's just Logan and me. I know with him here nothing can get to me. Nothing can hurt me.

"There was something different about the demons last night," I say with my face still in his lap, eyes closed, focusing on his touch.

“What was different?” He asks softly, still caressing my back as we talk.

“I’m not sure, but they were definitely stronger.” I turn my face up so I can look at him. “Why don’t you have scars? I saw you with claw marks the very first night you saved me from a demon. They didn’t scar you like they scarred me. Why?”

“I’m a Werewolf, as far as I know, the only thing that can leave a scar on us is pure silver. I don’t know why,” he shrugs. “But you don’t have scars on your arm from the attack by the lake.”

“You’re right. I hadn’t even thought of that. Why was this time different?”

“I don’t know,” he says softly.

I stay silent and think about it. Why was this time different? Was it because it had been a General demon? Or was it something else entirely? My gut is a mess of knots. Something isn’t right but I have no idea what it can be.

“Valmont saved me last night. He could have died but he chose to risk his life. To save me.” I keep eye contact to see how Logan will react, but he doesn’t seem to care.

“I’m glad he was there and I’m glad he risked his life. I don’t want to think about what would have happened if he hadn’t.”

“It doesn’t bother you?”

“Who knows why that Vampire does what he does, and no, I don’t care what his motivations are. All I care about is you,” he says gently as he brushes my hair out of my face.

I push myself up, my hand had been healed completely, and there’s no pain anywhere in my body. My cut shirt is barely hanging on my body at the neck. Valmont had cut it, but not quite all the way to the top. I take Logan’s face in my hands and kiss him deeply. His hands ran up my back and came around to the front, under my shirt and swept his hands lightly across my breasts. My body reacts quickly to that one simple touch, sending chills down my body and throbbing between my legs.

I reluctantly break the kiss. "I need to shower and try and get some sleep. My sister will be here later today."

Logan looks disappointed but doesn't say anything and just nods his head. He's always willing to put his needs and wants aside for me. He always puts me first and I love him for that.

I stand up and look back down at him sitting there, looking scrumptious, undressing me with those sexy green eyes, and my heart turns to stone in my chest. I came close to dying tonight. Or at best, being extremely injured. An experience like that reminds you to appreciate all you have in this life more than anything else can. I don't want to take one second for granted. I want to enjoy every second of my life and make the most out of it while I have it because tomorrow is never promised.

"Looks like you could use a shower too," I smile and reach my hand out to him.

He grins, his eyes light up, and my body becomes Jell-O, just like that. He takes my hand and stands up, never letting his peridot gaze off of me. His big body consumes the air and space around me, and it takes me a second to gain control of my body, but once I do, I lead the way down the hallway, through the bedroom, and into the bathroom. I step into the walk-in shower and turn the water on to heat up.

I come back out and Logan is standing where I left him, leaning against the counter, his arms holding onto it behind him. The heated desire in his eyes is piercing my soul. I can feel his want and need through our connection, and I send the same need back to him. I keep a hold of his heated gaze with mine as I reach for his shirt and start lifting it up but I'm too short to finish taking it off. He continues the motion, pulling the shirt over his head and throwing it to the floor.

I run my hands up his arms, feeling his muscles under my hands, and then down his chest and stomach. Logan closes his eyes, and exhales a heavy breath, as I slowly continue to trace the v-cut down until I find the button on his jeans. I unbutton them and slowly unzip them. I never take my eyes off of his as I reach my hand in and caress his already hard length. His hand grips my wrist, stopping my exploration, and he pulls the pants, and underwear off, tossing them away. He's standing naked in front of me and I slide my eyes slowly down his body, drinking him in. Every time I see his body, I lose my breath.

He's gorgeous.

Massive.

Strong and firm.

Perfection from head to toe.

He pulls me into him, my body presses against his, as he bends his head down for a kiss. I eagerly tiptoe to meet him. I can feel his hard erection against my stomach and I groan into the kiss. His rough hands are on my back again, and then the next thing I hear is a loud, *rip*, as he tears the shirt the rest of the way off me. I let out a surprised, *yip*.

"I wasn't expecting that," I laugh up at him.

"I could rip the rest off too, if you'd like," he smiles deviously at me.

"Or I can just take them off," I say as I climb out of the jeans.

We're both standing here, naked, staring at each other, but it isn't awkward. It's appreciative and loving. I think we're both taking in as much of this moment as we can. I'm trying to capture him, like this, in my mind forever. Even though I know, at some point, the memory will fade.

Logan walks towards me and backs me up, into the shower, until we're standing under the cascading water of the showerhead.

I reach for the bar of soap and start lathering it in my hands, then I move to Logan's body. I want to wash, and touch, and admire every inch of him.

As the water washes away the soap, I follow the trail of my hands with my lips and tongue. He's patient, and lets me worship his body, as he stands still under the water with his eyes closed. My hands wrap around his massive cock as I glide my hands up and down, squeezing him tightly, causing him to moan with pleasure. I massage his balls which causes him to open his eyes and watch me.

Once the water washes the soap away, I lower my body, balancing on the balls of my feet, and use his muscular thigh to steady myself. I look up at him, his body towering over me, but my eyes are locked on his as I lick and suck on his balls while I pump his length in one hand. I lick my way all the way up to his tip and take him into my mouth. My tongue licking up the pre-cum greedily, as I moan my pleasure around his cock, my pussy throbbing and soaking already. He's too big for me to take all of him but that doesn't stop me from trying as I swallow as much of him down as I can.

A growl rumbles deep in his chest as I get part of him down my throat before I have to come up, gasping for air. Before I can take him back in my mouth, he grabs my arms and lifts me up to stand in front of him. His chest is rising and falling with his heavy breathing.

"God, I love the way you look when I'm inside of you. In your mouth, in your pussy, but I love the way your look more when you're cuming and screaming my name," he says as he lathers the soap in his big hands. "Do you want me to make you cum, Amarah?"

"Yes," I plead, my body already hot and tense with anticipation.

His hands, slick with soap, glide across my skin easily. My heart is racing and my body is reacting to the feel of his hands on me. His hands slip over my breasts and my nipples harden under his touch. He caresses and gently squeezes them, then, as the water washes away the soap, he replaces his hands with his mouth, causing my stomach to twist and turn in desire. His hand slips between my legs and makes me catch my breath. It's like I forget how to breathe for a moment as his thick fingers rub soap across my clit and I finally let out a shaky moan.

I'm holding on to his muscular arms as the water cascades down my back and his fingers move relentlessly between my legs. I'm throbbing, soaked with need, and losing control. His lips and tongue are exploring my neck and shoulders. He keeps rubbing his slick fingers over my clit, back and forth, back and forth, then gently bites down on the space between my neck and shoulder, and my body gives up all its secrets. My knees buckle and I breathlessly whisper his name, as the pleasure takes over my body.

Logan's mouth finds mine and suffocates my cry of pleasure as he easily picks me up in his arms. He pushes me up against the tiled wall with a low rumble in his chest. He positions himself against my opening and starts pushing his way inside of me. My body is tight and he has to work for it. He gives me an inch and then he pulls back. He pushes again and gains another inch then slowly pulls out again. Over and over until he's almost opened me up to take it all.

"You're mine," he says, as he pushes into me one last time, giving me everything. All of him finally sheathed inside of me. It's almost impossible to take all of him, but somehow, I do, and it's perfect. Now his strokes are long and deep. I throw my head back, moaning my pleasure loudly.

His massive hand grabs the base of my neck and pulls my head down. His eyes hold mine and there's so much emotion in them, and what I'm feeling through our connection, brings tears to my eyes.

"Say it," he demands.

“I’m yours,” is all I can breathe out before he takes my mouth with his. We don’t need any more words, our bodies speaking for us. He steps away from the wall, taking all of my weight easily, as he wraps his arms around me and holds me tightly to his chest. He starts pushing harder and faster as my body falls onto him and I feel another orgasm building.

When my life is crazy and I feel like I’m lost at sea, Logan is my lighthouse. He always brings me back to reality. Back to myself. Back to my purpose. No matter how many waves crash down on me, he’s always there.

Guiding me.

Protecting me.

Healing me.

Loving me.

It’s like I’ve never lived at all, until now. Everything else I’ve ever experienced in my life, pales in comparison. There’s never been any danger like there is now. There’s never been so much uncertainty and yet, clarity, all at the same time. I’ve never felt love before. All the love I thought I had for people in my past is inconsequential to what I feel for Logan.

I’m finally *feeling*.

Finally understanding.

Finally living!

The emotions well up inside of me along with the pleasure. Logan lets out a moan and I know he’s close too. He pushes even harder and I cling to him like a life raft, letting the healing tears pour down my cheeks, hidden amongst the water running down my face, as we climax together.

Logan steps further into the water, and continues to hold me, my head buried in his neck, as we come down from our high. How he manages to still be standing is beyond me. He finally eases his hold on me and I slide down his body until I'm standing in front of him.

He cups my face in his hands and rubs his thumbs under my eyes, "Amarah, what's wrong? Did I hurt you?"

I shake my head, "no"

"Then what is it? Why the tears, babe?"

I smile brightly through the heavier emotions, "you just called me, *babe*."

He returns my smile, "I did."

"It's official, official now, you know. There's no going back once the nicknames have started."

"There was no going back the second I laid eyes on you. The second I touched you. The second I kissed you. The second I slid inside of you. The second you claimed my heart, my Wolf, my everything, Amarah."

"*Babe*," he adds with a wink.

More tears flow at his words and I laugh through the tightness in my throat. I gently punch him in the chest, "that's why I'm crying."

He looks at me with a confused look, his eyes darting back and forth between mine as he continues to wipe the falling tears away.

"*You*," I whisper. "Just you. You've changed *everything*. Everything I ever thought I knew about loving someone is a lie. You just appeared in my life, out of nowhere, and just completely *shattered* me. You've destroyed who I was, completely, and this new me is here, like I'm experience life and love for the very first time. Whatever else I felt before you, Logan, was all a lie. All false. Because what I feel for you and how you make me feel," I shake my head, trying to find the right words and struggling. "The way you look at me, the way you hold me…it's…"I place my hands on top of his, still cradling my face, "I've never felt anything more real in my life."

I move his hands to my chest, over my heart, "I've never felt more, in here. It's like I was a ghost, passing through this life unseen, unfelt, and unheard, until you found me, and brought me to life. The tears are because I *feel* that much every time I'm with you. You bring me to life, again and again, every second of every day."

He pulls me to him and hugs me tightly. He holds me as if I'm the most precious thing in the world, but also as if he doesn't hold me tight enough, I'll evaporate right through his arms.

"Not a second of this life will go by that I don't see you, feel you, or hear you, Amarah. You will never fade to the background or disappear as long as I'm here. As long as you let me love you. I'm here for you. *Always*, for you," he lays a gentle kiss on my head as he cradles me to him.

I nod against his chest, too overwhelmed with emotions and tears to say anything. Besides, words are inadequate to explain the level at which I love him and I struggle trying. Instead, I pour all of my love through our link and hope that he understands even a fraction of what I feel for him.

"C'mon, lets get out of here before we turn into prunes and get blasted with cold water," he says softly.

We both dry off with a towel and then Logan jumps straight into bed. Normally, I would have insisted on putting some clothes on, even if it's only underwear and a tank top, but today is different.

He lays on his side and holds the blanket up for me. "Come here, babe" he smiles at me.

I can't help but smile back and climb into bed. No arguing. No fighting. No insecurity. I let him pull me into bed, against his body, and it has nothing to do with sex. I stay facing him, resting my head against his chest, and wrap my arm around his waist. Our legs intertwine and he pulls me as close as he can. He lets out a heavy, contented sigh and rubs my back aimlessly, not paying any attention to the new scars adorning my back.

I close my eyes, focus on listening to his heart beating steadily in his chest, and the feeling of his fingertips on my skin. Under the soap, I can smell Logan, just Logan, woodsy, like a warm, clear summer night. It's his scent and his alone, and it comforts me.

I don't remember falling asleep but I know it had been quickly. I sleep like the dead and am grateful that I don't dream. It gave not only my body a chance to recuperate, but my mind as well.

I wake up to Logan looming over me, shaking me gently. "Amarah, your sister is calling," he hands me my cell phone.

I manage to answer the call before it's sent to voicemail. "Hello," I mumble into the receiver.

"Sister, are you ok?" My sister's voice sounds concerned on the other end.

"Yeah, everything's fine, sister. I just had a late night last night and finally got to sleep."

"Oh, ok. Well, sorry to wake you. I'm on my way and I'll be there in about an hour."

"No worries, I slept enough. Ok, I'll see you soon. Drive safe."

"I will. Ok, see you in a bit," she hangs up.

"My sister will be here in about an hour." I tell Logan.

"I know," he gives me a smirk, "I heard."

"Oh yeah, Werewolf hearing, how can I forget," I tease.

"Come on. Let's get up and get ready. I can't wait to meet your sister," he says with a devious smile. "I'll make coffee."

"Oh God, you better behave," I laugh.

"I'll be on my best behavior. Scout's honor," he winks as he pulls on some basketball shorts and heads out of the bedroom.

I'm left lying on the bed smiling like an idiot to myself. Logan is so calm and easy to be around. He's polite and respectful and great at small talk. Not to mention great to look at even if he isn't talking. How can anybody *not* like him? Besides, Logan is the last thing I'm worried about.

I have to decide if I'm going to tell my sister the truth about who I am. Suddenly, my light hearted mood is gone and I have no idea what the fuck to do.

"Oh, fuck me," I say to myself as I shake my head and get out of bed to get dressed.

"That can be arranged!" Logan yells from the kitchen.

"Best behavior! Remember?" I yell back

"Oh, it *will be* my best," he insists.

My body responds to the thought immediately. I shake my head and keep further comments and suggestions to myself. This is going to be an interesting weekend.

# Iseta Rhyn

Authority by Elevation Worship

I give my sister the biggest hug as soon as she gets out of her vehicle, and I immediately feel better with her here, all my childhood comforts coming back to me. It's been way too long since I've seen her. We keep in touch a good amount of time through social media, but it's just not the same as spending time with someone you love in person.

"How was the drive?" I ask as we walk inside.

"Oh, it was fine. Boring. You know how it is."

Boring, I think, my life is never going to be boring ever again. "Yea, I know, but I'm so glad you're here," I beam.

We walk inside and Logan walks over to meet us. Quite the gentleman, as always.

"Sister, this is Logan. Logan, this is my sister, Danelle."

They exchange pleasantries, Logan offers his hand and she takes it. When their hands met, I feel slight electricity in the air, and goosebumps break out on my arms. It gives me chills but I don't want to react or make anything awkward. They seem to be sizing each other up and I feel like I'm missing something, but I don't want to access my power or our connection, or do anything…Fey like. I'm not sure if I'm going to reveal the truth to my sister, so I keep everything locked up tight, even it means I'm a bit out of the loop.

"Well," Danelle gives a small smile, "aren't you special."

"Oh, I think we're all special in our own way, but yes, your sister puts up with me, so I agree" Logan says, without skipping a beat, and giving us a dazzling smile.

I'm looking back and forth between them. I'm *sure* I missed something, but I have no idea *what*, and I feel left out. Like a third wheel.

I shake my head, "come in sister, have a seat. Can I get you anything to drink?" I head into the kitchen and expect them to follow me. "Let's see," I open the door to the refrigerator, "we have water, sweet tea, white claw seltzer, wine, wine, and more wine."

When I don't get an answer or hear any noise behind me, I turn around and my sister is standing at the island, holding a piece of paper in her hands. It's the drawing of the symbol Andre had seen while visiting Aralyn.

"Where did you get this?" She asks, very seriously. The look on her face has me worried.

"Oh, don't worry about that," I laugh nervously. "That's just...ummmm...for a, uh, project I'm working on."

I try to take it out of her hands, but she moves it out of my reach. "Amarah, do you know what this is?" She asks in a lecturing tone.

"Yes, I know what it is, and it's not what you think, I swear."

"Well, you better damn well tell me what it is because this is not something you fool around with."

"Wait, how do *you* know what it is?" I cross my arms and stare at her.

She sighs, “maybe we should all sit down.” She walks around the island to a barstool and takes a seat, still holding onto the piece of paper. “And grab the wine while you’re at it.”

I pull the wine out of the fridge and get three glasses out of the cabinet. Logan takes over and starts pouring so I can sit down and give my sister all of my attention. I’m nervous because I have no idea what’s going on. I have no idea what happened when she and Logan shook hands, I have no idea how she knows about the symbol or what she thinks I’m doing with it, but most importantly, I’m nervous because I don’t know what the Hell I’m going to tell her.

Danelle places the paper down between us. Logan slides over her glass of wine, “thank you,” she smiles at him. She takes a sip and I follow suit. Nothing some wine can’t fix, right?

“I’m not into anything...*bad,* if that’s what you’re thinking.” I explain.

She just shakes her head, “maybe I should start.” She reaches over and takes my hand in hers. “Amarah, I’m not who you think I am. I’m not your sister.”

I let out a sigh of relief in my mind. All the stress and anxiety I had about whether I would or wouldn’t tell her the truth is gone. Then, my heart and mind start racing, trying to figure out how much she knows. How does *she* know that she isn’t my sister? Is she a threat? She doesn’t visit too often, so has she been sent here to kill me? I mean, there are easier ways to do that than sitting down to have wine, but I still can’t help the suspicion.

With no need to hide anymore, I let my guard down and open up my power. I sense her energy searching for something…*evil.* Perhaps a demon possessing her. No, no demon. Nothing evil that I can sense, but I do recognize her type of energy.

I let out a relieved sigh, but I’m still in shock. “You’re a Witch,” I blurt out, staring at her.

She takes another sip of her wine and gently sets the glass down. She's moving very slowly and easily, as if she doesn't want to make any sudden movements or scare me.

She nods her head, "yes, I'm a Witch. My real name is Iseta Rhyn, and I know exactly who and *what* you are, Amarah."

My mind is racing. "How...I mean..." I scratch my head, "you were there with me the whole time I was growing up. How do you know the truth?"

I don't care or focus on the fact that she said she knows *what* I am. I'll come back to that part later. Right now, I'm feeling a lot of emotions. Confused. Hurt. But mostly betrayal.

"I'll always be your sister, Amarah. Just because we may not be blood, doesn't mean that we aren't sisters. Surely you must know that."

"I just...I don't understand. How did you do it all these years? And how do you know about me?"

"Well, as you know, I'm a Witch. A Grey Witch to be exact. I don't belong to any group or Coven because I have different beliefs. My *own* beliefs. Yes, I'm a Witch, but I also believe in God. He's my Deity. So, when you were..." she glances at Logan and then back at me, "*conceived*, I received a message. I was to protect you, so that's what I've done. Or at least tried my best to do."

"Ok, well, I mean, that's good, that you believe in God. It would be bad if you didn't, considering..." it's my turn to glance at Logan now. He's watching us closely but he hasn't said a word. Smart man. He still doesn't know I'm half Angel. I shake my head, "anyway, what kind of message did you receive exactly?"

"Well, God sent Archangel Michael to visit me in my dreams the night you were, ummmm, conceived. They wanted someone they could trust, to watch over you in your most precious and weakest moments, when you were growing up and couldn't protect yourself. I was to watch over you, keep you safe, until you found out the truth of who you are. Which, I know now, that you have," she smiles brightly.

"Yes, I know who I am now. And how did you manage to hide in plain sight all of these years? How did you get everyone to believe you were part of our family? And what about Mom and Kizzy? Are they something other than what I thought too?"

"Well, honestly? I'm not entirely sure. Archangel Michael assured me that all would be in place. All I had to do was use some glamour to lesson my age and change it as the time went on to mimic that I was growing up alongside you all. Glamour, after all, is easy enough. Your mom and sister are human. They don't know the truth of you, me or this world," she shrugs. "And well, here we are now."

"So, who are you? Am I still seeing glamour now?"

"Actually, no, this is the real me. I don't know how much you know about Witches, but we're not like the Fey, we do age. We age slower than humans, yes, but still, this is inevitable. The white hair you see is indeed the truth. We do grow old and die. As it should be," she explains, seemingly at peace with it all.

I take a long sip of my wine and look over at Logan. He's been very quietly observing our conversation. "And I'm guessing you know that Logan is...also, not entirely human?"

She chuckles, "yes, sister, I know Logan is a Werewolf. However, I also sense something else." She studies him now, "he is...something *more*."

Logan smiles, "yes, I also have a Fey life-force inside of me."

"Hmmm," Iseta takes another sip of her wine. "I'm sure that's what it is then," she gives a weak, unconvincing smile.

I look at Logan and think about our connection. Is there more to him than I know? Is he *something* else? Would he keep the truth from me? After all, I'm keeping my truth from him. Now that I think about it, and contemplate the fact that he may be lying to me, I hate it. I don't want to be left in the dark on anything. What a hypocrite I am.

I open up our link again and he's wide open to me, he isn't blocking. He doesn't *feel* like he's lying or hiding anything. Shit. Looks like I'm the only guilty one lying to the person I love. How long is this relationship going to last if I don't tell him everything? The thought of losing him because of my lies cuts me to the core. I feel my eyes starting to water and have to look away from his handsome face.

Logan looks at me with concern on his face. "Amarah, are you ok? I feel...a lot of *emotions* coming from you."

I take a deep breath and pulled myself together. "I'm fine," I give him a weak smile. "It's just a lot to take in is all."

"Well, we need to discuss this," Iseta points to the piece of paper.

I sigh, "that's a symbol that was given to us as a possible lead. I'm sure you've heard of the Fey traitor, Aralyn?"

Iseta nods, "yes, I know about what's been happening around you. It's my job to know."

"Ok, well, this symbol was seen on a tin that Aralyn kept chocolates in. She gives these chocolates to other Fey and we think they're spelled to make them reveal all of their secrets. That's how she found out about the dragon scales the Fire Fey have, and we think she's been working with a Witch who was going to help her with her alliances and take over." I sigh, "I don't know too much honestly."

"Well, you know this symbol represents Lucifer, and I'm sure you were able to find out the *R* is Revna's mark. Neither is a good sign. This is dangerous even just to have written like this, on a piece of paper. It's pure evil, Amarah, just having the symbol in your house brings evil in. We need to destroy it."

"Do you know anything more about this Witch, Revna?" Logan asks.

"I only know that she turned from the light completely. I'm a Grey Witch, I work in both light and dark equally, again, as it should be, but with God as my chosen Deity, I do work more in the light. Revna has taken on Lucifer as her Deity of choice and has been in isolation ever since."

Why is Michael pointing me to Revna if everyone else knows she's evil? Why would I need her? Maybe it's only dark magic that can infuse the dragon scales? I don't know and I'm so confused with it all.

"Amarah," Iseta says again. "We need to destroy this, now."

"Ok, no problem," I grab the piece of paper and crumple it up.

"Amarah, don't be silly. That's not going to destroy it and you know it. I'll need to perform a spell to destroy it properly and cleanse your home. I'll go get my things."

"I'll help you," Logan offers.

"Thank you," she smiles and they head out the door.

Iseta told us to keep the door open, and went to sit cross-legged on the floor, surrounded by white candles and a burning bundle of white sage. She laid down some plastic, and had the drawing on top of it, on the floor in front of her. She holds a large white crystal in her left hand, she raises her right hand and starts...*praying*, is the only word I can think that fits.

"I call upon you, Lord, for light and strength. Give me the energy I need to destroy this evil." She reaches down and smudges the drawing, then reaches into a container, and sprinkles something black, in a solid line around the paper. My best guess is salt or sand, but what do I know? She sits there silent for a long time, the candles flickering and the sage steadily burning. She then moves her left hand, still holding the crystal over the drawing, and prays some more.

There's a sudden breeze that threatens to blow out the candles, but some how they remained lit. "With the power in me, through the white light, and the Angels surrounding me, I rebuke you! Be gone! With all the power in me from Above, you shall be returned below. She places the crystal on the paper and it burst into flames.

*Light cleanse this space*
*Where evil lay claim*
*Lend us your Grace*
*Protect us in Thy Name*

When the page is completely consumed by the flames, no more than a pile of ash, she removes her crystal, and gathers up the plastic, tying it tightly closed.

"This will need to be buried somewhere far away with black salt. I will take care of this on my way back home. For now, we just need it out of the house, and then I'll walk the house and cleanse every room. Leave the door open so the evil has a place to escape. Once I'm done, we'll close the door and I'll add protection to every entry."

I have no idea what to do or say. I've never seen *anything* like what just happened and all I can do is trust that she's doing what needs to be done to protect me. So, I just nod my head and agreed. What else can I do?

After all of the cleansing and protection is done, we're sitting in the living room, more wine in hand, and I feel relieved. The air and energy in the house does feel better. Plus, I'm relieved that I can talk about my life, my *true* life, with my sister. My feelings about her haven't change because I found out her truth. She's right, we'll always be sisters, no matter what.

"You've done so much for me already, I'm so grateful, but I have to ask. We've not been able to find a Witch to help us with the dragon scales. The Albuquerque Coven Supreme, said it can't be done. She said she doesn't know of anyone or any Coven strong enough to do the spell. Are you?"

Iseta sighs, "I do believe I can do the spell, but…" she shakes her head, "it would require blood. Blood magic is the only thing strong enough to do what you ask."

"Blood magic? Isn't that bad? And how much blood are we talking about? Would you need to *sacrifice* someone? Because in that case, Hell to the no!"

"Blood magic is just magic, it's how a Witch *uses* it that makes it good or bad, Amarah, just like everything else. Good and evil are choices one makes, not set in one thing or another. Normally, yes, I would say a sacrifice would need to be made. The magic you need is *powerful*. To protect against fire, especially for a Vampire, is not an easy task."

"Then forget it. I'll tell Valmont it's just not an option."

"You didn't let me finish," she scolds. "I believe that a decent amount of *your* blood, sister, would suffice."

"Oh," I say, taken aback.

"Why Amarah's blood?" Logan asks suspiciously.

"Don't you know how special she is?" Iseta counter.

"Of course, I know she's special, but why not any Fey's blood? Why Amarah's?"

"I'm afraid that's not my question to answer," Iseta looks at Logan and then at me.

"Amarah, what is she talking about?" Logan looks questioningly at me.

I slam the rest of my wine and get up to pour another glass. "Well, ummmm...there's just one *small* thing I haven't told you," I admit

*Shit, I'm going to need something harder than wine to have this conversation,* I think to myself.

All or nothing.

In this with Logan *completely* or not at all. Fuck.

Here we go.

# The Truth Always Finds The Light

Sweet Love by 112

"Wow," Logan sits back in the chair, he had left the couch to my sister and me. He's staring at me with a very confused look on his face. Iseta and I keep glancing at each other and then back at Logan. He's been silent for a while now, only muttering, *wow*, every once in a while, but I can see the wheels turning in his mind.

I can't take the silence anymore, "Logan? Are you ok? What are you thinking? I'm so sorry that I kept this from you, I swear I didn't mean to hurt you. It's just...the Queen and I thought it safer if..."

"No, it's ok. I understand why this is being kept secret."

I'm taken aback, "you do?"

"Yes," he lets out a heavy sigh.

"So..., you're not mad at me then?"

"I'll admit, I'm a little hurt that you didn't trust me enough to tell me."

"No, it's not that at all!" I plead.

Logan gets up from his chair and comes to kneel in front of me. "Amarah, this means you're even *more* precious than ever." His eyes are filled with a mix of awe and concern. "I've been around for a *long* time, I've seen a lot of evil people doing evil things for power, and I know the Queen well. She doesn't do anything without a good reason. It was right for her to advise you to keep this secret safe, and besides," he gives a teasing half-smile and caresses my cheek, "how can I be mad at an Angel?"

His smile and touch make me feel immediately lighter and better. "*Half* Angel," I say with a cheesy smile on my face.

"God, you're beautiful," he says staring at me.

It sends my heart racing and brings all the butterflies to my stomach. His eyes never fail to capture me completely. My eyes fall to his lips, my breath hitches, and I'm leaning into him without thinking of anything else.

"Ahem," Iseta clears her throat next to me.

We both jump, pulling away from each other, laughing and mutter, "sorry."

I blush to high Heaven.

Logan sits back down in the chair. "This all makes so much sense now. Why you're a Master of Fire, why you can look Valmont in the eyes. Who knows what you're capable of, Amarah! This is amazing," he's beaming.

"Don't get too excited or any crazy thoughts in your head. You know how much I struggle with my power. Maybe I'm capable of some really powerful stuff, but maybe not. We don't know what God has intended with me beyond killing demons."

"Oh, yeah! That's also why you can kill demons! Amazing!" He repeats in awe, as if he can't think of any other words to describe it all.

I laugh, “Ok, so much for not getting too excited.” I turn to Iseta, “so, you can use my blood and infuse the dragon scales? You’re sure?”

“Nothing is ever really certain when it comes to magic, but yes, I’m confident I can do what you need. I’ll just need to gather some more things before I’ll be ready for the spell.”

“This is such good news! Valmont is going to be thrilled, and I’ll finally have come through on my end for the alliance.”

“Don’t make him any promises, Amarah. I don’t know for certain if I will be able to do it. I think I can, but like I said…”

“I know, I know,” I interrupt her. “Nothing’s certain.”

We sit and talk until late into the morning hours. We share three bottles of wine between the three of us. We laugh, we cry, and it’s the best night I’ve had in a long time. It’s such a weight off my chest knowing I have someone from my human world also a part of The Unseen. And it’s another huge weight off my chest now that Logan knows my truth. I feel light and free! Although, that could definitely be the wine.

I make sure my sister is settled in the guest bedroom and then head to bed with a huge smile on my face, and thanks to the wine, not much on my mind. Logan and I get ready for bed and cuddle in next to each other.

Logan props up on his elbow to look at me, “so… your sister is a Witch.”

“I know, this is all crazy! I can’t believe the Witch I’ve been searching for has been right here, in my life, all along.”

“And you’re an Angel,” he scoffs and shakes his head. “A *real* Angel.”

I can’t quite read his face and the wine has numbed the connection a bit, “does that bother you?” I ask, concerned.

"No, it's just..." he sighs, "you're an Angel, Amarah. How do I compete with that?"

I push myself to sit up a bit, "what do you mean? Are you...*scared* of me now?"

"No," he blurts out. "Maybe, a little. I don't know. I know now that you're more precious than ever, what if I can't keep you safe?"

I feel the insecurity coming through our connection. "Logan," I hold his face in my hands. "It's just me. Little 'ole, newbie, have no clue what the fuck I'm doing, Amarah Rey. I'm the same person you've always known. Nothing's changed. Please don't pull away from me because of this. I *need* you. You make me strong. I can't do any of this without you."

"You make me weak."

I scoff and drop my hands from his face, "what do you mean?"

"Do you remember the first night we met?"

"Of course, I do."

"I was drawn to you and didn't know why. I still don't exactly know why. I think you being an Angel definitely draws people towards you. It makes sense, but... what I feel...it isn't something I can fight. It's intense. It's stronger than anything I've ever felt."

"I feel that too."

"Anyway, that night I showed you how to use your power, do you remember?"

"Yes. What does that have to do with anything?"

"The night I saved you, from the first demon attack, and we sat, talking in your kitchen. I told you that your power is unlike anything I've ever felt before. I told you that you could completely undo me. Completely destroy me."

"Logan, I don't understand. I would *never* hurt you."

"I told you it was your power that I was scared of, but the truth is, it's the way I feel about you. Since day one. Since I first laid eyes on you. You make me weak because all I care about is *you*. I will put myself, and anyone else, in danger long before I ever let anything happen to you."

I held his face in my hands again, "*nothing* is going to happen to me *or* you. Do you hear me?" I search his eyes for reassurance. The tables have turned and now it's my turn to be strong.

"When I said that you have the power to destroy me, I didn't mean literally your *power*, Amarah. If anything were to happen to you, I wouldn't survive. Do you understand? You make me weak in the worst way. I can't live without you."

His eyes hold unshed tears and I've never seen him this way before. It brings my own tears to my eyes and makes it hard to breathe. My chest feels tight and I had to swallow a couple of times before I find my voice.

"Logan, I..." I lick my lips and try again. There are so many things I want to say. I want to reassure him and tell him nothing is going to happen to either of us. That together, we're stronger than anything or anyone, and I believe it, but all I can say is, "I love you so much," as I pull him down to kiss me.

The kiss is hard and crushing and full of need. He moves on top of me, his massive body completely covering mine, and I grip his arms tightly. I want to protect him, to reassure him, to make him confident again. He's the strongest person I know and the only person I truly trust with my life completely. Seeing him so vulnerable and scared hurts my heart.

I slide my hands down his back and tug at his shorts. He breaks the kiss so he can sit up and take them off. For a split second, I'm embarrassed at the thought of my sister in the guest room down the hall, but that quickly leaves my mind at the sight of Logan. The need in his eyes. So, I ignore my inhibitions. Logan *needs* this. *I* need this.

He tugs on my shorts and I lift my butt off the bed to make it easier for him to take them off. He leans back down on top of me, his face inches away from mine, but he doesn't come in for the kiss. We just stare at each other, both with too much emotion to comprehend or even try to verbalize. His chest presses against mine every time he inhales, our breathing already heavy.

I pull my power out and press it around us. I haven't used it while having sex since the first time. It's not usually something I have time to think about before I'm lost to pleasure at Logan's touch. But tonight is different. The rush of power brings goosebumps to our skin and Logan shudders above me, momentarily closing his eyes as he enjoys the sensation.

It's overwhelming.

It's comforting.

It's heat on our skin.

Logan follows my lead and lets go of his Fey power and it immediately mingles with mine. That cool breeze that always seems to cool me from the inside out. The perfect match to my power. It's my turn to close my eyes and take it all in.

It's Logan.

It's us.

It's home.

Logan finds my lips with his and parts them with his tongue, taking his time with every stroke against mine. He kisses me so slowly it's almost excruciating. My body is on fire, I'm throbbing *everywhere*. I moan slowly and deeply into his mouth. His hand moves between my legs, his fingers slipping in easily.

He growls gently and pulls away from the kiss, “you’re already so wet.”

“You don’t understand how much just your simple touch affects me,” I admit.

When I finally open my eyes, I gasp in shock, but Logan speaks first, “your eyes. They’re glowing again, like honey fire.”

“Yours too,” I whisper, “emerald green fire.”

Logan keeps his eyes on mine, opens my legs wider, and pushes his way inside me the same way he just kissed me.

Excruciatingly slowly.

Inch by slow inch he fills me up. I inhale deeply and lift my hips to meet him. He stops when he’s all the way inside me, and just keeps staring at me, like he wants to memorize everything about this moment. All I can hear is my heavy breathing and my heart pounding in my ears. My hands are on his chest and I feel his heart beating hard beneath them, matching the rhythm of mine.

He slowly starts to move in and out, keeping a steady, but slow pace. We never once take our eyes off of each other.

It’s intimate.

It’s intense.

It’s beautiful.

The power is pulsing inside of me and all around me. We’ve had sex many, many times, but never like this. Never this raw with emotion. With unbridled love.

I feel the heat in my body starting to rise. My breathing getting short and heavy. My hips losing their rhythm. Logan keeps his steady pace, never faltering, in and out, in and out, over and over again, never breaking eye contact. The heat is a raging fire inside of me and I need it out. I hold onto Logan’s muscular arms and revel at the strength in them, but they’re shaking from the effort of holding himself up this long. I feel my body tighten around him and I can’t contain the fire anymore. I let out a loud moan, almost a cry. I bite into Logan's shoulder to stifle my screams of pleasure as my body spasmed underneath him.

He finally collapses on top of me, giving in to the pleasure and abandoning his slow and steady pace. He wraps his arms around me and hugs me tightly to him. I mirror him and wrap my arms and legs around him, holding onto him as tightly as I can. We We hold onto each other for dear life for what feels like hours.

Logan finally raises up enough to look at me. The fire in his eyes is gone but the intensity is still there. He stops moving above me and comes in for a kiss. It's long and deep and I moan into his mouth. He breaks the kiss and continued moving his hips again. He's back to the slow and steady rhythm and I can't take it.

"Logan," I say in a breathless whisper. "you're going to make me cum again."

He smiles confidently and finally closes his eyes. He listens to my body and knows when I'm close again. He grabs onto the headboard and pushes harder inside of me, causing me to gasp at the depth of him inside of me. I have to cover my mouth with my hands to keep from crying out again. Logan lets out a growl that's almost not entirely human, as he pounds so deep into me I feel like he's going to split me in two. I feel him get even harder right before the pleasure claims us both and we cum together.

Logan lets go of the headboard and collapses on his side next to me. We're both breathless and spent, even though he had done all the work.

I roll over and ran my hand through his hair. He opens his eyes to look at me and his eyes are the beautiful green with hints of yellow they always are. No power to magnify their beauty but they still enthral me and I never want to look into anyone else's eyes this way. Ever again. For my entire life.

"Well, that was... *wow*," I say with a giggle.

"I've never felt our power like that before. Not since the first night. And your eyes, they were like fire again."

"So were yours," I say. "What does it mean?"

He shakes his head, "I don't know."

Just then, I notice the bite mark I left on his shoulder. There's a small line of blood seeping out of it. "Oh my God, I'm so sorry! I broke skin!" I reach out to touch it then stop. "Did I hurt you?"

His smile is devious and confident, "I didn't even feel a thing. Come here," he reaches for me and rolls to his back so I can lay on his chest. It's our favorite position.

"I hope my sister didn't hear us."

"Shit, me too."

We both start laughing. I sigh and let myself fall into his embrace. This is all too good to be true. If anything life has shown me, it's that nothing this good lasts forever. The thought makes me sad and I quickly push it aside.

"You know, I've been so happy this past month, just being here with you, but I've been thinking," I sigh. "I need to get back to my training, and we need to elect a new Leader for the Air Fey. I can't stay in hiding anymore."

He sighs too, "I know. I've been thinking the same thing. At least we've gotten to enjoy this time together," he hugs me tighter. "Plus, it's not like we aren't going to still be together."

"You're right," I smile. "There's a lot to do and we need to get it done."

I think about my sister being able to finally help with the dragon scales and the alliance with the Vampires. I'm thrilled, but I can't help but still wonder why Michael had told me to find Revna.

"You know, there's one more thing I haven't told you," I confess.

I feel him tense just a little. “Oh? It can’t be anything more serious than finding out you’re an Angel,” he snorts. “Right?”

“No, no,” I reassure him. “But it is along the same line, and well, since now you know the truth, I won’t sound so crazy.”

“Alright, I’m listening.”

“Archangel Michael came to me in a dream recently. He told me that I should find the Witch, Revna. He said that she would be able to help me with the dragon scales, and I’m just confused as to why he would tell me to find her and not Iseta.”

“Hmmm...I don’t know. Are you sure the dream was real?”

“Yes, it was like the dream I had when I was prepared to fight evil. Remember I told you about it?”

“I remember.”

“Well, dreams aren’t usually that vivid or memorable. These two were.”

“Alright, well, did he tell you *how* to find Revna?”

“No. He said that a raven would lead me to her. He said I would know when it happened. I just don’t know why I’m being directed to her when everyone else, and my gut, is telling me she is evil.”

“I don’t know, Amarah. Your gut has always led you true, but why would an Angel mislead you? There has to be some reason we don’t know yet. I know your sister said she feels confident with the dragon scales, but what if she can’t do it? What if it does require something stronger? Darker?”

I sigh heavily, “this is my confusion. I just don’t know. I don’t know what to do.”

“Well, you have Iseta now and you know her so, trust her. Let her help you. Maybe she won’t be powerful enough after all and that’s why you need to find Revna. And if you happen to come across Revna, well...be careful and alert and see what she has to offer. You never know."

"That sounds like a solid plan. See? What would I do without you?"

"Amarah?"

"Yes?"

"No more secrets."

"No more secrets," I agree.

# Private Party

E.T. by Katy Perry, Kanye West

I enjoy the rest of the weekend with my sister, which consists of mostly drinking wine, long chats about life, reminiscing, and a ton of laughter. It's relaxing, stress-free, and one hundred percent just what I need. It's the best way to end my month-long hiatus before getting back to reality.

"I hate that you're leaving," I pout. "But we all have so much to do."

"I'll be in touch soon. I need to gather some things for the spell, but it shouldn't take me too long. In the meantime, *you* be careful, ok?" She's my older sister but honestly has always been more like a mother to me. And a best friend.

"I will, I promise," I assure her and give her a long, tight hug.

"And *you*," Iseta surprises me when she walks up to Logan and hugs him as well. "You make sure she stays out of trouble. I know how she is. Stubborn and doesn't like to ask for help. You keep her safe for me, you hear?"

Logan nods, "I will always protect her with my life."

Although *I* don't like the sound of that, Iseta seems satisfied.

"Good," she patted him on the arm. "Ok, well I'm off. You two take care of each other and I'll see you both very soon."

I watch my sister get into her vehicle and turn around in the driveway. She pulls out and waits for a few cars to pass before getting on the road and heading back home. I stand in the driveway and watch until I can't see her vehicle anymore.

Logan hugs me from behind, wrapping his arms around my shoulders, and I lean into him.

"You'll see her soon. Everything is going to work out just fine," he says softly.

"I know. It's just hard saying goodbye when you never know what tomorrow holds, but that's a burden we all live with, warriors or not." I sigh. "I need to go see Valmont tonight before we head out of town tomorrow. I need to update him on everything."

"Why not just give him a call?"

"Well, it's a lot to explain. I'd rather see him in person and see what his mood is like. He's been patient so far, but I need him to *remain* patient. We're so close to getting the alliance in place. I just feel like a personal touch will go further than a phone call."

"Whatever you think is best," he kisses me on my head. "Come on, let's go inside and finish packing for tomorrow."

We're all set to go to the Õhk Family, to designate a new Leader, as well as continue my training. I have no idea how long I'll be gone this time so, I reach out to Mariah, to house and dog sit for me again. She's the true Angel.

The clock turns to exactly 10:00 p.m. as I pull up to the Sandia Casino to see Valmont. The last time I had seen him, we left on...*awkward* terms. To be honest, I really don't want to see him and potentially be in another awkward situation, but business has to come before my personal feelings on this one. I owe it to him and I owe it to the Fey. We need this alliance solidified. We need Valmont.

I pull into the valet and a young man rushes to open my door for me. I let him.

"Good evening, Miss Andrews."

"Hey, Josh. A little late to be considered evening, isn't it?" I ask, as I hold out a tip.

"Not around here," he smiles and shakes his head. "You know I can't take that, but I appreciate the offer. I'll keep your car ready up front," he says quickly, as he hops in and closes the door so I can't argue.

I sigh and shake my head. I've become a regular here. Not something I'm proud of by the way. And because Valmont is...well, *Valmont*, he insists everyone knows who I am and treat me like I'm freaking royalty. It's silly and I don't like it, but there's nothing I can do or say to change it. I've tried and gotten nowhere so, I stopped trying. Besides, this is the last thing I should be spending my energy fighting.

I'm almost to the back of the casino, where the steps lead up to Valmont's office that overlooks the night club, when Emerson spots me. The ever-present and alert bodyguard.

"Hey, Amarah, you here to see Valmont?"

"What gave me away?" I ask sarcastically.

He knows I'm here to see Valmont. That's the only reason why I come to the casino. I know he's just making small talk, but for some reason, the rhetorical question bugs me. Having to see Valmont always gets me...*snippy*.

"He's hosting a private party. I'm afraid he's unavailable."

I cross my arms, even more frustrated now. "Is that so?"

"I'm afraid so," he gives me a hard, stern look. As a former Navy SEAL, he has a good one, but it doesn't faze me. I know he won't, and *can't*, act on it.

I look back, defiantly, into his piercing blue eyes, "I have news about the alliance. Trust me, you need to take me to him, now. I won't take but five minutes of his *precious* time," I roll my eyes.

"Amarah, trust me on this one. He's not in the best mood. I really think you should come back and see him tomorrow night."

"I can't come back and see him tomorrow night. I'm heading to the Air Fey and I don't know when I'll even be back. I need to see him tonight. Besides, it's good news so, it might help his mood."

He stays looking at me for a long time, his mind racing with the decision.

"This needs to happen Emerson. *Tonight*. I don't care what kind of...*mood* he's in. We're partners and he needs to make time for me. The party isn't going anywhere."

He sighs and shakes his head, "fine, but don't say I didn't warn you. Follow me."

He leads the way around the corner to where the entrance of the club is. There's a line twisting through the red velvet and gold rope barriers. Not surprisingly, the line consists of mostly women, scantily dressed, wearing high heels that are way too high, too much makeup, and too much damn perfume. Their high pitched talking and giggling is filled with anticipation for the party inside.

"Ugh," I mutter under my breath as I follow Emerson to the front of the line. I've never been that girlie girl and I just can't relate to it. At all.

There's a big standing sign off to the side that indicated this was a, *Private Party. Well excuse the fuck out of me, Mr. Boujee*, I think to myself, as the bouncer at the entrance nods to Emerson and lifts the rope to let us through. Of course, this doesn't go unnoticed, and shouts and screams of protest and anger erupt behind me. I smile to myself and continue following Emerson inside.

There's a narrow hallway that leads from the entrance and opens up to an enormous room. It's only a little after 10:00 p.m. and the place is already jam-packed. I have no idea how the others, waiting eagerly outside, are ever going to get in. The dance floor is in the center of the large room, and there are two bars on each side. VIP tables line the rest of the space along the walls, but the main VIP lounge is straight across from the entrance, and takes up the entire back wall. Of course, it's elevated to give you the best view of every inch of the club. No doubt that's where Valmont will be.

As soon I walk out of the hallway and enter the dance floor, all of my senses are accosted at once. I can't believe my eyes. Everywhere I look, Vampires are...*feeding*. The distinct metallic smell of blood hangs in the air and I can taste it on the back of my tongue. The air feels charged with energy. Devious, forbidden energy, with an undercurrent of sex. My immediate reaction is shock, but that soon turns into rage, as I imagine these innocent people being attacked.

"Emerson," I grab his arm angrily. "What in the Hell is going on?" I have to shout to be heard over the music.

Emerson leans down closer to me, "I *did* warn you. This is one of Valmont's coveted private parties."

"We have to stop this! This isn't ok, these people..." I look around me and realize that no one is scared. No one is screaming. In fact, everyone seems to be enjoying themselves. Emphatically.

"These people are what? Clearly enjoying themselves?"

"I don't understand. They're being...*eaten*," I have no words to describe the horror I see right in front of me. "Why aren't they scared?"

Emerson laughs, "man, how you ended up mixed into all of this is beyond me. You don't know much about Vampires *at all*." He shakes his head, "Let's go. Valmont is this way."

We start pushing our way through the crowd in the direction of the VIP area. There are too many bodies, everywhere I look, Vampires are feeding. Someone grabs my arm and spins me around. I'm suddenly being pressed way too close to a Vampire with blood dripping down his chin and crazy eyes.

He moves his face even closer to mine and the smell of blood is overwhelming. "Mmmm, don't you smell delicious," he says, as he breathes in deeply. He runs a finger down my neck, "what a treat you are. What do you say we go somewhere more... *private*?" His teeth snap at the end of the word.

I'm suddenly *terrified*, like I had been the first time I met Valmont.

I'm frozen.

I can't think.

I can't move.

My heart is in my throat.

The room is suddenly quiet, and all I can do, is stare at his mouth in horror. The red on his lips is too vivid. Too vibrant. Like a splash of color being spotlighted in the night.

Emerson suddenly looms over us, "she's not here for the party. Let her go."

The Vampire sticks out his blood-stained bottom lip in an exaggerated pout. "Boo. Maybe next time," he leans in and sniffs me. "Definitely next time," he smiles and shows his fangs, then finally lets me go and pushes back into the crowd.

Emerson is standing in front of me now. "Amarah, are you ok?" He snaps his fingers in front of my face and my mind suddenly comes crashing back to reality. The music is blaring in my ears again, I take a deep breath in, and my body shakes.

I have to swallow a few times before I find my voice, "I'm ok." I say the words, but I'm not sure they're true.

Still, I have to get a hold of myself. Nothing is going to happen to me here. Not with Emerson with me and definitely not with Valmont nearby. Then again, it would take less than a second for one of these Vampires to sink their teeth in me. I shudder at the thought and *not* in a good way. I've been spending a lot of time with Valmont and he makes it easy to think he's normal. Well, normal-ish. Seeing the Vampires like this, really solidifies what they are.

Predators.

"I'm ok," I repeat, stronger this time.

Emerson has a worried look on his face, but he nods once, and leads the way towards the back of the club, but this time, he doesn't let go of my arm. We come to a set of stairs that head up to the VIP area, some girls are hanging out on the rail, looking over the dance floor. They're dressed in very little, or very tight clothing, and they're all beautiful with voluptuous curves. Of course, Valmont would take the prettiest ones for himself.

I'm suddenly very aware that I'm wearing a pair of jeans, sneakers, and a tank top. Granted, they fit me well and show off what curves I do have, but I'm a four at best, compared to these women. I'm all of a sudden feeling insecure and out of place. Is this the type of girl Valmont likes? Considering what I know about him and his style, it does make sense. Why do I care?

"You'll find Valmont up there," Emerson points up the steps. "There are no other Vampires up there except him, you'll be safe. I'll wait for you here."

I look up the steps and I don't want to go up. I just want to run home, back into the safety of my home and Logan's arms. Why hadn't I done what he suggested? I could have easily made this a phone call instead of a visit. I'm kicking myself in the ass for being so damn generous.

"Amarah," Emerson gets my attention again. "Are you sure you're alright? We can go and you can leave your message with me. I'll make sure he gets it."

*C'mon, Amarah, you're the Võitleja. You can handle a little private party*, I say in my head. *You're better than this. You're stronger than this. You have allied the Vampires when no one else could. Put your big girl panties on and get up those damn steps!*

"No, I'm fine. It will just take me a few minutes to talk to Valmont. I'll be right back," I finally sound more like myself, but my feet feel like they're stuck in concrete blocks, as I push myself up the stairs.

I receive a lot of dirty looks as I mount the stairs and head further into the VIP area. I'm scanning the place for Valmont, but so far, I can't see him. I keep walking through the area and head towards the right side. I see a giant black leather couch against the wall and someone sitting on it in an immaculate white suit and shimmering silver-white hair. That has to be him. He's the only one I know who dresses that elegantly and has white hair.

As my reluctant steps draw me closer, I realize a woman is sitting sideways, in his lap. All I can see of her are her long beautiful legs stretched out on the couch, a radiant blue dress that barely covers her goods, and long, flowing blonde hair. Her hand is gently holding Valmont's head, and his face is buried, hidden in her neck.

I stop when I'm standing a few feet away and gasp when I realize what's happening. Valmont hears me and rolls his eyes up to look at me. His piercing turquoise eyes stare up at me as his mouth is pressed into the woman's neck. I try to hide the shock and horror off my face, but I'm sure I fail. Valmont seems to bite down harder on her neck as he keeps eye contact with me. The woman just sits there and moans her pleasure into his ear. I don't understand it.

Valmont slowly lifts his head away from her neck, his mouth stained with her blood. He keeps his eyes on mine, as he wipes the corner of his mouth with his thumb, then puts it in his mouth to clean the blood off. No matter how elegant Valmont is, how beautiful, exotic, poised and proper, he'll always be one thing above all else.

Someone…no, *something*, at the top of the food chain.

A predator.

He shoves the woman off his lap and onto the couch quite abruptly and not very gently. She doesn't seem to mind. Her face is slack and she has a lopsided, drug-induced, smile on her face. She's completely gone and no longer on this planet much less in this room.

"Amarah Rey, what are you doing here?" He asks in a tone that isn't exactly friendly.

I try to respond, but nothing comes out. My heart is blocking my throat and I can't speak. I just stare at him and the drunk girl sitting next to him.

I'm suddenly swept to a dark corner of the VIP area, my back slams into a wall. It's like I blinked once and was suddenly just somewhere else. Valmont is pinning me to the wall with his body inches away from mine, and both hands on either side of me, leaving me nowhere to escape.

Once again, I feel frozen in shock. My heart is beating too fast in my chest. My eyes are drawn to his lips, but this time for a different reason, other than admiring them. I can still smell his clean cologne with hints of bergamot, but now, I smell the blood, and I don't need Logan's Wolf senses for it. It's right there, fresh on his lips.

He grabs my chin and aggressively shoves my head to the side, "I hear your heart beating out of your chest, Amarah Rey."

He leans his head in, I can feel his warm breath on my neck, and my pulse beating frantically beneath it. His lips gently brush my neck and I can't help but breathe in a shaky, scared breath.

"Only this time," he whispers with his lips on my skin, "I can sense your fear."

He closes the gap between us and presses his body against mine. I swallow hard as I feel him, hard and ready. He's enjoying this, he's enjoying my fear, and as terrified as I am, my body still reacts to him against me. His fingers gripping my chin almost painfully, his body covering mine, and the feeling of his erection trapped between us. It all speaks to something dark, something dangerous, rooted deep inside of me. Something that scares me. Something that I don't want to acknowledge.

It feels wrong.

It feels bad.

It feels *evil.*

He gently and slowly licks a warm line up my neck, then closes his mouth over my throbbing pulse, and sucks. I close my eyes and the sensation of his mouth on my skin. The heat of it ignites my desire and send shivers down my body.

He thrusts his hips forward, pushing his erection harder into my stomach, as his fangs graze against my skin, pulling a whimper out of my throat. A whimper I don't even know is caused by fear or excitement.

His mouth leaves my neck. "I can taste your *desire,* Amarah Rey. Desire for *me*," he whispers softly in my ear.

He pulls back, jerking my face back to center so he can see me, and I have no clue what my expression shows. Yes, I'm terrified. Down to my bones. He scares me like no one else ever has, and yet, a small part of me likes the fear. A small part of me is attracted to it. To him. My body reacts to his body in a way that it never has.

He leans in as if he's going to kiss me, but I still can't move. I'm still frozen against him. Maybe I just don't want to move. Maybe I want this to happen. His hand comes up and caresses my cheek, his fingers slightly tremble as he trails his thumb over my bottom lip. My lips part at his touch, and I sigh.

He suddenly takes a giant step back away from me and closes his eyes, his jaw taut with tension. I let out a heavy, relieved sigh, and my body relaxes with it. I'm breathing heavily and I'm still scared, but I know the immediate danger has passed.

He finally opens his eyes, straightens his suit, and finally looks at me. "You didn't answer my question."

My mind can't remember a single thing that happened before the last sixty seconds. "What question?" I manage to get out.

"Why are you here?"

Why am I here? Yes, why *am* I here? I have to shake my head, which seems to be foggy, and remember why I came to see him.

"I… my sister…" I struggle to get it all out right. "We have a Witch to help us," I finally blurt out.

Valmont's demeanor changes ever so slightly. His rigid posture relaxes, the anger in his eyes dissipates, and his face softens. This is the Valmont that I'm used to dealing with.

"Who is this Witch?" He asks coldly, still distant with me, but I'll take him being distant over scary, any day.

"Believe it or not, my sister."

"Your sister? You mean, your *human* sister?

I laugh, "yes, she's actually *not* my sister. She's a Witch who's been looking over me since I was born." I shake my head and bring up my hand to stop his questions, "and don't ask me the details, because it's just as confusing to me. The only thing we need to focus on is that we can finally complete this alliance. You can finally have protection for you and your people."

"Well, now, not *all* of my people, Amarah Rey," he says, obviously still irritated.

I sigh, "no, not all, but I did the best I could."

"Well, maybe your best isn't good enough, is it?" He spits out, angrily.

It feels like a physical slap in my face to hear him say it. Him. Valmont. The Vampire who's been nothing but nice, or at least intrigued with me, from the very beginning. Damn the truth for being so hard to hear sometimes. I'm already insecure in myself as it is, I don't need to hear other people confirm it. I have to push past the tears harder than I've ever pushed before. I refuse to let him see me cry.

I hold my head up high, "maybe my best isn't good enough, but that's all you get, and I don't see anyone else lining up to give you protection against fire. I'll be in touch when she's ready to perform the spell and then we can be done with these meetings You can be done with me and my lack of…everything," I throw my hands up in the air, giving up on making any more effort. "I'll let you get back to your...*party*." I say, disgustedly, as I walk past him and back the way I came.

I don't look back and he doesn't try to stop me. When I reach the bottom of the stairs, Emerson is there, like he said he would be. He eyes me and his eyes narrow, but he doesn't ask anything. He just nods once and leads the way through the crowd, staying close to me, back to the entrance.

Once I'm out of the club, the air feels lighter and clearer, and I take a deep breath to steady myself. My mind is racing with everything that just happened. I was finally exposed to Vampires in their element, and something tells me, this is just the tip of the iceberg. I know deep down, that this very public party, is the *least* of what they do.

What they *are*.

And Valmont? He's never terrified me as much as he did tonight. The first time, I had been caught off guard. It was my first time meeting a Vampire, but *tonight*...tonight I was genuinely terrified of who Valmont is.

I shake my head and head out to my car as quick as my legs can take me without flat out running away. I want to put as much distance between me and Valmont, and that den of predators, as soon as possible.

Once this alliance is in place, I'll be done with Valmont, except for when *absolutely* necessary, for business. To handle the war. I can even let the Queen deal with the alliance going forward. I have enough on my plate to focus on anyway. So, why did tonight bother me so much? I don't want to admit the truth.

That a part of me enjoys the thrill, the threat.

No.

I won't admit it. If I need a thrill, my boyfriend is a damn *Werewolf* for fuck's sake. I can get all the thrill I need with him and be *safe* the whole time.

Maybe that's the difference? I don't want to be safe.

I throw these thoughts out of my head, turned up the radio, and drive back home.

To safety.

# The Happiness of Innocence

Mind On You by George Birge

On the road again. Is it just me that only hears Donkey's voice singing that song now? Anyway, we're on the road again, Logan and I. We're heading up North to the Air Fey's home. The Queen is already there because, in addition to my training, we'll also be selecting a new Leader for the Õhk Family.

Two main candidates are vying for the position and it will be the Queen's decision on who gets the title and responsibility. I feel bad for whoever takes over the role. The last Leader, and *traitor*, has tainted the honor of the family and set a long, dark shadow over them. It isn't fair to blame the entire Fey family for her crimes, and no one does, but...something like that isn't easily forgotten. Trust has to be earned again. Sad but true.

I'm completely relaxed in the passenger seat, holding Logan's hand solidly in mine, enjoying the beautiful New Mexico scenery and humming to the song on the radio. It's early October and starting to get a little chilly when the sun goes down. The leaves are turning their beautiful yellow, red and orange colors. It's almost time for sweats, hoodies, and warm fuzzy socks. I'm not a fan of winter and being cold, but I don't mind fall at all.

We're about an hour and a half into our drive. We've passed a lot of small towns along the way and are headed into the next one. We must be getting close. Again, I have no idea where we're going or what to look for. Then again, with glamour, I probably won't even see what's actually there anyway.

I look over at Logan, "are we almost there?"

He turns and gives me his beautiful green eyes, "yes, the town is just up the road maybe ten more minutes."

He keeps his eyes locked on mine and my heart starts to race. One, because he affects me so easily and two, because he's driving.

"Logan! Watch the road!" I break eye contact to look at the road and make sure we're still in our lane.

Of course, we're holding steady in our lane and I can still feel Logan looking at me. "Logan, I'm serious!"

He chuckles, "you don't trust me?"

"You know I do, but you need to see where you're going when you're driving, Werewolf or not."

He looks back at the road and then lets go of my hand. He lifts up the center console and raises his arm, "come here," he gestures for me to slide over to him.

I raise my eyebrows, "and taking my seatbelt off isn't safe either, Mr."

He looks at me again, this tie with his teasing half-smile, and eyes sparkling with humor. I can't help but smile back, and of course, comply with his request, as I unbuckle and slid over to him. Maybe someone has the will to defy this man, but it's not me. Especially when it gets me closer to his body.

He hugs me close to him and then give me his eyes once again. "I would never put you in danger," he says seriously.

"I know," I whisper as my eyes fall to his lips.

He pulls me in for the kiss and, even though I know it's dangerous, I can't fight it. I don't want to. It's nothing more than a press of our lips for maybe three seconds. Still, three seconds with your eyes off the road is three seconds too many.

I open my eyes and find him still looking at me. "Watch the road," I lecture, still drowning in his green eyes.

His eyes glance at the road and then, all of a sudden, his eyes widened and he jerks the steering wheel, making the truck swerve. My heart is in my throat and I gasp. I want to scream but nothing comes out. I quickly looked at the road, but nothing is wrong. We're still in our lane and there are no other vehicles around. I look back over to Logan and he's desperately trying to hide a smile and failing.

"You ass," I yell, as I punch him in the arm.

He busts out laughing, "you should have seen your face."

"I can't believe you would scare me like that on purpose! Are you trying to give me a heart attack?" I put my hand over my heart for dramatic effect and give him my best mean face.

He's trying to catch his breath from laughing so hard, "oh come on, I had to. It was too easy." He reaches up and caresses my cheek, the hints of laughter still tugging at his lips, "don't be mad."

I try. I try to be mad at him for his little prank, but the happiness in his eyes, and the smile threatening to break through, warms me all the way to my soul. My mean face slowly crumbles and his humor is rubbing off on me. I was being an easy mark and he played on it.

The smile spreads across my face as I relax next to him again. "Ok, ok, I'm not mad, but you're still an ass."

"As long as I'm still *your* ass. Here, let me make it up to you." He starts scrolling through the playlist on his phone.

*Mind On You* by George Birge comes through the speakers.

He hugs me tighter and starts singing. I pull back so I can watch him, swaying in his arms as he sings to me, with a smile on my face and love in my eyes.

I lean in to kiss him on the cheek. "I love when you sing to me," I whisper in his ear, then take his ear lobe gently between my lips. I start kissing down his neck and feel the goosebumps erupt on his skin.

"Mmmm," he moans and leans his head back. "I thought you didn't want us to wreck?"

"I don't," I say as my teeth scraped his neck and then I very gently bite down, slowly, tasting his skin.

"You keep doing that and I'm going to pull this damn truck over right fucking here."

I continue kissing him along his jaw and then pull back so he can see me. "Don't tease me with a good time," I bite my lip.

"Damn it, woman," he grabs my hand and places it on his hard erection. "You see what you do to me?" His voice is low, eyes full of heat.

I squeeze him through his jeans, feeling how big and hard he is, and it sends desire and need racing through my body at lightning speed. "So, let's do something about it," I say as I start to unbutton his jeans.

His hand stops me. "We can't. We're here."

I straighten in the seat and start looking around at the town as we approach. It looks like every other small, blink and you'll miss it, New Mexico town. The buildings are all old, mostly adobe, and look like they're falling apart. The surrounding land is all rolling hills and mountains off in the distance. This town is out in the middle of nowhere and looks deserted and overgrown.

"Welcome to Truchas," Logan sounds grumpy, as he pulls into a dirt parking lot in front of one of the old, ragged-looking buildings.

"This is it?" I ask, skeptically. "Are they using glamour to make it look like this?" Although, after I ask the question, I know they're not. I would have been able to feel the tingling sensation glamour leaves in the air.

"Nope. There's never been a need. This town has been where the Air Fey have lived for centuries. The look of it alone keeps most people from stopping. It looks deserted and there is no reason to stop here. It is just a pass-through town."

"So, no one has *ever* stopped here before?" I ask, and I know I'm being difficult.

"Of course, there's been a few here and there, but they use their glamour on themselves easy enough when it happens."

"This town reminds me of the small town I grew up in. It's the same way. Blink and you miss it."

"Maybe one day you can take me there and I can see where you grew up."

I snort, "not likely. I don't ever go there if I don't have to. There's nothing good about that place and nothing left there to give me a reason to go back. Come on let's get out. I need to stretch my legs," I say, changing the subject.

Logan turns off the engine, opens his door, and gets out without another question. He really is pretty great about knowing when to push and when to let go. I scoot over to the driver's side so I can follow Logan out. He turns around and steps up to the truck. I part my knees so he can squeeze in.

"I want to know everything about you, Amarah. Good, bad, ugly. It all matters because it made you into the person you are today. Don't be ashamed of your past, we all have one."

"I'm not *ashamed* of it," I say with a sigh. "It's just...there aren't very many *good* memories. Not that I can remember a lot either way. I have these blank spots in my memory. Like, a lot! I have a terrible memory of my childhood if I'm being honest," I chuckle, trying to lighten the seriousness of the conversation. I shake my head, "there *are* good memories, but there's a lot I don't care to revisit too," I shrug.

"I can feel your conflicting feelings," he says quietly. "Just know that I'm here for you, in every way, and I want to know every part of you. We have a lifetime to get there though, and I'm in no hurry." He moves my hair behind my ear and kisses me gently on the cheek before placing his lips on mine.

I wrap my legs and arms around him and kiss him back. He lifts me off the seat and steps away from the truck. I hold onto him tighter and he breaks the kiss, giving me his cocky smile, "I thought you needed to stretch your legs?"

"Then put me down," I whisper in his ear, as I gently take his ear lobe in my mouth again, and then kiss his neck. He groans in the back of his throat and his hands tighten where he holds my thighs.

I hear a door open and a bunch of little voices and hurried little footsteps. Logan sets me down just as a small group of kids come into view. They run as fast as they can towards Logan. He drops down to his knees, opens his arms, and the little group rams into him with all their excited energy. Logan sways with the force of their arrival but doesn't fall over. When he regains his balance and has given them all his attention, he stands back up, bringing the smallest of the children up with him in his arms.

She looks to be about five and the other kids are anywhere from eight up to twelve. I'm just standing here, watching the merriment, with a silly smile plastered on my face. I've never seen

Logan interact with kids before. He's natural with them and they all seem to love him. I've never been great with kids, and seeing Logan interact so easily with them, warms my heart.

"Hey, everyone," Logan says, getting their attention. "Let's not be rude and say hello to Amarah."

All their little gazes eagerly look up at me and I can't help but gasp. They're all fair-skinned and have different shades of blonde hair, but when they look at me, I'm startled to see their violet eyes beaming up at me. I've seen their families' eyes before but I'm still not used to it. Purple eyes are just not a color you see on a day to day basis.

"Hey guys," I say, smiling down at them. "I'm Amarah, it's so nice to meet you."

They all started talking eagerly at once and asking a million questions.

"Who are you?" "Why are you here?" "Are you a Werewolf too?" "What power do you have?" "Are you Logan's *girlfriend*?" That last one comes from one of the older boys in an, *ewwww, girls have cooties*, kind of voice.

I look up at Logan and we both laugh. The little girl in his arms is one of the sweetest little things I've ever seen. She still has her baby, chubby cheeks. Her hair is in loose, natural curls just past her shoulders, and her eyes are like deep purple amethyst stones staring at me.

I wave to her, "hi. What's your name?"

She shies away and cuddles harder in Logan's arms. "It's ok, Amarah is with me. You can tell her your name. She's very nice," he encourages her.

She looks at me and quietly says, "Tori."

"It's so nice to meet you, Tori," I say softly. "I hope that we can be good friends too. Like you and Logan are."

She smiles shyly at me and nods her head but leans in towards Logan again. The group of older kids are still trying to get our attention.

One of the smaller boys grabs a hold of my hand and says, "I'm Vic, I'll be your friend," he smiles up at me, his deep purple eyes sparkling with youth and innocence.

I smile back at him, still holding on to his small hand, "I'd like that, Vic."

"Come on," he says, as he pulls on my arm.

I look back at Logan and he's following us. "Looks like you've got some competition," I tease.

"As do you," he says, gesturing to the sweet little girl in his arms.

"Touché," I laugh.

Well, the kids are warm and welcoming. They seem to know Logan well and really like him. Then again, they're already liking me too, and they don't know me at all. Maybe they trust me because I'm with Logan? Maybe they're just sweet, happy kids?

As Vic holds onto my hand and leads me to the door they came running out of, I hope the rest of the Air Fey will be as happy and welcoming. Considering what they've recently gone through, with Aralyn, I doubt it.

I just have to remember that it's not me they're mad at. It's not personal.

Here we go.

# Getting Settled

Sweater Weather by The Neighbourhood

Vic eagerly pulls me into the building and I follow, my eyes scanning everything, on alert. Do I think anything is going to happen to me? No, not really. Not here, not with Logan and kids around, but still...I'm in an unfamiliar place and don't know what to expect.

The inside of the building is one massive room. It looks like it could be used for all types of events. It reminds me of a dance hall. There's a slightly raised stage at the back of the room, but it's currently hidden behind a large curtain, and the rest of the floor is just one big open space. People are walking in and out of the back door bringing in tables and chairs.

Vic lets go of my hand and runs off with the other kids across the floor and out the back door. "Are they setting up for the ceremony?" I ask Logan.

"Yeah, looks like. Come on, let's see if they need some help."

Still holding little Tori in his arms, he leads us across the floor and towards the back door where everyone seems to be coming from. We walk back outside and I see another building that looks like a garage, stacked full of tables, chairs, boxes, lamps, and all sorts of other supplies. I scan the people around me and no one seems to notice or care that we're here. No angry stares. No curious stares. No hostility whatsoever.

I finally recognize someone I know in the small crowd and smile as we head towards her. Even in this setting, dressed down, there's no mistaking her authority. She's still just as elegant as I've ever seen her, wearing a pair of light blue jeans, brown boots, and a long-sleeved peach colored blouse. Her sunflower yellow hair is pulled back loosely behind her, leaving stray strands around her face.

She looks up as we approach and her warm, grey eyes sparkle with love. "Logan, Amarah, I'm glad you both made it safely." Queen Anaxo, also my aunt, smiles at us and comes in for a hug.

I like when I get to see her like this, relaxed and at ease. I like when she's able to show more of being my aunt than when she has to be the Queen. Still, she commands attention and respect in either form.

Breaking the hug, Ana turns to the other woman she had been speaking to, "Amarah, this is Vyla Beck, she is the Õhk Family's Healer. Vyla, this is Amarah Rey Andrews."

Vyla looks at me with the same deep purple eyes. She looks a bit older than I'm used to seeing with the Fey. Even so, she doesn't look *old*. She looks to be maybe mid-40s and has some slight crow's feet and smile lines that show up when she smiles. It makes her look warm and inviting. Her blonde hair is braided expertly, not allowing any strands to fall around her face. Her hands are soft but strong as we shake hands and exchange hellos.

Vyla looks at Logan standing next to me and takes a step towards him. "I see my little one has already attached herself to you," she says smiling. She reaches her arms out towards Tori, "come on Viktoria. Let's give Logan a break."

Tori shakes her little head emphatically and leans back in towards Logan. Logan speaks softly to her, "be a good girl and listen to your momma, Tori, and later we can have some hot chocolate. With *extra* marshmallows," he whispers. "Deal?"

Her eyes light up and she giggles, "deal!"

Logan gives her a soft kiss on her cheek and hands her to her mom. I watch it all with a stupid look of awe on my face. This large, muscular Werewolf, who can transform his hands into claws and tear you to shreds, is a big *softie*. He's so gentle and sweet with Tori it makes my heart swell. I want to run into his arms and kiss him. I want to be *his* family. The urge is so strong, I bite my bottom lip and look away before I lose the battle of wills.

"We're setting up for the ceremony tomorrow night. Let's get this all taken care of and then I'll show you where you're staying so you can unpack and relax," the Queen directs us.

It takes us a couple of hours to get everything set up and ready for tomorrow, but everyone seems at ease and comfortable. Tomorrow is when everything has to be formal, which I'm *not* looking forward to, but as Võitleja, I have my own part to play. This will be my second formal meeting since discovering The Unseen and finding out my true identity. It hasn't been that long ago, but I feel so different. It feels like so much more time has passed than just two months.

We finish as the sun is setting and I can feel the heat being sucked into the Earth. I can feel the chill sneaking in with the shadows. It's colder up here than it had been in Albuquerque, and I'm grateful for Logan's insistence that I bring warmer clothes.

We're the last ones to leave. Ana, Vyla, Logan, and I, stand in the dirt parking lot, as the last little bit of light fades from the sky.

"I'll be staying with Vyla and her family since I'm only here for a couple of days. They have made up one of the extra homes for you to use since you'll be staying longer for your training," Ana explains.

"I have the keys for your place back at my house," Vyla nods in the general direction. "Come on, we'll head there now so you can unpack and get settled."

We follow Vyla across the street and head down a worn path that leads off into the land towards one of the mountains. Little squares of light spread out across the fields, indicating homes of the Fey, all within walking distance but far enough apart to give each other privacy. I like that the houses here aren't on top of each other like they are in the city.

We approach a small home that has a wooden fence, a little higher than my waist, around the property. Vyla opens the gate and we all walk through as she stays behind to latch the gate behind us. We wait for her to lead the way again as we walk up a couple of steps onto a front porch.

She opens the front door and walks in, then steps to the side, holding the door, "come in, come in, please, don't be shy."

I follow Ana and Logan comes in behind me. We're barely through the entryway when the kids come running over. Tori runs into Logan's arms again, and he obliges by picking her up. Vic is suddenly pulling on my hands trying to get my attention.

"Amarah, Amarah, do you wanna come and play with us?"

"Now, now, Viktor, Amarah, and Logan need to get unpacked and settled. You'll have plenty of time to see them."

"Awww," Vic hangs his head. I peg him to be about nine or ten.

"Hey," I grab his hand to get his attention. "I heard Logan promised Tori some hot chocolate later," I glance up at Tori and she's nodding her head in agreement. "So, why don't you give us some time to get settled, and later we can all hang out and have some hot chocolate. Ok?"

He perks up, but not quite as much as his sister had, at the Promise of hot chocolate. Maybe it's because I don't mention the *extra* marshmallows.

A man walks out of the hallway, "kids, listen to your mother and don't torture our guests. Why don't you both go and play awhile before dinner."

Logan lets Tori down and she runs off with her brother. He stands back up and greets the man walking up to us. "Hey man, good to see you."

They take each other's right hand and hug each other. Although, it's more like a quick bump and tap the shoulder than an actual hug. He's the same height as Logan, but his build is leaner

Logan turns to me, "Amarah, this is Jonathan, Vyla's husband, and your trainer. Jonathan, this is Amarah."

He offers his hand and I take it. It's a strong grip and he shakes my hand firmly. He has violet eyes too, but not as dark as Vyla's. The kids have their mother's eyes. His blonde hair is cut short on the sides, a bit longer on top, but not by much. It's styled with a side part and swept to the left. His face has a naturally stern look to it and the beard adds to the effect.

"It's a pleasure to meet you, Jonathan. You have a lovely family," I say with a genuine smile.

"Thank you, and please, call me Jon. I look forward to our training. I've heard good things."

"Oh, well, don't get your hopes up. My experience has shown me to be a harder student than I'd like to be, but I'll do my best."

Vyla walks over to us and hands Logan a set of keys. "Here you are, dear. You'll be at the house next door to our right. It's all yours."

"Thank you," Logan takes the keys. "We'll go get settled."

Vyla nods, "dinner will be ready around seven. Come on back when you're ready, no rush."

"Oh, do you need help with anything?" I offer, feeling way too useless.

"Nonsense," Vyla waves her arms at me, shooing me towards the door. "You two go get settled, Ana and I have it handled here. Plus, I'll make the kids help," she winks.

"Ok," I laugh, as Logan takes my hand and leads me out the door.

"They're so nice," I beam up at Logan. "Little Tori seems so attached to you. I didn't know you came here that often."

"I visit all the Families a couple of times a year. Since I don't have my own...family," he hesitates, "I spend a lot of time with the Fey. Tori has been attached to me since she was a baby. I have no idea why," he laughs.

My heart breaks for him because I know how hard it is for him to not have a pack. He's a Lone Wolf and has been for a long time. I feel that slight ping of pain through our connection and want to take it away.

"Well, I think it's adorable and you're great with her," I remember the feeling I had earlier, seeing his gentleness with Tori, and how it tugged at my heartstrings and I wanted to hug him and kiss him. I send that through our link to him and he stops walking, turning to face me.

"Do you know how hard it was for me not to grab you and kiss you when I felt this earlier?" He asks.

"It was hard for me too," I admit. I can't see his face very well because it's full-on dark now, but I can *feel* him and that's enough. "You're not alone Logan. I know I can't compare to a family, to a Pack, but you'll never be alone again as long as I'm alive."

"I know," he whispers. "Thank you." He hugs me to his chest and I welcome the warmth of his body. It's gotten a lot colder out as the night has set in and I'm not wearing a jacket.

I shiver, "let's get inside, it's cold out."

"Oh shit, I'm sorry. The cold doesn't affect me like it affects you and I forget."

"It's ok."

The next thing I know, Logan picks me up, and holds me sideways in his arms. I throw my head back laughing, "what are you doing?"

"This way you can cuddle in and stay warm."

"We're almost there, pretty sure I'd survive another minute."

"Maybe, maybe not. Let's not risk it," he says seriously.

I giggle and snuggle into him. He's warm and smells like the woods. Like a clean, crisp fall morning after a rain. I can feel the comfort of being next to him seeping into my body. I close my eyes and everything about him overtakes me.

His scent.

His warmth.

His muscles working as he holds me.

His heartbeat echoing in my ear.

The rise and fall of his chest.

I'm no longer cold at all.

I feel him climbing the stairs to the porch and he stops at the door. Before I can move, he says, "hang on to me," as he lets go of my back with his right hand. I hear the keys jingling as he manages to get the door unlocked and he walks us inside. It's instantly warmer inside the house, and a lamp has been left on in the living room, leaving a faint glow around us.

I lift my head off his shoulder so I can see his face. "Are you going to put me down now?"

"I don't want to," his voice comes out breathy but I know it has nothing to do with the effort of carrying me.

My heart starts racing and I can feel his heart beating Faster against his chest. "It hasn't gotten any easier to be next to you," I whisper.

"No, it hasn't," he agrees. "And I don't want it to."

"Me either," I barely get the words out before our lips connect.

His tongue finds mine and it set the butterflies in my stomach flying frantically. How can he still affect me so much? Just a kiss and I'm overtaken by passion. By desire. By heat. By need. My body responds to every single touch as if it will be the last time I feel him.

*Desperately.*

I'm drowning in him, his touch, his kiss, his scent, his strength, his comfort, his love, his need. I'm drowning in him, but he's also the only one who can save me from sinking.

We break the kiss, both breathing hard. We laugh and he finally sets me down. He hits a light switch on the wall and the house lights up. We're standing in a small entryway and the living room is directly in front of us. I quickly note the real fireplace off to the left. Considering how much colder it is up here, and the fact that we're coming into fall and winter, I'm happy to have it. I can see a small dining room table behind the living room and the start of the kitchen.

There's a door immediately to my right. I walk through and hit the light switch to reveal a bedroom with an attached bathroom. The room is a decent size, with a king-sized bed, and plenty of room to move around it. The bathroom is also a nice size and has an oversized tub and a separate stand-up shower. I don't normally enjoy baths, but only because a standard tub is too small. I can never get my entire body under water at the same time. But this tub on the other hand...I can see candles and bubbles in my future. With a naked Logan of course. Just picturing it stirs desire inside me and I bite my lip.

Logan comes up behind me and whispers in my ear, "you do know I can feel what you're feeling, right?"

I smile, "Oh yes, and I can feel that you're feeling it right back. That's what I love about our connection. No hiding. No games. Just pure, honest feelings."

"Mhmmmm," he mumbles an agreement and kisses my neck sending shivers down my body. "We'll use the tub, just not right now," he sighs and steps away. "I'm going to pull the truck back here to the house and unpack our things. You stay here, and stay warm."

"Ok," I say, turning around to watch him walk out of the room.

I throw myself on the bed and sigh. *He really is too good for me,* I think to myself. I don't know how I would manage any of this Warrior business without him by my side. We have one more night of ease, before business starts up tomorrow, and then my training. I sigh again.

Bring on the pain.

# Michael

She Talks To Angels by The Black Crows

I'm standing on top of a mountain. The wind up here is rough. It's whipping my hair all around and in my face. I'm only getting glimpses of my surroundings. I grab at my hair, attempting to hold most of it steady, so I can see where I am. I'm higher up than I've ever been and I don't remember how I got here. Standing at the edge of the mountain top, I feel like I can see the end of the world from this height. There are more mountains around me, and empty flat land stretched out in front of me, as far as I can see. I glance down and I can see a paved road and tiny dots that must be houses. They're so far below it's hard to tell.

I turn around and am shocked to see a huge, castle-like building reaching towards the sky. It's magnificent and although it looks ancient, it's in perfect condition. My eyes sweep over my surroundings and I'm drawn to a raised wooden platform to the side of the castle. More so, drawn to the person sitting in the middle of it.

"Hello!" I yell out, but the wind takes my voice and carries it away to the Heavens.

I take a step towards the platform and stumble, looking down to see I've stepped on the long white dress, billowing in the wind around me. It's similar to the one I remember wearing when I was in White Sands.

In a dream.

I pick up the material with my free hand, the other still trying to reign in my hair, and walk towards the platform. The material of the dress is thin and I'm barefoot...*again*. I should be been freezing up on this mountain, but I'm not. Other than the wind, loud in my ears, and whipping around me, I'm unaffected by the elements around me.

I make my way to the platform and climb the stairs to get to the top. I immediately recognized the man sitting cross-legged in front of me.

"Hello, Michael," I yell. Even this close, the wind is so intense, I have to yell to be heard.

Michael slowly lifts his head and devours me with his eyes, one slow inch at a time. When he finally settles on my face, his crystal-clear blue eyes sparkle with mischief as he smiles, "hello again, Amarah." He doesn't yell, but I hear his voice loud and clear. It caresses my skin and sends a shiver down my spine.

My feet carry me until I'm standing in front of him, still trying desperately to hold my hair against the wind, and my frustration from overwhelming me. Not one gust of wind or small breeze touches Michael. He sits there, completely calm and comfortable, looking like the regal Angel he is. His eyes never leave mine and he has a sly smile playing on his lips as I sit down opposite of him.

"Why is the wind not affecting you?" I ask loudly.

"Because I'm controlling it. You can too, Amarah," his Scottish voice floats steady and clear through the wind.

"I don't know how!"

He stares at me a bit longer and then holds his hand up and makes a fist. The wind stops instantly.

I let out a sigh of relief and my body relaxes. “Thank you. I really do dislike the wind,” I say as I try to right my hair and fail.

“Oh, a Fey that dislikes one of Earth’s natural elements?” He raises his eyebrows and smirks.

I duck my head, “hey, give me some slack. I did grow up believing I was human, remember? Maybe I wouldn’t dislike it if I could control it like you.”

“That's what you are here for, aye?”

“Here? As in right now?”

He chuckles and the sound send more shivers through my body, “here, as in, with the Air Fey.”

Why does he make me so nervous? “Oh, ummmm, yes. I will begin my training with them soon.”

Michael’s mischievous eyes still hold mine and I have to look away. I’m left looking at the devious smile, pulling at the corner of his beautiful lips, drawing me in. My breath hitches, and his smile finally wins as it lights up his already handsome face, making my heart skip a beat.

I realize I’m staring at him unintelligently, I clear my throat and sit up straighter, trying to gather the intelligent thoughts I know are in my mind...*somewhere*.

“I still haven’t found Revna.”

He shrugs nonchalantly. His demeanor is always so smooth and calm...and *inviting*. “You will when it’s time.”

“Why are you leading me to her? Everything I’ve found out about her, is that she’s *evil*. Why not lead me to Iseta?”

“There is a reason for everything I do, Amarah, you’re just going to have to trust me, and I’m not here to discuss Revna.”

“Oh? What are you here to discuss?”

"Tomorrow's ceremony. You're going to pick a new Leader for Air Fey, are you not?"

"Yes, how did you…"

"Angel, remember?" He interrupts with a dazzling smile.

"Right. How could I forget?" I shake my head and look down at my hands, needing to look anywhere else besides at him. *C'mon, Amarah! Pull it together! You're half Angel too, no need to swoon over him,* I lecture myself in my head.

Just then, as if he read my thoughts, Michael leans in closer to me, and gently lifts my chin. The touch sends a small spark on my skin, like static electricity, and makes me gasp. Then, I'm staring at his piercing blue eyes from inches away, which completely takes my breath away.

"Amarah," he whispers my name, "are you alright?" His face is utterly serious and caring, but his eyes are still sparkling, still teasing. He knows he makes me nervous and he clearly enjoys it.

I drop my gaze from his eyes and that's a mistake...*again*. They land on his rosy pink, perfectly heart-shaped, luscious lips. I let out a heavy sigh and I feel the heat crawl up my cheeks at the thoughts running through my head.

"Amarah?" He asks again, this time moving those lips even closer to mine.

They're so tempting, begging me to lay mine on them. They're beautiful, but Logan's lips are fuller. The thought of Logan brings me back to my senses. I slowly pull my head back, out of his gentle grasp.

I take a deep, shaky breath, "I'm fine." The words come out but I don't *feel* fine. I feel overheated, nervous, and like a damn teenager.

He leans back in his relaxed, easy manner, with that damn smile men get when they know how much they affect you, and I hate that he does.

Regaining my composure, I scowl at him, “so, what do you know about the ceremony tomorrow? I assume you’re here to give me information?”

“Aye, I’m here to tell you who the right Leader should be, and you need to make sure that it happens.”

I shake my head, “it’s not up to me. It’s the Queen’s decision, not mine.”

“Yes, but the Queen listens to council, does she not? After all, you did convince her to align with the Vampires. She listens to *you,* Amarah.”

I think about his words and I know them to be true. The Queen has always trusted my instinct from day one. Maybe because I’m her niece, or maybe because I’m half Angel. Whatever the reason, the Queen *does* listen to my advice.

“I may be able to convince her.”

Michael smiles another heart-stopping smile, “oh, I know you can. I have all the *faith* in you.”

“So, who is this rightful Leader and why?” I ask curiously.

“There will be two candidates that want this new position, one of them is hardly a choice. I imagine once you find out who it is, you will agree. However, just in case, I’m here to guide you toward Luke Meyer.”

“Ok, and why is this Luke guy the one who should be Leader?”

“There are always things at play, Amarah. Far more than you could ever comprehend or imagine. I’m afraid you’re just going to have to trust that I’m telling you this is the right decision.”

“I understand that everything always seems to work out and happen for a reason. I’ve seen it countless times in my own life. If that’s the case, and things are in play like you’ve said, then why not just trust that it will happen exactly how it’s supposed to happen? Why come to me to ensure it?”

“Again, you question me. You’re questioning the direction of an Angel? You must have some real trust issues, aye?” He asks mockingly.

“I don’t mean to question you or be difficult,” I shake my head. “I just want to understand, that’s all.”

He nods his head and leans in closer again, “you will see, tomorrow. Luke is the clear choice and I need you to make that happen. Can you do that for me, Amarah?” He reaches out and touches my arm.

I can feel the warmth of his gentle touch penetrating my skin. He slowly caresses down my arm as he moves back and out of reach again. He’s left a line of fire tingling down my arm and I have the urge to reach out after him.

I ball my hands into my dress to hold on to something and keep my hands to myself. I look at his eyes and they’re pleading at me to do this. “I will do my best to sway the Queen’s decision.”

He smiles and his face lights up again, “wonderful!”

The wind picks up again, full force. My hair is back in my face, obstructing my vision. I can’t see a thing. I wrangle my hair and when I can see again, I’m standing back where I started. The edges of my vision start to get blurry and everything around me slowly fades.

I open my eyes to a faint light peeking through the sides of the curtain in the window. I don’t recognize the room and it takes me a second to remember where I am. I’m in the home the Air Fey have made available to us. Once I remember where I am, I relax and focus on the dream. It's fresh and vibrant in my mind, more like a memory than a dream. I can still feel the wind on my skin and in my hair.

Maybe when Michael cists me, it's more than just a dream?

But what? And how?

I look over my shoulder and smile when I see Logan asleep beside me. His bare chest is moving in a steady rhythm, up and down, as he breathes deeply in his sleep. I quietly get out of bed and head toward the kitchen. My left arm has a light tingle exactly where Michael had touched it in the dream. I shudder and rub at it with my hand, willing it to go away, and then busy myself with making coffee.

The ceremony is going to happen tonight and I'm not looking forward to the formal event. Me and formal never really go well together. I sigh and think of my dream again. Who's the other person up for the Leader position? Why are they not a good choice? How will I know if I'm making the right choice?

More importantly, what will happen if I make the *wrong* choice?

17

# Who's It Gonna Be

Whose Side Are You On by Tommee Profitt, Ruelle

I had showered and now I'm getting ready for the ceremony when Logan comes back to get me. He had gone out to help with the last little bit of preparations. I see him come into the bathroom behind me through the mirror I'm currently standing in front of. He's in a similar outfit as he had been the first time we attended a formal meeting. Basically, just leather pants. My eyes fall to his bare chest and work their way down to the v-cut that disappears under the pants.

I swallow hard and lean against the counter to steady myself. Of course, Logan notices and I know he could feel my desire through our connection. He gives me a flirtatious half-smile and runs his hand through his hair, making my chest, and other things, tighten even more.

"Like what you see?" He teases, as he saunters towards me.

"You know I do. And so will every other woman that has eyes." I grumble, a little irritated that he's put on display the way he is.

Shirtless and poured into leather pants that leave nothing to the imagination. Possessiveness courses through my veins.

He's mine.

No one else's. And yet, every other woman with breath in her lungs and eyes in her head, are going to be fantasizing about him tonight.

"The only pair of eyes are care about are yours, Amarah."

I turn around to face him and he takes the time to slowly look me up and down.

I'm being a total hypocrite because I'm also wearing a pair of leather pants that hug all of my curves, black combat boots zip up to my knees, and a leather tank top that also zips up with a black zipper, and fits like a second skin. My hair is pulled back in a high ponytail and I darkened my normal non-existent eye makeup. When his eyes reach back up to mine, I can see the heat in them.

"And every man is going to be undressing you with their eyes," he barely maintains the rumble in his chest. I feel his possessiveness too, along with a scorching hot desire to take me. Now. To claim me. To put his scent all over me.

He stops just out of reach in front of me, "we better put up our blocks. Just seeing you in the outfit is going to be hard enough without feeling each other's desire too."

My heart is racing, my hands grip the counter tightly, but they desperately want to reach out and touch him. Feel his skin against mine. Feel his muscles move underneath my hands. Underneath my naked body.

"And what do you desire?" I ask bravely.

He takes the last step towards me and reaches his hand out to the zipper on my shirt. He slowly unzips it until my cleavage is visible. He leans down and licks a slow line, tracing the mound of my breast with the tip of his tongue as his hand palms my breast. I swallow hard, close my eyes, and use all my willpower to put my shield up. I just imagine encasing my frantic beating heart in cement, cutting it off from all feeling. That isn't the case exactly, I'll still feel how I feel about Logan, which in itself is all-consuming and overpowering, but at least this way, I won't have to feel *his* desire, too.

My body is still on fire from his one simple touch, but with the block in place, I feel empty and colder inside. I'm so used to being connected to Logan and his feelings too, that it leaves me feeling like a piece of myself is missing. His absence leaves a massive Texas-sized hole in my chest.

"What I desire? You, Amarah. Always you."

He slowly zips the shirt back up. "This stays zipped *all* the way up," he demands, as he takes a step away from me. I know how hard it is for both of us to fight this connection. As hard as it is for me to put my shield up, it's just as hard for him to step away from me. We're like magnets to each other.

I sigh and release my death grip on the counter. "Is everything ready?"

"Everything's ready. Are you?"

I nod, "I just need to put on my weapons."

"Let me help you," Logan offers.

"Even with the shield up, I still want you, Logan, that doesn't change. So, as much as I would like that, it's probably best if I do it myself, or we might not make it to the ceremony," I chuckle.

He agrees and watches me strap on my thigh holsters for the daggers. Then I pull the sword over my head and adjusted the strap so it sits tightly across my chest. Anytime I'm in leather, with weapons, it reminds me of Selene, from Underworld. It's not my first choice of attire, but I can't help feeling fucking badass in it. I do feel, and look like, a Warrior. Logan on the other hand doesn't have to add any weapons to his outfit. He *is* the weapon.

We walk back to the town hall and it's buzzing with energy and noise. We make our way inside and everyone makes room for us. There are head nods and acknowledgments in our direction as we head toward the stage. The curtain has been lifted to reveal the throne.

Much like the others I've seen, this one is just as large and magnificent. It resembles stone, but I've never seen any natural stone shimmer as this throne does. Unlike Hallana's throne, which is stark white and cold, this one is shades of greys and blues and emits warmth. Even though it's more inviting, there's no mistaking the power it holds. You know it's meant for the Leader and the Leader alone.

The throne sits alone and imposing on the stage. Unlike at Headquarters, there's no seat for me or Logan. So, I'm not sure if we're going to be on the stage tonight or not. My question is answered as I continued to follow Logan up the stairs onto the stage. He walks behind the throne and takes his spot to the left, standing a step behind it. I follow his lead and take up my spot directly across from him on the right side of the throne.

I don't know what to do with my hands, so I clasp them in front of me and ready myself for the events to come. I use this time to observe the crowd in front of me. There are tables off to the sides, against the walls that are currently empty, but I assume they will be overflowing with food and drink for the celebration to come afterward.

There are more tables spread out across the floor, with chairs on all sides, but they leave an aisle open directly to the stage. People are sitting down, trying to find a spot to take for the ceremony, or lingering towards the back, talking with one another. Everyone is dressed elegantly and it takes my breath away at how beautiful the Fey are. Yes, they're all using glamour, their shimmering skin and wings are hidden, but you can still tell they're magical beings. There's no hiding it once you know what the truth is. They're so much... *more*, than humans. It's in their energy, their pride, their uniqueness. How can anyone not see how magical they are?

I spot Vyla, Jon, and the kids, sitting at a table to my left, close to the stage. Tori is sitting in her dad's lap, taking in all the excitement with wide, wandering eyes. Vyla is talking to another lady who's sitting at their table, and Jon is partially turned in his chair, talking to a couple that sits at the table behind them. My eyes continued moving across the crowd and I see another familiar face.

Caleb, one of Aralyn's victims, standing off to one side, in the back of the room. I haven't seen him since he led the demon attack on the Fire Fey, was captured, and then told us everything he knew about Aralyn and her plans. Which, unfortunately, wasn't much. From his current situation, standing utterly alone, it was clear his people haven't forgiven him for his treachery. I feel sorry for him, but his actions and naivety cost six Fey their lives. Families that will never recover from the loss of their loved ones. That type of loss, heartache, and betrayal, isn't easily forgotten and even less likely to be forgiven.

He must have sensed my eyes on him, because he looks up at me, and dips his chin in acknowledgment. I nod in return. He's a victim, yes, but what he did is almost unforgivable. He has a long road ahead of him before his people will trust him again. I know his intentions were good. Misguided, but good. He believed Aralyn and thought he was doing something that would help the Fey. Unfortunately, love can be blinding. I know he feels regret for his part in Aralyn's plans. He probably also feels a lot of shame in his naïve actions, but not all of them were his alone. He had also suffered some of Aralyn's spells. Not all of them being Witch spells either. Love is a powerful spell in and of itself.

A hush comes over the crowd and I follow everyone's gaze. The Queen is making her way over to the stage, looking like pure goodness and light, all golden and glowing, from her gold gown that hugs her upper body tight, then billows around her, the sleeves are slit at the elbow and strips of golden fabric hang to the floor, to her spiked, golden crown that resembled the rays of the sun. Even amongst this elegant crowd, she's a magical spotlight that outshines anyone or anything else.

That spotlight moves down the aisle and climbs the few steps onto the stage. She smiles and nods to Logan and me, then turns slowly and sits on the throne. Everyone else rushes to find their seats, some stay standing in the back, but everyone's attention is on the stage, and not a single person makes any noise. Not even the children.

"Thank you all for being here with us today." The Queen's voice is loud and strong, carrying to every corner of the building. "The reason we are gathered here today saddens me greatly. We have all been cut *deeply* by Aralyn's betrayal."

The Queen pauses and there's finally some stirring in the crowd at the mention of our traitor.

"I understand how hard it is to move forward when betrayal comes from within. From the ones we love and trust. I know that's even harder to move on when the enemy has not been caught and held responsible for their crimes, but we *must* take the steps to a new future. We must come together. We must unite. We must move forward, as one, as a family, with new hope and energy. That starts by electing a new Leader."

There are head nods and murmurs of agreement all around. The Queen holds up her hand, commanding everyone to silence once again.

"Those of you who are ready to dedicate your life and efforts to Leading your people now is the time to step forward."

The crowd comes to life again, as people start talking and looking around at one another, waiting to see who is going to step forward. Two people head toward the aisle and slowly make their way to the front of the stage.

The man is fairly short, at about 5'9, but his confidence is ten feet tall. He's dressed just as elegantly as the rest of the crowd, wearing a soft grey suit with a pastel lavender dress shirt. His tie is silver and has matching lavender swirls embroidered into it. The lavender shirt matches his eyes, which are such a light lavender that they seem almost void of color.

His long blonde hair is swept up and back away from his face. His hair has the same effect as his eyes, so light that it almost has no color at all. It's unnatural and yet, magical and still beautiful. He wears a confident smirk that lights up his face and eyes. It makes me think of Andre but, where Andre is all friendly teasing, this man's smirk is just arrogant. His entire look is spectacular but all of it is just shy of being...*invisible*. As if you look away, he'll disappear into thin air. It's a bit unnerving.

The woman standing next to him is a tiny thing, close to 5' flat, but her energy is just as big as his. Where he's all glitz and show, she's humble and simple. Her straight sandy blonde hair, with streaks of silver, is pulled half up and half left down. She doesn't appear to be wearing any makeup, and her almost white cheeks, are flushed naturally.

The dress she wears has sleeves that barely hang over her shoulders, a gentle swoop across her chest, and falls loosely to the floor. It hugs her curves without being skin-tight. It's also lavender, but not pastel. No, it's solid and bright, just like her eyes. There's no smile gracing her lips, and although she's petite and soft, there's an unmistakable hardness in her purple eyes.

They both bow to the Queen and the Queen nods at both of them. "Luke Meyer and Arabella Armada, thank you both for stepping up to take on this responsibility. As you know, there can only be one Leader, so we must decide which one of you it is going to be."

Armada? I glance at the girl standing before the stage, in shock, as I learn her name. I'm outright gaping at her and she must feel it because she turns those cold, hard eyes on me. I hold her gaze as I use my power to *sense* her, to feel her energy. I sense anger, betrayal, and determination, but the anger is hot and feels alive. So much *hate*.

"Why should I crown you as the new Leader of the Õhk Family?" The Queen asks them both.

Luke bows in Arabella's direction. "Ladies first," he smiles brilliantly.

Arabella doesn't even glance in his direction. She raises her chin and addresses the Queen. "Your Highness, I am very well aware of my position and what it must look like." Her voice is loud and strong for such a little thing. "Trust me when I say that no one is more horrified or embarrassed than I am. I have been betrayed not only as a member of the Air Fey Family but also *personally*. I have more reason, than anyone else, to do what's right. To set all that has been wronged, *right*. It's my only purpose now, to fight for the Fey, to bring honor back to my family, my name, and do right by *everyone* who has been affected by my sister's betrayal."

My heart starts to race at the mention of our traitor. The traitor who tried to have me killed. The traitor who conspired with

Vampires and Witches in secret, trying to gain the crown. The traitor with Fey blood on her hands.

So, this is Aralyn's sister. I can sense Arabella's energy. I know she's frustrated, embarrassed, betrayed, and angry. Really angry! But how can we trust her? She is Aralyn's *sister*. Her blood. I think about my own sisters, my family. What would I do for them? What lengths would I go to? Can we trust that she isn't working with her sister, even now?

It makes me uneasy, nervous. I have a gut feeling that something isn't right. I send my power out, searching, past the building and out in a perimeter around us. I'll sense any energy that approaches us. Aralyn is still out there, somewhere, and if she wants to attack us again, this is as good a time as any.

I'm suddenly very anxious.

Why hadn't I thought of this earlier? I should have been on high alert since the beginning. I'm getting too comfortable with the Fey. With Logan. I need to be the *Warrior* they need. I scold myself and then refocus my energy.

Luke is talking now, "I'm a strong Master of Air, a fierce fighter, and I have no..." he glances at Arabella," *tainted* history. My life has been dedicated to the Air Fey and I will not falter as the new Leader. I will be ruthless in our protection and I will do what is needed to bring the traitor, and her followers, to justice. When the time comes, I will *not* hesitate or show mercy. Can you say the same, Arabella?"

I focus on Luke as he's talking, sensing his energy. His energy is definitely strong, definitely arrogant, but something in my gut clenches. A warning. What is his motivation? What is he hiding? I think about Michael saying there's more in play than I know. Does Luke know something we don't? Could he possibly know where Aralyn is? Is he just waiting for the chance to be the one to bring her in? To be the hero? Is that the reason I feel like he's hiding something?

Arabella still doesn't look his way. She squares her shoulders, standing taller, her lips are set in a hard line, and her eyes are piercing the stage. "Yes, as a matter of fact, I can. There's more to being a Leader than just being *ruthless*. There are other disconcerting issues that need attention, and no one, including you, *Luke*," she sounds disgusted just saying his name, "seems to want to investigate."

Luke chuckles, "if you're talking about the *missing* Fey, you just haven't come to terms with the fact that they abandoned us. They are followers of *your* sister, and have fled with her. There's no need to...*investigate*," he spits the word out. "You just want there to be another explanation other than your traitorous sister."

Just then I hear a growl coming from Logan and I feel a familiar prickling energy from my power prowling along the perimeter outside. We both step forward at the same time, and I pull my sword from its scabbard. There's a rush of nervous energy and hurried voices coming from the crowd.

I look at Logan and his eyes have turned Wolf amber. His hands are no longer human, they're claws. He *is* the weapon. It still unsettles me to see Wolf's eyes staring back at me from his handsome face. I shake my head to clear my thoughts and grip my sword tighter. I pull my energy back to me and into the sword. The engraved crosses flared to life.

The Queen is on her feet and standing between us. "What is it?" She asks calmly.

"Demons," Logan and I say together.

## Another Betrayal

Can You Feel The Heat Now by Tommee Profitt

There's a surge of energy and emotions as the crowd hurries to prepare for the attack. Glamour is thrown aside, and I watch as the Air Fey come alive, making the room appear brighter as their skin and wings shimmer.

"Guard the children and the Queen! Stay inside and stay together! You, take some fighters with you out the back and guard the entrance. You...," I hear a strong, authoritative voice giving commands, as Logan and I run out the front door together.

One good thing about being out in the country and not in the city, is that there's no need for glamour, or to worry about protecting innocent humans who could get caught up unknowingly in a magical war. One bad thing, it's pitch-black outside, and I can barely see a few feet in front of me. I can't see the demons yet, but I can definitely feel them. The hair on my arms raises against the evil, prickling energy in the air.

"Can you see them?" I ask Logan.

"I see them," he growls in a voice I hardly recognize. "About fifty yards out and closing fast.

"How many?" I ask calmly.

"Maybe twenty here in front. I don't know about behind us."

"We'll be ready," a voice to my right grabs my attention.

Luke wields two long swords in his hands. His wings are out but he's still standing solidly on the ground. A gentle rustling noise above me causes me to glance up into the night sky. A few Fey are levitating in the air, ready for the attack. I recognize Caleb as one of them. A bright light out of the corner of my eye makes me focus my attention back on the world in front of me.

Fire.

The demons are sending fire our way. There's a gust of wind and the balls of fire slowly get smaller, and smaller, before they disappear completely before even reaching us. Then the demons are on us and my world narrows down to my fighting zone. I need to hold my ground, I can't be distracted by the fight around me. These are all fighters and people who can handle themselves. Shit, probably way better than me. I have to just focus on keeping my own ass alive.

A demon comes charging directly at me, red eyes glowing, mouth snarling. It swings its arm and massive claws at me, I steps to the side and have to drop to the ground, to maneuver under the demon's arm. I barely have time to stand before the demon turns around and is back on me. I pull my sword into a two-handed grip, holding it out in front of me. The demon charges me again, but this time, I get my sword out in front of its body before I have to duck again. I feel my sword connect but it's a shallow cut and didn't faze the demon.

It's moving faster than I remember them moving before. The demon's tail comes out of nowhere and whips at my feet. I stumble and go down, but not completely, as I catch myself with one hand on the ground, but that's all the time it needs. The demon is over me in a second and kicks me square in the chest. The air whooshes out of my lungs and I'm flung flat on my back. I still hold my sword in my hand but all I can think about is trying to breathe. I'm trying to fight the paralyzing, slow wave of panic that comes from not being able to draw in a breath.

The demon crawls over me and snarls inches above my face. I notice the same mark on its forehead that I had seen on the other demons in the city. I can't do anything with the sword from this angle, but I manage to pull a dagger free from my left thigh. The demon throws its head back and shrieks loudly, displaying its razor-sharp, dagger-like teeth. I don't hesitate. I take the dagger and jab it as hard as I can through the top of its mouth. I crawl backward on my elbows until I'm out from under it.

I get my feet under me, pull in a big breath of air, "arghhh!" I scream as I ram my sword into the demon's chest with all the force I have in my body. When I feel the sword come out the other side, I yank it back. The demon falls to the ground, bursts into flames, and in seconds, is no more than a pile of ash.

I retrieve and replace my dagger, then take a look around. A nearby tree is fire, lighting up the parking lot, and I can see there are fewer demons, but the fight is still going strong. I briefly glimpse Logan and Luke, still on their feet and holding their own. Caleb launches off the ground, and I'm helpless to watch as a demon sends a fireball directly at his back and hits one of his wings. The wing falters and he falls to the ground with a deafening crunch, before the demon is on top of him.

"Caleb!" I run forward to help him and completely miss the demon coming at me from the side. It tackles me and I hit my head, hard, when my body is crushed on the ground. I feel a stabbing pain behind my eyes as I momentarily see black. My vision snaps back into place just as the demon is bringing his teeth down towards my face. On sheer instinct, I raise my left arm up to block my face, and the demon's teeth wrap around my forearm.

"Ahhhhh!" I scream in pain. My power had gone out in the split second I lost consciousness. I feel the teeth sink into my skin like a hot knife sinks into butter, and I swear, I can hear its teeth grating against the bone. I fumble for the dagger strapped onto my right thigh.

I can barely think past the pain, but I manage to grab the dagger, and sink it hilt deep into the side of the demon's head. The only problem is, it falls on top of me when it dies, trapping me under its heavy body, as it bursts into flames.

I throw my right arm over my face, turning my head to the side, protecting my face the best I can. I scream when I feel the fire melt the skin on my arm, from where the demon's bite still holds tight, even as it dies. My clothes catch fire and I scream again as I feel my skin burning the entire length of my body. The demon's body is gone, no longer weighing me down, and I know I should roll over to suffocate the flames. You know, stop, drop and roll, as we're taught as kids, but I can't think past the excruciating pain. I just scream one long scream after another.

I manage to make out Luke face through watery eyes as he rushes to my side and kneels beside me. "Don't worry, Amarah, I got you."

The flames grow smaller and finally die out but the pain doesn't die with them. My body is still burning as if the flames are still alive and licking at me.

"We need to get her to a healer, now!"

I've lost all sight to the pain, I'm on the verge of passing out, and I vaguely register that I'm still screaming, as my body is lifted off the ground. I smell burned flesh and sweat, but under all that, I smell the familiar scent of woods on a warm summer day.

“Logan,” I barely croak through a raw throat. I think I hear a raven, *kaaaa*, right before I finally pass out from the pain.

# 19

## A New Leader

Ready To Play by Club Danger

The noise of people bustling around me comes to me slowly, their energy, calm and hushed. My eyes flutter open and I'm immediately greeted by Logan's worried face. His eyes are locked on my body and he doesn't notice that I'm awake. The look on his face pains me and worries me in equal measure. I can feel his hand held tightly and solidly in mine. On the other side, The Queen and Arabella kneel next to me, holding a sheet just above my body. A sheet? Why are they holding up a damn sheet? Their expressions match Logan's and send my heart racing.

Something's wrong.

Vyla is kneeling on my right, next to Logan, her hair pulled back in her usual tight braid. Not a single piece of hair astray to get in her way. Her face, unlike the others, is calm and focused. I let my gaze follow where theirs are trained and reality bitch slaps me right in the face. As soon as I see my naked and burned body, the memories, along with the pain, come flooding back.

"Ahhhh!" I cry out in pain, as my brain registers the trauma, alerting everyone that I'm very much awake again.

Logan leans his face down over me, consuming my blurry vision, his features now schooled, but it's too late. I saw his concern.

I saw my body.

I didn't even feel the tears streaming down my face as he wipes them away with hushed words of comfort I can't comprehend. All I can register is the intense pain radiating from every inch of my body.

"Amarah, hey, Amarah," my eyes connect with his and they hold me steady. "Hey, it's going to be ok. I'm here," Logan says as he strokes my face with his free hand. "Vyla is going to heal you. The pain will be gone soon, I promise."

"It burns! Everywhere burns!" I cry.

"I know, Amarah, I know." He can no longer fight the tears as they well up in his eyes, "I'm so sorry. Just focus on me, look at me. It will be better soon."

I try to focus on him but everything is blurry. I can't see him clearly. And since I can't focus on sight, I focus on feeling. And all I feel is pain. The worst pain I've ever felt in my entire life. More than the claws to my back, more than the insignificant burns I received through my Fire Fey training, more than any heartbreak I've ever known. I have nothing to compare this pain to, and I wish desperately that I can pass out again, just so I can be oblivious to it once more.

It feels like hours pass before Vyla finishes healing me, even though I know, it's only been minutes. The sheet the Queen and Arabella had been holding to shield my naked body from the room, is now wrapped around me, as Logan cradles me in his arms.

"Alright, Amarah, how are you feeling?" Vyla kneels down next to me, such calm and care in her deep purple eyes.

"Just exhausted. A little weak, but other than that, fine. Thank you," I manage a weak smile.

"Good," she pats my arm. "Well, let's start with the good

news, shall we? I was able to heal all of the burns. You won't have any burn scars," she smiles brightly, then it falters. "As for the bad news, I'm afraid I couldn't keep the bite marks from scarring."

The memory of the demon's teeth sinking into my arm come rushing back, my arm throbs as my brain recalls the pain. I pull my arm out from under the sheet to examine it. I hadn't had a chance, or desire, to look at my body once I was healed. Now, I tentatively touch the fresh, pink scar tissue adorning my left forearm.

"It's ok, Vyla, it's not my first demon scar and I'm sure it won't be the last. There's nothing you can do about that, but thank you for the rest. I'll gladly sport a few scars on my arm versus my entire body having burn scars," I admit and mean it.

She smiles sadly and nods, "I'm going to make my rounds and see to everyone else."

"Oh my God, Tori and Vic, the other children…" a wave of panic hits me. I'm so mentally exhausted from the pain that I haven't even *thought* about everyone else. A wave of guilt quickly follows the panic.

"They're fine, Amarah. Everyone is fine, don't worry," she smiles reassuringly. "Your injuries were by far the worst, but there are some other scrapes and bruises I need to attend to. You just relax, Doctor's orders."

I nod and settle back into Logan's embrace. That seems to satisfy her, as she stands back up and heads out into the room of the surviving Air Fey.

"I've sent someone to bring you some clothes," the Queen takes Vyla's spot and kneels beside me. "Oh, Amarah, you sure had us all worried," she grabs my hand.

"I'm ok," I give her hand a reassuring squeeze. "Just tired. It's all part of the job. Although, I do hope I get better at it sooner rather than later."

The Queen lets out a heavy sigh, "I do wish things were different. I wish you had come to us in a peaceful time. I wish you you had more time to learn everything, to *train*."

"There's never a perfect time in life for anything. All we can do is the best with what we've got and have faith that everything happens for a reason. We don't always see the forest through the trees, but I do believe that his is where we're all meant to be. All of us. Right here, right now. We can't change it and it's *not* your fault, Ana."

"I'm just glad you're ok," she smiles. "We'll give you some time to get dressed and get your bearings, but we do need to finish the ceremony. We need to pick our Leader."

Oh yeah, that.

I forgot we were in the middle of something important before the attack. "What are your thoughts so far?" I ask.

"I'm really not sure. Both are Masters and both have the potential to be great Leaders. I hate to admit it, but I do hesitate with the relationship Arabella has with her sister, but is it fair to condemn her for her sister's actions?"

"Of course, it's not, but how can you *not* take that into account? I sensed her energy, I know how betrayed she feels, but you can feel betrayed by someone without turning your back on them. Being betrayed doesn't mean you stop *loving* them, caring for them, and believing the best. It sure as Hell doesn't guarantee you stop *helping* them."

"Yes, definitely wise words, Amarah. It's a lot to consider."

I can see the concern to do the right thing weighing heavily on her. I don't envy her and the weight of being Queen. How Aralyn, or anyone, could want this responsibility fails to register for me. I would never want it.

"And what of Luke? I don't know much of either of them. He

seems very arrogant to say the least, and my gut says to be weary, but I don't know why. He did hold his own tonight and protected his people," I shake my head. "I just don't know. Logan, you know them better than I do, what are your thoughts?"

"I agree that both are good choices."

I feel his chest rumble through me as he speaks, and I want to lean into him more, to fall into the warmth and safety of his arms. I want to fall into him and forget about reality for a while, but I have to be strong right now. I can fall into his arms later. With the promise of that happening later tonight, I make myself sit up straighter, as he continues.

"I've known them both for a long time and I don't have anything bad to say about either. However, I do hold the same hesitation about Arabella. I know it's not fair. Nonetheless, it's there."

The Queen nods and I can see her contemplating everything we've said. After a few moments of silence, it's decided.

"I think we have our answer then."

A teenage girl comes barrelling up the stairs to the stage, where we still remain, and bows before the Queen. "Here are the clothes for Amarah," She huffs, as she sits them down next to me. "I'm so sorry, I had to go through some of your things to find you some clothes," she says nervously.

I smile up at her, still clutching the sheet around me, thankful I'm going to finally be dressed again. "It's really ok. Thank you for getting these for me. I appreciate it."

Everyone is brought back to their seats and asked to get settled, while I head into the little office to get dressed. There's a pair of clean underwear that I put on, followed by a pair of dark blue jeans and a black t-shirt, that leave my shiny new scars staring up at me. Torturing me with their memory. I force myself to look away as I sit down to put on my socks and shoes when there comes a gentle knock on the door.

"You can come in," I instruct.

Logan comes in, holding my weapons. I stand up and go to him, my hands gliding over the weapons in his hands, examining them. They still look as new as the day they were forged. You'd never be able to tell they were in any type of battle much less a fire. A demon fire. Fire from Hell, literally.

"How?" I look up in surprise.

He shrugs, "I'm not sure."

I take the scabbard and slide it over my head, amazed that there's no damage to it whatsoever. I strap on the thigh holsters with the help of Logan this time. I feel better once my weapons are back on me, but I'm still feeling a little scared and insecure, although I'll never admit it aloud. As always, with Logan, I don't have to always voice my feelings. Some emotions come through our bond, loud and clear. Just like I can clearly feel the guilt he's feeling, even though, he has *nothing* to feel guilty about.

"Amarah, I'm so sorry. Come here," he reaches to pull me into a hug.

I place my hands on his chest, holding my ground, and shake my head, "no. Not yet. If I let you comfort me right now, I'm going to break down, and we aren't finished with business yet. I need whatever strength I have left to get through the rest of the night."

He hangs his head in defeat, "I'm sorry. I should have protected you."

I take his face in my hands, "no, Logan. Your job is *not* to protect me. Your job is to protect the Fey, and you did that tonight. I'm the Võitleja. It's my job to fight in this war. It's my job to tip the scales and start making some progress. If anyone has failed tonight, it's me, not you."

"You're still not completely trained. You still don't have

complete control of your power. No one is expecting you to tip the scales yet."

"Maybe, maybe not," I shrug. "But you know I'm right."

"Right or wrong, I don't care. I'm not trying to be right. I know who I am and I know what my duty is to the Fey, but honestly, fuck it, fuck them, and fuck everything. You're my world, Amarah, plain and simple. You're the only thing that truly matters to me. I told you I would never let anything or anyone hurt you, and I failed you," he grabs my forearm and runs his fingers over my new scars.

I remove my arm from his hand and lace our fingers together instead, "Logan, I want you to listen to me. I love you, and I'll do anything in my power to keep you safe, too. I get it, I do. I don't know what I would do if something were to happen to you. I don't even want to think about it, but we can't forget the people around us. We've talked about this. How our connection and pull towards each other can be dangerous. I never want innocents, like Tori and Vic, to become victims of our selfishness. Do you understand me?"

His Adam's apple bobs, and tears pool in his eyes as he nods his head. I squeeze his hand in mine, reassuring him that everything is ok.

After a moment, he clears his throat, "I'm just glad you're ok."

"Ditto," I tiptoe to reach his lips and he leans down to meet me. His lips feel good on mine. Solid and real. Seeping life and energy back into me. It's a simple, sweet kiss, but still stirs my heart.

We leave the comfort and solitude of the little office and I'm a little embarrassed to see everyone waiting for us. I feel everyone's eyes on me as I make my way back onto the stage. Logan and I take our posts on the sides of the throne and we all pick up right where we left off.

"Will Luke and Arabella come forward again, please?" The Queen orders.

They walk back down the aisle, both looking no worse for wear, even though I know Luke fought by my side, and I assume Arabella had as well.

"If this night has proven anything, it's that a strong new Leader is surely needed. Someone to not only lead but to protect. Someone we can trust to do the *right* thing. Someone we can trust to do what's *needed.* Someone who is ready to not only fight the war on the demons, but to fight the war against our traitor, because there is no doubt in my mind that she is the one behind tonight's attack," the Queen's voice is hard and cold at the mention of Aralyn's treachery.

"This makes *two* attacks against the Fey. We're lucky no one was taken from us tonight," her eyes drift to me for a moment, the emotion raw in her eyes, then she steels herself again and continues.

"Our new Leader's first order is to find the traitor and bring her in for justice. She must pay for her crimes." There are nods and murmurs of agreement all around, and some more enthusiastic shouts of support from the back of the room.

The Queen raises her hand, demanding silence, "however, I will also accept the traitor *dead*." No one says a word. I see Arabella swallow hard but force herself to stand straighter. Luke just smirks with his arrogant approval.

"It's with this is mind that I select Luke Meyer as the Õhk Family's new Leader."

More nods and agreements sweep through the crowd again but I keep my eyes on the two candidates, watching them closely. I expect to see defeat in Arabella, but her eyes only seem more determined. She stands tall and still, only a small twitch as she clenches her jaw, lets me know she's pissed.

Luke looks just as smug as ever, his cocky smile split across his face, as he bows to the Queen.

The Queen stands, "join me."

Luke walks up the stairs, stops in front of the Queen, and bends down onto one knee. He bows his head and then meets her eyes.

"Luke Meyer, do you accept the role as Leader of the Õhk Family, and do you swear to do what's right for this family at all costs? Even if that cost is your life? Do you accept this honor and responsibility?"

"I do," he says confidently.

The Queen reaches for her crown and pulls one of the spikes free. "Give me your hand."

Luke raises his palm up to her. She holds it in her left hand, but her eyes address the crowd once more. "On this night, I, Anaxo Andrews, Queen of the Fey, have selected Luke Meyer to lead each and every one of you, the Fey of the Õhk Family. If there is to be an objection, let it be stated now."

Her gaze passes over a silent crowd. She allows plenty of time for anyone to step forward and be heard. No one does.

"Air has accepted you, Air has held you, and when the time comes, may Air keep you." With the spike of the crown, she cuts a line across his palm. "Rise, Luke Meyer, Leader of the Õhk Family, and accept your throne."

Luke bows his head once more before he climbs to his feet. He walks to the throne and presses his bleeding palm against it. There's an immediate gust of wind that emanates from the throne and encircles him in it. His glamour is stripped away, his wings suddenly visible, and his skin shimmering like it's made up of a million tiny crystals. The throne matches his skin and they both start glowing. The wind raged harder and he bends his body into the throne, fighting to stay standing, fighting to keep his palm connected.

Then, as suddenly as the wind appeared, it stops, along with the shimmering glow. The throne is back to being warm and beautiful, but not *alive*, as it had just been. Luke's skin is still shiny, like pixie dust has been thrown on him, but no different than any other Air Fey. He slowly removes his hand from the throne and I see a glowing mark in the palm of his hand.

He turns around to the crowd, lifts his palm above his head, showing them his glowing palm. The mark of the Õhk Fey Leader. There's an eruption of excitement, clapping and yelling. All their faces are filled with relief and hope.

This is an important night and I know I've just witnessed something truly special. Something that doesn't happen often. The selection and appointment of a new Fey Leader. I know I should share in the excitement of the others, so why don't I?

What Michael said needed to happen, happened. I know I should trust him. I knew he's an Angel and see things I don't. So why is my stomach in knots? Why do I feel like I've just watched the crowning of the devil?

# Who to Trust?

Us by James Bay

Food and drinks are brought in and the demon attack appears to be out of everyone's mind. Everyone is in good spirits and celebrating the fact that they now have a new Leader to bring them out of the darkness Aralyn created. I understand their delight and renewed hope but I can't share in it.

I'm sitting at a table alone, staring at the pile of food on my plate, mentally parenting myself. *You need to eat, Amarah. You need to gain some strength and energy back.* Yet, I can't seem to bring the fork to my mouth. I should also be celebrating, not only the new Leader, but the fact that no one died tonight. Everyone is alive. *I'm* alive. But I have no energy to even try. My eyes keep lingering on the new scars that decorate my arm, and my mind keeps replaying the feeling of razor-sharp teeth grating against bone.

"Amarah," a voice next to me brings me out of the memory. "May I have a moment?"

"Sure," I sit up a little straighter as Arabella takes the seat next to me.

"Luke is the wrong choice," she says curtly and straight to business.

It feels like a punch to my gut and fuels my own doubt about him, but I can't let anyone see that. "Oh? And why is that?"

"I don't trust him."

I scoff, "and we should trust you?" I blurt out and immediately feel bad about it.

She lifts up her chin and her eyes tighten, "I know where I stand among everyone's opinion. If I had any doubt before, tonight made it *perfectly* clear."

She isn't wrong and I don't know what to say. It isn't necessarily right to keep her in her sister's shadow, especially if she is innocent of any wrong-doing or assistance, yet, here we are.

"Your opinion of me doesn't matter. No one's does," she says coldly.

"Then why are you sitting here?"

"Because regardless of what you and everyone seem to think about me, I care about my family, and I'm not talking about Aralyn. I'm talking about *this* family," she raises her hands gesturing to the crowd around us.

"Luke has changed since everything has happened," she sighs and I finally see a hint of her tiredness. "I don't know how to explain it, but he isn't the same. He's different somehow. More arrogant. More…" she circles her hand in the air as if trying to find the right words, "more demand for attention and power. I know it probably doesn't make sense to you."

"Then why are you telling me this? Why aren't you talking to your people, to the Queen?"

"I have," she grits out, her anger back in full force. "Seems my sister has destroyed any hope of me being trusted, Hell, even just *heard*."

"I'm sorry..."

"I don't want your pity," she cuts me off. "I heard what you did for the Fire Fey guy, Andre, that was accused of being a traitor. You sought the truth regardless of what it meant. The truth here is that something is going on. Fey are disappearing and I know it is *not* because they're following my sister. Luke refuses to acknowledge this, so does everyone else, and it's leaving us open to whatever is going on here. He is *not* the right choice. I don't trust him," she repeats.

My stomach is in knots as I sit here and listen to her talk. Is she telling me the truth? Does she genuinely care about the missing Fey and protecting them? Or is this an act? A ploy to get me to walk right into her sister's arms somehow? I'm too mentally exhausted to have this thrown on my plate right now.

A headache is starting to form behind my eyes, I sigh, "I don't know what you expect *me* to do about any of it."

She scoffs and stands up to go, "my sister did have one thing right, I don't know what everyone sees in you. Clearly, you're just like everyone else, only more human and *weaker*. You've been warned. Do what you will with the information. I *will* find out the truth behind what is happening here and you can continue playing at being our...*Warrior*." She looks me up and down with disgust and storms off before I can wrap my head around all her hateful insults.

"What was that about?" Logan asks as he watches Arabella disappear into the crowd.

"Sore loser is my best guess," I shake my head and the headache explodes, sending any thoughts I may have had about what Arabella said, out the window. I squeeze my eyes shut and grab my head.

"Amarah, what's wrong?" Logan kneels beside me.

"Just a headache. I need to go lie down and call it a night."

"Let's get you out of here then," he moves to pick me up and I shake my head causing more stabs of pain.

"No," I use my words. "I can walk on my own." Arabella's words, *human and weaker,* echo in my head. I'm not going to give her the satisfaction of seeing me being carried out of the hall.

I hold my head up high as I slowly push through the crowd and make my way outside. The cool night air bites at my skin but it does nothing to cool down the fire that's exploding inside my head.

We pass beyond the reach of the light from the open door, but I keep walking across the road, and into the darkness of the field. When I'm sure no one can see me, I finally let my legs give out from under me.

Logan is walking right next to me and catches me before I hit the ground. His speed and strength always take me by surprise. He scoops me into his arms effortlessly and carries me the rest of the way to the house. He could have scolded me for being stubborn and proud but he doesn't. He doesn't say a word as he carries me into the bedroom and gently lays me down on the bed. I try to open my eyes but that just sends more stabbing pain through my head.

I feel his hands on my ankle, and gentle pull, and then my foot comes free from my shoe. Then the other one. He proceeds to remove my jeans and I don't protest or fight. He leaves my underwear and t-shirt on, knowing I don't like being naked and exposed. He walks around to the other side of the bed and moves the covers aside then walks back around and lifts me up again. He lays me down again and then I hear his footsteps head out of the bedroom. He didn't pull the covers over me and I don't have the energy to do it myself.

It's cold but it's a small discomfort next to the pounding in my brain. I hear him come back into the room. "Amarah, you need to take these. It will help your headache."

My back is to the side of the bed and I can feel his big body hovering over me. I know he's right. I need to take something for the pain but my body feels like it weighs a ton and the slightest movement causes my head to explode.

"I can't," I whisper weakly.

"Here, let me." His hand slides under my head and gently lifts it up. Gentle or not there's still piercing pain from him moving me. "Open your mouth." I do, and feel pills land on my tongue, then a glass is pressed to my lips. "Drink," he orders. I manage to swallow down the pills and he lays my head back down.

He still hasn't covered me and I hear him shuffling around the room some more. Then the light goes out and I feel him climb into bed behind me. He pulls the covers over us both and melds his warm body against mine. Even through the pain and exhaustion, my heart and stomach stir as I feel his skin on mine, but I have no energy to even move a muscle. That's how I know I'm really hurt and exhausted. When I don't want to jump Logan's bones. No, correction, when I *can't* jump Logan's bones.

My skin is prickled in goosebumps, as I try to fight the earlier chill. Logan rubs my thigh, and then my arm, creating some friction and trying to warm me up. When the goosebumps finally fade, he moves his hand to my temple, and gently starts caressing my hair in small repetitive movements.

"You're too good for me," I manage to whisper.

"Says the half Angel," he chuckles. "I love you, Amarah. More than I've ever loved anything or anyone. It breaks my heart seeing you like this, in pain, and seeing you tonight. The way you were burned…I felt so lost. So helpless. I wish I could take all of it, all of your pain and scars, and bear it for you. I would if I could."

"I know."

He's quiet for a long time and I can feel his strong chest

rising and falling against my back. His hand has stilled and rests in my hair. I think he's fallen asleep, but he slowly moves his arm down and encircles my waist, pulling me even closer to him. I can't get much closer unless he pulls me into his body.

"I was terrified and I can't remember the last time I've ever been terrified," he admits quietly. "Seeing you like that. Seeing your body…" his voice breaks and his body shudders. Is he crying? "I can't lose you, Amarah," he whispers and hold me tight.

I grab his arm and hug it to my chest as fiercely as I can. I realize I can't feel him through our link. There's still a hole in my chest even though I had long since dropped any and all shields, which means, he's shielding himself from me.

"Stop blocking yourself from me. I need to feel you," I say, my voice coming out stronger finally.

He opens our connection and I'm flooded with emotion. I feel his helplessness and his doubt. His doubt that he isn't good enough. His doubt that he can protect me. Logan has always been my rock. My strength. The reason why I can move forward after all of this shit. Feeling his insecurity like this makes my heart ache.

"Don't you know I can't do any of this without you?" I ask desperately.

"That's the thing, Amarah. What am I really doing? You've been hurt, *badly,* more than once, and where was I? What good am I to you if I can't keep you safe? If I can't even keep you from getting hurt, how can I keep you from being…" he trails off and doesn't finish the thought out loud.

"I am *not* going to die, ok? I'm not. I don't think God made me just so I can die before I even do anything. I believe that, in my heart, and I also believe that you're not going to die either. We may not be able to protect each other the way we want but someone *is* protecting us. I believe that and I need you to believe it too."

Logan stays silent behind me, clutching my body to his as if he's afraid to let me go.

"You know what's even harder than protecting me?"

"What?" He whispers.

"Being here to pick up the pieces. Being here to deal with all these emotions and feelings. Dealing with the trauma. Being strong enough to get through it and come out stronger on the other side. And we will, Logan. *Together.* But I won't be able to face it, any of it, without *you*."

I feel him nod his head but he doesn't say a word. He doesn't have to. I feel his emotions ease. I feel his body settle next to mine. I feel his breathing getting heavier and I match mine to the rhythm of his chest. My headache is a distant ache as I fall into a deep, dreamless sleep.

# More Training, More Failing

Try Again by Aaliyah

It's been a few weeks since the demon attack and since Luke was selected as the new Leader. I've started training with Jon and learning to use the air as part of my arsenal. As usual, that part comes harder for me than the physical combat training. Jon is just as good as Andre when it comes to fighting, but unlike Andre, he doesn't take it easy on me.

"Come on, Amarah, faster!" He urges as we practice with dull daggers.

"I'm going as fast as I can," I say through gritted teeth, concentrating with everything I have on the man in front of me.

"No, you're not." He picks up his speed even more.

I'm barely able to defend myself against him much less be on the offensive. I'm so focused on blocking his assault that I don't realize he's slowly backed me up, step by step. I feel my heel step over the side of the raised platform but it's too late to stop. The momentum of my body and his attacks send me over the edge.

I gasp as I feel my body falling, my heart in my throat, as I wait for the impact of the ground to knock the air out of my chest. It never comes. I've stopped an inch above the ground.

I look up at Jon standing on the edge of the platform, expecting to see disappointment on his face, but I never do. He's a tough-as-nails trainer and teacher, but he has patience for days. Perhaps it's all the training he's done over the years or because he's a father, either way, he never looks disappointed in me which I appreciate. I've been improving but not as fast as I'd like. What's new?

"What happened, Amarah?" He asks, still holding me suspended above the ground.

"I lost track of my surroundings," I sigh.

"And what happens when you lose track of what's around you?"

"People die."

He doesn't respond, just stares at me, making sure I'm not just telling him what he wants to hear. He's making sure I'm taking this seriously, which of course, I am.

He nods and I feel the hard ground under my back as he finally releases me. "Next time, I'll let you fall. Maybe that will teach you," he scolds. "Get back up here."

I groan as I pull my achy body off the ground and walk back up the stairs onto the platform. It's the same platform I had been on in my dream with Michael. This is where the Air Fey train, way up on this mountain peak, where they can control and manipulate wind with no one being the wiser. Even the fairy tale castle is real, though, I have yet to be inside of it. Jon says it's mainly used for storage and training in the winter months. It's also a hideout, if and when, the Air Fey ever need to use it.

Walking across the platform, I see that Jon has laid his training daggers off to the side and is sitting in the middle of the

Platform, much like Michael had in my dream. I walk over to him and sit down, mirroring him.

"Let's work on your air control."

I sigh in defeat because I know how this is going to turn out. Can you guess? Yeah, not great, but I keep my mouth shut and do my best to follow his instructions.

"Close your eyes and feel the air around you. Concentrate on it. Feel its power."

I close my eyes and I try, I *really* do, but I can't *feel* anything. How do you feel air? I'm struggling because I can't see it. I can't feel it. How can I possibly manipulate it?

I sigh, "I don't feel anything." I open my eyes and Jon is studying me. "I'm sorry, I just can't see the air. I can't feel it," I wave my hands in the air, "how am I supposed to control something I can't see or feel?"

"How did you start using your power?"

"What do you mean?"

"You can access the power that's within you easily, and use it anytime you want, right?" He asks.

"Yes. I don't understand how that matters when trying to touch air?"

"Well, your power isn't something you can see or feel with your hands. How did you learn to use it?"

"Hmmm," I think out loud, "that's a really good question. Well, when I was training with the Fire Fey, I started using the ground as a gateway to my power. I can *touch* the ground. I can feel it under my hands, and I was able to feel the natural magic that's in the Earth," I shrug.

"I see." I can see the wheels spinning in his mind. "So, we need to get you to feel the air."

"Sure," I shrug. "But how do you plan on doing that?"

"Wind."

"Wind?" I repeat back to him.

"Wind is just air in motion."

"Yes, but I've felt wind before and I've never felt...*connected* to it."

"Because you weren't trying. Using the elements requires focus, concentration and belief, Amarah."

"Alright, well, let's give it a go, shall we?"

When the wind comes at me all fast and furious, I'm thankful that my hair is wrapped up in a bun on my head. I can feel the wind blowing across my skin. It's just as real as if something or someone was touching me. It's physical. I concentrated on the way it feels. I lift my hands up and let the wind flow in between my fingers and over my hands. It's all around me, but I still can't sense the *magic* in it. The essence. It's just annoying and aggravating, wind.

The wind assaults me for a solid ten minutes, non-stop before I finally throw my hands up in the air, "It's no use!" I yell in frustration. "I can't do it."

The wind stops and Jon looks at me with the calm, patience of a Saint. "It will come, Amarah. It's your first time trying with wind. I'm confident you will figure it out."

"That makes one of us," I mutter under my breath.

"Let's call it quits for the day and pick up tomorrow," he stands up and offers me his hand.

I take it and let him pull me to my feet. "Thanks for trying, Jon. And thanks for not losing your shit," I chuckle. "I would've lost mine a long time ago if I was in your shoes."

"I'll only lose my shit if you stop trying. Unless that happens, I'm happy to be here with you."

I shake my head, "too much on the line to give up. You have my word."

He nods, "why don't you and Logan come over for dinner tonight?"

"Oh, no, that's ok. I don't want to put you and Vyla out."

"Nonsense. She loves having people over. Not to mention Tori and Vic would sure enjoy it."

I can't help the genuine smile that splits my face. The Beck family is perfect and I've come to care for them deeply. I understand why Logan likes visiting so much. It doesn't hurt that seeing Logan with Tori tugs at my heart strings. I'm not great with kids myself, but I do my best. Vic seems to like me and even Tori is coming around to me. I must be doing *something* right.

"We would love to," I beam up at him.

"I'll let Vyla know. Are you ok getting back on your own?" Even though he knows I am, he always asks.

"Of course. We'll see you later."

"See you later."

I watch him walk to the edge of the peak, his wings emerge in a graceful flutter, as he dives over the edge and out of sight.

"Must be nice," I sigh as I head to the small enclosed cable car.

The aerial lift lets us, non-flight beings such as myself, up and down the mountain. It's also used for the kids. The Air Fey are not all born with the ability to fly, it has to be earned. They earn their wings once they become a Master. So, in the meantime, to be able to get to the training grounds, the lift it is. We're so high up in the mountains that it will take me another twenty minutes to reach the bottom.

Jon and I are typically the last ones to leave. To say he pushes me hard is an understatement. I'll have just enough time to get back and shower before we head over to the Beck's for dinner.

I let out an exhausted sigh as I start to climb into the cable car. Then I hear it, “kaaaaaa.” My heart jumps in my chest, I take a few steps away from the cable car so I can get a good look up at the sky. I see a black speck in the sky, getting larger, as the raven flies closer. It swoops down and lands on the top of the cable car.

“Kaaaa.”

“Well, hello to you too. I would pinch myself but I know I’m not dreaming. I wasn’t sure if I really heard you the night of the attack or if I imagined it. I’ve been waiting for you to make an appearance.”

Am I really talking to this bird? Do I think it will answer me back? No, obviously. Do I think it can understand me? Maybe.

Ok, yes. I do.

“I can’t follow you anywhere now. You’re going to have to come back and find me another time. When I’m not training and preferably not when the sun is about to go down.”

I stand here and stare at the raven. Even weirder, it stares right back. It keeps cocking its head from side to side and shuffling its wings. For some reason, I don’t want to get too close to it, and I’m not sure why. What’s it going to do? Attack me? Maybe. Probably not. Still, it makes me nervous.

I take in a big breath and let it out. I walk to the cable car, get in, and hastily shut the door behind me. I hit the switch to get it moving down the mountain and I notice the raven flying nearby. I watch it swoop up and down as it travels along, slow and steady, with the cable car.

I shake my head and lean back against the seat letting my body relax from the onslaught it taken over the past, however many hours, Jon spent kicking my ass. I’m finally used to the slight rock of the cable car on its line. At first, it made me nervous, and I was scared I was going to drop right out of the sky. Now, I let the slow rock, side to side, soothe me into a peaceful lull.

The jolt of the sudden stop at the bottom jerks my body and

mind out of it's relaxed, sedentary state. I climb out of the car and immediately search the sky for the raven but it's nowhere to be seen. I still have a bit of a trek to get from the base of the mountain, across the field, and back to the houses. I set my mind to it with the promise of a hot shower awaiting me.

Preferable one with Logan in it.

# When You Least Expect It

Masterpiece by Jessie J

"So, how is training going?" Vyla asks as we all sit around the table in their dining room.

"Not good," I say at the same time as Jon says, "not bad."

Vyla is sitting across from me, and looks from me to Jon and then back to me, with a curious look.

"Jon is being polite," I shake my head. "I don't think Jon could say a mean thing even if he wanted to."

Vyla chuckled, "oh you'd be surprised. My husband wouldn't say it if it wasn't true." She reached over and clutched his forearm with a smile and look of complete adoration in her eyes.

It made me smile and I couldn't help but glance at Logan. He was sitting next to me on my left with Tori in his lap. Vic was across from them and next to Vyla. Jon was at the head of the table to my right.

Logan reaches out and brushes my hair behind my ear, "Amarah is just being hard on herself like always."

I shake my head, making my hair fall in my face again, "I

wish that were true. Sure, I may be getting better at the hand-to-hand combat but it's been *weeks* and I still can't even slightly control air."

"You're from the Müstik Family. The ability is inside of you, Amarah, you just have to believe it. It's a part of you and just another addition to your power. It *is* there. I'm sure it will come to you soon," Vyla says confidently.

"I hope you're right," I sigh and focus on my plate of food as the conversation turns into idle chatter about the kids and their day.

I help Vyla clean up the dishes and the kitchen while Logan and Jon go outside to cut some firewood. The kids are running around, playing, and keeping each other entertained. It's amazing how kids are so easily entertained by even the smallest thing. Adults just complicate everything.

The men are still outside when we've finish cleaning up. I'm standing with my back against the counter and watch as Vyla brings out some wine glasses.

"Would you like some wine?"

"Yes, please. Wine sounds terrific."

"Any preferences?" She asks.

"Something sweet, if you have it, would be great! You have such a beautiful family. Thank you for letting me be a small part of it while I'm here. I can see why Logan loves coming here," I say as I watch her select a bottle of wine from the pantry and proceeds to uncork it.

She hands me a glass of wine as she looks at her kids, "yea, Jon and I are very Blessed." She has such love in her eyes, a mother's love, and I can't help but wonder if my own mother had a chance to look at me the same way before she died. The fact that I'll never see that look directed at me sends a crushing pain to my chest.

"Logan is part of the family, and now, you are too," she

smiles brightly at me. "Cheers."

I return her smile as our glasses clink together and I take a sip of the red, slightly sparkling with little bubbles, wine in my glass. "Oh, my goodness. This is delicious!"

"I'm glad you like it. So, do you and Logan plan on having a family of your own?" Vyla looks at me with a sparkle of her own in her eyes and an eager smile.

The direct question takes me off guard and I choke on the sip of wine I'm taking. I cough to clear my throat, "ummm, no. I mean, uh, we haven't talked about anything like that," I laugh nervously. "We've only known each other a couple of months. I don't think that's a conversation we'll have for a while. Plus, it's not like either of our lives are exactly family material."

"I've lived a long time, Amarah, there's never a perfect time to start a family and you'll never *feel* ready, but when two people love each other, truly love each other, nothing else matters. And let me tell you, that man loves you, Amarah."

I feel my cheeks getting warm and it has nothing to do with the wine. I wasn't expecting this topic of conversations and don't know what to say. Before I can think of anything, Vyla continues.

"I've known Logan a long time and I've never seen him this...*peaceful*, before. Logan has always struggled with his happiness. He's always had this...I dunno, deep anger that he kept suppressed. If you knew him well enough, and knew what to look for, you could see it. He hid it well though. Shit, centuries of practicing and anyone would be a master of their emotions, but I used to see it in his eyes. The loneliness, the *anger*, that always haunted him."

She shakes her head and then looks at me, giving me intense eye contact, "he no longer has that haunting look, Amarah. The only thing I see when I look at him now is love. And I've seen the way you look at him too," she says with a teasing smile. "You're good for him, Amarah, and he's good for you. Don't take it for granted."

Just then, the door opens, and in come the men in our lives. They're both holding an armful of firewood, talking about chainsaws, and taking a trip to gather more firewood for the upcoming winter. Logan makes eye contact with me and straight up stops my heart with his radiant smile. No matter what else is going on around us, we're always connected. That crushing pain I felt in my chest a minute ago, turns into a heavy, overflowing pour of emotions.

"I won't," I answer Vyla's last comment absentmindedly. My focus now elsewhere.

The men set some wood in the fireplace, and I get to show off my fire skills, as a Master of Fire. I may not be able to control air, but I excel in fire. How I've become a Master of Fire, when I'm not supposed to be a Master of *anything,* is beyond me. My best guess is the Angel part of me give me a leg up. My own Divine power that's within me is very similar to fire. Only it's pure and white and feels completely safe.

Tori and Vic are kneeling next to me, their little bodies eager with anticipation, as I call the fire to my hand easily.

"Oooo," Tori's eyes light up.

"Cool!" Vic exclaims. "Can I touch it too?"

I turn the fire in my palm into the pure white flame I used back in the attack on the Fire Fey. "Go ahead, you can touch the white flame, it won't hurt you."

Vic's smile widens but he's hesitant. Smart kid. He slowly moves his hand toward the flame, trying to sense the heat. He then quickly pushes his hand through the flame and pulls it back. When nothing happens, he tries again. This time, he puts his hand slowly in the flame and lets it linger.

"Wow! This is so cool! Try it, Tori!"

Tori shrinks back and shakes her head vigorously but her

eyes are still in awe of the flame.

"The fire doesn't hurt me because it's a part of me, just like air is a part of you. Fire, real fire, is dangerous and hurts the absolute *worst* when you get burned. Trust me, I know first-hand. So, you must both promise me to *never* try and touch fire any other time, ok?"

They both nod their heads and I proceed to light the logs on fire. When the awe of the fire has passed, the kids go back to playing and entertaining each other, as we sit around the living room drinking our wine.

"How is Luke doing with his new position?" I ask. With all of my time spent training I haven't had much time to see how anything else is going.

"Good, as to be expected, I assume," Vyla shrugs.

"He's put together a small team to search for Aralyn. As you know, the Queen has made finding her a priority, and that seems to be what he's focused on," Jon says, as he throws his feet up on the coffee table to get more comfortable on the couch, next to Vyla.

Logan and I are sharing the oversized chair, his arm resting on the back of it, so I can cuddle in on his side. The fire is burning warmly to my left and I can see the open kitchen in front of me.

"I don't know how he plans on finding her if Ethan and the other Leaders couldn't track her the night she disappeared. Her trail is more than just cold. It's like it has been completely wiped clean. No traces," Logan shakes his head. "The Wolves should have been able to track her."

"She disappeared almost as if my *magic*," I scoff.

"What are you saying?" Jon asks, sitting up, and coming to attention.

"Just that. I think she used magic to disappear," I shrug. "It's the only thing that makes sense."

"Why would a Coven get involved with Aralyn and her

treachery?" Jon continues asking questions.

"From what I know of Witches and the Covens, they *wouldn't* get involved. In fact, they're frustratingly selfish. But a *solitary* Witch...why not? I'm sure you've heard that's what we think happened with Andre and some of the others she was using. She used magic against them. I'll say it again, it's the only thing that makes sense."

Movement in the kitchen catches my attention. "Ummm...guys," I point toward the kitchen. "Tori is climbing your cabinets," I laugh.

Vyle waves her hand, "don't worry, she does this all the time. She's going for the cookie jar," she laughs and shakes her head lovingly. "Only one, Tori!" She calls back without even looking.

"Ok!" Comes the excited little voice of Tori from the kitchen.

Jon continues probing me, "so you really think Aralyn found a Witch to help her?"

"I do. I mean, she was bold enough to approach the Vampires. There's no doubt in my mind she has other sinister plans and plenty of people helping her." I'm trying to focus on the conversation but Tori is making me nervous. She's on top of the counter now.

Jon is stroking his chin, "it is an interesting theory. If you're right, do you think she's still close by?"

"Well, ummmm..."

"No Vic!" Tori's voice interrupts me.

She's standing on top of the counter clutching a round canister to her chest, which I'm assuming is the cookie jar. Vic is standing in front of her trying to take it from her.

"Kids!" Vyla and Jon say at the same time.

They seem completely comfortable with what's happening in the kitchen, as if it happens often, but it's making *me* extremely nervous, but hey, they aren't my kids. I have to trust that Vyla and Jon know best in this situation.

I try to continue, my eyes shifting from the kitchen scene to Jon's eager gaze, "yeah, I do think she's close by. In hiding of course, and I don't think…"

"I said, NO!" I hear Tori's voice pierce the air, as I look up just in time to see her stumble backwards from the force of jerking the canister out of Vic's prying hands. Then, her tiny little body is falling off the countertop, and I'm on my feet before I even have the thought.

"Stop!" I scream as I hold my hands out helplessly in front of me. I squeeze my eyes shut so I won't see Tori hit the floor. There's the sound of a glass breaking and then absolute silence. No crying from Tori. No talking of any kind.

"Amarah, it's ok. Everything's ok," Logan's voice is soothing as he places his hand on my back to comfort me. "Open your eyes."

I slowly open my eyes to see Tori suspended in the air and everyone's eyes on me.

"Am I…"

"Yes," Jon beams up at me from his seat on the couch. "Yes, you are," he laughs happily.

I can feel it now. There's tingling in my hands and arms, almost as if they've fallen asleep, but not as stinging and uncomfortable. I can *feel* the weight of the air holding Tori, keeping her from hitting the floor. It's like I can feel all of the microscopic, invisible particles in the air. Like on a humid day, when you feel the thickness of the air, before and after it rains. I slowly lower my hands and feel the thickness underneath Tori moving and changing.

Tori sits on the floor, where I've placed her, and doesn't seem fazed by anything that's just happened. She just sticks her hand in the cookie jar, pulling one out and quickly shoving it into her mouth. I consciously let go of the power and the tingling in my arms stops.

I fall back into the chair, Logan takes his seat next to me, and grabs my hand. Vyla gets up and walks into the kitchen. She snatches the cookie jar from Tori and places it back on the counter. She scolds Vic for picking on his sister and he storms off down the hallway to his bedroom.

"Are you ok?" Logan asks quietly.

I just nod, still in a daze at what's happened. Vyla comes back holding a broom and dust pan.

"Shit!" I say with feeling. "I'm so sorry about the glass. I'll replace it."

"Oh hush! No need to apologize and no need to replace the glass. I have plenty," she bends down and sweeps up the broken glass into the dust pan. She places her hand on my knee, "thank you for protecting Tori. I knew it would come to you," she winks as she gets up and heads back into the kitchen.

"Looks like training will be a Hell of a lot more fun tomorrow," Jon says, with too much excitement in his voice, and a gleam in his eyes.

"I don't like the way you said that," I scowl at him. "Should I be worried?"

His smile widens and a hint of something devious passes through his eyes, "you'll see."

"Great," I groan.

# Learn To Trust Yourself

Little Me by Little Mix

The wind is gently blowing the strands of hair that escaped my bun across my face. I can feel the wind but it's different now. It isn't just solid wind, no, I can feel each individual particle that floats on the breeze. Almost as if I can reach out and pluck them out of the air, but when I open my eyes, I still can't see anything. Again, how do you *see* air?

"Good, Amarah, you're getting better," Jon says from his seat across from me. "Now change your focus. Do something else with the air."

I close my eyes again, it helps me focus on what I can *feel*, since I can't see it with my eyes. I feel those particles, direct them towards Jon, and feel the breeze leave my face. I lift my right hand off my knee and start making a circle in the air with my index finger. Jon says I don't need to physically imitate what I want to do but it seems to help me.

I open my eyes as my finger continues making circles in the air. Jon is now sitting in the middle of his very own gentle tornado.

His hair and clothes are being whipped around as the wind circles him.

"How am I doing?" My voice is serious but I can't help the amused smile tugging at my lips.

Since I'm usually the one being blown away by the wind, I can't help but enjoy the fact that I'm in control, and it's now Jon that's at its mercy. At my mercy. Granted, I'm being gentler than he had ever been with me, and he's allowing me to do this. He can take over control of what I'm doing at any time. He's a Master of Air and I'm just a young grasshopper, learning to wax on and wax off, like the Karate Kid. The happiness and the silliness of the situation finally has me cracking up.

"Very funny, Amarah, ha ha," Jon says sarcastically, but there's a slight smile playing on his lips as well. "That's enough of that," he says sternly, and the wind instantly stops.

"What's it like to be a Master of Air? What can you do with the air? I mean, in addition to having wings and flying."

"Hmmm, well, just like any other Master, you have that element within you. For example, you can call fire from within you when there is no fire around, right?"

"Yes," I say, as I produce a flame in my palm, letting it flicker through my fingers before calling it back again.

"I can also call the air from within. I can create air in a space where maybe air is limited. I can also take the air completely out of a room and suffocate those in it. Furthermore, I can take the air straight from someone's lungs."

As he says this last part, my eyes widen, my hands rush to my chest as it tightens, and I'm suddenly gasping for air. It doesn't last long, and I'm sucking in fresh air a few seconds later, but he succeeded in causing me panic. It's a terrifying example of his power.

"Holy shit," I say through gasping breaths. "That is definitely useful." I rub my hand across my chest as I continue to take in slow, deep breaths, "and terrifying."

"Controlling air may seem like one of the lesser talents. It's definitely one of the less showy ones, but it's one of the most deadly. Everyone needs air to survive and a Master can easily take that away from you."

"I see that now," I laugh nervously.

"Call your fire again," he instructs.

If anyone else was sitting across from me, I probably would have been scared to do anything else after that little stunt, but I trust Jon completely. I know he won't hurt me. What reason would he have? Not to mention he's had plenty of chances over these past weeks if he wanted to.

I call the fire again, and let it burn bright and strong, the red and orange flames dancing in my palm. Then, they're gone, and I hadn't called the fire back. It's like it was *taken* from me. It feels like a violation of my power somehow.

"What? How? Did *you* do that?" I ask in surprise.

Jon just nods his head.

"But you're not a Master of Fire! How can you control *my* fire?"

"What do fires need to thrive?" He asks patiently.

I think about it for a second and then it dawns on me. "Ohhhh, I see. You're not controlling my fire but controlling the air around it! That's why the fire that the demons used in their attack never reached us. Someone had controlled the air before the fire got to us," I'm talking more to myself as I figure it all out in my head.

"Exactly. Fire is useful and can be very dangerous, but all the other elements can easily defeat it. Air, you saw, Water obviously, and Earth, well, through enough dirt on a fire and that suffocates its oxygen too. Needless to say, the Fire Fey have always had a bit of a chip on their shoulder when it comes to the others because of this," he chuckles.

"Well, that makes sense. At least I know now why Hallana is so hot-headed all the time," I laugh. "It is a bit unfair now that I'm thinking about it."

"We all have our strengths *and* weaknesses, Amarah. No one is more powerful or stronger than anyone else."

*Well, except me*, I think to myself. At least the part of me that's Angel.

Jon continues, "at the end of the day, we can all get hurt or worse."

"Can we try something?" I ask tentatively.

"Sure, what's on your mind?"

I pull the fire back into my palm, but this time, I use *my* power and produce a beautiful, pure white flame. I turn that into a ball of glowing white energy, resting gently in my palm.

"Can you suffocate it?" I ask, but my eyes never leave the ball in my palm.

I stare at it for what seemed like forever, waiting for it to get smaller and disappear in my hand, but it glows steady and solid. There's not even the slightest flicker or waver in my power.

The silence is loud and I finally look up at Jon. He's staring intently at *me* and not the ball of light in my hand.

"What's wrong?" I ask nervously. The look on his face isn't exactly comforting.

"What is this? Some kind of magic?" He asks sternly.

I shake my head, "I have something…" I hesitate, not sure how to explain it without sharing my secret, " *else,* in me. It's hard to explain. It's part of the fire but it's also just...a part of me. I think? This is what I used when we were attacked by the demons at the Fire Fey home."

"Whatever it is, it's powerful. Maybe it doesn't need oxygen to thrive. Hell, maybe it's not fire at all but something else entirely."

We both sit completely still and stare at the swirling ball of light in my hand. It isn't just light either. It has energy to it. I can feel it radiating off the swirling ball as if waiting to be commanded into action. I know it's powerful and I know it's all mine.

"What can you do with it?" Jon finally breaks the silence.

"To be honest, I'm not entirely sure," I let out a heavy sigh and pull my power back inside of me. "I don't know what I'm capable of, Jon. Not knowing yourself and what you might do is *not* a great feeling. What if I hurt someone with it? I think that's why I'm struggling so much with the elemental stuff. I'm scared," I admit.

He rubs his beard and nods his head, "I can understand that, but Fey are connected to the Earth, Amarah. We're the most natural beings on Earth. You shouldn't fear the power itself. The power is wielded by us, as individuals. Ultimately, *you* are in control of what happens when you use your power. Your power *is* you. It's a live and intuitive thing, Amarah. As long as your heart and your intentions are good, you don't have to worry. Does that make sense?"

"Yes, it does. The Queen mentioned the same thing when I first met her. I understand that everyone has the choice to use their power for good or evil, but I also don't deny that I'm not perfect. What if I'm not completely in control? What if my emotions make me...*reckless*? I haven't had centuries of practicing my control. It makes me nervous."

"I think being concerned and nervous is a *good* thing, Amarah. It means you're aware and that you care. See, good intentions already," he smiles and reaches out to lay a hand on my arm. "Learn to trust yourself, Amarah. I know you'll do the right thing," he squeezes my arm reassuringly and then stands up. "Now, let's get back to using weapons, shall we?"

"Yeah, sure." I push myself up and start to walk over to where the practice daggers lay, near the end of the platform, when two of them come flying at my head. I have to throw myself on the floor to avoid being knocked unconscious. Or worse.

I whip my head around and see Jon grab the daggers right out of the air. "Whoa!" I say in awe, as I stand back up.

Jon smiles wickedly, right before he throws one of the daggers right at me. It comes hurtling at my face so fast I don't even have time to blink much less get out of the way. The dagger stops an inch from my face, pointed right between my eyes. My heart is in my throat and I have to push it back down before I can speak.

"How..." I move to grab the dagger but it's gone again and back in Jon's hand before my hand reached it. I just stare, unintelligently, at Jon.

"Close your mouth, Amarah, you may swallow a bug," Jon laughs. "Why do you look so surprised? You pretty much did the same thing when you saved Tori from her fall."

I had to think about it. "Yeah, I mean, I guess but...I never thought about how it could translate into combat! Plus, I didn't really know what I was doing, it just happened instinctively."

"Well, now you've been practicing with moving the air. This is just another piece to it. You use that same feeling you had earlier when you had me in my own little whirlwind, but you apply it to lifting and controlling weapons."

"Why do I think that's easier said than done?" I cross my arms over my stomach.

Jon chuckles, "because it does take a lot of control. It's one thing to suspend something in the air," he lifts and holds the dagger in the air with his power. "It's another thing entirely to control its movement in the air. You're not actually focused on the weapon itself, but the air around it. It does take some getting used to."

"Of course, it does. Story of my life. Nothing is ever easy."

Jon sends one of the daggers floating over to me, slowly this time, hilt facing me. "Your turn," he says, as the dagger falls from the air.

I catch it in my hand easily and just stare at it for a while. It feels good in my hand. I like the feeling of holding and wielding weapons. I'm pretty good at it too, and that always excites me, and makes me feel strong.

"Why can't I just stab demons the old fashion way?" I ask.

"You kill a demon by any means necessary, but you need to learn to use the air to move things too. It doesn't always need to be a weapon. It will come in handy in all sorts of situations. Especially one where you may be tied up and can't physically use a weapon."

"Ok, you have a point there," I sigh. "Here we go."

I concentrate on the dagger in my hand, willing it to lift off my palm, and suspend in the air. When nothing happens after several minutes of trying, I grab a hold of the dagger, and drop my hand to my side.

"It's not working."

"Stop concentrating on the weapon. Remember what I said? Concentrate on the air *around* the weapon. Try again."

I let out a frustrated grunt but pick up my hand and try again. This time, I close my eyes and focus on feeling the weight of the particles in the air instead of the weight of the weapon in my hand. I can feel them surrounding the dagger, so I focus on them and will them to move, to lift the dagger into the air. I open my eyes to see the dagger a couple of inches off my palm, floating in the air.

"I did it!" I say excitedly.

"That's the first step. Now, take a hold of that feeling, feel the air holding the dagger and move the air around the dagger. Send it to me."

I concentrate on the air, like he instructs, I use my palm to mimic the movement of pushing the dagger towards Jon. I feel the air move but the dagger clatters to the floor.

"That's ok, it was your first try. Try again," Jon encourages me.

I pick up the dagger a thousand and one more times, before I finally throw my hands in the air, "that's it! I give up! I obviously *can't* do it, ok."

Jon walks over to me and picks up the dagger, "you *can* and you *will*. Keep practicing when you can, on your own, and we'll continue trying together in our training." He holds the dagger hilt toward me again.

"I'm done trying today, Jon, I don't want to try again right now."

"I know. I thought we'd get some of that frustration out of you before we call it a day?" He makes it more of a question than a command.

I smile, but it feels more like a snarl, "bring it on old man!" I say, as I snatch the dagger out of his hand, and attack instantly.

After about twenty minutes of going full-out, physical exertion, I'm mentally *and* physically exhausted. I climb into the cable car as the sun is getting close to the horizon. I made progress today, and I know I should be happy with myself and my efforts, but what I'm more focused on is my revelation.

I'm scared of myself and my power.

Finally admitting it out loud feels like a weight has been lifted off of me. I replay Jon's words in my head. I need to trust myself. As long as my intentions are good, I won't hurt anyone.

"My intentions *are* good", I say out loud. I smile to myself as I take the first step in not only learning to trust myself, but also truly believing in myself.

# You're My Angel

Angel by Aerosmith

I walk into the house, kick my shoes off by the door, then turn to lock it behind me. I'm instantly welcomed by the smell of something cooking for dinner and my stomach is suddenly alive and yelling at me that it's hungry.

"Something smells delicious!" I yell from the entryway, but when I turn around to face the rest of the room, I'm left speechless.

The lights are off, candles are everywhere, and there's a fire roaring in the fireplace. All the flickering lights, bouncing off walls, creating shadows, and giving the room a warm, intimate glow. I head through the living room and notice the small dining table is covered in a white tablecloth with two place settings and a couple of tall, white candles illuminating it.

Turning the corner, I see Logan standing at the stove, taking up way too much space in the small kitchen. His body and presence always overwhelming any space he's in as if nothing can contain him. My heart instantly starts racing. He's barefoot, has on a pair of dark blue jeans, *no shirt*, and an apron that says, *kiss the chef*, written across the front. He looks scrumptious and I'd be happy to just have *him* for dinner.

"What's all this?" I ask in astonishment.

Logan finally looks at me and gives me a sly, half-smile. He unties the apron and lays it on the counter. He picks up a bottle of wine as he walks towards me oozing sex appeal. He runs his hand through his hair and his muscles put on a show that I soak in. He doesn't even have to do anything other than stand there, and my body goes limp and into overdrive, all at the same time.

He stops once he's inches in front of me, towering over me, and invading my personal space. I can feel his body heat on my skin and my breath quickens. He still hasn't said a word. He takes a swig of the wine right out of the bottle and then leans in for a kiss.

The kiss is solid but soft and gentle. The taste of wine on his lips is one of my favorite things. His tongue runs across my bottom lip, sending the butterflies in my stomach flying hectically, and then he pulls away. I sway on my feet as I try to follow his lips with mine. My hands pressed against his massive chest is the only thing that keeps me standing. I lick my lips, already buzzed off his wine flavored kiss.

"Hello, beautiful," he finally says with that half-smile still taunting me. "Would you like some wine?" He asks, as he takes the few steps to the table, grabs a wine glass, and leaves me pleasantly confused and wanting more. He offers me the glass of wine and I take it as he pours himself a glass too. I take a sip and the flavor only reminded me of his lips on mine.

"Not that I'm complaining, trust me, but what is all this about?" I wave my hand around trying to distract myself with everything else in the room.

"Do I need a reason to spoil you for a night?" That damn smile still playing on his lips, tugging at my heartstrings and things lower in my body.

"No, but… I dunno, I'm just not used to this."

He pulls his phone out of his back pocket and a few seconds later, *Angel* by Aerosmith, comes blasting out of the speakers. He takes another sip of his wine before he sets his glass and phone down on the table and holds out his hand out to me.

I raise my eyebrows, my own smile threatening to break through. I place my hand in his and he takes my glass of wine, setting it on the table next to his. Then he pulls me in close and starts dancing with me.

I have a silly grin plastered on my face, "oh my goodness, what has gotten into you?"

"Shhhh, my part is coming up."

"What…?"

And then he starts belting out the chorus to the song. I throw my head back and laugh, as he gently pushes me away, spins me before pulling me back in, and dipping me. He holds me in a dip, as he finishes the chorus and then crushes me with a kiss as he pulls me back to standing, my body fully pressed against his.

He keeps a firm hold on me, his arms possessively around my body, and his eyes intent on mine. We keep dancing, swaying our way through the song, until the next one plays. It's *Angel* by Theory of a Deadman. He starts singing it right away and caresses my face, matching the lyrics.

Then he holds up a finger, "wait here," he gives me a quick peck on the cheek, then hurries off towards the bedroom. Coming or going, Logan is always a meal for the eyes. Fuck a snack. The man is a whole meal plus dessert! I watch, hungrily, as his muscled back disappear into the bedroom.

I'm too stunned and speechless to protest. I just pick up my glass of wine and head into the kitchen to see what he's cooking.

I open the oven and see a casserole of some kind and it looks and smells amazing. My stomach growls at me again.

Logan comes back into the kitchen, offering me his hand again, as he nods in the direction of the bedroom. "Come on."

"Where?" I laugh as he picks up his phone and pulls me through the living room, through the bedroom, and into the bathroom.

"Wooowww," I drag the word out with wide eyes, taking it all in.

Logan is drawing a bath filled with bubbles and rose petals. Candles line the back of the tub where there's a built-in shelf. There are also candles on the counter, leaving the entire bathroom engulfed in a beautiful golden glow.

"This is breathtaking, Logan, really....I don't even know what to say."

"The only breathtaking thing in this room is you, Amarah," his voice is husky and low. "You don't need to say anything, just enjoy this with me."

"What about dinner?"

"Dinner has another hour."

His smile melts my body and all I can do is whisper, "ok," as he takes my glass of wine out of my hands for a second time. I start to take my shirt off when Logan shakes his head.

"Nuh uh. I want to undress you."

The look in his eyes is pure, hot passion. It makes my heart race and I swear it can be heard beating from a mile away. His body is almost touching mine and I have to lean my head back to look into his eyes. He slides his fingertips under my shirt and begins to lift it, as his fingertips gently grazed my sides, sending chills all over my body. I close my eyes and shiver. He stops when my shirt is covering my eyes and trapping my arms above my head.

I feel the absence of his body heat right before I hear the light squeak of the bathtub handles as he turns the water off. I can't sense his movement and I can't see anything. All I can feel is the rise and fall of my chest, as my body reacts to being pinned, and unable to see. Not knowing what Logan is doing or what will happen next sends anxiety and excitement racing through my veins.

Then, I feel the warmth of his body behind me. He doesn't touch me. He doesn't have to. His body heat is caressing my skin as if it were his fingers. I feel the warmth move around me and I know he's standing in front of me again. Then I feel his warm breath on my mouth and my lips part, waiting for the kiss, but it never comes. I feel his breath on my neck and a moment later, his soft, wet tongue leaving a burning trail down my neck and to the top mound of my breast. Then a gentle blow along the wet line, cooling it off, and sending a shiver down my spine.

Still pinned and still unable to see, I feel heat coming through my bra as he covers it with his mouth and gently bites down, pinching my nipple between his teeth through the fabric. My stomach tightens and I sigh in pleasure. Then his heat moves again and he's standing behind me. I feel his fingers graze against my skin as he unhooks my bra, but it's trapped on my body, with my arms pinned above my head. I don't have time to think about it as I feel his warm tongue again. It starts at the bottom of my neck and slowly draws a line straight down my spine sending goosebumps to cover my skin.

"I love the taste of your skin," he declares in a deep voice, full of desire. I hear a zipper and then the sound of his jeans hitting the floor.

His chest presses solidly against my back, and his hands slip under the bra, his calloused hands gently scratching the sensitive skin on my breasts.

"I love the feel of your skin."

My nipples harden at his touch, and he gently squeezes each one as he pushes his hips into me, letting me feel his hard erection. I cry out with the sensory overload. Not being able to see is causing everything else, every small touch, every small breath and whisper on my skin, to be heightened.

His hand travels lower along my body. His left hand rests on my stomach, almost covering it completely, pulling me into him harder, as his right hand slips under my leggings. A low growl rumbles through his chest, as his fingers part me and slip inside of me, taking the breath from my lungs. He removes his fingers and rubs lazy circles around my clit. His fingers slick with my desire.

"I love how you're always so wet for me," his voice is a whisper next to my ear.

"Always," I breathe out as I rock my hips against his hand. His fingers still circling my clit, building up my desire and ripping a moan from my throat.

"I want you to cum but not like this."

He removes his hand and brings his fingers to my lips. I open my mouth and close my lips over his fingers, licking and sucking them, tasting myself on him. It's his turn to moan behind me. "See how sweet you taste. I want you to cum with my mouth on you. I want you to release all that sweetness right on my tongue."

My body is tingling all over as the shirt is finally pulled off. My bra is off next and then then the workout leggings. No buttons or zippers to fuss with. He pulls them down and I grab onto his shoulders to steady myself as I step out of them. He sweeps his arm behind my legs and lifts me sideways in his arms then steps into the enormous tub before he slowly sets me down.

His lips fall on mine, and the sensation of the deep kiss with the feeling of him hard and ready trapped between our bodies, makes me moan and move my body against him. He starts singing again with his mouth still on mine. I hadn't even heard the music much less which specific song is playing, but now I pay attention as he sings along to, *Lips of an Angel* by Hinder.

I pull back so I can see his face. "Did you make a playlist with every song that has the word angel in it?" I ask, smiling.

"Of course. Because you're my real-life Angel, Amarah."

I laugh, "you are absolutely ridiculous *but*… I'm going to thank you for all of your thoughtfulness tonight."

I slowly sink down into the steaming hot water. It's almost too hot, almost, but I know it will just last longer if we start this hot and there's no way I'm complaining about anything right now. I look up at Logan's gorgeous, muscular body towering over me. Everything about him makes me feel so small. His eyes are shining in the candle light, eagerly watching me. I keep eye contact with him, as I lick him from the base of his cock to the tip before, I take him in my hands to angle him toward my mouth.

My hair is still up in a bun and leaves a clear view of what I'm doing. He watches as I take him in my mouth and then back out again. I circle my tongue around the tip of him, tasting his pre-cum, and then take him in my mouth again, over and over, until he's slick from my mouth. I have to use my mouth and both hands to cover every inch of him. He finally closes his eyes and tilts his head back moaning with pleasure.

His hands settled on the back of my head, as he starts to move his hips, taking control of the motion. He pushes inside of my mouth and hits the back of my throat. He's huge, and I have to force myself to relax, and take every inch he gives me. I swallow as much of him as I can, and moan and the feeling of him down my throat, but I still can't take it all. I hold onto his hips for balance and bring a hand to caress his balls as he fucks my mouth. I can feel him getting even harder, and I could barely fit him in my mouth, when he lets out a groan that turns into a growl in his throat.

He pulls out, we're both breathing hard, "Damn. I need a minute. This is not how it's going to end tonight." He pulls me out of the water and leads me to the edge of the tub where he gently pushes me to sit down.

It's his turn to kneel in the water. I have a split second to register the cold tile against my back, before Logan is putting my legs over his shoulders, and I'm completely exposed to him.

"You're mine." He keeps eye contact with me as he lays a kiss on the inside of my thigh, then another, and another, slowly getting closer to my core. To where my body throbs with need.

I love that he claims me, not only physically, but with his words too. He does it every time as if it's his obligation to remind me. I don't need reminding, but it turns me on to hear him say those words.

*I am his.*

He watches me watch him, as he licks me right up the center of my core, slowly. "Mmmm, how can you taste so good?" He draws slow, lazy circles with his tongue around my clit, teasing me. He knows where I want his attention but he refuses to give it to me.

I move my hips against him, trying to get his tongue where I need it. He chuckles and then finally moved his tongue over my clit, then sucks.

"Is this what you want?"

"Yes," I rest my hands gently in his hair as he makes more teasing circles.

"Ask nicely."

"Please," I breathe frantically.

He stops teasing and gives me what I want. He moves his tongue flat over my clit back and forth, back and forth and then with a hard flick, again and again, taking his time building me up to climax. I watch him, as he watched me, until I can't fight the pleasure anymore and have to give into it completely. I throw my head back against the tile and close my eyes. I focus on his warm, slick tongue as he devours me.

"I'm close," I pant.

He slides one finger inside me, as he continues to caress me with his tongue, and then another. He's working in a slow steady rhythm, listening to my breathing, listening to my moans of pleasure. I move my hips in a matching rhythm to his tongue strokes and his fingers, pumping in and out of me. It feels so good I never want it to stop, but the pleasure is building like a dam inside me, and I know I'm going to break. My legs begin to shake with the pressure, tightening around his head.

"Oh my God. You're going to make me cum," I say, as I dig my hands into his hair, hanging on for dear life. He never changes his rhythm. His tongue rubs against my clit as his fingers curl up inside of me, hitting that spot that brings me to the edge.

Then he shoves me over.

My body jerks as the dam inside of me breaks, my pussy spasming as it releases my orgasm on his tongue like he wanted, and I cry out in pleasure with his name on my lips.

He pulls me off the edge of the tub, and down into the water with him, before I can recover from the mind-blowing pleasure. He kisses me hard and hungry and I can taste myself on him and it makes me moan into his mouth.

"I want you, now," he growls, as he turns me around, leaning me over the tub.

He doesn't give me any time to prepare before he shoves himself in me all at once. It sends a small shock of pain through my body. He's never been rough with me and it catches me off guard. Not to mention, he's not small, and he just forced all of himself into me in one hard shove. I register what happened and a part of me likes it. A few strokes later, my body opens to him, and it's nothing but pleasure.

A loud *smack* splits the air as his hand lands on my ass. I gasp in surprise, again, I'm caught off guard, but the feeling and the sound of it, send a wave of pleasure crashing through my body.

"Again."

Another *smack* cracks through the air as his hand comes down on the same spot. I feel the instant heat of my skin reacting to the hit but the pleasure of him pumping inside of me is still overwhelming. I moan and push my hips back, meeting his hard strokes with more force.

I want more.

I *need* more.

"Fuck me harder," I demand.

He pulls my hair free from the bun, fisting it in his hand, and pulls me into him, making me arch my back and straining my neck with the force of it. We're sending water and bubbles sloshing over the edge of the tub but neither of us seem to mind. I'm just focused on the feeling of him inside of me, his large body slamming into mine from behind. His massive cock pounding deeper than he's ever been, hitting the end of me, causing a small shock of pain at the end of each stroke and yet, building pleasure inside of me at the same time. Consuming me in every way. It feels amazing but I want to ride that fine line between pleasure and pain.

"Bite me."

I feel him hesitate behind me, "Amarah, I don't want to hurt you."

I turn my head so he can see my eyes and know that I mean it. That I want it.

"Do it."

Whatever he sees in my eyes, he doesn't hesitate again. He leans forward, takes the skin of my back into his mouth, and bites down. His grip on my waist becomes bruisingly tight, as he pounds into me, building me up to another orgasm. I'm on the edge again when I feel his rhythm falter and I know he's close.

"I'm close, Logan. Don't stop," I plead.

He growls as he continues to slide in and out of me. He pulls out until the tip is barely inside of me before he rams into me. Then pulls out and does it again, again, again, until I cry out in pleasure.

Logan cums with such force that I feel it unleash inside of me. He bites down just a little harder as he loses control and it sends me over the edge one final time. He slowly releases his bite, leans his forehead on my back and I feel the wetness of both of our orgasms running down my thighs. He slowly pulls out of me, my body clenches around him with a final shudder of pleasure, and we both collapse. The water has started to cool but it feels great on my burning skin.

"Amarah," he's trying to catch his breath. "I'm sorry, I didn't mean to break skin."

I reach back and feel where he bit me. My hand comes away with a small amount of blood. "It's ok, I promise. I asked for it," I say with a devious smile as I slide further down into the water.

Logan reaches for me and cups my face in his hands, "what was that about?" It's his turn to ask.

Staring into his questioning green eyes, I suddenly feel insecure about my actions. What if he doesn't want what I want? What if he thinks I'm weird or crazy? Have I scared him away?

"Technically, you started the rough play," I give a weak smile. "You're not going to break me, Logan." I shrug, "I like a little pain, along with *a lot* of pleasure. Not always, but…" I shrug again and drop my eyes to the water, not knowing what else to say, and not wanting to look at him. I don't want to see the disgust on his face for what I asked for.

"Amarah," I can hear the smile in his voice. When I look back up, I'm greeted with a huge smile that melt my heart and eases my insecurity.

He shakes his head, still holding my face in his hands. "You never cease to amaze me," he chuckles. "But you have to promise me you'll never let me hurt you. You have to tell me to stop if something gets out of hand."

I bite my lip and nod, "I will. I promise."

He drops his hand to my shoulders, turns me around and pulls me into him, so my back is against his chest. He wraps his arms around me and hugs me to his chest.

"You wanna know a little secret?"

I nod again, not trusting my voice not to break in this moment.

"I like a little pain too," he whispers in my ear.

A huge smile splits my face at his admission and I finally relax and lean against him. His phone is still playing music and, *Calling all Angels* by Train, is now coming through the speakers.

I laugh, "God, how many songs were you able to find about Angels?"

He chuckles, "you'd be surprised, but it did take some searching."

Just then the oven timer beeps and Logan lets out a disappointed sigh. "I better go take care of that," he kisses the top of my head and gets out of the tub. He stands there, water cascading down his chiselled body, dripping water all over the floor as he stares at me.

"I love you, Amarah."

My heart becomes a stone in my chest again, weighing too

much to possibly be able to carry. It's too full of love and every other emotion I have for him. I love him so much it physically hurts my heart. What's a little pain with all that love?

"I love you, too."

My eyes follow his naked, dripping body, and I'm *starving.* An insatiable hunger that I have for this man...no, Werewolf. I smile to myself as he wraps himself in a towel and heads out of the bathroom.

I sink down until my body is fully submerged in the water and I take a moment to literally soak up my life. It's imperfectly perfect, and for the first time in a long time, I feel whole. I'm finally content and happy and it came in the form of a dangerous new world.

My stomach yells at me for the millionth time and urges me to get out of the bathtub and get food inside of me. Looks like I can't sustain myself on having just Logan for dinner after all.

But that won't stop me from trying.

# Hide and Seek

Hide And Seek by Klergy, Mindy Jones

I can't stop yawning as I pour my coffee and head out onto the small porch. I pull my coat tighter around my body as if that will help keep the chill at bay. The world is just beginning to wake up with that slight, pre-sun morning glow. I look toward the horizon and know the sun is going to make its appearance soon and chase the chill away for a few more weeks.

The sound of the truck door closing brings my attention back. Logan and Jon have been loading up their trucks with supplies for a day of wood cutting. They're going to gather more firewood to carry them through the upcoming cold winter months.

Logan climbs up the stairs to join me on the small porch. "We're all set and ready to head out." He has a big smile on his face and I know he's looking forward to spending the day out in the woods.

"Alright," I can't help but smile at his genuine happiness. "When should we expect you guys back?"

"Hopefully before dinner. Depends on how quickly we can

get the two trucks loaded but Jon and I are both pretty quick at cutting and chopping. What about you? What are you going to do with an entire day off from training?"

"Absolutely *nothing* and I'm so looking forward to it," I laugh. "I'll probably spend some time with Vy and the kids and just relax."

"Ok, well, enjoy your day and don't worry about us. We'll be back this evening," he pulls me into his warm embrace. He's only wearing a thin, long-sleeved t-shirt but his body is warm. He's always warm. I sink into the hug without meaning to and my heart feels a bit heavier in my chest.

"What is it, babe?"

"I just realized this will be the first time I'll be without you since we've been together." I try not to sound sad and co-dependent. Just stating facts. But I know he can feel what I'm feeling and I'm going to miss him. He hasn't even left yet and I already miss him. It's fucking terrible.

"I'm only going to be gone for the day. It's the same as when you go and train all day."

"It's different. I'm going to be alone, nothing to occupy and distract me and you won't be here. I know I'm being *completely* ridiculous but I'll miss you."

He pulls back from the hug and lifts my chin so he can look at me. "I'll miss you too, my Angel, but I'll be back soon. I promise."

I nod my head, "I know." I give him a weak smile but it's the best I can do.

He leans in for a kiss and I tip-toed to meet him. It's supposed to be a quick*, I'll see you soon kiss*, but it turns into an, *I don't want to leave you kiss*. His hands travel to my back to pull me closer against him. My chest is solidly pressed against his and my hands hold his face and run through his hair. His lips are melted into mine, our tongues desperate to stay together. We finally pull away, both breathless.

Logan leans his forehead on mine and whispers, "God, Amarah, what have you done to me?"

"It seems we've bewitched each other."

"Jon's waiting. I have to go but I'll be back before you know it. I love you," he lays a kiss on my forehead and starts pulling away.

I hold on as long as I can, until our fingertips are the last thing to touch, "I love you too. Be careful."

Be careful? It sounds silly once I say it out loud. He's a powerful and strong Werewolf that fights and kills demons. He doesn't need to be careful gathering firewood. Nonetheless, my heart constricts with fear that something will happen.

I watch him climb into his truck and he looks at me one last time through the windshield. I blow him a kiss and he pretends to grab it, placing his closed fist to his heart. We both smile at each other and I watch him follow Jon's truck out of the field and towards the road. I watch the taillights fade and stand here staring out at the road long after they've disappeared.

The sun is coming up now and I can feel the slow warmth beginning to build around me. It's quiet. The type of quiet that you only get in the country. There are no cars, no honking, no sirens, no city sounds to interrupt the peaceful morning. It's still early enough that everyone else is comfortably tucked into their beds and dreaming.

My phone pings with a new notification. I pull it out of the jacket pocket and unlock it. I smile when I see Logan's name and I open the message.

Logan: Fuck, how can I miss you already? I don't know what you've done to me, Angel. Play this on repeat because it's a promise.

Spotify Link: I'm Gonna Love you by Murphy Elmore

I sit down on the step and follow the link to listen to the song. I bite my lip just imagining what tonight is going to be like. I love when he gets all intense, lovey-dovey. I love that he doesn't care about being vulnerable and acting on his emotions. I do as he says, and play the song again as I type back my response.

Me: So, you're gonna love me like I ain't ever been loved, huh?

Logan: Every day. For the rest of my life.

Me: Sounds like a perfect life to me, Logan Lewis.

I wait for his response as I listen to the song for the third time but no reply comes. He probably lost reception already, Hell, it's even spotty here. I'm just about to walk back inside when I see movement out of the corner of my eye. Someone is walking across the open field, heading towards the mountain range in the distance. I can't make out who it is but it strikes me as odd. No one is up this early, much less heading to the mountain to train. My gut instinct tells me something isn't right.

I hear Arabella's voice in my head, *the truth here is that something is going on. Fey are disappearing and I know it is not because they're following my sister.*

I stop debating whether or not I should listen to my gut and run inside to change as quickly as possible. I throw on some dark blue jeans, sneakers, and a black long-sleeved t-shirt. I quickly strap one of my daggers to my right thigh and am pulling my hair into a ponytail as I run out the door. If there's something going on, I'll do my best to find the truth. Besides, what else do I have to do today?

I see the lone figure off in the distance and I do my best to follow in a low, stealthy stance. I don't want to get too close but I also don't want to lose sight of them. They're heading past the cable car and along the base of the mountain range. They keep walking at a quick pace but don't seem rushed or worried about being caught. Maybe it's nothing? Just someone out for an early morning walk?

The initial adrenaline of the chase is fading. I've been following this person, along the mountain range for what has to be over a mile already, and nothing suspicious has happened. I'm just getting ready to scold myself for being paranoid and start heading back when they disappear. One minute they're there and the next minute they're gone.

I pick up my pace and stop where I saw them disappear and that's when I feel it. *Glamour*. I can feel the tingle of the magic in the air on my skin. Something is definitely going on if there's glamour out here in the middle of nowhere. Why is it here? Do I want to take this next step and find out? What will I find? What if it's a trap? All these thoughts race through my mind. I've come all this way, am I really going to just turn around? Fey are going missing and Aralyn is still out there. Still close.

"Come on, Amarah, you have to find out what's going on. No one else will," I take a deep breath and step into the glamour.

I'm suddenly standing in the midst of trees. Not a forest, exactly, but tons of trees everywhere, the sound of running water close by. I look around, trying to figure out which way the person I was following has gone, but I've lost sight of them.

"Shit," I whisper in frustration. I decide to just keep walking in, straight ahead, and keep my eyes peeled for any sign of movement or life. Other than the water I can hear running nearby, it's completely quiet. No birds, no animals, no twigs snapping. Nothing.

The water gets louder and eventually I see a river. It's only about thirty feet wide and doesn't look to be very deep. The water is gently flowing around rocks that are spurting out here and there. Again, it's so...*peaceful.* Almost too peaceful. It doesn't feel or look like anyone has come this way.

I stand at the edge of the riverbank and sigh, "way to go, Amarah. Real smooth."

I look up and down the riverbank for any signs of a trail or disturbance in the ground. Nothing. I sit down, feeling tired from the adrenaline spike, and the trek out here. Might as well just rest a bit before heading back empty handed and none the wiser about who's out here. Maybe I can watch for someone coming back? Yeah, that's what I'll do.

I get up to head back when I hear it. The familiar, *kaaaa*, of the raven. I look up into the distance where the noise had come from. I hear it again and start heading towards where I think it's coming from. I walk along the riverbank following the raven's guiding, *kaaaas*, before it finally makes an appearance.

It flies across the river and *kaaaa'ed* again urging me to follow. I look at the river and it seems to be even more shallow here. I can see rocks that I can step on to cross. I hesitantly put one foot on the closest rock and step out over the water. Ok, I can do this. I take a shaky step onto the next rock, then the next. Before I know it, I'm in the middle of the river, but the next rock is too far out of reach for me to step onto it. I'm going to have to jump for it and the rocks are slippery with whatever slimy algae is growing on them.

I look back over my shoulder and debate just turning back. Why am I following this raven anyway? Do I really need to find Revna now that we have Iseta? What if Iseta can't do the spell? I'm here for a reason, right? I've been led here and I need to follow through and find out why.

I take a deep breath and jump towards the next rock. I land on it, my left foot hitting first, and...I slip. I catch myself with my hands gripping the rock in a low squat but my left foot is fully submerged in the ice-cold water.

"Son of a bitch!" I pull myself up and finish crossing the river. The raven is waiting patiently for me on the other side. It cocks its head to the side and *kaaaas* at me again.

"What are you looking at?" I ask angrily, as if it can understand me. "Well," I throw hands up in frustration, "where to now?"

The raven continues to fly low from tree to tree as I follow. All I can hear is the squishing sound that my foot makes every time I take a step. My foot is beginning to feel numb from the freezing water, sending needle pricks through the bottom of my foot with every step. I grumble to myself about how stupid I am for following a raven out in the middle of nowhere. I don't even know where I am anymore much less where the person I was following is.

I finally see a small house up ahead. It's surrounded by the trees but has a pathway that leads up to the front door, and a golden glow of light shining through the window. I stop to crouch behind a tree and watch the house for any sign of movement inside or out.

I shake my head, "this is ridiculous. This is like Hansel & Gretel only I'm following a bird instead of crumbs. This is for sure the house of a Witch and where I go to die."

I stay crouched behind the tree for what feels like forever, watching the house for any signs of life. Nothing happens. No one moves inside or out. I'm either going to go knock on the damn door or head home. Decisions, decisions. The raven flies down from a tree and lands in the middle of the pathway. It looks directly at me and *kaaaas* for the millionth time.

I look around me one more time, “oh, what the Hell.”

I head toward the path and my heart starts to race. I try to steady myself so I can hear other things besides my heart beating loudly in my ears. I’m a few steps away from the raven but it hasn’t moved from the path and I don’t want to get closer to it. I’m about to step around it when it flaps its wings rapidly and rises into the air. I move my hands up to shield my face from its wings when the noise and flapping stop.

I’m suddenly standing in front of a woman dressed in skin-tight, black leather from head to toe. The leather hugs all of her curves and her ample cleavage looks close to spilling out over her corset style top. Her arms are covered in intricate designs and symbols. She’s quite a bit taller than me and I have to look up to see her face. She has long, straight black hair and cold black eyes rimmed in thick black eye liner, against stark white skin. Black lipstick finishes off the very emo look, and speaking of looks, she looks… *young.*

“Hello, Amarah.” Her voice is crisp with a matching coldness to it. She takes a quick step towards me, her hands reaching out to each side of my head.

I feel an ice-cold shock to my temples. I let out a gasp as my body starts to fall to the ground. I’m caught by unknown hands and feel a solid chest against my back. The woman’s face swims in and out of view as my vision slowly fades.

“I’ve been waiting for you,” she says with a wicked smile.

My world goes cold and black.

# Revna

You Should See Me In A Crown by Billie Eilish

My mind is screaming and I squeeze my eyes shut against the pain. I try to move my hands, to cradle my head, but they're jerked back painfully. That's when I feel the heavy, cold steel around my wrists and hear the clanking of the chains. I slowly open my eyes and find myself I'm lying on my back on a hardwood floor. I look down at my body and see that I've been shackled at the wrists and ankles.

The memory of following someone, the glamour, the house, the raven, the woman...all comes flooding back to me. My heart starts racing and the panic sets in. *Calm down, Amarah. You're no good to anyone if you panic,* I think to myself. I try to slow my breathing and focus on my surroundings instead. I need to know where I am, who's here, scout for any potential weapons or tools to free myself, and I can also use my power to escape. *I'm not helpless!* I think again, this time, with stronger conviction.

I roll onto my side, putting the wall I'm chained to, at my back. The rest of the house is laid out in front of me. It isn't very big. I can see a bed off to one side, and a small couch on the other side, next to a fireplace. Straight ahead is a small kitchen. There are things cluttering every surface. Books, baskets, bowls and jars of all sizes, plants and herbs everywhere, even hanging from the ceiling. Yes, there's no doubt in my mind this is a Witch's house and definitely where I go to die. But why? Why am I being held like this? She knew my name. So, if she knows who I am, then she must know I'm only seeking her out for help. I'm no threat to her! So, why chain me up?

I listen for the sound of anything or anyone moving.

Nothing.

No movement.

No breathing.

I slowly push myself into a sitting position, sending my head into fits of stabbing pain, and I'm thankful the wall is here to support me. I pull my knees into my chest and lay my head on my arms willing the pain to stop. I can't think past the pain behind my eyes and I need a clear head to get out of here.

I don't know how long I stay sitting in this position. I must have dozed off because I jump when I hear the door slam closed. I yank my head up and notice the pain is still there but thankfully, not as bad.

"Good, you're awake," that same cold voice I remember sends chills down my arms.

"Why the fuck am I chained up? What do you want?" I ask as my eyes adjusted to the dim light.

"Now, Amarah, is that any way to address your host? Where are your manners?"

"*My* manners?! If you're the host, is this how you always treat your guests? Knock them out and put them in chains against their will?"

"Only the powerful ones," she says with a hint of a smile in her voice.

She walks towards me, swaying her hips in all that leather. It looks like she's walking to a beat only she could hear. When she gets closer, I can see she's holding a jar in one hand and a knife in the other. My heart starts racing again and I know I need to do something. I reach for my power but I can't feel it. I close my eyes and try again, desperately trying to keep the panic at bay, and failing.

She kneels down in front of me, the overwhelming smell of patchouli making me reel back in disgust, "I hear you've been looking for me."

"Revna," I look her directly in the eyes, trying not to show my fear, or my repulsion.

"Ding, ding, ding! We have a winner! Now, what should your prize be?" She asks as she tips my chin up with the side of the knife.

"I was told you could help me. Apparently, that's not the case. Are you going to kill me?"

"*Could* help you, Amarah. I *could* help you...if I wanted to, and it turns out, I don't," she shrugs her shoulders. "As far as killing you," she looks at the knife turning it this way and that way dramatically. I notice it has black designs etched along the blade on both sides, similar to the marking along her arms, "why on Earth would I kill such a powerful weapon?

Before I can blink, she swipes the knife across my arm, holding the jar underneath to catch my dripping blood inside of it. When it's filled, Revna places her hand on my open wound, mutters something I can't understand and her touch turns ice cold. When she removes her hand, the cut is gone.

"We can't have you bleeding out unnecessarily now, can we?" She says, as if she knew I was going to ask her why she healed me. "Not when your blood is so potent."

"Shhhh," she puts a finger to her lips, even though I haven't said anything, and leans in closer to me. "I'll let you in on a little secret," she whispers, as if there's someone else who will hear us, even though we're the only ones in the house. "I know what you are but don't worry, your secret is safe with me," she winks. "No, no, I will not waste a single drop," she smiles as she stares at the jar of my blood.

I can see the deep-rooted evil in her stare. I don't need my power to feel the evil coming off her in waves. She's cold and frozen to the core. Just being close to her sends a chill into my bones that makes them ache.

"Why are you doing this?"

"*This*...as in?? What, Amarah? Keeping you hostage? Taking your blood?" She inspects me from head to toe with a disappointed look on her face. "I'm not sure why He wants *you*," she sighs. "But a deal is a deal. I give you to him, I get immortality. Really, it's no brainer. Not to mention in the meantime, I get to play with your blood. Surely, you *must* know your blood is very powerful." She stands up and heads back towards the kitchen.

"I must admit, I'm extremely excited to see just *how* powerful it is. Human blood is ok, it can lend itself to a number of spells, but you often have to use all of it in order to get any results. You know," she makes eye contact with me, as if making sure I'm paying attention, "you have to *kill them* and take every last drop. Anyhow, Fey blood is better, obviously. More *magical* and with more... *umphhh*. Don't you think?" She makes a show of showing off her face and body. "You didn't think I looked this good because of good genes, did you?" Sha laughs maniacally, "Oh, you silly goose. I bet you can't even get *close* to guessing my age. Go on!"

"What?" I ask in confusion.

"Guess my age!" She says eagerly.

I'm stunned at her nonchalant, talkative demeanor, not to

mention, I'm still trying to clear my head from whatever she did to it before. Before I can say anything, she continues.

"I'm well over a hundred but a lady never tells her age so don't bother asking. Now, where were we before you so rudely interrupted?" She crosses her arms, and taps her cheek with her index finger, as if trying hard to remember something. "Oh yes, *blood*! Fey *and* Angel blood," she turns to look at me. "*Your* blood, Amarah, I cannot wait to see what I can do with this." She kisses the jar and sets it down on the counter.

"You're the one who's been taking Fey blood. You're the reason they've gone missing."

"Well, gee, aren't you a smart cookie. What am I going to do about all these prizes you're winning? Huh?"

"Who wants me? Who is *He*?"

She sticks her bottom lip out in a pout and puts her hand on her hip, "awwww, I thought you were smart and had it all figured out. I guess not the smartest cookie after all. What a shame. Well, that just means more surprises," she says with a devious smile.

I just glare at her from across the room and hope she can feel my hatred through my stare. The fear and panic are gone now that I know she intends to keep me alive. That's going to be her last mistake.

"You are an evil, twisted, bitch and I'm going to kill you," I say clearly and calmly.

Revna's face falls into something cold, and extremely scary, as she stares at me from across the room. If looks could kill, I'd definitely be a frozen meat popsicle. Thanks, Bruce Willis, for that image by the way.

Just when I think she's about to mutter a spell to murder me, she throws her head back, and...*laughs*. It's a chilling thing to hear, and stirs just a little of that fear I had pushed down, back up. She stomped back over to me, no swaying this time.

She kneels in front of me again, all the humor and playfulness gone. "You have one thing right, Amarah. I am an evil bitch and you do not want to fuck with me. Keeping you alive doesn't mean I can't and won't hurt you. I don't need you conscious to take what I want from you. I don't need you walking. I don't need you talking. I only need you breathing."

She puts her hands on my head again and I feel that same cold spark take hold. Her voice is back to light and playful when she speaks again, "now sleep. We have company coming over later and you need your rest." She gently pats my cheek.

I stare into the empty black pits that are her eyes, "I. Will..." I blink rapidly trying to keep the darkness at bay. "Ki.." and I don't get to finish my threat before I'm pulled back into the chilling darkness.

I slowly come back into consciousness to the sound of voices arguing quietly. The piercing pain is back full-force in my head. What the Hell is she doing to me when she knocks me out? It better not have lasting effects. I'll be pissed!

A woman is speaking, and I swear, I've heard her voice somewhere before. "She's powerful. Untrained, sure, but nonetheless, we shouldn't underestimate her."

I recognize Revna's voice. "Stop worrying, both of you. I put a spell on those chains, using *her own* blood, so she can't use her power as long as she's wearing them."

Shit. That's why I couldn't use my power earlier. This is

definitely going to be a problem. I mean, what else do I have? I glance at my thigh, suddenly remembering I had strapped a dagger to it, before I left. Of course, it's wishful thinking. The first thing she would have done is remove it. No, the first thing she did is knock me unconscious, disarming me was step number two. I stay silent, laying on my side with my eyes closed, listening to the conversation.

"But we don't truly know what her powers *are*. We don't know what she's capable of," the other woman insists. Is that fear I hear in her voice?

"Not to mention, she'll be missed. People will come looking for her. Logan will come looking for her," this from a male. Again, I know that voice from somewhere but the pain in my head is making it hard to think straight.

Logan. My heart skips a beat at the sound of his name. Logan sure as Hell *will* come for me.

He will find me.

He *will* save me.

There isn't a doubt in my mind about that, about *him*, and I need to focus on that.

*Logan will save me.*

"Oh please," Revna scoffs. "I can handle a few Air Fey and an oversized dog. That's if they can even find her here. Plus, I'm working on the spell for the demons and a couple of other tricks up my sleeve. No one is going to be able to beat us with her blood powering my spells. Speaking of, I need more. Go get some."

I refuse to be approached laying down and in pain. I make myself sit up again, pushing through the noise of the jack hammer in my head.

"Well, hello there, sleeping beauty. How nice of you to finally join us."

"Luke," I spit out his name, as if it leaves a bad taste in my mouth. “Arabella was right about you.”

“Oh, how is my dear sister doing these days? I hear she didn’t take the loss to Luke very well.”

Aralyn comes gliding into view. Her purple eyes gleaming with mischief and evil thoughts. I knew I had heard that voice before.

I look up at both of them, standing before me, and I can’t keep the disgust off my face or out of my voice. “Why? Why are you guys doing this? How can you kill your own family and friends?”

Aralyn shrugs her dainty shoulders, “it’s a war, Amarah. There will be casualties. It can’t be helped.”

“Yes, it can! *You’re* doing this and you can stop it!”

“Why on Earth would I want to stop now when I’m so close to getting what I want?”

“You’ll never be Queen. The Fey will not follow you after all you’ve done. Not to mention the other groups. You’ll have no allies.”

“I beg to differ. You see, fear is a great motivator. They will accept me as their Queen and they *will* follow me for fear of what I will do if they don’t.”

“And what’s in it for you?” I ask Luke. “Why are you doing this?”

“Isn’t it obvious?” He smiles that arrogant smile and pulls Aralyn against him and kisses her. “I’m going to be King,” he says, as he caresses Aralyn’s face.

They look at each other with something other than evil in their eyes. Love. They love each other. It’s clear to see but I can’t think of them as a couple in love. I can’t normalize them on any level. They are demons in my eyes and I kill demons. It’s my job.

“You’re both mad, just like the Witch over there is, and I *will* stop you. Your happy ending doesn’t exist as long as I’m alive.”

“Now, now, children,” Revna pushes between them, “that’s enough of that.” She takes the knife and jar from Luke. “Apparently, if you want something done around here you have to do it yourself." She kneels in front of me again, and too quick for my eyes to see, cuts open my arm to fill her jar. She lays her hand on my arm and sends that cold power to close the wound again.

I can't help the shiver that violently shakes my body. "They *are* looking for me and Logan *will* find me," I say with as much confidence as I can. "And when I'm free," I lean closer to Revna, "I will kill you. I will kill all of you."

"Now, now, that's definitely enough of that," Revna says as she touches my head…again. I know I can't fight it. I have no control over my situation. The only thing I can control is myself.

I won't cower.

I won't back down.

I won't be weak.

I won't be a victim.

I hold my chin higher, in defiance, "Logan will find me."

I try to reach out to Logan through our connection but I can't feel anything inside of me. I settle on a silent prayer before I'm lost, once more, to the darkness.

# The Power Of Love

Not Alone by Red

I'm in and out of consciousness more times than I can count. The stabbing pain in my head is a constant thing now. The pain never leaves. I remember bits and pieces of being awake. Someone pouring water down my throat, the smell of food, undistinguishable conversations, daylight, moonlight, all just a blur of reality. Hell, maybe it's all bee a dream. I can't tell at this point.

In addition to the lightning storm between my ears, my body feels weak. I feel drained. How long have I been here? Hours? Days? Weeks? How much of my blood has she taken?

I'm lying on my side, back pressed solidly against the wall behind me, the hardwood floor I've been laying on for who knows how long, is sending pain through my shoulder and hip. I've definitely had been in this position for way too long. I register the pain but there's pain radiating all over my body, all competing for my attention, and I'm too weak, too tired, to do anything about it.

A bright white light starts shining through the cracks in the front door that sits between the kitchen and the living room. It's so bright, it's like staring into headlights from inches away, but it doesn't hurt my eyes. The light keeps growing, getting bigger and stronger, until it consumes every inch of the house and all I can see is white light.

"Amarah, you need to be strong. You're stronger than this. You need to fight." A female voice speaks to me but I can't see anyone. It's like her voice is coming from every direction and all around me.

I'm overwhelmed by the smell and feel of a hot summer day. I close my eyes and I swear I can feel the sun and its warmth on my skin, sinking into my bones, chasing the bone-deep chill of Revna from my body. I can smell the trees, the flowers, and freshly cut grass.

"Who's there?" I try to speak loudly but my voice is a soft rasp, struggling to escape my dry throat.

"Amarah, listen to me. You need to reach out to Logan through your link. The link is more powerful than either of you realize. Just concentrate on Logan. Feel him. Sense him. Be open to him and listen for him. He *will* hear you. Do you understand?"

"No, I don't understand. These shackles...I can't. I can't use my power."

"Your connection with Logan is deeper than your power, Amarah. I need you to trust me." The voice is soft and sweet, but also authoritative, but I'm not afraid. I know I need to listen to this person.

"Who are you? Show yourself."

I feel a soft hand gently touch my cheek and a face slowly comes into view above me. I recognize that face. I would know that face anywhere because I burned it into my memory. The unconditional love I feel for her is instant. A connection and love like no other. There's no mistaking who she is.

"Mom?" My heart starts to beat faster. I choke back a sob

and blink back the tears that are threatening to blur my vision. No. I need to see her face clearly.

I lift my hand, to place on top of hers, but all I feel is my own skin. Her face starts to fade and my tears are unleashed. "Please don't go. Mom! Stay with me, please! Help me," I beg.

"I love you with all my heart, Amarah. I'm *always* with you," her voice drifts further and further away, receding along with the light.

"Don't go! Please!"

"You're destined for greatness, Amarah. This is not your ending. Call out to Logan."

The light disappears completely, along with the warmth from my body, and I'm left lying in cold darkness once again. The only warmth I can feel is the lingering feeling of my mother's hand on my cheek and the warmth of my tears sliding across my face.

"Don't leave me here. Come back," I whisper through my sobs.

I hold myself as I cry, until there are no tears left. I thought I was weak and drained before, but now I feel utterly empty inside, all alone. I have nothing left to give.

No power.

No blood.

No tears.

I think of everyone, everything, I'll leave behind. How will people remember me? Who will miss me? My sisters that aren't really my sisters? The Queen, my aunt, and only living true family I have? Logan?

God, Logan. I think about the last time I saw him. I watched him leave not knowing it would be the last time I would see him. Just when I think I can't possibly cry any more tears, they pour again, at the thought of never seeing Logan again.

From the moment I saw him standing across the street, I knew I was drawn to him. The first time I saw his green eyes piercing my soul. The first taste of his lips on mine, when the world disappeared, and it was just us. The jealousy of thinking of him with anyone else. The first time he told me he loved me. His body on mine and the way he smells of the woods and comfort. The way he always made me feel safe and loved. Oh, so loved.

At least I'll die knowing I had the love that most people only dream of. "I love you, Logan Lewis," I whisper to myself, as my heart begins to break.

*Amarah?! Is that you? Can you hear me?*

I bolt up into a sitting position, my eyes scanning the house, "Logan? Is that really you?"

*Yes, I'm here, Angel. Where are you? We've been searching for you but we can't seem to find you.*

"Logan, where are you? I can't see you!" I start to panic.

*You're talking to me through our link. I'm in your head, Amarah. Now please, tell me where you are.*

*Oh,* I say in my head, *how are we doing this?*

*That's a question for another time. Angel, I need you to focus and tell me where you are.*

*Ummmm, yeah, I'm being held in Revna's house. I followed Luke here and I thought...* I shake my head, *I thought Revna would help us but she's evil, Logan. She's helping Luke. And, Aralyn is here too! They're all working together!*

*We will worry about that later, first we need to find you. Tell me how to get to you.*

*I followed Luke north hugging the mountain range for a long time. I don't know how far. There's a spot with trees and a river, it's hidden by glamour. I don't know where exactly, but her house is across the river.*

*Ok, good. Good. I followed your scent across the river but we can't find a house. We keep going in circles out here getting nowhere. She must have put a spell on the house so we can't find it.*

*We? Are you out there now?! Logan, please find me!*

*I'm going to follow our connection. I will find you, Angel. Stay with me, ok?*

*Ok, please hurry. I don't know where everyone is but no one is here right now. They could be back any minute.*

There's silence.

Five seconds…

Ten…

Twenty...

*Logan!*

*I'm here. I'm with you.*

*Watch out for the raven. Revna is the raven.*

*Ok, I'll let the others know. You feel close, Amarah, real close now. I'm going to find you.*

*Hurry, Logan. I'm weak and I don't know how much longer I can hang on to consciousness. Talking to you this way is taking a lot out of me.*

I feel the pain in my head starting to build again. I try to push the pain aside and focus on my connection to Logan, but it's hard. The pain is *fierce* and I don't have much strength left to fight it. I know I'm going to pass out when I start seeing white dots in front of me.

*Logan.*

*Amarah, stay with me. I'm close, I can* ***feel*** *it. I can feel* ***you****. Hang on, ok. Stay strong for me.* His voice is calm in my head even though I know every nerve in his body must be on fire.

*I love you. I love you…withhhh…alllllll...*

I don't get to finish telling him how much I love him before I lose the connection, and all control, over my mind.

The door slams open, causing one last rush of adrenaline to pump through my body as I try to see who comes in, but it's too dark to make anyone out. I hear voices, men talking to each other.

"Keep an eye outside for anyone coming. Search the house," Logan's voice is strong and authoritative.

I'm fighting for consciousness when a familiar face comes into view and all the fear leaves my body. I'm safe.

"She's alive," he says.

Déjà vu hits me hard. "How are youuuu..." is all I get out, before I give up all my strength, and pass out again.

My body is being carried by strong arms. My head is gently rocking against a solid chest. I know this body. I know this scent.

Logan. It's Logan and I'm home. I'm safe. The only sound is the sound of footsteps and the occasional twig snapping. I can hear others walking alongside us but I can't move my body to see who else is with us.

"Logan," my voice isn't even a whisper, but he hears it.

"Shhhh, Amarah, you're safe. We're almost home. Just relax, I've got you and I'm not going anywhere." His voice rumbles through his chest and he hold me tighter.

The window curtain has been left open and the morning sun is shining directly on my face, waking me up from my dreamless, dark, cold sleep. I throw my arm over my face so my eyes can adjust to the brightness. I recognize that I'm in the bed I've been sleeping in for the past few weeks. I'm back in the Air Fey's home that Logan and I have been using.

The pain in my head is still there, but it's a dull aching pain, instead of the intense stabbing it has been. It feels like a normal headache and not like I'm getting a lobotomy while I'm wide awake. I roll over and realize I'm in bed by myself. Logan isn't here and a quick shot of adrenaline, and fear, rushes through me as I imagine something bad might have happened to him. I sit up in bed, wide awake, listening for any sound. I sigh as I make out his voice coming from the living room.

"There's no way I could have known she'd go chasing after Luke, and Hell, I didn't even know Luke was involved," he says, with a tone of frustration.

I throw the covers back and pull my legs to hang over the edge of the bed. I stand up and immediately feel like Bambi, trying to use my legs for the first time. I get my shaky legs as steady as I can underneath me, my head throbs harder with the movement, but I ignore my ailing body and heads toward the voices.

"I'm just saying, she's special, and you're supposed to keep her safe."

I come to the doorway and stop, holding on to the doorframe, to gather more strength. Logan is pacing the living room and my heart skips a beat at the sight of him…and at the sight of who he's talking to.

"You don't think I know she's special? I know better than you just how special she is." He growls angrily and runs his hand through his hair in frustration. He looks up when he finally hears me and runs towards me.

"Amarah! You shouldn't be out of bed. You need to rest." I notice the dark circles under his beautiful green eyes. His hair is a tousled mess, and it looks like he hasn't slept in days.

"I feel like all I've done is sleep," I say, but I still feel the exhaustion pulling at my body. I fight it. I need to be awake. I need answers.

I lean on him as he helps me walk to the couch to sit down. "Can you get me a blanket, please?" I'm cold down to my bones, with the kind of cold I don't think a blanket will help against, but I have to try.

"Of course," he smiles, but his eyes catch the man sitting at the other end of the couch, and his jaw clenches as he leaves to get me a blanket.

"Hey, love," Andre sends a teasing smile my way, dimple on full display, but it doesn't quite reach his eyes. His eyes show the worry he won't vocalize. "Seems like I'm destined to always rescue you," he winks.

I can't help but smile at his attempt to make light of the situation. "Thank you, Andre. It's good to see you," I say honestly. "I wish it was under better circumstances."

"Well, no worries. I'm here now and we can make them better whenever you want," his flirting is over the top and bound to piss Logan off.

I just shake my head, "how are you here?" I finally ask the question I tried to ask back at Revna's house.

"I couldn't just sit by and do nothing when I heard the news of you going missing. I came as quickly as I could, to help find you."

"Thank you for coming," I reach my hand out to him and he takes my hand in his. My eyes travel up his muscular, tattooed arm and stop at his beautiful, deep brown eyes. "I don't deserve it, but thank you."

Logan comes back and eyes our hands but doesn't say anything. I let go of Andre to grab a hold of the blanket and pull it around me. "Do you think we could have a fire too?"

"You can have whatever you want, Angel. I'll start one right away," Logan sets about placing logs in the fireplace. "A little help?" He asks Andre.

Andre stays in his seat but sends a fireball into the fireplace causing the wood to blaze to life. Logan comes back to the couch and gently moves me enough so he can sit beside me. He puts one arm over my shoulders, and I lean into his embrace, appreciating the additional warmth of his body. I'm too tired to be concerned about hurting Andre's or Logan's feelings at this point. They can both just grow up and deal with whatever happens.

"Since Andre is here, that means I was missing for…a while. How long was I gone for?"

I hear Logan swallow hard behind me, "four days. Today

would have made five. Valmont came too," he says, as he points to the coffin against the wall. I had literally walked right by it and not seen it. Yeah, tired may not cover it. Not good.

"I feel like I was there forever. I lost track of time because I was in and out so much. Revna kept knocking me out," it's my turn to swallow hard, "and taking my blood."

"Your blood? What does she want with your blood?" Andre asks. He can flirt and tease at the drop of a hat, and most people miss the intelligence masked in all the over-the-top remarks, but he's more perceptive than anyone gives him credit for.

I can't tell him why my blood is more important than anyone else's. "She wants to use it in blood magic. She's been using Fey blood for a while now."

"So, she's responsible for the missing Fey," Logan puts it together.

"Yes. Luke has been helping her, and Aralyn is with them, too. They're together, him and Aralyn, I mean. They want to be King and Queen."

Andre scoffs, "well that's never going to happen."

"I don't know what they have planned. I wasn't awake long enough to hear their plans. All I know is whatever they're using my blood for isn't good. Whatever spell Revna is coming up with, it's going to be extremely powerful. We need to get to her before she has more time to do whatever it is she has planned. We can't let them kill more innocent people."

"Don't worry, Amarah. We aren't just sitting by idly waiting for another attack. The Queen is here and so is Princess Hallana, Prince Vadin, and Prince Emrick. They each brought a handful of their best fighters. We were waiting to see what you know before we started planning our attack, but it *is* going to happen, so don't worry."

"Why are we waiting?" I start to get up but Logan holds me

back. "Logan, let me go. I need to talk to the Queen. We don't have time to waste."

"Amarah, listen to me. You're in no shape to plan anything right now. You need to rest and you need to eat and get your strength back."

At the mention of food, my stomach growls angrily. I don't remember the last time I ate and I know I've lost some weight in the four days I was held captive. I must look exactly like I feel. Like a big pile of steaming, stinking shit.

I sigh in defeat because I know he's right. "I am starving actually. I would like to try and eat something. And shower."

"Leave it to me, love. I'll whip up something delicious for you to devour and then we can discuss that shower," he winks as he gets up from the couch and heads into the kitchen.

"If he doesn't stop flirting with you and winking at you, I'm going to snatch his eyes right out of his head," Logan says through gritted teeth.

I couldn't help but smile at the fact that Andre can still get under Logan's skin, even now. "You know he does it on purpose to rile you up, and the more you react, the more he'll do it."

"Yes, but I also know how he feels about you."

I turn so I can face him and throw my legs over his lap. "What happened to not caring about what others feel because we can't control them?"

He doesn't say anything, just sits there, fighting all his emotions. I can feel them.

Relief.

Anger.

Frustration.

Fear.

Hopelessness.

Desperation.

But above all else is love. Always love. His love for me. Nowhere in there is jealousy.

"I know what you're feeling, and I'm sorry."

"It's not your fault, Amarah," he says quickly.

"I know, but I should have been smarter than that. I should have trusted my gut and none of this would have happened."

"You're safe now, that's all that matters," he holds my face in his hands and looks at me so intensely, it takes the air right from my lungs. "When I got home and you weren't here, Vyla said you had never stopped by, I knew something was wrong. I went looking for you immediately. I found your trail but I couldn't find you and…" his voice cracks and his eyes tear up, causing mine to do the same.

I place my hand on his chest. I can feel his heart beating hard against my hand. "Were you out there in those woods the whole time? It looks like you haven't slept in days."

He nods and holds my hand in his, against his chest. "Amarah, I thought the worst. After days of searching with no luck, I thought I'd never find you. I couldn't *feel* you. I thought..."

I know he can't bring himself to say he thought I was dead. I can't bring myself to say it either. I had given up. I had welcomed death, and now, sitting her next to Logan again, I hated myself for giving up so quickly.

"I wasn't strong, Logan. I tried to be, but I wasn't," the tears fall down my cheeks as I think about being held hostage. About losing all hope.

"Oh, Angel, you're so much stronger than you know," he gently wipes the tears from my face. "What you went through was not easy, but here we are. Still here, together, and I'll be here with you and we will overcome this. I'll always find you, Amarah. I'll always come for you. The only thing that will ever keep me from you is death itself. Hell, even then I'll probably never leave your side."

I let out a strangled laugh, trying not to break down completely, and I just nod. I lost hope in everything inside of me, everything I am, but I never lost hope in Logan.

He leans in, still holding my face in his hands, and lays a gentle kiss on one cheek and then the other. Then his lips brush mine, almost hesitantly, as if he's not sure it's the right time for a kiss. I crush my lips to his and my heart feels like it explodes in my chest. In those final moments, I was saying goodbye to him, and I'm not ready to say goodbye to him.

We need more time.

I vowed to *never* give up so easily ever again. I have something, someone, to fight for. He fought harder for me than I did for myself. For us. That won't happen again.

We break the kiss, he pulls me onto his lap, and holds me tightly. "God, Amarah, I thought I had lost you. I've never prayed so much in my life."

"You almost did lose me. I had given up. I'm so ashamed and disappointed in myself for that."

"If you had given up, why did you reach out to me? How *did* you reach out to me like that?" He asks, still holding me.

"I saw my mom," I smile at the memory. "My mother, Alexandria, came to me. She told me to reach out to you through our link. She said our connection is stronger than either of us know. I just started thinking about you, from the first time I saw you and all of our time together since, you're all I thought about, and I just prayed you'd hear me, and you did."

"What does this mean?"

"I don't know," I whisper.

I shiver, still fighting the cold that seems to be gripping me, refusing to let go. Logan pulls the blanket around me and hold me tighter. I can hear the strong, steady beat of his heart against my ear. A sound I've come to recognize and find the most comfort in. I snuggle into his neck and take a deep breath, settling in his lap. We sit here, in silence, holding each other. I feel his body relax, and his breathing deepens, as he finally allows himself to sleep.

I can't imagine what he went through out there, for four days, looking for me. I had at least been unconscious for most of my time, but Logan had to live with his fears the entire time, and yet, he hadn't given up.

I feel the exhaustion on my body and mind finally pulling me under. I say a quick prayer of thanks, to God, and to my mom, and fall asleep in Logan's lap.

Food and a shower are just going to have to wait.

# A Piece Of My Heart

The Night We Met by Lord Huron

Logan and I slept through the entire day. I'm not sure how we eventually made it to the bed, but Logan never let go of me, even in his sleep. His large body is pressed solidly behind me as he hugs me into his chest. It feels like he's trying to pull me inside of him. My body has finally warmed up but the headache is still there. I don't want to get out of bed but the headache is persistent in its need for food and water.

I gently lift Logan's heavy arm and scoot out from under it. He's still in a deep sleep and I don't want to wake him. I know he needs the sleep after missing four days straight of it. I walk into the living room and immediately notice the fancy coffin I had missed earlier. It's shiny white, almost silver, just like Valmont's hair. *Boujee*, I think. We have a complete boujee Vampire in our group. I smile and shake my head, not at all surprised.

Andre is passed out on the couch. One leg hung off the side and a tattooed arm thrown across his face. I can see the rise and fall of his chest as he breathes deep in his sleep. I don't even know when

Andre arrived and I wonder how much sleep he had missed too. Everyone had come out here and sacrificed everything to find me. I'm Relieved, and thankful, but I also feel guilty.

I sigh and head into the kitchen. I immediately poured a glass of water and down some ibuprofen. Then I go to the fridge and examine what we have to eat. I don't want to cook anything, or warm anything up in the microwave, because I don't want to make noise and wake everyone up. Also, I'm too hungry to wait for anything to cook. So, I settle for making a sandwich. I hop onto the counter, sandwich in hand, and rest my head against the cabinets, closing my eyes as I scarf down the food.

"I love a girl who's not afraid to eat."

My eyes shoot open, and I gasp, which causes me to choke on the bite I'm swallowing. I launch into a coughing fit, chug some water, and finally get the food down. Andre s leaning on the counter across from me, arms and feet crossed, smirking at me with humor in his eyes.

"You ass! You could have killed me! I could have choked to death," I whisper yell, so I won't wake Logan, but try to sound as shocked as I feel.

"I was kind of hoping I was going to have to give you mouth to mouth," he smiles, dimple on full display, but it isn't humor I see on his face anymore.

He shoves off the counter and steps towards me. He pushes himself between my legs, causing them to widen more, to allow his body to fit. He places his hands on the cabinets on either side of my head and leans his body into me.

We're eye to eye and I see the hungry, heated look in his eyes, and then his gaze drops and lingers on my lips. I swallow hard and close my eyes, trying to steady my heart beat that's determined to race at that look and the closeness of Andre's body.

I've always been attracted to him, and just like he's tattooed, the time we spent together is tattooed on my heart, in my skin, and in my memories. My body remembers the memories, the feelings of healing each other, and being what we each needed in that moment. A part of me will always love and care for him, but I can never give him what he wants. What he *deserves*. I had never been *in love* with him. Not to mention, Logan is asleep in the other room, and if he walks in on this, he will no doubt kill Andre. Without hesitation. I need to be strong and stern no matter what my body is saying.

"Andre," I curse myself silently as his name comes out a breathless whisper.

I open my eyes and gasp. He removed his glamour, and stands in front of me like he had before, with his Fire Fey scales on full display. The memory of seeing him like this and touching his skin for the first time comes crashing back. My heart is pounding in my chest and I hate my body for betraying me. Betraying Logan.

"I thought I had lost you," he whispers back, just as breathless, and his hand drops to caress my cheek. "And..."

both of his hands slowly trail down my arms and stop, resting on my thighs. His eyes find mine and I'm brought back to the memory of us in the tower. Only this time, there's no fear or caution in his eyes. He knows what he wants and he knows how he affects me. He also doesn't seem to care if we get caught.

"...and I was furious with myself for letting you go so easily. For not fighting for you. For not fighting for what *I* want. And I want you, Amarah."

He licks his lips and that brings my focus to them. I remember how they felt on mine. How soft they are, and how desperately I had sought to comfort him, and myself, in that kiss. Just remembering the emotion behind it causes my hands to betray me as

I caress his arms, feeling his soft scales under my touch. I'm suddenly overwhelmed by his smoky scent.

It's his turn to close his eyes. He whispers, "Amarah," as he digs his hands into my thighs and pulls me closer to him. I gasp with the sudden aggressiveness he's showing. My heart is racing, and again, I hate my body for reacting to him.

He leans in, as if to kiss me, but I lower my head and our foreheads meet instead. I can feel his breath on my face. We're both breathing hard, hearts pounding like caged animals, trying to reach each other. It would be so easy to give in and fall into his kiss. The memory of what it had been, wanting to experience it again, pulls at something in me. I want to caress his heart, his soul, with my lips on his. I still want to soothe him and care for him, but unlike last time, I no longer need the same healing. My heart and my body are taken.

"Please, don't do this," I whisper. I don't want to see him hurt. I don't want to be the one to continue hurting him.

"Amarah, this is right. You can't lie, I know you feel it too. Your heart beats for me," he places a hand on my chest and puts my hand on his, "just like my heart beats for you."

I could feel his heart thumping in his chest, against my hand, matching the beat of my own pounding heart. Our time together had helped heal something in me and I know I healed something broken in him too. What we shared was so much more than anything physical. I know what we shared is special. I can't deny it. But it was fleeting. It wasn't meant to be anything other than what we needed in those moments. What I have with Logan is so much… *more*, and nothing, and no one, is *ever* going to come close to what we have.

Not in this lifetime or the next.

Andre moves his hand from my chest, and lifts my chin up, so I have to look at him. "Why do you fight it?" He searches my eyes for an answer. He genuinely doesn't understand that the racing heart he feels in my chest is more about betraying Logan then it is for him.

"Andre, I…"

"Amarah!?" Logan's voice sounds frantic, as he yells for me from the bedroom, and his worry for me feels like a painful slap across my face. I feel like I've betrayed him somehow. That my body still reacts to the memories I shared with Andre. Maybe I have.

I pull back from Andre. "It's ok, Logan, I'm in the kitchen," I call back, hoping I don't sound as out of breath as I feel. I push Andre in the chest, hard. "Get over there, now!" I'm not happy that he's put me in this situation but I know he's doing what he thinks is right.

Fighting for love.

And I can't stay mad at him for that.

He smiles deviously, dimple taunting me that he isn't finished, but he backs away and resumes his easy stance against the counter. Only his eyes betrayed his nonchalant demeanor. They're confident and determined. I'm struck with the same thought I had when I first met him. He's going to be a pain in my ass. Andre's glamour is back in place and he looks like, normal, teasing Andre by the time Logan walks in.

Logan looks at me, then Andre, trying to decipher what's going on, but finally makes his way over to me. He gives Andre his back as he comes and stands exactly where Andre had been a moment before. Only Logan is much bigger and completely blocks my body from Andre's view. Where I had been face-to-face with Andre, I have to look up to see Logan's eyes, and just like that, those green eyes capture me, like gravity, and I'm pulled into him.

I'm his.

Completely.

How can anyone not see that?

He comes in for a kiss and I know he's doing it on purpose.

He wants to rub Andre's face in the fact that I'm *his* to kiss. I don't like flaunting, especially when I know how Andre feels, because I've never been one to be outright cruel. Still, Logan deserves everything and more, and if he wants a kiss, he'll get a kiss, no matter the
reason.

He holds my chin in his fingers, my hands rest on his chest, the kiss is tender, but claiming. His tongue sweeps across mine, and I have to fight to keep down the moan that wants to come out, but I can't help my body melting in his hands.

"I don't like waking up without you," he admits out loud.

What I say out loud, "I needed to eat," I pick up my half-eaten sandwich that had fallen, forgotten on the counter, "and I didn't want to wake you. I know you needed the sleep."

And with our new found mental connection, I whisper into Logan's mind...

*I'm yours.*

That earns me a body melting smile and he steps to the side so he can see both of us. "It's almost dark out and Valmont will be up soon. We should get ready so we can all head over to the meeting as soon as we can."

I hadn't showered in days, and neither had Logan, for that matter. "Good point. I think we all desperately need showers."

"Let me know if you need help getting the water temperature right, love. I'd be happy to help," Andre winks. He's back to calling me, *love*, like he calls every girl he flirts with, but his eyes aren't empty and careless. He's keeping up his act for Logan's sake but I know the difference.

Logan growls a warning at Andre and the tension in the small kitchen rises.

I sigh and hop off the counter, "I'm a big girl, Andre, I know how to handle a shower." I don't look at him, or Logan, as I walk out of the kitchen.

"I'll be right there, Amarah, and I'll make sure *our* shower is nice and *steamy*," Logan says from behind me.

I don't comment, because his statement is directed at Andre, not me. I just shake my head and keep walking. Being between these two for who knows how much longer is going to be a problem. I don't need a steamy shower.

I need a cold one.

# Next Steps

About To Get Crazy by Oh The Larceny

Logan and I sit on the edge of the stage, legs hanging over the side, as we face a couple of tables that had been put out for our meeting. All of the Leaders are here, Princess Hallana and Andre from the Fire Fey, Prince Vadin from the Water Fey, Prince Emrick from the Earth Fey and now, Arabella, who has taken the position of Air Fey Leader. The one who *should have* been elected in the first place had I just listened to my gut, and of course, Queen Anaxo is sitting at the head of one of the tables. For whatever reason, Ethan and the Werewolves aren't here.

Each of the Leaders have brought a handful of their best fighters, Healers and Masters. Jon and Andre are the only non-Leaders to sit in on the meeting though. I can feel Andre's gaze on me, filled with too much I don't want to see, so I avoid his gaze altogether. That just leaves me dealing with everyone else's eyes on me. Since I had been taken as a hostage by Revna, everyone seems to be looking at me for answers. I feel the heavy weight of their eyes on me.

Waiting.

Expecting.

They're going to be sorely disappointed.

I shift my body, as if I'm trying to get comfortable, but really, I just want to lean my thigh solidly against Logan's. He immediately reacts to my need for his touch and places his hand lazily on my thigh. The smallest, simplest touch from him always soothes me. Comforts me. It's like he has, not only a key to my heart, but to my body as well. Everything about him speaks to everything about me, and now I'm ready to take on the world, with Logan by my side.

"Arabella was right," I admit. "Fey *have been* going missing because of Revna and not because they left on their own."

"As much as I would like to say, *I told you so*, I really just want to stop her before anyone else is taken."

"Why has she been taking Fey?" Valmont asks, from where he's leaning against the wall, hidden in the shadows. He's always so still and so quiet I had forgotten he was here.

"Revna works in dark, blood magic. Any blood will do, but Fey blood is more potent, more powerful. The stronger the blood, the stronger the spell."

"And do we know what kind of spells we might be up against?" Prince Vadin's sapphire eyes lock on mine from across the table.

I let out a sigh, "I'm new to The Unseen, I don't know much about Witches and their spells, but I have been thinking about one thing. Has anyone here fought demons recently?"

Head nods and murmurs of agreement spring up around the Leaders.

"And has anyone noticed marks on their heads? That they

seem stronger? Faster?"

Again, nods of agreement all around.

"Well, I think the mark is a spell made specifically from Fey blood. A spell that makes them stronger and harder to kill. This is, of course, a theory. I don't have proof but if we want more answers and suggestions, I think we should call in my sister."

"Your sister? You mean your *human* sister?" Princess Hallana crosses her arms, clearly unimpressed.

"About that..."

"Amarah's oldest sister is actually the Witch known as, Iseta Ryhn," the Queen addresses the Leaders.

Both mine and Hallana's eyebrows shoot up and we both question the Queen at the same time.

"Seriously?"

"You knew?"

"Yes, I'm serious," the Queen addresses Hallana. "And yes, I knew," she turns to address me.

Voices erupt from the tables and everyone starts talking at once. Seems this is a larger topic of discussion than I had known it would be. Why is it so shocking to everyone? The Queen holds up her hand and calls for silence.

"She's not *actually* my sister. I mean, I thought she was when I was living as a human, but she was placed into the family, same as me. To watch over me."

"By who? And why did you need protecting?" Hallana asks no one in particular. Her eyes dart between me and the Queen.

Since they *still* don't know about my birthright or what I am, I don't know how to answer that question. I start to stumble over my words, and thankfully, I'm saved by the Queen.

"That is a discussion for another time and hardly our priority right now. We need to stay focused on what we are up against and how we plan on moving forward to stop this, once and for all. Amarah, what else can you tell us?"

I sigh and run my hands down my face, "not much. I know that Luke is working with Aralyn. They want to become King and Queen together. As far as *how* they plan to do that," I lift my hands, to show them empty, with no answer.

"All I know is that we need to attack Revna before she has any more time with my blood." I glance at the Queen because she knows what it means for Revna to have *my* blood. A look of fear flashes across her face before she takes control of her features and hides it.

"I have no idea how much of my blood she actually took. My guess is...*a lot*, and whatever she has planned for it...it isn't good for us."

"There's another problem," Logan finally speaks up from his seat beside me and everyone's eyes go to him as he speaks. "Revna's house is also spelled. When we were searching for Amarah, we circled around it for days, and never saw it. We were always right there close to it but we couldn't see it. Revna has spelled it so we won't be able to find it on our own. I second the suggestion to bring Iseta in."

"Plus, she will be able to help us complete the spell that will give Valmont protection against fire. Having him next to us in this fight, with his speed, will heavily increase our odds of winning."

I see uneasy eyes dart to the Vampire, standing in the shadows, and I sense their uncertainty about having him here. Having him as an ally. The Vampires and the Fey have never worked together, so their hesitation is warranted, but this isn't the time for hesitation. Then again, I have seen another...*side* of him, that scared the shit out of me recently. The memory of his body pressed against mine, the smell of blood on his breath, sends a shiver down my body.

And as mad as I am about our last encounter, I still come to his defense.

"Valmont has done nothing but prove worthy of this alliance. He's already stepped up to the plate, to assist us, without even having the alliance complete. I know it's a foreign concept to be working with the Vampires but they've done nothing to dissuade us. If you're having a hard time trusting him, I'm asking you to trust *me*. He will not betray us."

"You're so certain in him?" Vadin asks the question I'm sure is on everyone's mind.

"Yes," I say without hesitation and as much conviction as I can put into that one simple word.

Vadin holds my gaze, as if he's trying to read my soul, but he eventually gives a slight nod and I nod back. I can feel Valmont's gaze, heavy on me, even from across the room. I meet his eyes even though I can't see them from where he stands in the shadows. He places his hand on his chest, over his heart, and gives me a small nod, similar to the way Vadin had. I know he's thanking me for backing him and taking on the responsibility of his actions.

I nod back to Valmont and then address the table once again. "Now that everything is on the table. What's the plan?"

"Well," the Queen speaks, "I think the first step is to call Iseta and get her here as quickly as possible. Once she has completed the spell for the Vampires, if she can, we will proceed to Revna's. We will use glamour to hide our forces and hopefully, Iseta will be able to get through Revna's spell, and get us to her house. The goal is to capture them all, *alive*, so we can question them about their plans and alliances. However, if it's your life or theirs, do not hesitate to take it. I will discuss a few more details with Iseta once she's here, but that's all for now. Go and prepare your people."

"More waiting. I fucking *hate* waiting," Hallana grumbles but does as the Queen asks.

The other Leaders get up without a word and head out the door. Logan and I stay put because I know we have more to discuss with the Queen. Once everyone leaves, it's just us and Valmont.

"Valmont, would you mind giving us a few minutes?" The Queen asks politely.

"Of course," he pushes off the wall effortlessly and glides out of the meeting hall to join the others outside. Although, I'm sure I like the thought of that. I shake my head, they're all adults, surely, they can behave.

The Queen sighs, finally showing her stress and exhaustion, as her shoulders slump slightly. "Tell me about what happened when you were taken, Amarah. All of it."

"I honestly don't know much more than what I told the others. I was kept unconscious most of the time, but I know her main goal was to collect my blood. She knows what I am and..." I feel a chill run through me thinking about her cold, icy stare, and her cold power running through my body, but what sends goosebumps across my skin, is remembering what she told me.

"Amarah," Ana gets up from her seat and walks over to me, pulling my hands into hers, as she stops in front of me. "It's just us here now. Tell us what happened."

"She wanted my blood, obviously, but..." her words come back to me, still chilling even in memory. *I don't know why* he *wants you.* I shiver, "she said someone else wants me. She said she was going to give me to *him*."

"You didn't tell me any of this." Logan's body goes taut with adrenaline at just the mention of another threat. "Who is *he*? Who wants you?" His voice is heated and *not* from passion.

I just shake my head. "I don't know, but... I'm scared," I whisper.

"Oh, Amarah, honey, we aren't going to let anything happen to you," Ana pulls me into a hug and I let her. I close my eyes and let her scent wash over me. Sunshine and summer. That's what she smells like. That's what my mother smelt like. I cling on to her tightly and continue with my revelations.

"I saw her, Ana, I saw my mom," my throat is tight and I feel the emotions and tears bubbling up to the surface with just the slightest mention of the memory.

Ana pulls back to look at my face, "you saw Alexandria? When? How? What did she say?"

"I don't know if I was dreaming or if it was real. I was so out of it from being in and out," I shake my head, thinking about the memory. I lift my hand to my cheek, I could feel her soft, warm touch, as if it had just happened. "She said I was destined for something great and that this wasn't my end." The tears stream down my face, "she told me she loved me and that she was always with me."

Ana pulls me into a hug again, and my quiet sobs shake my body as she holds me, letting me cry on her shoulder, as she rubs my back and whispers soothing words in my ear. When I finally stop crying, I pull out of her comforting embrace, ready to face the world again.

I square my shoulders and continued, "only *we* know what my blood is and how dangerous it is for Revna to have it. We need to stop her, now, before anything worse happens."

"I know. We will. We just have to do it right. We can't go in there blind and unprepared."

I nod in agreement. I don't want to wait, waiting is always the hardest part, but I know she's right. "She had me in shackles that were spelled too, with my blood. I couldn't access any of my power. Maybe we can use them or Iseta can do something similar so we can take her and not fear her magic."

"Yes, that's a great idea. It will be one of the details I work out with Iseta when she gets here. Why don't you give her a call? Let's not waste any more time than absolutely necessary."

I nod again and realize I don't have my cell phone on me. "My phone is back at the house," I move off the stage and Logan follows me. I'm heading towards the door but hesitate.

"Go, Amarah. There's nothing more we can do at this moment. Try and get some rest while you can. We're all going to need it."

I know she's right, yet again, but I also know there's no way I'm going to be able to rest. Not until Revna is captured and I can find out more about who wants me. And more importantly, *why* do they want me? There are too many enemies. Too many unknowns.

As if he can read my mind, and Hell, maybe he can, Logan pulls me to a stop before we reach the house. "Why didn't you tell me? What Revna said about someone wanting you?"

"Because I don't have any answers. It means nothing more to me than it does to you."

"Amarah, this means that there's more we don't know and a bigger threat to *you*. Whether we have answers or not, it is a very important piece of information."

"There's always some kind of threat when it comes to me, Logan." I throw my arms up in frustration, "It's not like we don't know that! It's old news and there's nothing we can do about it!"

"I'm not going to let anything happen to you. You know that, don't you?"

"I know. It's just…there's a lot at play, a lot of unknowns, and you can't always be there to keep me safe, Logan. It's not your responsibility, so please, don't take it on. It's an impossible task."

"Watch me," his voice is deep and determined.

I reach up and hold his face in my hands. His eyes are a dark green in the soft light from the stars and the moon. Almost another full moon I notice. I smile at the thought of how I notice the moon now, because of Logan.

"Logan, if something happens to me..."

"Don't even go there, Amarah. Don't say it."

"Please let me finish." I feel his jaw clench under my hands. He's not happy about this conversation. "If anything happens to me," I continue, "I want you to know that I was completely happy with you. That I felt a love only few people ever get the chance to feel. Our love is such a Blessing but I know it can also be a curse. I don't want our love to be a curse, Logan. I don't want it to be the end for you. I don't want it to ruin you. I need to know that if something happens to me, you will move on. I want you to be happy, Logan, always. Promise me you'll try."

"How can you stand here and ask me to be happy without you? Don't you know how impossible that is? Don't you know that you are *all* of me? Don't you know that you are the reason I'm truly able to live and not just survive? Before I found you, I was empty, Amarah. The only emotions I knew were anger and emptiness. I was a hollow weapon for the Queen and this war. That changed the instant I saw you at that club. It's like you shocked my heart back to life."

It's his turn to hold my face. I can see the overwhelming love and emotion in his eyes. They sparkle in the moonlight showing all of his emotion. His heart, right there on display in his eyes. That look takes all the air out of my chest.

"I'm the person I am today because of you, Amarah, only you. My Angel. You can't ask me to be this person without you. Who I am only exists because of you. Without you," he closes his eyes and swallows hard. "Don't ask me to promise something I can't."

I don't know what else to say. I think about my life before

him.

Meaningless.

Empty.

I can't imagine being without him and I haven't lived with the emptiness as long as he had. Can I ask him to promise something I can't promise either? I realize it's unfair and cruel to ask him for so much. And yet, I still want it. I want him to be happy even if it isn't with me.

"Fine," I manage to say. "Be a miserable old man then."

We both laugh, taking the tension and seriousness down a notch. "You know we don't age, so technically, I already *am* an old man. And I plan on being a happy old man with you as a happy old woman by my side."

I look at his face and see the seriousness in his eyes. He means it, every word, and more than that, I can feel it. I feel his conviction. The truth of his words. I remember my own conviction and my own promise. I will fight harder for this. For us. Either one of us dying is just not an option.

"Be careful what you wish for. I'm going to be a pervy, old lady, always using you for this amazing body," I tease.

"This body is yours to use whenever, and however, you want," he guides my hand down his stomach, to feel his cock stirring.

My body reacts instantly to his. Five days. It's been five days since I felt him, since I had him completely. Five days too long, and I want him. I need him.

"If I remember correctly, you did promise to love me like I've never been loved," I say, as I rub his hard cock.

"A promise I intent to keep. Right now," he picks me up and I wrap my legs around his waist, as he walks us the rest of the way to the house. Once we're inside, he shuts and locks the door behind us.

"Call Iseta first but, Amarah..."

"Yes, Logan?"

"Make it a quick call," he commands, as he pulls his shirt off, over his head, tosses it at me, and walks to the bedroom unbuttoning his pants.

"Yes, sir."

# Beautiful What-Ifs

If You Met Me First by Eric Ethridge

Standing back out on the porch, watching yet another sunrise, only this time, Logan is with me. I lean into his firm chest, hand on his strong forearms, as he hugs me from behind, wrapping his arms around my shoulders.

He grounds me.

He strengthens me.

He supports me.

How can I ever think about either of us moving on? I quickly shove those awful thoughts from last night out of my head as I spot Iseta's vehicle pulling off the road and driving across the field to our house. Déjà vu hits me yet again, as this is the exact position Logan and I were in, the last time I watched her leave.

I smile and pull away from Logan, walking down the steps as she gets out of the vehicle, and practically tackle her in a fierce hug.

"I'm so glad you're alright, sister." She squeezes me tighter before she lets me go.

"I'm fine," I give a weak smile that I know isn't quite so

convincing. “Thank you for coming so quickly. We have a lot to do and we need to move as fast as we can before Revna has too much of a head start.”

She nods, “I agree. Which is why I’m going to leave right away to investigate what we’re up against. I need to see where Revna lives, and feel what type of magic she has in place, so we can be prepared. Then we can work on the spell for your Vampire tonight.”

“What? No! You can’t just *walk up* to her house! Especially not alone!”

“She won’t know I’m there, Amarah. I’ll shield myself from her view, don’t worry. I promise this is only going to be an information gathering visit but we need to know what we are up against. We can’t just walk in blind and expect to figure it out when we get there.”

“I know but...how can you shield yourself? Won’t she sense your magic?”

She shrugs, “maybe, maybe not. It depends on how powerful she is, but I promise, I’ll be safe. She isn’t aware that I’m here and helping you. She won't be expecting it or looking for another Witch. I’m not going to get close.”

I can see there’s no arguing with her. “Fine, but you’re not going alone. I’m coming with you.”

Logan and Iseta speak at the same time.

“Absolutely not.”

“I don’t think so.”

I cross my arms and glare at both of them. “Well, you’re definitely not going *alone*!”

“I’ll go with her,” Logan offers.

“What? Why you and not me?”

“Because I can help keep her safe, just in case something happens, and Revna doesn’t want *me*.”

"He has a point, Amarah. I'll cloak both of us. She won't know we're there. I just need to get close enough to detect her magic wards, that's all. I promise you, it will be a quick, simple trip, and we'll be back before you know it."

I let out a heavy sigh and throw my arms up in defeat, "fine. I know I can't change your mind. When do you want to leave?"

"Right now," Iseta's eyes are set and determined.

I scoff, and my heart takes a little tumble, thinking about Iseta and Logan heading off towards danger. Alone. I want to be there with them, to help protect them, but I also know I'm more of a liability. I don't like it. Any of it.

"But first, I need to use the restroom. I've been on the road for five hours."

"Yea, of course. First right, through the bedroom."

Iseta heads inside, leaving Logan and I standing here, ready to erupt into an argument. Well, I am anyways. Maybe she did need the bathroom, or maybe she knew we needed a moment to ourselves, to discuss what had just been planned out of the blue.

"I don't like it. I don't want you to go." I sound like a pouting child and don't even care.

"Amarah, it'll be fine, I promise. Besides, now we can keep in touch all the time through our link. I'll keep you posted the entire time," he smiles.

*You know, having our own private conversation whenever we want is going to be a lot of fun.* His voice echoes in my mind and he wiggles his eyebrows at me.

I laugh and think back, *are you seriously thinking about being a **perv** in my mind when other people are around?*

*You've gotta admit, it would be kind of exciting.* His smile is devious and tugs at my stomach, and lower, sending my heart racing.

*You're absolutely terrible! I can't believe you're even thinking about **that** right now, with everything going on.*

*Angel, the only thing that will stop me from wanting to touch you,* he caresses my cheek, *to kiss you,* he leans down to put his lips on mine. He kisses me as he continues speaking in my mind, *to feel every inch of your naked body against mine, to be deep inside of that tight, wet treasure of yours,* the thought of it makes me moan into his mouth, *is if I'm dead in the ground, Amarah. **Nothing else** will keep me from wanting you. Not Witches, not demons, not a war.*

And just like that, the rest of the world becomes insignificant. The world narrows down to only us. Only his lips on mine. His hands on my body. And it isn't enough. I want to ignore all of our responsibilities. I want to undress him, and let him take me right here, on the steps of this rickety porch. I feel him growing between our bodies and he finally breaks the kiss. I hate him for it. For leaving me throbbing with need. For starting something we can't finish.

I fall back on my heels and let out a frustrated groan.

"I know," he chuckles.

"I can't believe you're just going to leave me here...*like this*," I say angrily.

The front door closes and helps to break our sexually charged connection. Iseta comes to stand next to us. She seems to feel the tension, although, I don't think she realises it's *sexual* tension.

"You two ok?"

Logan assures her that we are, while I just grumble unintelligibly, and glare at him.

"Alright then, shall we?"

Logan nods. I don't want him to leave thinking I'm mad at him because I'm not. Not really.

I grab his hand, "please be safe and hurry back."

"We will," he leans down to kiss me, quickly, nothing embarrassing in front of Iseta, but as he pulls back from the kiss, his voice whispers in my mind again. *I can smell your desire. I know how wet you are for me.* He gives me his cocky half-smile, that promises all the pleasure in the world is to come, as he turns to walk away. *I promise, I'm coming back as quickly as I can, so I can devour you with my mouth, and make you beg for me to push my cock inside of you.*

Even though I know his words are in my mind, I can't help but blush at the thought of Iseta being right here, as we have this naughty, private conversation. Her eyebrows raise up, but she doesn't comment, as she turns to follow Logan.

*I expect mind-blowing orgasm with that cocky mouth of yours. You better come back and claim me,* I whisper back. *I love you, Logan Lewis.*

*I love you too, my Angel. We'll be back soon.*

I walk over to the porch steps and sit down with a heavy sigh. Less than a week ago, I was on this same porch, same time of the day, watching Logan leave. This time, I know the danger that's out there, and they're heading straight for it. I can't stop myself from worrying. From thinking that the absolute worse can happen. I sit here, alone on the porch, and watch their backs grow smaller and smaller, until they disappear from view. And still, I sit here. My eyes never waver from the *exact* spot I saw them last.

The front door opens and then closes behind me. I finally pull my eyes away from that spot to glance at Andre as he settles on the step next to me. I had honestly forgotten he was inside.

"You ok?" He asks softly.

"I will be once all of this is over."

"It will never *all* be over, Amarah. There will always be war, people to fight. Only in a perfect world would there ever be peace. You've gotta learn to dance in the rain or else you'll just drown."

I sigh because I know he's right. Life has never been, and never will be, easy. "How have you been, Andre? How is Hallana treating you?"

He shrugs, "as to be expected, I guess. She tries to avoid me as much as possible, but when I do see her, I see the disappointment in her eyes."

"It wasn't your fault, truly, she knows that too." I reach out and touch his arm, trying to comfort him, "it will just take time."

He looks down at my hand on his arm. "I think about you, Amarah. Every second of every day and night. You consume my thoughts when I'm awake and my dreams when I sleep." He places his hand on mine, "your touch healed me." He looks up and meets my eyes, "your eyes saw me," he reaches up and cups my face in his hand, then gently runs his thumb over my lips, "your kiss saved me, and yet, I'm completely lost."

His eyes move to where his thumb still sits at the edge of my lips, "I hunger for another taste, another touch, another look," he drops his hand and meets my eyes again, "my heart aches for you and it is the most..." he closes his eyes and his jaw clenches, "...*torturous*...ache."

He takes in a big breath and lets it out slowly. He looks at me again and it's hard to meet the look in his eyes. I can clearly see that he loves me and I can't accept that look. I want to look away because I know my eyes don't reflect what's in his, but I hold his gaze, I don't turn away from him but he deserves so much more.

"You saved me from a hollow, cold existence, and I will forever be grateful. You set me free. I'm free to *feel* again but nothing, and no one, can even come close to what I feel with you, Amarah. Trust me, I've tried. I've tried to erase you. To replace you. I've tried but it's pointless. All I want is you."

His words should move me. They should stir my heart, but as I sit here, looking into his beautiful, vulnerable, and honest eyes, my heart is a mile away with someone else. I can still feel the wetness between my legs. My desire for someone else. But it does hurt my heart, to sit here next to Andre, knowing what he feels and unable to do anything about it. What can I say? What can I do? I'm utterly useless in this situation and that breaks my heart for Andre. I never wanted this to happen. I never wanted to hurt him.

"I want to kiss you again, Amarah."

"Andre..."

"I know, I know. You're fiercely *loyal*." That earns me a small smile but it fades quickly. "That's just another thing to add to the long list of things I love about you. But..."

He gets up from his seat to stand in front of me. He leans his body into me causing me to lean back. I feel the hard angles of the steps pressing into my back and I have nowhere else to go. He places both of his hands onto the step above my head, like he had done in the kitchen. His body is inches away from mine.

He looks at me again and there's a burning fire in his eyes. A fierce determination I've never seen before. "...you have no idea how hard I have to fight myself not to *take* it. To take what I want and damn the consequences. Because if I can just kiss you one more time, if I can feel your lips on mine, your body against mine, I know it will ease this pain."

I swallow hard, my heart finally beginning to race at his words, but not in a desire kind of way. In an, *oh shit what is he going to do*, kind of way. I can feel my chest rising and falling harder with my heavy breathing. I know he notices it too and I wonder if he thinks it's out of desire.

He leans his head in closer to mine and I slightly turn my head, trying to avoid a kiss but also not trying to be outright hurtful. He rests his cheek on mine, sighing at the touch, and his next words are a whisper in my ear.

"You want to know the only thing that keeps me from taking you?"

When I don't move or answer right away, he lifts his head up, his lips grazing my cheek ever so softly, his eyes searching mine, desperate for an answer.

"What," I finally manage to breathe out.

"The fact that I know you would hate me and that would kill me," he hangs his head and takes a seat on the step below me. I let out a shaky breath I hadn't realized I had been holding back. My heart is pounding in my chest and I bet he can hear it too. I wonder if he knows how much he just scared me? Not scared for my life, but terrified he would try to kiss me, and make me reject him.

He's staring off into the distance. "Do you remember the first time we met? When we were escorting you to the Fire Fey for the first time?"

"I remember," I say softly, getting control of my breathing and my voice.

"You asked what Logan and I had talked about when we hung back. Did he ever tell you?"

I shake my head and realize he doesn't see my response. "No."

"I asked about you. If you and him were...an *item*. He said no but he threatened to remove my hands from my body if I ever touched you," he chuckles at the memory. "I've always been drawn to you, Amarah. I've always known you're special." He looks at me and smiles sadly.

"I told him that you had the right to decide who you wanted to be with. I told him that if you chose me, and he did something to hurt me or ruin us, that you would hate him. And vice versa. He knew I was right and I think that's the only reason we've both behaved as well as we have. We don't want to risk your hate, and therefore, lose you completely." He sighs, "I know it might not make sense but I believe that as long as you don't hate me, there's a chance."

The silence grows between us. I think about everything he just said. I do care for him. I cherished our time together, and if there wasn't anything between me and Logan, I had no doubt that I could eventually fall in love with Andre. It would be a different kind of love, not an all-consuming love like I have with Logan, but it would be love.

Then again, love is never the same. You get it once, completely different with each person. All these thoughts are beautiful what-ifs, but I know if he did do what he wanted against my wishes or consent, I *would* hate him. He's right. There would be no chance for beautiful what-ifs if he crossed that line.

"You haven't said much, Amarah. You can be honest with me. No lies between us, remember?"

I smile, "I remember, Andre. I remember everything, and I want you to know that I cherish the time we had together. It will always warm my heart. *You* will always warm my heart. And you're right. If you were to do anything without my consent, I would hate you for it. I understand that you control your desire. I see the effort it takes you to lock it away with the idea that forever is a long time, we live a long time, and things change. I can't make any promises to you, Andre, but I do know that one never knows what the future holds."

And that's the best I can give him.

He just nods, still staring off into the distance. My heart hurts at the thought that he's holding on to a very *small* what-if. Just like I want Logan to be happy, if the time ever comes that he has to live without me, I want Andre to be happy too.

"Andre, I need to say something, and I don't want you to take this the wrong way."

He hangs his head again and I can't help but reach out and take his face in my hands. I pick up his head and beckon him to look at me. He rolls his eyes up to meet mine, reluctantly, but he holds my gaze.

"I want you to know, and to *see*, how much I truly care about you. It breaks my heart to see you struggling and to know that I'm the cause of your pain." I feel my eyes watering and close them, trying to gain control. I still held his face in my hands. When I open my eyes again, Andre's stare has softened.

"I hated seeing you broken and empty, the way you were before, but I hate seeing you hurting even more. I need you to try and move on from me. I need you to be happy. Whatever that looks like for you, I need you to try. Keep a place for me in your heart but don't let me *consume* it. I don't deserve that and neither do you. So, you want me not to hate you? Then I need you to *promise me* that you will try to move on and be happy. Because if this continues," I shake my head, "if I have to continue seeing you in pain, I will hate *myself.*"

Now it's my turn to search his eyes for an answer. "Promise me you'll try," I whisper.

He nods his head and gives me a weak smile, "I promise."

I don't know if he truly means it or if he's just telling what I want to hear. I don't want to think about it. I just want to take his promise and wrap it around my heart to stop the hurting. I want him to take his promise and keep it. To find something or someone to make him happy. Someone who can love him the way he so desperately deserves.

He gets up from where he's sitting and heads back inside without another word. I hear the door shut behind him and I'm left alone once again. I close my eyes and say a silent prayer that he'll find peace. Then I open my eyes and focus on the horizon where I had last seen Logan and Iseta.

*Come back to me, Logan.*

# Time For Change

Regulate by Warren G

The sun is high in the sky, my butt is numb from sitting for so long, so I've started pacing in front of the steps when I feel it. The link that tethers me to Logan. I snap my head up in the direction I had seen them last and can barely make out two small dots across the field.

*Logan.*

*I'm here, Angel.*

I have the urge to run and I don't think twice. I take off like a bat out of Hell, hurling my body down that link.

When I can see Logan's features, I'm rewarded with a body-melting smile. My heart soars and I feel like I can fly. In that moment, I swear that I do. I see him plant his feet, as I never slow down, and fly into his arms. My body crashes into his with such force that he has to take a step back to absorb the impact.

His laughter rumbles through his chest and into mine as I cling to him with legs and arms wrapped around his body. My head is buried in his neck and he smells *so good*. I want to rub my skin all over him. I desperately want his scent on me. I don't want to let him go. He would happily carry me the rest of the way back if I wanted him too, but we aren't alone, and I need to be considerate of Iseta. I reluctantly let go and slide my body back down to the ground.

"Have you been out here waiting this whole time?" Logan asks, still filled with genuine laughter.

I shrug, "what else was I going to do? So… how did it go? What did you guys find out?"

Logan grabs my hand and kisses it, before settling his large hand in mine, as we walk back to the house. He may as well have been holding my heart instead of my hand.

"Well, she definitely has some strong wards up, which we knew about. Luckily, I can work a spell that will allow everyone to see *through* her magic."

"That's good news. How will that work?"

"Oh, the tedious details don't matter, but I will need to see everyone who plans on going on this mission. I also need to work on the dragon scales. I have a lot to do and prepare for us to be ready," she sighs. "It's going to take a lot out of me and I'm not sure how much help I'll be when it actually comes to the fight."

"You're doing more than your fair share helping us against magic. Trust me, it's more than enough. Besides, I'd rather you not be involved in the actual fighting, if at all possible. One less person to worry about."

"I'm stronger in a fight than you might realize. I'll be there, Amarah. You need me in case she decides to use more magic, which she will. I'll be ok."

I just nod because I know she's right. "So, you guys didn't see anything else? Anything that could help us understand what they're planning?"

I suddenly feel...*vicious.* I feel the need to sink my teeth into flesh and feel warm blood gush down my throat. The feeling is so overwhelming, so real, I stop walking and have to close my eyes against the feelings I'm having. It's like a different kind of *desire*. It warms my body and sends a satisfying shiver down my back.

It's intoxicating.

It's powerful.

It's terrifying.

"Amarah? What's wrong?" Iseta stops alongside me.

I hear her concern but I can't answer. I can't form any other thoughts much less words. I'm lost in the need to chase.

To hunt.

To *kill.*

I let out a small growl that I've never heard come out of my body before. It's jarring and makes me gasp. I look up at Logan just as his eyes are changing back to their gentle green from Wolf amber.

"She's feeling my Wolf."

"Jeeessuuuuussssss!" I say breathlessly. "I have *never* felt it like that before."

"I'm so sorry, Amarah. It's a full moon tonight and when you asked us what else we discovered..." he sighs and runs his hand through his hair, "I'm sorry. I'm holding him back again."

"What did you discover to make your Wolf so...*provoked*?"

He clenches his teeth and snarls, obviously still affected, and fighting for his control. "Demons. The place felt like it had been overrun with demons."

"Shit. That's not good. When they attacked the Fire Fey, there had to be close to a hundred. If they did that once, they can do it again. They're definitely prepping for a battle."

We all just stand here, in our own thoughts. Thinking about what the Hell else they have planned and what the Hell are we going to do to stop them. At least that's what *I'm* thinking.

"Come on," Iseta breaks the tense reverie. "We need to get back and tell the others what we know and get prepared."

Logan heads off to the meeting hall to discuss what they've found with the other Leaders. I don't know where Andre is but he isn't in the house, and Valmont is still snuggly tucked away in his coffin. He'll be...waking? Rising? I don't know what to call it, in a couple of hours when the sun sets to make way for the night.

Iseta is setting up everything she needs for her Witchcraft in our living room. I sit on the chair across from where she sits on the couch. She has all kinds of candles, crystals, what looks like dirt or sand, a small curved blade, bowls, and jars of all colors and sizes, all spread out over the coffee table.

"Thank you, again, sister, for coming. I don't know what we would have done if we couldn't get through Revna's magic."

"Of course, I would come. It wasn't even a question. Yes, she's *very* powerful. I could sense all the dark, blood magic she's been using," she shivers. "That woman has abandoned anything to do with the light."

I swallow, remembering her cold touch and how I knew, looking in her eyes, she is pure evil. "Her power is...*cold.* Every time she touched me, or used power on me, it left me freezing, and aching in my bones." It's my turn to shiver. I almost feel the cold seeping back into my body again just the thinking about it.

"Yes, I felt it too. Cold and dark." She's silent for a moment and then stops what she's doing and looks at me. "How much of your blood did she take?"

"I'm not sure honestly, but I know it had to be a lot. I was there for four days."

Iseta nods, "that scares me. The things she can do with it. The power of what your blood is…" she shakes her head, "we are going to have a Hell of a fight on our hands."

"Do you have any idea what she might have planned?"

"Not really, no, but whatever she does, whatever magic she uses, it will be amplified by your blood."

"Is there anything we can do to fight against it? Can you use my blood to make *us* stronger?"

"I really don't know. It's hard to try and counter something you don't know is coming. I'm going to need a bit of your blood for this spell though. I'm going to make an ointment that will help everyone see through her magic. Your blood will make the effect stronger since she used your blood in her magic to begin with. I also had to take something that belonged to her." She holds up a knife and I immediately recognize it.

"That's the blade she used to cut me."

"I know. I sensed your blood on it, that's why I took it."

I narrow my eyes at her, "sister...how did you get it?"

"I went inside and took it," she says plainly.

"Are you crazy? You said it was simply going to be an *investigating* trip! You went *inside* her house? You could have been caught! What were you thinking?"

"I knew she wasn't home, plus, Logan kept a lookout. It took me two seconds. I was in and out in a jiffy. Besides, I needed something that belonged to her for the spell to work. In order for us to see through her magic, we needed a piece of her. Something we could take her...*essence* from. If that makes sense at all."

"I swear. All of this stress is going to be the death of me."

"You've never had an easy life, Amarah, why would this one be any different?" She sighs, "I hope you know that I tried to make your childhood the best that I could. I couldn't interfere too much, but I did try to give you good memories. I did and do love you, Amarah."

"I know," I smile at her.

"Besides, you can handle it. God only gives battles to his strongest Children. Now, come here so I can take some of that precious blood."

I walk over to the table grumbling but complying. I give her the same arm Revna had cut again and again. She picks up the knife Revna used and sliced a line across my forearm. I wince at the stinging pain but it's over quickly.

"Have you learned how to heal yourself?" Iseta asks as she continues going about her task.

I sigh, "no, unfortunately. That trick has kind of fallen through the cracks amongst *everything else* I have to learn."

"It really is simple. I'm surprised no one has at least walked you through it yet. All you have to do is access the power inside of you. Focus on your injury and tell your power what you need it to do. Our power is like our auras, our essence. It *is* us. It wants to protect us and heal us. It's very intuitive."

"The Queen told me that once. That my power showed me what I wanted to know even though I hadn't even realized it myself consciously."

Iseta nods her head in agreement, "exactly. So, just let it be. Just let it do what it is meant to do. Stop fighting against it. Send your power to your injury and command it to stitch the skin back together. It's a very small, shallow cut, and will be easy. Go on."

I look at the cut and it is small. It's about an inch long and not very deep. Just enough to open the skin and receive the blood running underneath it. I feel my power inside of me, pull it out, and sent it down my arm. I concentrate on the cut and I imagine the skin being pulled back together.

My eyes widen in astonishment as the cut starts to close right before my eyes. "Holyyyyy shhhh....." I look at Iseta and lifte my arm for her to see. "It worked! I did it!" I laugh joyfully.

I'm rewarded with a big smile from Iseta, "told you. The worse the injury, the harder it is to heal it. It will take a lot more concentration and force of will, but it can be done. I'm proud of you, sister."

I know she isn't *really* my sister, not by blood anyway, but I've always looked up to her and always will. Her telling me that she's proud of me, warms me up from my head to my toes, chasing away any lingering coldness in my blood. I sit back on my heels, and continue to watch her work in awe, content silence.

When she was finally done working her spell, we alert the Queen, and let everyone know they have to come see her. I sit on the couch and watch as one by one they step up to Iseta. She holds a small bowl in her hand, filled with what looks like a white cream, inside of it. She dips a finger into the bowl, getting a small amount of the cream to rub over each eyelid, of everyone who will be going with us to fight.

"It's a cream to help you see the truth. To reveal what's underneath the magic," she explains to everyone.

I had gone first, so everyone could see that it was *harmless*, Logan followed, and then the Queen. Let's just say not everyone trusts easily. The Fey are not used to working with anyone other than the Werewolves. The Witches and Vampires have always kept to themselves. It's hard for some to believe that they suddenly want to help us. I understand their suspicion, but just because something has always been a certain way, doesn't make it right, and doesn't mean it has to *stay* that way.

Things are changing. Aralyn has turned on her own people, a first in Fey history, I graciously reminded them, while trying not to roll my eyes. So then, why not have other firsts? Just because Valmont is a Vampire and Iseta is a Witch, doesn't mean they have ill intent against the Fey. I know it. Logan knows it. The Queen knows it. But still, some need convincing. Sigh.

So, either willingly or reluctantly, all of the Fey who will be part of our mission, are finally prepared with the truth cream, or, whatever you wanna call it. Of course, we won't know if it works until we're there, but I know it will. I trust Iseta. And if it doesn't? Well, we're still going to do our best to stop them. In the end, there's no other choice unless we want to be ruled by a couple of psychopaths with a demonic, evil Witch on retainer. No, not an option. So, we come together. We trust the people we wouldn't normally think to trust. Create new alliances and do the dirty work.

Regulators! You know what to do.

## Trial By Fire

Play With Fire by Sam Tinnesz, Yacht Money

When the last person leaves the house, it's just Logan, Iseta and myself, sitting in the living room. The sun is setting and we're all on edge. Anxious to get moving. Nervous that they'll attack us before we we're prepared.

Iseta is bent over the coffee table, still working, restlessly. She sighs heavily, "well, everything for the dragon scales is set. All I need is fresh blood from you, Amarah, a hair from Valmont, and the scales."

I nod, "Valmont has the scales with him. He should be...ummmm, *waking up*, soon."

Just as I say it, the coffin door swings open and captures all of our attention. Valmont sits up, then steps out smoothly and elegantly. I mean, as elegantly as one can climb out of a coffin. I notice that the inside of the coffin is the same turquoise color of his eyes and looks plush and soft. Hell, it looks...*inviting.* I shake my head, boujee Vampire indeed.

He's wearing black jeans, black boots, and black button up

shirt. His silver-white hair gleams against the black. I've never seen him in anything less than a three-piece, tailored, expensive ass suit. This is a shocking surprise. One I didn't think he could pull of quite so well. It's casual, but still oddly elegant. I don't think he'd ever be caught dead, pun intended, in a t-shirt. I'd whistle if it wouldn't cause an unnecessary scene, or, if I could whistle.

He's fussing with his cufflinks and smoothing out his shirt. God forbid he let anyone see him sporting a wrinkle! We're all watching him, but he doesn't seem fazed in the slightest. He smoothes his shirt down his chest one mor time then finally looks at us.

"Speak of the devil," I say with a smirk.

"Good evening, ladies," he inclines his head and gives us a charming smile. "Logan, pleasure to see you, mate" he nods.

Before I can say anything else, he's striding over to Iseta. He offers his hand and she takes it.

He brings it to his lips, gently kissing the back of her hand, "you must be Amarah Rey's lovely sister, Iseta."

She nods, "yes," but I notice she never looks directly at him.

"Well, it is my absolute *pleasure* to meet you. I must say, I'm very...*excited,* to see what you can do. We've been waiting a long time for this moment. Haven't we, Amarah Rey."

"You know how difficult this spell is based on what Mae and every other Witch has told us. Don't get your hopes up, Valmont. I told you, there's no guarantee that this is going to work."

He looks at me then, and I'm grateful I can meet his eyes, but I also don't like what I see in them.

Eagerness.

Anticipation.

Hope.

A fierce need for this to work.

He's lived how many centuries fearing fire? And now to have that security so close. Just within reach. I'm worried what he'll do if it doesn't work.

As if he read my mind, "it *will* work, Amarah Rey," he says with such conviction that I can't help but believe him.

Iseta gathers all the dragon scales that we have and places them in an extra-large mixing bowl we found in the kitchen. She takes Valmont's hair, my blood, and begins working at the coffee table with all of her ingredients. I have no clue what she's using, or what words she's muttering, but I feel the heaviness of magic fill the air. I hadn't felt anything when she created the truth cream, so I know this is potent magic. Powerful magic.

That power hangs thick in the air, and I can feel it pressing against my skin, trying to climb down my throat to suffocate me. It's very similar to what I felt when we visited Mae but this is even *stronger.* I have to pull my power out and create a buffer between myself and the magic that threatens to consume me. I glance at Logan and Valmont. Other than their tightly clenched jaws, I can't tell if they're struggling. Maybe they aren't.

A sudden burst of fire roars up from the table and brings my attention back to where Iseta is still working and chanting. The fire burns bright red, then turns to orange, yellow, blue, and finally pure white. Then, as quickly as it had roared to life, it's gone. Iseta hangs her head and slumps tiredly against the couch. I can see her chest rising and falling with the effort this spell has taken. This has all been hard on her and it worries me that maybe I asked for too much.

I'm about to get up and go to her when she raises her head. She looks pale and exhausted. It looks like it takes all her effort just to stay sitting upright and speak.

Her voice comes out a mere whisper, "pour this over the scales," she motions to the bowl in front of her.

I walk over to the table and peer inside the bowl. It's filled with a clear liquid that looks like water, only slightly thicker. I tentatively touch the bowl, expecting it to be hot from the fire, but it's cool. Almost cold. I lift it up and pour the liquid over the scales until there's nothing left to pour.

Iseta points to a large wooden spoon, "stir them and make sure they are each coated well."

I didn't question her, just quietly follow her instructions. When I'm certain that all of the scales have been thoroughly coated with the liquid, I set the spoon back down on the table.

"Now, they need fire to bind them together. Amarah, use your fire. The fire will die on its own once the magic has all been absorbed into the scales."

I glance up at Valmont. His eyes are trained on the bowl, face completely blank of any emotion, and I'm pretty sure he's done that creepy thing he does.

Stopped breathing.

I nod, again, not questioning what she needs me to do. I call on my power and create a fireball in my palm. I send it into the bowl, and the scales catch easily, like a flame to gasoline. As the fire slowly dies down to reveal the scales, I notice that they all glow beautiful, iridescent shades of reds and gold. They looked like fire opals. I keep staring at them, expecting the glow to eventually fade, but it doesn't. They remain glimmering.

Enchanted.

"They're beautiful," I whisper in awe.

"It is done," Iseta says quietly. I can hear the tiredness in her voice but she's sitting a little straighter.

Valmont glides over and looks into the bowl with me. "How do we know if it worked?"

"How else? We test it. Trial by fire," I suggest.

I see the fear dance across his eyes before it's gone in an instant. "Well, we can't test it on you, Valmont, obviously. If it doesn't work, you'll die."

"You can test it on me," Logan offers and walks over to where we're standing. He reaches into the bowl and grabs one of the scales. It looks tiny in his large hand. Just a small, inch by inch, unassuming square. "As long as I'm holding it, or it's on me, it will work, right?"

"That's the idea," Iseta says, not very convincingly.

"Alright," Logan takes a step away from Valmont. "Whenever you're ready, Amarah. Give me your best shot."

I laugh, "I'll hardly give you my best shot. I'm just going to aim some fire at your hand. Are you ready?"

He nods. I look into his sparkling green eyes and there's not a single trace of fear. He's faced much worse than a simple burn. It makes me feel better as I pull another fireball into my palm.

"If this doesn't work, at least we can heal you," I say, as I throw the fireball at his hand.

He never blinks.

Never flinches.

And the fire never touches him.

It looks like the fire hits an invisible wall and is sucked in, evaporating into thin air. I can't help the immense feeling of accomplishment, and relief, that washes over me. A huge smile splits my face as I look over to Valmont.

"Valmont! It works!" I exclaim.

He has a look of pure awe and shock on his face as he stares at where the fire has disappeared. He finally looks at me, and takes the few steps between us, to stand in front of me. A little taller than Logan, I really have to crane my neck to look up into his face, but I'm glad I do. His eyes hold a lot of emotions, but what I see mostly is the same thing I felt, *relief*. A burden has been lifted off his shoulders.

He cups my face in his hands, I'm still smiling like an idiot as I look into his handsome face. His eyes glow, but not from him trying to use his power on me, he knows it doesn't work on me. No, his eyes glow with reverence and elation.

"Amarah Rey, I have *never* been more grateful to meet someone in my entire life. It was the best decision I've ever made to seek you out and propose this alliance. You have given me what I never thought possible. I'm at a loss of words to explain how grateful I am. I will owe you a debt for the rest of my life. I don't know how I will ever repay you but I will live the rest of my life trying."

The smell of his skin is intoxicating. Sea, bergamot, peppermint, and the faint metallic smell of blood. I can also smell something else. Something new.

Desire.

I can smell his *desire*.

It suddenly hits me that I'm feeling Logan's Wolf again, and all the sensations, all the anxiety of it, sends my heart pounding in my chest.

Iseta clears her throat, "technically, *I* did this for you but hey, potato-potahto."

"Yes, thank you, Iseta." Valmont acknowledges her with words, but he never takes his hands from my face, or his eyes from mine. I'm amazed at his glowing turquoise eyes and don't want to look away. His eyes reflect the same urge rising inside of me.

Hungry.

I hear a growl and finally look over to see amber eyes in Logan's handsome face. He also has the massive claws I've seen before, protruding from his hands. His voice comes out a low, warning growl, that seems to hit me right between the legs, "I need you to take your hands off her."

"Ok, that's my que," Iseta says and slowly stands up. "I'm gonna go." I see her walk toward the front door and I don't blame her. I wouldn't wanna hang around for this fight either.

Once she's safely outside, I focus on the two men in front of me. It isn't jealousy but outright *possession* I feel through our link. I'm his, and his *alone,* to touch. I know his Wolf instincts are taking over, pushing his normal, *logical*, human feelings, aside. Still, it makes me wonder if this is truly how he feels. It sends a different kind of thrill through my body and I shudder.

He's fierce.

He's dangerous.

And a part of me is drawn to that danger.

"Take. Your. Dead. Hands. Off. Her. Now," Logan says, barely in control now.

"Of course, mate." Again, he says the words but never takes his eyes off of me. He slowly lowers his hands and steps back. He put his hands up and out in front of his body, to show that he's not a threat.

Logan bounds for me and a hard breath is forced out of my body, as his shoulder slams into my stomach. I'm over his shoulder, being carried away, before I even register he moved. He walks into the bedroom, slams the door shut, and throws me down on the bed. He's on top of me before I can react to anything, barely able to catch my breath. When I meet his eyes, they're his beautiful, but normal, peridot eyes staring back at me.

"I'm barely in control, Amarah. The moon is rising and I need to go." He closes his eyes and I can see, and feel, how much the fight is taking a toll on him.

I feel his Wolf as if he's inside of me too. My body burns with the need to be free.

To run under the moonlight.

To hunt.

To feed.

But there's another need now.

The need to mate.

The need to claim what belongs to me. I pull his head down and rub my face all along his cheek and neck, trying to rub his scent all over me. His arms are straining with tension, as he holds himself above me, my nails clawing at his skin. I know my scratches draw blood because I smell it as it starts trickling down his arms. He lets out a growl and I scream in a mix of pain and pleasure as he bites my neck, right where it meets the shoulder, at the same time that he pushes his massive erection between my legs. He isn't gentle and I know he's letting me know…

*HE. IS. ALPHA.*

I let out a whimper of submission and need. I need him. I need his body on mine, skin to skin. I need him inside of me. I need him to claim me. Claim my body. In this moment, I need him to completely dominate me. He removes his teeth from my skin and I know, without a doubt, there's teeth marks in my skin. I smell the fresh blood as it trickles down the back of my shoulder. He lets out another growl but this one isn't aggressive. It's letting me know that he'll always take care of me. I wince as his tongue licks up the blood and then something like a purr escapes my throat.

He pulls his head back and his amber eyes are looking back at me. "You're mine," he growls again, and in an instant, he's gone. The bedroom door slams against the wall and the front door is left wide open in his departure.

I lay here, panting. Pissed that he left me in this state of need, yet again, but knowing that I didn't stand a chance against his Wolf. Once he gives up control to the Wolf completely, he would kill me. Not because he means to, but because I'm not a Werewolf. I can't survive a *Wolf's* love and I sure as Hell don't want to even try. My body chills at the thought. I know I should be scared of Logan. In that moment, when he fought so hard for control. I should have been scared. But I wasn't.

My hand touches where he bit me, at the same time, I hear his beautiful howl in the distance. And even though I know it's insane and not logical, *at all,* my body shudders with desire.

# Out Played

### A Storm Is Coming

A short while later, our small group is gathered in the field outside, geared up and ready to attack. There's a lot of tension and anxiety pulsing through the air but no fear. We're all armed to the teeth with weapons. It's quite the sight to behold, and I pinch myself, as I stand off to the side taking it all in. Seriously, how did this become my life?

Even the Queen has a sword strapped to her back, daggers on her thighs, and her sunflower hair pulled back in a tight braid. I've never seen her look so...*deadly.* I've always seen her inner strength, her command for respect as Queen, but this is different. I see the warrior. The Queen who refuses to hide behind her people. The Queen that chooses to fight right alongside them. A true Leader. Not a dictator. My heart swells with love and pride. She's my Queen. She's my *blood* and I respect her even more for fighting alongside us. It's clear she's earned the title and responsibility of being our Queen.

Valmont pulls away from the crowd and stands next to me. I raise my eyebrows, amused at the large sword peaking over his shoulder. I see that a dragon scale has been placed on a chain and hangs around his neck. It sparkles under the moonlight, faintly glowing, like a red ember of protection.

"Go ahead, say what's on your mind, Amarah Rey. You always do."

"I didn't expect to see you carrying a sword. Do you even know how to use it, Mr. Boujee?" I tease.

A smile plays on his lips, "I'm an expert at… *many things*, Amarah Rey." He says as his eyes slowly slide down my body and then back up again. "Some of which I would eagerly show you."

A small amount of heat creeps into my cheeks but I just shake my head. He looks utterly relaxed and at ease yet… *devious.* Still, he's always easy to be around...well, when he isn't in a *mood.*

I ignore the flirting like I always do. "Thank you for being here, Valmont. The others might be a bit nervous about you being here but I feel better with you by my side."

"There's nowhere else I'd rather be," he says seriously.

His eyes still show his awe and desire as he looks at me, the smile still playing on his lips. For being terrified of it, he sure likes to play with fire where I'm concerned. The thought of Logan's warning sends a shiver down my back and I feel the bristling of fur, instead of skin, on my body. Then I hear the low growl from behind me.

*I'm here.* Logan's voice comes through, loud and clear, in my mind.

I turn around and am momentarily stunned and speechless. This is the second time I've seen him in his Wolf form but the first time I hadn't been in my right mind. I had only glimpsed him before passing out. Now, standing before me, he's *huge*. Just like he is in real life, he takes up all the space ad air around me. There would *never* be any chance of mistaking him for a normal, everyday, wolf.

His amber eyes are eye level with mine and are fully aware and intelligent. Not the look of pure animal, but not human either. A strange mix of the two together. I've seen these same eyes on Logan's face before but they're even more impressive now. His fur is almost lost in the darkness of the night, but the moon reveals that it's the same rich, dark brown that I see on Logan every day. I want to run my hands over it and through it. I want to wrap my arms around his massive neck and get lost in the feel and scent of his fur.

Of his Wolf.

Of him.

I can feel his concern radiating through our link. He's worried about how I'll react to seeing him like this. He's worried that I won't accept him. *All* of him. It isn't as strong of a connection now that he's in his Wolf form, it's still between us, but it's dampened. The Wolf is more in control now, his thoughts, and his needs. Animal instincts, not human, although Logan is still in there. I know it and feel it. Again, such a strange mix of the two.

He doesn't say a word or move a muscle, as he stands in front of me, letting me take it all in. Maybe he's treating me like prey, he doesn't want to scare me and send me running, screaming in the opposite direction. But if that's the case, he couldn't be more wrong. I'm connected to him. I've felt his Wolf before, and I feel like his Wolf is also, somehow, a part of me. And I know Logan is still conscious in his mind. I know he won't hurt me. Besides, his Wolf chose me too.

*You're beautiful,* I whisper into his mind as I take a slow step towards him.

He lets out a huff and I know it's relief at my words. His amber eyes track my movement with deadly accuracy. I take another step towards him, and then another. He still doesn't move. Doesn't even twitch a single muscle, and still remains silent in my mind.

I stop when I'm only inches away. I'm vaguely aware that we have an audience but I don't care. This is about us. This is about Logan. I need him to know that I accept him. All of him. I need him to know that I trust him completely.

*Logan, I know you're in there. I know you won't hurt me. I'm not scared of you and I never will be.*

*You should be, Amarah. When I first shift, he is in control. Until he…I… until I get what I want, until I satisfy my animal instincts, the human side of me is not in control. I can hurt you accidentally in the initial turn. I* ***need*** *you to know that.*

I shake my head, refusing to believe, and let him believe, that he'll hurt me, *you'll never hurt me, Logan.*

*Amarah*, he lets out a low warning growl, needing me to understand. I hear the gasps and murmurs of concern from the crowd behind me. They have no idea what's happening or that the growl isn't meant like they think.

I reach out and gently touch the side of his muzzle. His eyes close as he lets out another huff. I take another step closer as I run my hand along his massive neck.

*Your fur is so soft...and thick, and beautiful.*

I do what I've been wanting to do since I first turned around and saw him like this. I slide my arms around his neck, press my body into his, and bury my head in the fur on his neck. The warmth coming off of him in Wolf form is intensified. I feel that warmth seep into me as I cling to him. I rub my face in the fur, and inhale deeply, taking in his scent. Yes, he smells like animal fur, but underneath it all, I still smell Logan. I still smell the woods and freshly rained on Earth.

*You smell like home.* I'm rewarded with another low growl of approval. *I know you're worried about me seeing you like this but I love you, Logan. All of you. You'll never be a Lone Wolf again. I'm yours and you're mine, completely.*

*Thank you,* he finally whispers back. *I don't have any other words. Thank you. I love you.*

I take a step back so I can look into his eyes again. His eyes roam over the bite mark, already bruising, on my neck. *I should say I'm sorry for that bite. I should hate myself for doing that to you, Amarah, but I'm not and I don't. I marked you because you're mine and I want* ***everyone*** *to know it.* His eyes move to Valmont, who'ss standing a few steps behind me. He let out a vicious growl, *especially that handsy Vampire.*

I laugh out loud. I know I must look utterly insane to everyone watching us. They don't know that Logan and I can talk to each other this way and I don't care if they all think I've lost my mind.

*I know you're not jealous. I feel your Wolf's instinct to protect me. To claim me, but just in case, let me remind you.*

I lay a kiss on his muzzle and am rewarded with a low purr. He drops his head, and I let out a small hiss of pain, as his big, rough tongue sweeps across the bite at my neck. A tongue designed to clean meat off bone and yet, he's delicate when he licks me.

*When this is over, we are going to finish what we started.*

The thought of what that statement entails sends the butterflies loose in my stomach and I shiver.

"Ahem," I hear the Queen clear her throat getting our attention. "Amarah, is everything ok? Are you both ready?"

Even in Wolf form, Logan consumes my senses. To Hell with anyone or anything else. I sigh as I remember, we are in fact, not alone. We have an audience and we're all gathered here for a reason. Being so consumed by Logan is dangerous and we obviously need to work on it more. At least I do. Turning around to face everyone, I can't stop the heat from creeping up my cheeks.

"Yeah, we're ready. Logan will run ahead and let me know if there's a threat." At least my voice is steady and firm and not breathy and heated with desire.

"How is he going to do that, exactly?" The Queen asks, confused.

"Ummmm, well, Logan and I can still communicate when he's in this form. In here," I tap the side of my head.

The Queen narrows her eyes at us, "we'll discuss this more at a later and more appropriate time." She shakes her head, "well, if we're all ready..."

"I'll join Logan," Iseta steps forward.

"There's no possible way you can keep up with him. I'd rather you stay with the safety of the group," I argue.

"Are you sure about that, little sister?" Iseta gives me a wicked grin I've never seen on her before. "My magic will cloak you all until we get close. Revna's magic will see through mine once we cross her threshold, but you will also be able to see through hers. We will at least be playing on even ground. Logan and I will see you there."

Without another word, Logan takes off, his giant strides and speed eating up the distance across the field. Iseta sets out on a swift, but human, speed behind him. There's absolutely no way she can keep up with him. And then, in a flash of white wings, she's a snow owl, taking to the skies. The rest of the group heads out at a brisk pace behind them.

I have to take a minute to pick my jaw up off the ground, "well, fuck me. What the Hell else do I not know about my sister?"

Valmont is by my side again and lets out a whistle, "bloody Hell, she's a Shapechanger. Powerful indeed."

"A what?"

Valmont chuckles, "so much you still don't know, Amarah Rey. It is endearing."

I scowl at him, "now is not the time to make fun of me, Valmont. I may just accidentally slice you up in the confusion of the fight we're about to be thrown into."

He outright laughs at me this time, but doesn't say anything else, as we make our way as quietly as possible towards pure evil. Everyone is focused and on high alert as we reach the mountain and travel quietly alongside of it. The group stops just before crossing into the glamour.

"What's the report?" The Queen asks.

*Logan? Anything?*

*Nothing. It's quiet. Too quiet.*

"He says there's nothing."

The Queen nods, "let's go but everyone be ready. Stay alert to magic and anything that looks or feels out of the ordinary. Trust your instincts."

*Iseta and I have eyes on the house. Someone is inside. We'll wait here for you and let you know if anything happens. And, Amarah?*

*Yes?*

*Be safe. Be alert. The presence of demons here is overwhelming. It's the most I've ever felt.*

*I'll let the others know. You be careful too, Logan. Please keep my sister safe.*

A low growl in my mind is all I get as a response.

"Be careful. Logan says this place has an overwhelming presence of demons."

I get head nods and murmurs of understanding as the group slowly starts to disappear through the glamour. I notice Andre stops and waits for me.

He gives me his teasing half-smile, "you've come a long way from the first time we asked you to walk through glamour."

I think about the first time I saw Nicholas disappear through the glamour. I was in such awe and wonder at something so *magical*. I feel so much older now with everything I've experienced since then.

"It feels like a lifetime ago. So much has happened since then. I don't even feel like the same person anymore."

"That makes two of us," he says quietly.

We stand here, the only two left standing on this side of the glamour, and I look at him. *Really* look at him. He has changed. His eyes used to only hold humor, as part of the mask he wore. He still hides behind his humor and teasing but his eyes are different. His eyes are alive with feelings and emotions. I wonder if anyone else notices? I wonder if anyone else sees the real Andre? The one behind the shameless flirting. The one worth loving and getting to know. A small part of me wishes it could be me but it can't.

"We should catch up to the group," I say quietly.

He nods, "I know you don't need protection but I'm going to be right by your side tonight and we'll kick ass just like we did the first time." His eyes fill with humor, the mask he can so easily slip on. He gives me a dazzling smile, dimple on full display, "let's go kill some demons, shall we, love?" He winks and disappears through the glamour.

"Pain in my ass like always," I can't help but laugh to myself as I follow him through the glamour.

Once I'm on the other side, I feel it. The magic is heavy in the air, almost suffocating, even though we're outside. I have to pull on my power to shield myself from it. I can hear the quiet footsteps of our group, and the gentle trickle of water from the river nearby, but that's it. Logan is right, it's quiet. Too quiet.

Our group crosses the river quickly and easily. We're heading directly towards Revna's house. I see people breaking away from the group and sliding into the trees on each side. Some of the Air Fey are taking to the sky. They'll circle around the house, so we can surround them, and hopefully prevent any type of escape this time. The goal is to capture Revna, Luke and Aralyn, to not only stop them, but interrogate them and find out who else is working with them. We have to eliminate the threat. All of it.

The small house becomes visible and I wonder if everyone else can see it too.

"Can you see it?" I ask Andre who's next to me.

"Yes," he whispers.

Iseta's truth cream works. We can all see through her magic. My heart starts to race. The adrenaline finally kicking in and gearing up for a fight. The magic in the air is tingling my skin and I feel the familiar *cold* of Revna's magic seeping into my skin. The memory of that piercing cold pain, shooting through my head every time she put me to sleep, making me shudder.

"Amarah, are you alright?" Andre whispers.

"I'm fine. Just remembering the last time I was here."

"That's not going to happen again." His voice is a command. Certain.

I look at him, the seriousness of his face and the words he speaks, calms me. I'm thankful I'm not here alone this time. "I know."

As we encroach on the house, the front door opens, flooding light from within onto the worn path. We all stop, hands on weapons, ready to deflect and use the elements we have at our fingertips. Everyone stills. There isn't a rustle, a twig snapping, Hell, there isn't even a breath to be heard. Utter, chilling silence, as we wait for what's about to happen.

Revna saunters out of her house, clad in a similar black leather outfit I had seen her in before, her curves on full display. The stark whiteness of her skin stands out and almost glows against all the black she wears and the darkness of the night. She stops at the edge of the light, but with the only source of light coming from behind her, I can barely make out her face. It's hidden in shadows. Only her long, black hair is visible as it glints in the light.

She crosses her arms and examines her nails on one hand, looking bored. "Well, you guys sure took your sweet time." Her icy voice sends a shiver down my spine.

Queen Anaxo steps forward a few paces, head held high, her voice strong and commanding. "Revna, this madness needs to stop, *now*. We've never had any conflicts with the Witches. Why are you siding with a traitor and hunting our people?"

"No, of course not. The perfect Fey Queen and her perfect people. You could never be bothered with anyone else but yourselves. You and your...*kind*, are utterly arrogant. For that reason alone, I'm happy to work with Aralyn, but that's not the reason I've played my part." She shrugs her shoulders and flips her hair behind her, "no, I could care less about who is Queen and who isn't. You, Aralyn, a fucking monkey, I don't care. My role has only ever been about... *her*."

I can't see her eyes but I feel her cold stare on me instantly.

As if her gaze *touches* me. It's almost like I can feel her cold hands caressing my skin. I break out in goosebumps, and my breath hitches, just from her icy, evil stare. Andre's hand grips my elbow and steadies me. I swallow hard, trying to gain my composure, and meet her stare through the darkness.

I feel Logan walk up on the other side of me, so close his fur tickles my skin. His fur is raised, head low, and he's baring those massive teeth in the most vicious growl I've ever heard. Then I hear the beat of wings as Iseta flies down from the tree she had been perched in. She lands on her feet in front of me, back in human form.

She's also wearing all black leather, like the rest of us, but the night and the darkness don't consume her like it does Revna. As she strides up to where the Queen is standing, she almost illuminates the space around her with light. Of course, there's no light coming off of her but it's like the darkness just can't touch her. It moves with her and around her in complete balance with the light.

Iseta looks at the Queen, the Queen gives her a small nod, and Iseta takes a few steps in front of her. She quietly asked for permission to deal with Revna and not be disrespectful of the Queen's position. Iseta and Revna still stand a good distance apart but there's no denying the stark differences between them.

"Well, well, if it isn't the *righteous*, Iseta Ryhn." Revna drags out her name, *Izzzettttaaaaaa Raaaiiiiinnnnnn*, with sarcasm and disgust. "So, you're the reason my magic cloak didn't work. What do I owe this unpleasant surprise to?" She crosses her arms and pushes out her hip.

"If you want my sister, you're going to have to go through me." I've never heard my sister sound so... *powerful*. It's like her voice also holds a physical essence to it. It booms through the air and rustles the trees, but where Revna's voice is chilling and cold, Iseta's is a mixture of both. Cold and hot. Light and dark. Completely balanced.

Revna throws her head back and laughs. It's so cold it feels like ice flurries hitting my skin. "Oh, that's priceless. Really it is. I mean, it makes sense that *you* would be chosen to protect her. After all, what she *is* and who your Deity is, it makes sense, but *my* Deity wants her and has promised me immortality if I give her to him. So, you see, there really aren't any other options. I *will* give her to *him* and I *will* get my immortality."

My mind is racing. I'm thinking back to the time when Iseta first told me about Revna and the symbol. Her Deity is Lucifer. The Devil.

*The Devil wants me.*

My blood turns cold at the revelation. My knees buckle and I fall to the ground, my heart pounding with fear in my chest.

Hands are on me instantly and I hear voices around me, asking me what's wrong, if I'm ok, did she use magic on me. I hear Logan's concerned voice through my mind but I pay attention to none of it. I kneel here, on the cold ground, gasping for air. Lucifer wants me. Me! What does he want from me? What will he do to me? The thought of it alone is the most terrifying thing I've ever felt.

I feel a cold nuzzle on my neck as Logan tries to get my attention. *Amarah, I need you to breath. Listen to my voice. Come back to me. Touch me, breath me in. Come back home.*

I reach out and grab onto his thick fur. Even in Wolf form, he's still Logan. He's always my strength. He always grounds me and makes me feel safe. He's lying on the ground in front of me and I finally find those amber eyes with mine. For just an instant, I see concerned peridot eyes looking back at me through the Wolf. Just an instant and then they're gone. But I know Logan had pushed through

His Wolf to get to me.

*Logan,* I whisper.

*I'm here. I will always be here. You're safe. No one is taking you anywhere.* His growl reverberates through my hand into my chest. I remember to breathe. I focus on the world around me, slowly coming back to the present, and all that's happening. Istea and Revna are still talking.

"Oh Revna, you're so naive. To think that your Deity will keep his word. To think that he *cares* about *you*. You're just another one of his slaves."

Revna scoffs, "my Deity is known to me. He talks to me, he shows himself to me, he gives me power. What does your Deity do for you? Has he ever even spoken directly to you?"

"He doesn't have to. That's not how Faith works."

"Classic," she chuckles. "Well, are we going to stand her bantering all night or are you going to do something?"

"Where are Aralyn and Luke?" The Queen asks. "They're the ones we want."

"You're all so damn predictable and so easily distracted. You're all wanna be heroes, racing to save the day. It's quite amusing that you thought you were being proactive and smart coming here. That we would be sitting ducks just waiting for you."

"Where are they?" The Queen's voice is so low and cold, I almost don't recognize it.

Revna's smile is malicious and sends another cold blast through my body. "I hope you didn't bring all your fighters with you. It would be such a shame to leave so many weak and innocent Fey back at the town...*unprotected.*"

The Queen's face falls and I see the fear in her eyes. My heart sinks in my chest, as I think of Tori and Vic, and all the other children.

A piercing howl erupts next to me and I scream into his mind, *Logan, go!*

He's off faster than any Wolf should be able to run, meanwhile, my world slows down. Everything feels disconnected, far away. I hear the Queen yelling orders to get back to the town, as Air Fey take to the skies, no longer trying to remain hidden. Everyone else is running back the way we came, with speed that only comes from pure terror. Revna's cold laughter pierces through all the chaos and madness, making me shiver and sink further into myself. I watch her transform into a raven and take flight. Iseta is right behind her in her owl form.

Valmont is shaking me by the shoulders, "Amarah Rey!" Then he slaps me across the face.

The sound echoes in my head, the world around me slams back, full force. I look around, and it's just Valmont and I, alone in the darkness.

"Amarah Rey, we have to go help them in the fight, *now*. Are you ok? Can you fight?"

I nod my head, the anger setting in, pushing the fear aside. "One of your powers is speed, right?"

"Yes."

"Get me there as fast as you can."

He doesn't hesitate, he scoops me up in his arms, and the world blurs by. I prayed that we won't be too late.

# Angel Blood And Vampire Bites

Pray For Me by The Weeknd, Kendrick Lamar

I hear the screams and yells before I smell the smoke. My panic and fear are trying to claw its way back up but I will them deep, deep down and hold them there. It's a struggle but no amount of panic or fear will help us now. Valmont comes to a stop before we reach the town.

"What are you doing? We need to get in there now! Let's go!"

"Think, Amarah Rey. We can't just go recklessly, headfirst into a trap. We need to see what's happening so we know how and where to infiltrate." His gaze is locked onto the town, sweeping across the madness that awaits us.

I have to force my head to turn so I can see what's happening even though I don't want to see it. It's what I expected to see but still rips my heart from my chest. There are demons everywhere. The Air Fey who had been with us, are starting to land amongst the demons, but Valmont and I had passed the others who are constrained to the ground.

"*You* strategize," I yell. "Just get me the Hell in there!"

His eyes scan the chaos and seem to settle on something. I don't know what he sees that I don't, but the world blurs again and the next thing I know, we're in the middle of the town. Valmont found a safe space for us to settle and prepare to fight. He releases his hold on me, setting me down on my own two feet, and I quickly take in my surrounding. The fighting is all around us and I don't know where to focus. Where to attack first. The decision is made for me as Valmont and I quickly attract attention from the demons around us.

I hear the metal of Valmont's sword being pulled from its sheath and I follow suit, unsheathing my own. I send my power into the sword and the crosses etched down the blade flared to life. Valmont raises his eyebrows but only swing his sword in response.

An evil smile splits his face. "Are you ready to see the full force of our alliance?"

Before I can say anything, he winks and vanishes. One second, he's standing in front of me, and the next...he's gone. The air starts to fill up with black mist as demons are sliced through by an almost invisible sword. He moves so fast, all I can see is a glint of silver as his sword catches the light, and small glimpses of his silver-white hair as he moves like the wind.

All the demons near us are suddenly gone. I stand in the middle of black mist dissipating all around me. I'm frozen in shock and disbelief at what I just witnessed. If I hadn't been terrified of Valmont before, I *definitely* am after that display. He swings his sword to rest over his shoulder, dripping with something that looks like blood, but is black and much, much thicker.

Out of the corner of my eye, I glimpse a ball of fire hurtling my way. I pull my power as a shield around my body but the fireball never touches me. Valmont is suddenly by my side, the fire stops inches away from his body, and it looks like it gets sucked into a vacuum and vanishes. The dragon scale around his neck glows red, pulsing with magic, and seems to absorb the fire that's been thrown at us.

"Bloody fucking Hell, it works! I still wasn't sure it would," he lets out a relieved laugh that quickly turns into joy.

"You weren't sure it was going to work and you still stepped in front of me?"

"Always," he says softly, and then that evil smile replaces any and all emotion. He changes so quickly I'm not sure I even saw the emotion at all. "Well, are you going to fight or just stand there with your jaw on the ground?" He chucks my chin and disappears again.

I watch Valmont run into the demon masses and continue fighting, at a more normal speed, but still faster than I'll ever be. Screams and shouts filled the air. The others have finally arrived and everyone is fighting. The demons are everywhere. *Everywhere!*

I suddenly remember, Vyla and the kids are unprotected, and my body finally snaps into motion. I'm running towards their house, demons coming at me, but I'm finally focused now. Finally in fight mode. I maneuver around them, slicing them with my sword as I go. Some burst into flames from a killing blow, others just fall to the ground or stumble, but get back up. I don't have time to stop and finish them off. I need to make sure Vyla and the kids are ok.

I get to their house and barge through the front door. "Vyla!" I call out as I start to search every room. "Tori! Vic! It's Amarah! Are you here?" I stop and listen for any sound, any small voice answering me.

Nothing.

They aren't here and the house doesn't look like it's been touched. A small amount of relief washes through me. They aren't here. They got away in time. I have to believe it.

I run back out of the house, across the field, and towards the center of the fight. It's madness. Chaos. My eyes skim across the fighting. I spot the Queen swinging her sword, her bright yellow braid flowing behind her. Logan is fighting next to her. All teeth and claws as he rips apart demons. I hear screeching high above my head and look up to see a tangle of black and white wings as Revna and Iseta fight each other in the skies.

That's when I notice the moon. Not just a full moon but blood red, looking down on all of the destruction and death, as if it's right in the middle of it all getting coated in blood. I finally register the powerful magic that hangs in the air. I shiver and continue running towards the fight.

I fight and slice my way through the demons. My world narrowes down to a five-foot circle around me. Where one demon bursts into flames, another takes its place. There are just too many! We're overrun by even more than when they attacked the Fire Fey. Way more and they're stronger. Faster. Harder to kill. The adrenaline is racing through my veins giving me the energy and strength, I need to continue wielding my sword, but I'm starting to feel the weight of it in my hands. I'm weak from my time at Revna's and still haven't fully recovered. My arms are starting to shake with the effort it takes to continue holding it.

Slicing.

Cutting.

Jabbing.

Spinning.

Ducking.

Rolling.

Trying desperately to maintain my circle.

"Amarah!" I recognize the voice before I see Andre fighting his way to me. "Thank God you're ok."

We go back-to back instinctively. I take a second to sheath my sword and pull out my daggers, giving my arms a bit of a reprieve now that I can fight back the demons one or two at a time, with Andre's help.

"Well, this brings back memories," I grunt between blows.

"Not exactly the memories I want to remember with you."

"Are you seriously making jokes right now?" I can barely talk through my concentration to *not* get killed.

"Always, love." I hear the smirk in his voice.

"At least you're consistent," I manage to say through my heavy breathing. My arms and shoulders are burning from wielding the sword, and now daggers, for so long. My forearms and fingers are cramping from gripping so tightly. It takes everything I have, not to drop my arms, even for a second of relief.

Then, all of a sudden, the demons surrounding us stop attacking and take a few steps back. I keep my arms up, refusing to drop my guard for *any* reason. I let my eyes drift past my own circle and see that *all* of the demons have done the same thing. The sudden quietness is deafening. It's as if everyone is holding their breath, waiting for the next strike.

"What's going on?"

"I don't know," Andre says beside me.

"Well, well, well, isn't this fun?"

I spin around towards the voice I recognize. Aralyn and Luke are walking side by side, weaving through the demons, as they approach us. They stop far enough away that we can't reach them, but close enough to taunt us.

"Aralyn, Luke, what are you guys doing?" Queen Anaxo demands. She's out of breath and splattered with thick, black blood. She looks fierce and radiant with power. "This is madness! Look at all the people you're hurting! You're killing your own family!"

"This can all stop now. No more killing or destruction. No one else needs to get hurt. All you have to do is give your crown to me.

Make me your new Queen and this all stops." She smiles sweetly, as if she's speaking at a fancy party, and not standing in the middle of a battlefield.

"You've really gone insane," this comes from Arabella, who pushes her way towards her sister. She looks the same as we all do. Exhausted, splattered in blood, and one of her wings is ripped and bleeding. Still, she stands defiantly in front of her sister "How can you do all of this," she motions around us with her hands still clutching daggers, "to your own people, and expect us to *follow you*? To *bow* to you?"

"I do, yes, because you don't have a choice, dear sister. It's either this or you will all die and I will get the crown anyway."

"You're no sister of mine. I don't recognize the person standing in front of me. I will stop you, even if that means I have to carry the burden of taking your life." Arabella holds her head high, no hesitation in her voice or eyes as she says those words.

Aralyn just laughs her sweet laugh, "well, you can try, and you can die." She raises her voice so everyone can hear her, "you had your chance to surrender, I won't offer it again. Now, you'll all die." She turns to leave and, as if her words are the trigger of the spell, the demons began attacking again. I lose sight of Aralyn and Luke with the surge of demons. Arabella rushes towards her, but she has to fight to get through the line of demons, and she isn't going to make it in time.

*Logan, you have to go after them! Don't let them escape.*

*I have to protect the Queen.*

*The Queen can handle herself and no one will let anything happen to her. Please go! You're the only one who can track them. She can't get away again.*

A growl in my mind is his only answer, as I see him launch in the air, over the demons, and then disappear.

"Amarah, a little help here," Andre struggles to maintain our circle.

"Hold them off, Andre. I'm going to finish this."

I sheath my daggers and kneel down, placing my hands on the Earth. I've used my power like a white hot, Divine bomb against the demons and the Witches, I know I can do it again. End this fight before anyone else gets hurt or worse, dies. I breathe deeply, in through my nose, and blow it out slow and steady through my mouth. I steady my body and my mind, focusing on the power the Earth offers up. I can *feel* it alive and eager under my hands. I start to pull that power into me, adding to my own power, building it up to unleash it.

"Oh, Amarah, I don't think so." That cold voice seems to fly around me on an invisible wind sending chills down my spine.

It breaks my concentration and I look up to see Revna landing on her feet from her raven form. Iseta is nowhere in sight and panic grips my chest. Where is she? Revna is making her way towards me, the demons part before her, leaving a straight shot to me.

"You don't think I'll allow you to do what you did last time, do you?" Her hands came together, some kind of magical lightning flashing between them. "Oh yes, I heard all about how your power destroyed the demons in the Fire Fey attack. I won't allow that to happen here."

Iseta finally lands and stumbles behind Revna. She looks exhausted and I can see blood dripping down her right arm and on her chest.

"Revna! No!" She pulls a dagger from the belt at her waist but she's going to be too late.

I have a split second to make sure my power shield is still in place before that ball of lightning is thrown my way. I brace for the impact, but once again, it never comes. My body is being covered by another body, and all I can see is silver-white hair, as Valmont's body jerks, and he screams. He screams out in such pain I feel it like a blade through my chest. His body collapses to the ground and I can't seem to process what happened. It all happened too fast.

"Valmont!" I scream his name and roll him onto his back. I move the hair from his face, his eyes stare up into the sky, lost to pain. His skin is covered in small cuts that are all bleeding profusely. I watch as his body tries to heal them but they just reopen again and again.

"Valmont, look at me. Can you hear me?"

I cradle his head in my lap and watch as his eyes slowly focus on mine. The world and the fighting around me disappear. A demon could come and kill me right now and I wouldn't fight it. My attention and immediate concern are fully taken by the agony in Valmont's eyes.

He tries to reach his hand up to my face but it falls onto his chest. "Amarah Rey," is all he manages to say before he starts coughing up blood.

"No, no, Valmont. You're stronger than this. Heal yourself, please!" My voice cracks and tears start to blur my vision.

"Can't," blood bubbles out of his mouth.

"Damn it, Valmont! Why are you always saving me?!" The tears unleash, pouring down my cheeks.

"Amarah," Iseta kneels on the other side of Valmont, her hands, and the dagger in her hand, now covered in blood. "You need to give him your blood. Your blood was fueling Revna's magic tonight, it's the only way to save him."

I grab a dagger from my thigh and cut a line on my arm without hesitation. I don't even feel the sting of the blade as it slices my arm open. I *will* save him. I refuse to let him die protecting me. Not if I can save him.

Iseta places a hand on my arm before I can move it over his mouth. "He'll know," she whispers. "He'll know what you are." Her words and eyes hold caution, letting me decide if my secret is worth his life.

Valmont coughs up more blood followed by swallowing and choking sounds. His skin is covered in blood from the cuts that keep closing and opening. He's losing too much blood too quickly. He's literally bleeding out. What happens if a Vampire loses all of the blood that sustains them? I don't want to find out.

I look back up to Iseta's eyes, "I don't care. Not if it means I can save him." Whatever she sees on my face, she releases my arm.

"Valmont, take my blood." I put my arm against his mouth but he hesitates. I know he doesn't want to cross this line with me. Not under these circumstances. Not when he knows I don't want to be fed on.

"Valmont, damn it! Do it! You're going to die." The tears are running freely from my eyes, "please." I press my arm harder against his lips. I see the sorrow and regret in his eyes even as he lay here, in pain, dying.

Then, his lips part, and his hands came up to hold my arm to his mouth. He keeps eye contact with me as lips closed around my cut and he sucks. His eyes widen in shock and I know the instant he knows what I am. I swallow down my worry as his mouth works at taking my blood. It's like a vacuum is attached to my arm. The sheer strength at which he holds on and sucks is unnerving.

I feel his fangs brush against my skin and gently press down, causing my heartbeat to quicken. His chest is rising and falling as if he's struggling to control himself too. I know he doesn't have to bite me to get my blood, he's already healing, but I see the desire in his eyes. As I hold his gaze, his eyes start to glow, and I know he was going to do it.

"Valmont," I try to put authority into my voice but it's nothing more than a faint whisper.

His fangs sank into my arm with a sudden pinch of pain and then a warm wash of pleasure bursts over and through my body, taking all the air from my lungs. I moan loudly, as I collapse on top of his chest, my body instantly languid with pleasure. My whole body is tingling, I'm throbbing and wet, as if I've been worked up to an orgasm, just from the bite. I feel it the second he removes his fangs and my body instantly cools. The throbbing between my legs eases and I'm suddenly extremely embarrassed but also too relaxed to care.

Valmont raises up from the ground into a sitting position and helps me up too. Iseta is no longer kneeling beside us and I'm grateful for that. Maybe she knew what was going to happen and didn't want to stick around for the show?

Valmont's eyes are shining but not with his normal glow of power. They're just...*radiant.* "Amarah Rey, you're..."

"Yes," I interrupt him with a whisper.

"It all makes so much sense now." He looks down at my arm, the cut is barely bleeding, and now it's I have two neat puncture marks next to it. "Amarah Rey, I'm sorry. I couldn't," he closes his eyes for a minute and then opens them again to meet mine. "I couldn't stop myself. It took all of my control to pull back. To not keep drinking you. I could have killed you." He lets me see the honesty and sincerity in his eyes. He lets me see his fear. He's truly scared he wouldn't be able to stop.

"You can't tell anyone," my voice is still a whisper. I'm still reeling over how his bite felt. I'm just as scared as he is because I didn't want him to stop either. I would have been content letting him drink me to death as I orgasmed. I've always been terrified of Valmont as a predator but now, now... I'm terrified of how he made *me* feel. How his bite made me feel. It's like a drug and I know I'm going to be chasing that feeling until I have it again.

He picks up my arm and brings it to his mouth. My heart is racing again, I'm practically panting, desperate for him to bite me again, and terrified that he will. He continues to keep eye contact with me as he slowly licks my cut and his puncture marks. He groans as tastes my blood again and that sound, coming out of his throat, makes me throb again. He closes his eyes and shudders. When he opens them again, he looks at me, "your secret is safe with me." His eyes slide to my arm and mine follow. He brushes his thumb over perfect skin. There's no sign of the cut or his bite.

"How?"

"Our saliva heals our bites and small wounds."

We make eye contact again as he continues rubbing his thumb back and forth, back and forth, gently across my skin. We just sit here, staring at each other. Drunk off each other. My eyes move to his lips. I imagine what they would feel like trailing along my skin, followed by the piercing of his fangs into my skin again. I don't know how long we sit like this but everything else has completely disappeared except for the Vampire sitting next to me and the promise of another bite.

Dangerous.

This is so dangerous.

"Amarah!" Andre's voice cuts through my reverie. "Now would be a good time to use your power!"

Again, the world seems to come crashing back around me. There are still way too many demons. It's like they're never ending. I shake my head and reluctantly push away from Valmont. I place my hands on the ground, like I've done before, and start pulling the power inside of me.

This time, no one stops me.

When I'm so full of power and feel like I'm about to explode, I open my eyes. I know if I could see them, I would see nothing but a white flame where my eyes should be. The same flame is already in my fists and flicking up my arms. I think one word as I push all of that power out as hard as I can.

*Die.*

# 35

## Empty, Cold, Nothingness

Give Me A Sign by Breaking Benjamin

The world around me explodes. I feel my power burst out of me with the force of a bomb. I feel the exact moment when it hits the demons but something isn't right. It doesn't feel like it did the first time. It doesn't...*destroy*. No, my power doesn't even *touch* the demons. My power slams into a magic shield and then is thrust back at me with equal force. My power comes slamming back into me, throwing me to the ground, knocking the air out of my chest.

Valmont and Iseta are by my side in an instant. My eyes are wide, I'm chocking on my non-existing breath, and I know I look as panicked as I feel. I'm gasping for air, trying desperately to fill my lungs. They feel like they're on fire and every breath is a searing pain.

"Breathe, just breath, Amarah."

"Is she going to be alright?" Valmont asks worriedly.

"What... the fuck... happened?" I ask through my gasping breaths.

"The demons are all protected by magic. Magic fuelled by

*your* blood."

I'm finally pulling full breaths into my lungs, "the marks... on their foreheads."

"Yes."

"How can we win then? There's nothing else I can do and there's no way we can fight them all."

"Your power broke their shield, Amarah. I no longer feel the magic. We should be able to fight them easier now."

Iseta looks around us. I sit up and followed her gaze. The demons and the Fey are all sprawled on the ground, affected by either my initial eruption, or the blowback. I'm thankful to see them getting up. The Fey that is, not the demons.

The only ones who don't seem to be affected by the ripple of magic are Iseta and Valmont. I see Jon getting to his feet, a little unsteady, but he swings his sword at the closest demon and it dissipates into black fog. The demons seem to be more stunned from the power of the blast and the taking of their magic than the Fey.

A coughing noise gets my attention. Andre is laying on the ground a couple of feet from me, only, he isn't trying to get to his feet like everyone else.

"Andre?" My chest constricts again, as I see him lying there, unmoving. My body jerks awake and I crawl frantically to his side.

"Andre? What's wrong?" I'm kneeling at his side with my heart in my throat. His eyes are wide, scared, and I can hear him wheezing as he struggles to breathe. "Where are you hurt?" I look him over, desperately searching his body for a wound, but there's nothing to find.

"Oh, God," I swallow hard, and the tears come pouring down again, as I pick his head up and cradle him in my lap. "I did this to you. This was my power."

"Amarah," he wheezes and starts coughing. His eyes meet

mine and they focus. He holds my gaze and I see the love take a hold of him, replacing the fear. He brings a hand up to cup my face and he wipes my tears away with his thumb. I lay my hand over his.

"Don't cry, Amarah," more coughing wracks through his body, this time, blood trickles out of his mouth and fear sinks its claws into my chest and squeezes. Tightly.

"Don't try and speak, Andre. I'm going to heal you." I look away from him, scanning for Iseta. "Iseta! Help me!" She comes hurrying over and kneels on the other side of Andre.

"What can we do? What can *I* do?" I close my eyes to steady the rising panic. I need to be calm and focused for Andre's sake. I can't let him see how terrified I am.

"You can try to heal him, Amarah, but you've never been trained on it. His wounds seem to be internal. It won't be easy."

Iseta holds my gaze and lets me see the truth in her eyes, that this is beyond me, but I have to try. "I can do it. I can do it." I steady myself and meet her honest gaze with determination of my own. I have to do this! But what if I can't? "Find Vyla, please! Get here over to help me, now!"

Iseta nods and immediately runs off to find the Healer. I look down at Andre. His eyes are still glued to my face and his hand still pressed against my cheek. I move our hands down to his chest and I look into his beautiful brown eyes, my heart breaking, but I don't let it show.

"Hang on, Andre." I pull my power out and send it down into Andre's chest.

I have no idea what I'm looking for or how I'll even know if anything is wrong, but then I feel it. My power, my aura, senses his. I *feel* the pain as if it's in my own chest. The pain and struggle to breathe steals my own breath away. His lungs have collapsed and they're filling up with blood. I know how to imagine a cut in my skin sealing together, to heal, I have no idea how to fix the broken mess inside his chest.

I try to be strong. I try to be strong for Andre, but a small cry escapes my throat, and the tears are unleashed again. I know I won't be able to heal him. I just don't know how.

"Amarah."

Andre's voice is wet and raspy. I clench my eyes shut and shake my head. I don't want to see him like this. I can't bear to see him like this. I shake my head and heard myself mumbling, "no, no, no," over and over again.

His hand on my cheek again, "Amarah, please look at me." His voice is barely a whisper.

I open my eyes to face him. To face what I've done and the failure of not being able to save him. Being half Angel has to count for *something!* What good am I if I can't save him?

"Andre, I'm so sorry. I don't know how to save you."

"You saved me months ago," his eyes hold mine and there's no fear. No panic. I only see peace and love reflected back at me. That look, that knowledge, continues to strike my heart, ripping it apart.

I shake my head, tears falling, "no. you have to fight this, Andre. The Healer is coming. I just need you to hold on until she gets here, ok?"

"Amarah, listen to me," more coughing, more blood. Another cry escapes my throat. "I have lived more in these past few months than I have in years. Because of you. I know you love me because it was your love that saved me." He smiles broadly, even through the pain and the knowledge that he's dying.

That smile takes the broken pieces of my heart and destroys them completely. Utterly destroys them. I caress his cheek, my thumb circling his dimple, "I do love you, Andre."

"I know, love," he wheezes and coughs again. "Logan is a good man. I hate him for having your heart, but he's a good man. All I want is your happi…" he coughs up so much blood, I know he doesn't have much longer. I desperately want to look around and see if Vyla is coming. I want to shout at the top of my lungs for her to hurry but I don't want to take my eyes away from him for a second.

"Andre, please…" my voice cracks, "hold on. Just hold on. I love you. You have a piece of my heart, too, and I need you." I feel his hand getting cold against my cheek. I grab it with mine and press harder into my face. Willing the warmth back into him. "Please," I beg.

I lean down and press my trembling lips to his. His hand clenches on my cheek and his lips gently press back to mine. I can taste the copper of his blood and the salt of my tears. "Please don't go," I whisper against his lips.

"Thank you," he whispers back.

I pull my head back so I can look at him. "For what?"

"For easing my pain," he smiles weakly. "I love you, Amarah."

His chest stops moving and I watch as the light and life slip out of his eyes. I'm still holding his hand against my cheek but it's gone completely cold and dead.

That cold seeps into my skin.

Into my heart.

Into my soul.

"Andre! Andre! Please breath! Please wake up!" I look up to the sky, "God, please! Don't take him from me. Save him please! Please! I'll do anything, please!"

*Oh, My God, Amarah! What's happened? I'm coming!* I hear in my mind as a howl pierces the air far away.

I fall onto his chest, the tears flow like an unleashed river, and the crying painfully wracks my body. There's an agonizing scream that splits the air, crushing my chest, and I realize it's coming from my throat. I scream, and I scream, and I scream into his chest.

"Amarah Rey, please stop screaming. Please," I feel hands gently pulling me up and away from Andre's body.

I sit on the ground, staring at Andre's lifeless body, still clutching his cold hand in mine. I don't feel anything. I feel completely broken and numb. I tear my eyes away from his body and I look into Valmont's concerned turquoise eyes, still sparkling from the power in my blood. I look around us. Everything is happening in slow motion.

The fight is still raging around us. I realize that Valmont must have been protecting me, keeping me safe as I've sat here, completely unaware of anything and anyone, as I watched Andre die. There are still so many demons. Not as many as before, but God, there must have been hundreds in the initial attack for there to still be so many.

I return my gaze to Valmont's eyes. "The demons. Finish it, Valmont. My throat is already sore from screaming. My voice is a low rasp. Cold and empty. Completely void of emotion.

Valmont just gives me a nod and is gone in an instant. I see a blur of silver-white as black mist begins to fill the air. I close my eyes and lay my head on Andre's chest again.

No tears come.

No sobs or screams escaped my throat.

No thoughts or emotions flooded my mind.

My heart feels empty and doesn't even feel like it's beating in my chest. I close my eyes and let the empty, cold nothingness claim me.

# The Aftermath

Recover by Ruelle

I vaguely remember Valmont picking me up. His hands are covered in that thick, black blood up to his elbows. I hear him speaking, his voice echoing through me as my head is cradled against his chest, but I don't hear a word he says. He lays me gently on the couch, a fire is blazing in the fireplace, and he pulls a cover over me. I see a blur of faces and murmur of voices as people come and go but I don't register anything. I don't know whose faces I see.

I don't sleep but I'm not exactly awake either. My eyes are open but nothing makes sense. All my eyes can see is the life fading from Andre's eyes. All my body can feel is his cold hand pressed to my cheek.

I'm cold.

I'm so cold and empty.

I don't know how much time passes, but I stay here on the couch, staring out into the world, seeing and hearing nothing, until Logan's face takes up my entire vision. His lips are moving but I still don't hear a thing.

*Amarah, hey, I'm here. Can you talk to me?*

Logan's voice comes through loud and clear in my mind. There's no other sound or thought to compete with. I blink, finally *seeing* him, kneeling in front of me. His green eyes are full of concern.

*Logan,* even my thought is a mere whisper. Barely there.

*Yes, my Angel, I'm here. You haven't moved or spoken to anyone for hours. Everyone is worried about you. Please, tell me what you need.*

*Don't call me that.*

I feel his hesitation and his confusion but he's always known when to fight and when to let it go. I don't want to feel his emotion. I don't want to feel anything. I throw up a wall around my heart and sever our link but I still see the worry and disappointment in Logan's eyes. Still, he doesn't fight.

*Ok, my love. Whatever you need. Please just tell me how I can help you.*

*Bring him back.*

He sighs, *I can't.* He reaches out and moves the hair off my face.

*I'm so sorry, Amarah, I know what you're feeling. It's never easy to lose someone. This is a war and there will always be losses, but we will get through this. Together.*

Logan has lived a long time. Maybe he does know how I feel. But this isn't just a casualty of war. *I* killed him. *Me. My* power. *I* took his life. And not only did I take his life, I caused him pain before he died. I'm supposed to be special. How special can I be if I couldn't save him?

I.

KILLED.

HIM.

I can't be half Angel. I'm nothing remotely good. There's nothing Logan, or anyone, can do or say that will make any of this ok. There's nothing short of turning back time and saving him that will make me feel better.

My eyes start to water but I don't want to feel the pain. I don't want to feel the piece of my heart that's been shattered beyond repair. It can *never* be put back together. I close my eyes and shut it all out. I push down all the thoughts and all the pain. I reach for the bleak, empty, nothingness and pull it around me.

Cold.

So cold.

*Aamrah, you're shivering. I'm going to get you in a warm bath and then we can lay down and rest. Ok?*

I keep my eyes closed. I don't say yes. I don't say no. I don't care. Nothing else matters. I feel Logan's strong arms gently pick me up and carry me to the bathroom. He keeps me in his lap as he sits down on the side of the tub and starts to fill it up with steaming water. I let him undress me and undo my hair. I don't fight him. I don't help him. I'm just empty.

Numb.

Nothingness.

Logan gently lowers me down into the steaming water, then he undresses and climbs in next to me. He grabs the soap and starts cleaning my body. My body doesn't react to his hands on me as he washes away the dirt, blood, and demon gunk off my skin. He's washing away all the effects of our battle but no amount of soap can wash away my memories of Andre. I can still taste his blood in my mouth. I can still see his eyes, so full of love, fading away. I can still feel his cold hand in mine. The bath warms my skin but I still shiver. The cold is in my soul and no amount of warm water can fix that either.

He thoroughly washed my skin and hair with such gentleness. Such love. Such care. He hasn't said another word and is just being here for me. With me, but giving me space. Giving me time. I don't know if giving me space is a good thing or not. Do I want to talk about it? No. But am I worried I'll never recover from this emptiness if I stay in it? Yes. Do I want Logan to fight for me? To keep me safe? Yes. Do I deserve it? No. It's all too much to think about so, instead, I just chose not to think about anything.

After drying us both off, he picks me up again and heads into the bedroom. He pulls the covers back, lays me on the bed and slides in behind me. We're both naked but, for the first time, there's nothing sexual about any of it. He pulls me close and wraps his big body around me.

Loving me.

Comforting me.

Protecting me.

*I'm here, Amarah. Nothing is going to harm you. I love you. Try and get some sleep.*

I don't respond. I haven't said a word. I want to tell him thank you. I want to tell him that I love him too. I can't imagine if he had been the one who fell in the fight instead of Andre. A small amount of relief floods through me and I instantly feel terrible for it. Guilty for the relief that, if I had to choose between him and Andre dying, I would choose Andre. I hate myself for this thought. Andre is dead. *I killed him.* I'll never see his smiling face ever again. I'll never hear him say my name ever again. None of it's fair. None of it seems right. So, I say nothing. I close my eyes and give in, once again, to the empty, cold, nothingness.

I'm haunted by that blood curdling, agonizing scream. I hear it blaring in my head over and over again. It terrifies me but I can't stop it. I'm at its mercy. Again and again, I hear that scream.

My scream.

*Amarah! Wake up! It's all over, Amarah! Wake up!*

I bolt upright in bed, panic flowing through my body. My eyes dart around the room, frantically trying to remember where I am and what happened. Logan's hands grab my face, steadying me. My gaze locks on his and his eyes are filled with so much worry. That look pierces my chest and pokes at an already bleeding heart.

"Logan," I manage to get out. My throat feels like it's on fire as a sob catches in my throat and he wraps his arms around me.

"Shhhh, it's ok. I'm here. It's going to be ok." His words are soft and reassuring.

He holds me and strokes my hair as I cry in his arms. My body shakes violently as all of my emotions claim me. I feel like my body is breaking right along with my heart. I cry until my body hurts with the exertion. I cry until I can't cry any more, and Logan holds me through it all.

Murmuring soft words.

Consoling me.

Protecting me.

Always protecting me.

But he can't protect me from *me*. From what I've done.

When I finally stop crying and lift my head off his chest, I look around and realize we slept through the entire day. It's dark outside and I can feel that darkness pressing in on me. I shudder, still cold, despite the sweat on my skin from being cuddled against Logan.

Logan brushes my hair off my face, "how do you feel? What do you need? Are you hungry?"

Just the thought of food causes my stomach to flip, threatening to make me sick. I close my eyes and swallow against the nausea, willing my stomach to be calm. How do I feel? Physically, I feel drained, sore from head to toe. Emotionally, I feel crushed. Destroyed. Mentally, I feel terrified. Terrified of the memories that flash behind my eyes. Not only of Andre, although those memories are the strongest, but also of Valmont, Iseta, Ana, Jon, Arabella, everyone who fought and was injured.

"Everyone else.... Did anyone else..." I close my eyes. I can't bring myself to say the word. Die. Did anyone else die? I don't want to know but I have to.

"Let's get settled in the living room and we can get all the details and piece everything that happened together, ok?"

I nod my head. Logan gives me a smile, but it doesn't remove any of the worry from his eyes. He leans in and gives me a soft, gentle kiss, just a press of our lips. I return it and feel that bloody stump, that's supposed to be a functioning organ in my chest, ache.

Logan presses his forehead to mine, "I'm so happy you're here, Amarah. I was so scared. When I felt your pain, I didn't…" his voice is barely a whisper. "I can't…" he swallows hard, "I love you." He lays a kiss on each of my cheeks and then another on my lips.

I'm torn between being grateful Logan is alive, and feeling utterly disgusted with myself and the thoughts that come with the gratefulness. He's here. He's alive. Someone else isn't, and yet, I'm grateful? What I am is selfish. I'm selfish. I'm cruel.

I push down all those thoughts and all my emotions and manage to whisper, "I love you, too."

That earns me another smile, this one easing just a bit of that worry in his eyes. "C'mon," he grabs my hand and we climb out of bed.

I realize we're both naked, and the sight of Logan standing in his birthday suit before me, pure love and concern all over his face, makes my aching heart throb with desire. I want to pull him back into bed. I want to make love to him and I feel his need to do the same through our connection. I want to feel his hands and lips on me. To feel his body, alive and whole on top of me. I want to feel it and know it's real. That we're alive. That' we're together. I want to celebrate our survival.

Our survival.

I want to make love to Logan while others are dead. How can I even be thinking about having Logan in my arms when less than twenty-four hours ago I held Andre's dying body in the same arms?

I sever our link again because I'm sure I can fight the desire if I also feel it coming from Logan too. We get dressed and head into the living room together. Iseta and Valmont are sitting at the small kitchen table, talking in hushed tones. They stop and stare at us, at *me*, as we walk out of the room. Logan leads us to the couch and sits us down closest to the fire. The blanket is still on the couch and Logan covers me without needing to be asked before he sits next to me, pulling me into his arms, and holding me gently, but firmly, against him.

Iseta joins us on the other end of the couch and I can't help but remember Andre sitting in the same spot just a couple of days before. I close my eyes and push the memory away. Valmont moves to sit in the chair across from us and lounges absolutely elegantly. His eyes catch mine and they flare to life. The memory of what happened between us causes my heart to race, and my body to remember the intense, instant pleasure. My lips part and my thighs clench in response. I pull my legs up and curl them under me, holding myself more tightly, thankful that I blocked my connection to Logan. I don't want him feeling what I'm feeling right now. I just don't want to explain it or deal with it.

I realize I'm still staring at the damn Vampire and lower my gaze. I know Iseta and Logan have to see the exchange between us, even as brief as it was. How could they not? Still, this is the least of my problems. I pull the blanket tighter around me and snuggle closer into Logan. He squeezes, holding me tighter, and doesn't ease up on his hold as we sit here.

Iseta finally breaks the awkward silence, "how are you feeling, sister? We've all been so worried about you."

I snort in disgust, "worried about me? Why? I'm sitting here...*alive*, aren't I? That's more than I can say for others."

"Amarah, that wasn't your fault." Iseta's voice is soft. She's trying to be comforting but there's nothing that she, or anyone else, can say that will *comfort* me.

"Whose fault is it then?"

"You know who's responsible for everything. This is *not* on you. None of it is."

"I think Andre would beg to differ. If he was here to voice his opinion. But he's not. And you know why?" My voice is cold, angry, barely above a whisper. I continue, before anyone can even attempt to answer, because I didn't ask the question expecting a response. "Because *I* killed him. Not Aralyn. Not Luke. Not Revna. *Me.*"

I hold her gaze as I let what I said sink in for everyone around me. I let them *feel* my words and the truth that *no one* is going to say anything to change my mind about how I feel.

"Why, Iseta? Why did only he die when my power rebounded?" Andre's eyes, full of love for me, resurface in my vision. Blood pouring out of his mouth. I close my eyes to the memory and shiver. The coldness taking hold again. "I don't understand," I whisper.

Iseta lets out a heavy sigh. "Revna was using very powerful magic last night. Blood magic, Amarah, that was fuelled by your blood. Your *Angel* blood."

Logan's gaze snaps to Valmont, sitting ever so still and quiet, observing everything.

"He knows," I whisper to Logan.

Iseta continues, "you were right about the marks on the demons' heads. It was an upside down cross, drawn in your blood and powered from her Deity, Lucifer. It was a spell to not only make them stronger, faster, and harder to kill, but they were *protected* by your blood, therefore, shielded from your power. When you unleashed your power, it destroyed their shields, but didn't get past it. With nowhere to go, your power was pulled back to you with equal force. Thankfully, the other Fey only felt the slightest effects of your power. They were thrown to the ground, as if a bomb had gone off nearby, but they weren't harmed because they weren't the target of your power. You were the target as it rushed back to you, Amarah. Andre, due to his proximity to you, was directly in its path when it boomeranged back to you. He got the full force of it."

I just here, quietly, listening to everything she says. All I can do is shake my head. I don't want to believe that my power killed Andre. My power isn't supposed to hurt anyone. Ever. It's always been instinctive, a part of me, how did this happen?

"You and Valmont were just as close to me when this happened. Why only Andre?"

"I wasn't affected because I'm a powerful Witch and had my own wards and shields in place, which your power stripped away too, I might add. Valmont was not affected because your blood coursed through his veins, therefore, protecting him against your power."

"Wait, what?" Logan asks as he looks between me and Valmont. "He *fed* on you?" His voice dips and I hear the anger laced in it.

"He jumped in front of me when Revna tried to...*attack* me, kill me... I don't know what would have happened," I shake my head. "Valmont saved my life and he was dying, Logan. There was no other choice."

"There's *always* a choice," his voice is low. "Did you bite her?" His voice rumbles and I can feel his body strain with anger as he looks at Valmont.

Valmont lounges in his chair like a lazy cat. He doesn't say anything and gives off a seemingly innocent attitude but the smirk that plays on his lips and the gleam in his eye says more than words.

I'm suddenly sitting alone on the couch and Logan is on his feet before I even realize he moved. "You son of a bitch!" His voice is a low growl and my eyes immediately fall to his hands, that are no longer his hands, but his Wolf claws.

Valmont unhurriedly lifts his body out of his chair. A lazy, *lethal*, feline indeed. He takes a step towards Logan, not an ounce of fear in his eyes or body. "I tire of your threats, *mate,*" he drags out the word, "I haven't made you pay for those threats because of what it would do to Amarah Rey." His gaze slides past Logan to where I'm sitting on the edge of the couch.

"Don't fucking look at her!" Logan growls.

Valmont smiles enough to show his fangs, "but I must admit, I am losing my tolerance for your threats."

Logan's body tenses and I know he's close to losing all control. I'm on my feet before I can think. I step in between them with my arms out, "stop it, both of you." I want to shout but my voice is barely a whisper. I don't have the energy to cut through this testosterone. "Someone I care about has already died because of me. I won't survive it if anyone else dies. Please," my voice cracks and my vision becomes blurry.

I look at Valmont and see his hand start to reach for me despite all the warnings and pleading. It's as if he's moving without even thinking of the consequences. His hand stops midway and he blinks, a look of shock and realization flashing across his face. He drops his hand and takes a step back. I turn to Logan, his amber eyes bleed back to green, and his claws retract. He walks around the table, pulls me into his arms, and I let him.

"No more killing. No one else dies. Not because of me," I whisper against his chest.

"I'm sorry. We'll get through this, too. We'll deal with this together."

He leads me back to the couch. Iseta also walks back to the couch from where she had been standing as far away as possible. I was so focused on these two dominate males that I hadn't even seen her move. Valmont is back to his relaxed position in the chair, as if we had just been talking about hugging puppies and not having his life threatened. I swear, I don't think anything fazes him. I feel Logan's body, still tense and straining beside me, but he slowly starts to relax as he pulls me against him possessively.

Since we're on the topic, I have to ask, even though I dread the answer. "How many others?"

"Sixteen," Iseta says quietly. "Five from Prince Emrick's group, four from Prince Vadin's, two from Princess Hallana's and five from the Air Fey."

The tears quietly seep out of my closed eyes. "Vyla and the kids? Ana?"

"Safe. Scared and exhausted, but safe."

I let out a shaky breath of relief that they're safe, but the knowledge that sixteen others have died, guts me. "What else happened? Did we get them? Is it finished?"

"I was able to finally get Revna as she was distracted trying to hurt you. I know we wanted to get them alive if possible but I was too drained. She was kicking my ass and my only opportunity came when she was distracted by you. She left me no choice. I killed her."

I just nod, understanding her position, and not upset in the slightest that Revna is dead.

Iseta continues, "The alliance with Valmont couldn't have been completed at a better time and your blood in his veins…" she shakes her head, "*unbelievable*."

I look up at Valmont and he's still lounging, still smirking. "What does that mean? What happened?"

He shrugs, making the sloppy move look graceful, "I finished it. Like you asked."

"With his *bare hands*," Iseta explains. "He tore the remaining demons apart. *With. His. Hands*. Faster than anyone could follow. The rest of the demons were just...*gone*."

My eyes widen as I look at Valmont. I remember seeing the demon blood covering his hands and arms up to his elbows. I hadn't registered what it meant at the time.

"What did my blood do to you?"

"Increased all of my strengths," he answers calmly as he holds my gaze.

His demeanor doesn't change, his words are flat, normal, but I know how it must have felt to have that amount of power running through his veins. A Master Vampire, already stronger than most, made even *more* powerful. It really must have been like a phenomenal drug but he isn't letting onto anything.

Centuries of schooling his face, his body, and his emotions, makes it seem like what he's saying is no big deal. It doesn't matter. Doesn't faze him. I know it's all a lie. I swallow hard as a bit of fear creeps into my chest. I realize, he'll want that strength *again*, and what that means for me. This is why the Queen told me to keep my secret. I'm pulled out of that realization as Logan speaks.

"I followed Aralyn and Luke but they took to the skies. I tracked them but..." Logan runs a hand through his hair, "Luke distracted me. He stayed and kept me busy, fought me just long enough." He sighs, "Luke is dead but Aralyn got away."

"Again," I sigh. "So, it's not over. Which means she'll attack again. Again, and again, until she claims the throne or she's dead. If she...*when* she attacks again, more people will die. I can't handle any more death. I can't." I close my eyes to shut it out. I shut it all out. I lock down all my emotions because if I don't, I won't survive.

"We'll get her, Amarah. We will." Logan sounds so sure. So confident. That makes one of us. "She's losing her allies. Luke is dead, her Witch is dead. She's losing her advantage."

"We don't really know what or who she has, Logan. We're completely blind to her plans, her connections. We are always reacting and surviving her attacks, *barely,* and now we have no one left alive to interrogate. We have no answers and are no closer to stopping her than we have been since day one."

"We keep fighting, Amarah. There's no other choice."

"You just said there is always a choice," I argue.

"What are you saying? Give her what she wants?"

I shrug.

"You can't be serious?" He looks and sounds shocked.

"If they had what they wanted no one else would have to die," I say softly.

"If you think her being in power would stop anyone else from dying, you're wrong. Aralyn would not make a benevolent Queen. She would not rule as Anaxo does. If I'm sure of anything, this is it. It would be constant war and death with her on the throne and *him* by her side. And to think of you being wielded as *his* weapon..." his face tightens in anger, "it's not an option, Amarah. There is no choice but to fight. To do, and sacrifice, whatever is needed to stop them."

"Sacrifice *anyone*, you mean? Anyone except me." I look at him, gauging his reaction.

His jaw tightens but he holds my stare. His silence says enough. I already know his stance on the matter. He'll let the world burn if it means saving me. I know he said as much, but a part of me didn't believe he meant it, until now.

"Even you?" I whisper.

"That won't happen," he says through gritted teeth.

"So, what you're saying is, as long as I'm safe, it doesn't matter who else dies?" I spit the words at him. I'm angry. I don't mean to be but I am.

"There are going to be more deaths, Amarah. There's no

stopping that. As much as I wish I could stop it. As much as I wish I had the power to keep everyone safe…" he stares at me for a moment before continuing. His voice is softer now, "as much as I wish I could bring him back, Amarah, I can't. But I won't let you sacrifice yourself to anyone. Hell, not just anyone, the *devil*, Amarah. No," he shakes his head adamantly. "If that makes me selfish then so be it."

I know he's right. I'm not angry at him. I'm angry at the situation. At the truth of it all. I'm chastising him for putting me above others when I would do the exact same for him. I *will* do anything to save him. To keep him from Andre's fate. Even if that means giving myself to Lucifer to keep him, and everyone else safe. Isn't it worth it? One life, my life, for everyone else's?

*Amarah, please. Stop. Just stop with thinking like that. You know that's not an option and you know that wouldn't stop the war. I know you feel guilty about…*

*You have no idea how I feel!*

His jaw tightens again and his eyes are full of worry as he looks at me. *I would if you let me in.* He sighs, *I'm scared of losing you, Amarah. Not just if you died but I feel you pulling away from me. Shutting me out. Shutting everything and everyone out. You don't need to do this alone. Let me help you, because I can't lose you, Amarah. If you love me, if you* *want me to survive, I **can't** lose you. Don't push me away.*

My raw and bloodied heart burns in my chest and my throat tightens up. I have so many conflicted thoughts and feelings that I can't make sense of them. I don't know how I should feel. I don't know *what* I feel. So much has happened. So many things have changed and it's all a muddy, bloody mess. I don't know what to do. I don't know what to say.

So again, I sit here, pushing it all down, willing it all just to go away. I sit here, next to Logan who's pouring his heart out, trying to reach me. I can't handle the love and desperation in his eyes so, I look at my hands in my lap, and I don't say anything.

# Saving Logan

Heavy by Linkin Park, Kiiara

Valmont leaves immediately after our discussion and debrief ends. There's nothing more for him to do and he has a business and a territory to get back to running. He has Pierce and Emerson to handle things while he's gone, but he still only left when he absolutely had to, and only stayed gone as long as was necessary. He claims that young Vampires have to be...*handled,* and that he's the only one who can really keep his Vampires in line and his territory safe. I don't know a thing about it and I don't know a thing about what had happened between us.

We never had a chance to discuss any of it. A certain Werewolf has stayed glued to my side and didn't allow us a moment alone. Considering how Valmont's bite made me feel, and the fact that my blood seemed to sing in my veins at the thought of it happening again, I can't say I blame him.

Iseta had stayed one more day to help with as much as she could. Her magic is truly a gift. She helped with a lot of healing. Not only physical wounds, but she created tinctures and balms, energized crystals, and worked on healing the wounds that couldn't be seen. Even with all the help, it's not nearly enough. Healing and rebuilding is going to take time and patience, but the effort was appreciated by most. Not everyone took advantage of her offer, myself included, but what she did went a long way. Iseta fighting beside us had quelled the fear and uncertainty the Fey had of her.

She's now appreciated and respected among them and it made me happy to see my sister in my world. *Accepted* by my people. She left hesitantly. I know she's worried about me but there just isn't anything she can do. I have to get through this on my own. In my own way.

Logan and I stayed another two days and helped with the clean-up. Luckily, the battle had taken place mostly on the main street of the town. The buildings along the road were burnt and damaged, some beyond repair, and would need to be taken down and completely rebuilt. The only Blessing is that the houses off in the fields beyond hadn't been touched. The families had all been safe because we had arrived in time to keep the demons focused on us and the fighting. Thank God demons aren't the smartest creatures.

The trip back home is quiet and strained. The complete opposite of when we had come to the Air Fey. I had been at ease, happy and eager to meet everyone, to train and to have Logan by my side. I wasn't completely care free then but it wasn't overwhelming. With Logan by my side, I was happy, always. With Logan by my side, I was fearless. I could conquer anyone and anything.

But it doesn't matter who you have by your side when your personal demons rear their head and you have to figure shit out on your own.

I still haven't removed the block from our connection and Logan hasn't forced the issue. He also hasn't tried to be intimate. He's being thoughtful of my needs, not to mention, it just wasn't the time or place while we were with Air Fey, mourning. I know it has to be frustrating Logan but I just don't want to feel *anything*. I'm struggling with my own feelings. Struggling to keep them locked down so I won't completely succumb to them. I can't handle feeling Logan's feelings too. Not right now. Not when I know I'll feel his confusion. Hurt. Pain. But mostly his desire. His need. His love. Love that I don't deserve after what I've done. I feel like everything has changed and I don't know how to fix it or even if it *can* be fixed.

We pull up to the house and I let out a sigh, and it isn't a sigh of relief to be home, it's a heavy sigh of dread. I know that everything we haven't talked about is going to now bubble up to the surface and I'm not prepared for it. We take our bags in the house and I'm greeted immediately by Griffin. I'm thankful that Mariah, who had been watching him and my house, had left before we arrived. I scoop him up in my arms and let his little tongue kiss my entire face before I put him down.

I think about my life before all of this and a small part of me wishes I could go back. Even knowing that I hadn't been happy. That I hadn't been whole. If I can just turn back time and change everything, Andre would still be alive. My heart soars at the thought. But...I wouldn't know Logan either, and in an instant, my heart plummets back into darkness. So many conflicting thoughts. See why it's just easier to not think at all?

I sigh, "I'm going to shower."

I head down the hallway and into the bathroom before Logan can respond. I didn't invite him to shower with me and I hurried away before I could see his face. Before I could fall into his eyes, his arms, his kiss.

I step into the shower, the cold water is a shock as it hits my skin, but I continue under it. I grab the soap and wash my body, then my hair, moving with detached awareness. My body is moving out of habit and reflex. When I'm done getting clean, I just stood here, letting the ice-cold water rain down on me as I let the world slip away.

"Amarah? Are you alright?" I hear Logan's worried voice as he walks into the bathroom. "Jesus, Aamrah!" He steps into the shower, still fully clothed, and turns off the water. He grabs a towel and wraps it around me as he picks me up. I don't remember when I sat down or how long I've been sitting here.

"Jesus, you're freezing!" He's quickly trying to dry off my wet skin with the towel. Once he says the words out loud, I feel my body shaking uncontrollably, and my teeth chattering violently.

Logan walks to the closet and finds a long-sleeve shirt and a pair of sweatpants. He then moves to the dresser and pulls out a pair of my many fuzzy socks. He comes back over to me and starts dressing me. I help as much as I can but my body is shaking too much to control. He gets me dressed then pulls off his cold, wet shirt and jeans until he's in nothing but his boxer briefs.

He pulls me onto the bed and wraps his body around me. We always fit so damn perfectly. Like he's meant to hold my body against his. Like he's made for me and I'm made for him.

"I'm...sorrrryyy...." I say through my chattering teeth.

"Shhhh, it's ok. Don't apologize. You never have to apologize to me, Amarah." He kisses my temple and lays his head against mine.

My body slowly stops convulsing and I can breathe normally again. I feel Logan's body tense slightly behind me and I know what's coming.

"Amarah, we need to talk about this. About everything that's happened. You can't keep going on like this."

"Like what?"

"Like you don't care if you live or if you just...fade away.

You're not just hurting yourself anymore, Amarah, you're hurting me too," he whispers.

I swallow hard at his words and my chest constricts. "I don't want to hurt you, Logan. You're the last person I want to hurt."

"I know," he says softly as he rubs my arm soothingly.

"But…" his hand stops and his whole body stiffens against me.

"But what?"

"I *am* going to hurt you," my voice cracks. I take a minute to push the emotions down. I focus on the emptiness. I need to get through this. "Eventually, I *am* going to hurt you." I slide out of his arms and he lets go, reluctantly.

I sit up and turn to face him. God, he's gorgeous. He's everything to me and I hate seeing this look of anguish, pain, and uncertainty in his face.

"What do you mean, Amarah? I know you would never hurt me."

"Not on purpose but..." I shake my head, "things have happened. Things you don't know about. Things that if you knew, I don't think you'd want to be with me."

"That's not fair of you to make that decision for me. What things?"

I feel the emotions trying to claw their way back up my throat and I shove them down again. I look up at the ceiling, not wanting to meet his demanding eyes. I don't want to look into another set of eyes and see things I don't want to. Another set of eyes that will haunt me.

"What things, Amarah?" His voice is quiet.

I finally meet his gaze and I don't flinch as I tell him, "I kissed Andre." I see his jaw tighten as he clenches his teeth together but that's his only reaction. "I kissed him and told him that I loved him as he lay dying in my arms." His eyes close and he lets out a sigh.

"Amarah," he opens his eyes and reaches out to cup my face in his hand. "I'm *never* going to hold that against you. I know you cared for him. I know you loved him in your own way. We *are* connected, remember? I've felt everything that you felt for him. Yes, you loved him but you weren't *in* love with him. You chose me again and again. I've never doubted your love for me. What you did for him, as he was..." he shakes his head, "that was a *gift* for him, Amarah. That's nothing I'm going to take away from you."

Why is he so perfect? So understanding? I can't say I would feel the same why if the roles were reversed, but I see the truth in his eyes. I know that if I open our link, I'll also feel the sincerity of his words, but I don't dare. This isn't over. Far from it.

"There's also what happened with Valmont. I know you know what it means when a Vampire bites someone. The way you reacted..."

He drops his hand from my face and runs a hand through his hair. "I reacted badly and I'm sorry. The Wolf was still close to the surface. That's no excuse but..." he sighs, "Valmont *knew* what his bite would do. He knew and he *chose* to do it anyways. I'm not mad with you, Amarah, I'm pissed at him. You didn't know any better."

"Still. It happened. And..." I hesitate, not wanting to admit this out loud, especially not to Logan, "it felt like a drug." I close my eyes remembering the quick sting of his fangs sinking into my skin and the wave of pleasure it brought afterwards and I shudder. "That feeling terrifies me, Logan. I am beyond terrified because...because, I *enjoyed* it." It takes everything I have to meet his gaze. I see the pain in his eyes at the truth of my words. Already, I'm hurting him, and I hate myself for it, but I have to be honest with him.

"I'm terrified I will seek it out again and what it could lead to. I'm completely terrified of what I might do. That I won't be able to fight that craving and...and...what that will do to you," I whisper.

"I'm beyond pissed," his voice is so low and an angry growl trickles out of his throat. "But again, I'm not pissed at you. We can't make decisions based on things that may or may not happen. It terrifies me too, Amarah, but that's a bridge we cross if we ever get there and then, we handle it together."

"That's not a bridge I *want* you to have to cross for me, Logan. Ever! I don't want to hurt you in that way. I know what it feels like and I *never* want to do that to you. To what I did to Andre when I let him fall in love with me only to turn around and choose you. And you know what is even *worse?* Andre is dead. I killed him and my main thought is that I'm *relieved* it wasn't you!"

Logan reaches for me again, "Amarah..."

I scoot back and get off the bed, standing on the other side, away from him. "No, Logan," I shake my head. "How can I possibly be relieved that someone died? And not just died but...but *murdered...* by me. How selfish and evil am I?

"You're not evil..."

"You don't know me, Logan. You barely know me! There's this small part of me, deep down, that's always been excited and drawn to the dark things. The thrill of danger. Enjoying pain. That terrifies me too. And I can't help but wonder if my power knows it? You, Hell everyone, has told me that my power *is* me. Well, that's a part of me too, Logan. Maybe that's why my power killed Andre. Maybe my power is dangerous. Maybe *I'm* dangerous. And if I am, then I can't be anywhere near you!"

I start backing up away from the bed. Logan quickly gets up and walks to me. He grabs my arms, gently but firmly, to stop my retreat. "Amarah, I don't know what you're insinuating but don't think for one minute that I'm going to let you walk away from me with this bullshit excuse. I'm not afraid of you."

I look up into his eyes and I know he isn't scared. But I am. I'm shaking my head realizing the truth of my words. I've never spoken them out loud and they hit me like a sledgehammer in my chest.

"You should be," I whisper.

He reaches up and holds my face in his hands. "Amarah, I know you better than you think. I've literally been inside of your emotions for months. I know what's there and what's not. You're not evil. You're not dangerous. You are everything that is good in the world. You have such a big and caring heart and you are *so* brave. So brave. We will face anything and everything together. Don't run away from me." He's searching my eyes, pleading with me to hear him. My heart feels like it's being ripped from my chest with a blunt object.

All I can do is shake my head, "you're the one that's good, Logan. Even now, after everything I've confessed, knowing what the future might hold for us, struggles, heartbreak, *death*... you still believe in me. You still only see the best in me. You're such a good man. You're honorable and courageous. You're loyal to a fault. You love so deeply and...fuck me, you have the body of a God. You're everything I've ever wanted and I don't deserve you." I feel the emotion rising, refusing to stay down. My eyes start to water.

"Amarah, I've lived over three hundred years. Don't think that I've been a good man throughout all those years because I haven't. No one is perfect, no one. I've done things too, things I'm not proud of, we all have. That doesn't mean we don't deserve love. You deserve love, Amarah. Let me love you."

I blink rapidly but it's no use, the tears flood down my cheeks. He wipes them away as they fall, and he comes in for a kiss. His lips brush mine and my heart splits open. A sob escapes my throat and I pull back. "I love you, Logan. I love you so much that I know I need to let you go," my voice cracks, "because I'll only destroy you in the worst way."

"Amarah, you don't know what you're saying. You're in shock and grief from everything that's happened. You're not thinking clearly. You would *never* hurt me, Amarah, *never*. I know it with all of my heart. You're a freaking Angel for Christ's sake!"

I shake my head again and step out of his grasp. "Even Angels fall, Logan."

I turn and head out of the bedroom and down the hall. I reach for my keys hanging by the door. I don't know where I'll go but I need to leave. I need to go somewhere where I can think and sort through all of this clearly and that won't happen while I'm with Logan. Because I did speak the truth, every word.

Logan hesitated, thinking about everything I said, but when he hears my keys jingle and the garage door open, he comes running. He grabs my arm as I'm opening the door and spins me around, "Amarah, what are you doing?"

"I need to just...go. I need time to think about everything that's happened. I need to think clearly and I can't do that when I'm with you."

"I'm not letting you walk out of here." I see the panic and determination in his eyes.

He's doing what he thinks is right. I know that he's holding me back from leaving because he loves me. That part of me that wants to fall into him, to forget all the darkness and demons inside of me, is fighting its way up.

Images of Valmont and Andre, bloodied and dying in my arms flash across my mind. That's the truth of what happens to the men in my life. That's the truth of what will happen to Logan. And I won't survive it. I know that I won't survive it. What I can survive, is him, *alive*. Living and breathing. Even if it isn't with me. So, I shove it all back down and hold on to the fact that I'll save him whether he wants me to or not. Whether he understands it or not. I *will* save him.

"Let me go, Logan." My voice is cold and steady.

"No," he says firmly, his jaw tightens along with his grip on my arm.

I reach for my power without even thinking about it. Before I can hesitate. "I'm not asking," I shove it into his body with a lot of force. His eyes widened in shock as he's thrown back and his body hits the floor.

I'm out of the house, backing up my car, before he makes it back to the door. I pull out of the driveway, refusing to look at him. I pull onto the road and never once look back.

# 38

## Broken

The Other Side by Ruelle

Even though I know I'm doing the right thing, my already injured heart completely collapses in my chest. Not even just broken and crushed, no, it's completely obliterated into nothing. I's driving aimlessly, holding on to that familiar nothingness. I feel utterly numb and empty. I refuse to cave to the emotions, because if I do, I don't think I'll ever recover. So, I stare blindly and numbly out the windshield.

I have no idea where I'm going or even where I can go. The next thing I know, I'm on the freeway, heading towards Headquarters. That's also a home for me, if I wish. I have a room there that's mine and mine alone. I've never stayed there but I haven't had a reason to until now. All I need is just one night to myself. Once night to try and get my head straight. It's not like I can stay there forever. I do have a house and Griffin. There's a tug on my chest as I think about leaving Griffin but I'm not going to be gone forever. Just a night. Just until Logan can gather his things and go back to...Headquarters. Shit, that's where Logan used to stay before he started staying with me. Going there now is out of the question.

Muscle memory takes over and before I realize it, I'm taking another familiar route. When it dawns on me where I'm headed, I hesitate, but where else do I have to go? The answer solidifies my decision. I have nowhere else to go. The heartache threatens to take me down, but I push all the feelings down as far as they will go, and hold on to that emptiness that's been a part of me since Andre died. I rely on it now to get me through the next minute, the next hour, the next night. If I don't have to feel anything, I can survive the night. I have to believe that's true.

I pull into the familiar valet lane and am grateful to see my ever-reliant valet rushing to greet me. "Miss Andrews, what a lovely surprise," he says as he holds the door open for me.

As soon as I step out of the car it dawns on me how I must look. I'm dressed in a baggy, long-sleeved shirt, sweatpants, and fuzzy socks...I hadn't even remembered shoes. My hair is still damp from the shower and I know my eyes are red and puffy and my cheeks stained from tears. To his credit, his smile never falters.

"I'll keep it parked up front for you."

"Thank you, Josh," my voice is so low I almost don't hear myself.

Josh just gives me a small head bow as he gets into my car to move it out of the way and park it. I hurry across the parking lot and into the casino, hoping that no one else will notice my dishevelled self, and...fuzzy socks. No such luck. As soon as I step into the casino, a security guard is on me.

"I'm sorry Miss, but I'm afraid I can't let you in. We have a, ummmm, strict dress code." His voice is calm but firm.

I sigh, "I understand but I'm not here to gamble. I'm here to see Valmont."

"You will have to come back when you're dressed more...*appropriately*. Do you need me to call a ride for you?"

Great, does he think I'm on drugs? Hell, if I was security and I saw me, I would definitely think I was on drugs.

"No, no, I have a car. I'm fine, I'm not on drugs or drinking or anything," I say, frustrated. "I just need to see Valmont. I'll head straight to his office."

"Miss, you need to leave and come back, like I mentioned. Please don't make me escort you out." His voice is still calm, not escalating to my frustration, as if he's had a lot of practice dealing with crazy people. Not that I'm crazy. Although, I know I *look* crazy.

"That really won't be necessary. Just tell Valmont I'm here. If I can't go to him then just call him on your radio or whatever."

The guard look at me like I'm indeed crazy, and then he grabs my upper arm, in an attempt to lead me back out of the doors.

"Hey!" Now my voice carries and I'm angry. I don't care if people start to notice us. "Get your hand off me!" I start to struggle.

"What's the problem here?" A deep, familiar voice sounds behind me. I turn and see Pierce heading our way. "Amarah, what's going on?" He asks as his gaze sweeps over me, "what in the world happened to you?"

"You know this young lady?" The guard, still holding me, asks.

"Yes, release her now and make a mental note to remember her face and never lay a finger on her again. Understood?"

I jerk my arm out of his grasp and he lets me go. He looks at my face, as if he is indeed memorizing it, and then looks down to the floor as he takes a step back.

"Yes, sir," and then he's gone. Back to his post I'm assuming.

I rub my arm where he had held me, "thank you."

"You're welcome. Not that I blame him. He's just doing his job."

"I know."

He looks me over again and his eyebrows rise, "what happened?"

"I'd rather not talk about it. It's personal. I just need to talk to Valmont."

He nods, "come on, I'll escort you to his office so no one else stops you." He doesn't wait for me to acknowledge him before he strides off across the casino floor.

We take the long way to Valmont's office and keep to the outskirts of the playing floor. The least amount of people to see me here like this the better, I guess. We reach the stairs that lead to the office on the second floor, looking over the club. Pierce doesn't say another word or wait for me to climb the stairs before he takes off back towards the casino floor.

I climb the stairs and unease trickles into my stomach. I stop in front of the door with my hand up, ready to knock. What am I doing here? What am I going to say? What do I expect *him* to say? This is a terrible idea. Just when I'm getting ready to turn and leave, the door opens.

"Amarah Rey, couldn't stay aw..." the smirk is wiped off his face as he takes in my appearance. "Bloody Hell," he holds open the door for me and ushers me inside his office. "What on Earth has happened?"

I take a step just inside the door as he closes it behind us. He comes to stand in front of me, his eyes roaming my face. "You've been crying. Why? What's happened?"

I don't know what to say. I don't know where to start. I feel the emotions I've been cramming down, fighting to break free, just as hard as I'm trying to keep them buried.

"I..." My voice is barely more than a whisper. I start shaking my head, too fast, too frantic.

Valmont closes the gap between us and reaches for my face, stopping the frantic shaking. His hands are soft and warm against my cold skin. “Amarah Rey, talk to me. What has happened?”

His worried eyes search mine for answers. His voice...his touch, is so gentle it’s threatening to break me. All of the emotion is breaking through the surface. My eyes start to water and my throat is burning from trying to hold it all back. I step out of his grasp and hit the solid door behind me. All of the emotions flood through me at once, my knees give out, and I slide to the floor. I put my head in my hands, hiding as much as I can, as I can no longer stop the tears and sobs that escape my body. I end up laying curled on the floor, in the fetal position, fighting for control of myself.

I feel Valmont pick my shoulders up off the floor, and the next thing I know, my head is cradled in his lap. Valmont is sitting on the floor with me, in his expensive ass designer suit, comforting me. He holds me, strokes my hair, and whispers soothing words that I don’t hear. The tenderness of it all breaks me. I give into it. All of it. I let every feeling wash over me and through me.

Anger.

Fear.

Hate.

Loss.

Grief.

It all tears through me like a hurricane. But what cuts me the deepest...heartache. It’s an emotional and physical pain. I can feel my heart being ripped in two, brutally, by someone’s bare hands. It’s the worst pain I’ve ever felt and I know there’s no coming back from it. Can you die from a broken heart?

Yes.

Yes, you can.

# Darkness

Deep End by Ruelle

I don't know how long I cry but Valmont never moves. He lets me lay in his lap, breaking into a million pieces, while he strokes my hair and tells me everything is going to be ok. It's a lie. I know it. He knows it. But he says it anyway and I let him. The only time the tears and sobs stop, is when my body caves in to the exhaustion and pulls me into unconsciousness.

I vaguely register being picked up, there's an elevator, and then I'm being laid down in a bed with luxurious silk sheets. Sheets that are cold against my skin and match the coldness in my soul. I shiver as blankets are pulled over me, then I feel a caress of silky hair on my cheek, a gentle kiss on my temple, and the smell of peppermint and bergamot. Then I'm back into the darkness.

The darkness slowly fades and a dim light illuminates the world around me. I can barely see a couple of feet in front of me but I'm surrounded by trees, dead trees, that tower over me on all sides. The darkness that surrounds everything is deep and powerful. I can feel it pushing in all around me.

Whispering to me.

Coaxing me.

Calling me.

Urging my body to move.

I take a tentative step, my bare foot catches my eye, a flash of white in the darkness. I look down and see that I'm in another dress. Silk as black as the darkness surrounding me. Thin straps, barely visible on my shoulders, hold the bodice of the dress tight to my body until it loosens and flows from my hips down to the floor.

I take another step, then another. My steps growing more confident as I instinctively follow the pull of the darkness. I weave through the dead trees and maneuver over exposed roots. Gnarled branches seem to reach for me but nothing touches me, the roots don't trip me, as I make my way through the dead forest. I'm graceful in the darkness. Almost like I'm floating instead of walking.

The whispers keep urging me on. The tug in my stomach leading me forward. So, I walk and walk through the darkness. The trees start thinning and I finally reach the edge of the forest. All I can see is endless darkness ahead of me. Still, the whispers call to me. The tug in my stomach says to keep going. I do. I walk into the darkness.

Now free of the dead trees, the darkness seems to caress me. I feel it like a fantom hand running down my naked arms.

Soothing me.

Welcoming me.

The darkness is whispering that there's nothing to fear. The darkness isn't going to hurt me, but instead, love me.

Comfort me.

Keep me safe.

The dim light reflects off something ahead of me. I don't realize what it is until I'm standing at the edge of a lake. There's no rippling of water. No sound of water trickling on to the shore and receding. It's so still and quiet. Soundless. Motionless. It looks like a large black mirror.

I kneel at its edge and look in. I can barely see my face, pale against all the darkness. My eyes have no color. They look as black as the lake I'm staring into. My lips are also covered in black. It's such a stark difference compared to my skin. I look at them again and don't recognize them. I don't recognize the eyes looking back at me.

They're empty.

Cold.

Nothingness.

I run my hand over my reflection and gasp as I feel the warmth against my skin. It's so warm against my cold skin it sends a shiver of pleasure down my spine. I let my hand sink further in. It's thick. Warm and thick, unlike any water I've ever felt. Like it can hold me. I place my other hand into the lake and close my eyes, swishing my hands back and forth, relishing the warmth and the thickness of it. I want to walk into it and let it coat my body. I want to feel the warmth against my skin, let the thickness hug my body. It would be so comforting and relaxing.

"The darkness suits you, Amarah."

I'm startled at the sudden sound of a voice behind me but I recognize it immediately. I stand up and slowly turn around. Michael is standing about five feet in front of me. He's dressed all in black as well. The dress shirt, silk like my dress, is unbuttoned at the top, showing a sliver of his throat and chest. It's tucked into black slacks that ended against black dress shoes. My eyes roam over his body and my heart beat quickens. I've never seen him dressed so...*fancy*, and it suits him.

I slowly make my way up his body, appreciating every inch,

until my eyes make it back to his face. His sky-blue eyes are lost to the shadows and look just as black as mine do except, his teasing humor is still there. His slight smirk turns up the corner of his beautiful lips. He's just as stunning as the first time I saw him but now I see the danger lurking under the surface. The danger that I've been oblivious to in the beginning because I wanted him to be someone he isn't.

"Hello, *Michael*," I say sarcastically. "Although, we both know that's not your name. You lied to me."

His smirk turns into a grin that brightens up his whole face.

Light.

Beautiful.

Breathtaking.

*Lies.*

He throws his head back and laughs. His laughter seems to touch me and caress me, sending a shiver down my spine and butterflies loose in my stomach.

"Although, I have been known as the Prince of Lies, technically, I never told you I was Michael. You came up with that ridiculous idea all on your own. As if he, or any other Angel, would actually visit you. I just didn't correct you."

"Fine."

What else can I say? He's right. I had assumed who he was when he said he wasn't and *Earthly being.* I had assumed he was Michael since Michael is the one who Blessed my mother. He had only smiled when I asked him if he was Michael. He never said a word, and instead, let me run with the idea that I wanted to believe.

"What do you want? Why am I here?"

"I'm here for you, Amarah, of course. Why exactly *here*," he shrugs, "this is *your* dream, *your* creation this time, not mine. Although, I did dress for the occasion." He slips his hands into his pockets and stands there looking absolutely at ease. “I must say, I’m rather impressed though.”

The realization that this is my dream, my creation, scares me. This darkness is in *my* head. This darkness is what *I* feel. I shiver again and close my eyes. I need to focus on the man...no the *demon*, standing in front of me.

I open my eyes and gasp. He’s standing closer to me and I didn’t even hear him move. I start to take a step back but the lake is directly behind me. I still my racing heart and lift my chin.

“What do you want with me?” I hate that my voice is a little shaky.

“Shall I be honest with you? Or perhaps you would prefer more pretty lies, eh?” I can now see the blue of his eyes and they sparkle with mischief.

“You’re the devil. Why would you ever be honest with me?”

“The devil,” he takes a hand out of his pocket and waves it in the air, as if he’s waving away the word. “A word used to describe me by religious people who follow blindly and ignorantly. People who forget that I, too, am an Angel. People who fail to see the balance of the world. For you cannot have good without evil. You cannot have light without darkness. I am equally as needed in this world as He is,” he exclaims. “Yet, I’m constantly referred to as the bad guy.”

I just stare at him, not knowing what to say. There’s truth in his words but he *is* the bad guy.

“I’m sorry, Amarah, all that to say, please, call me Lucifer.” He slides his hand back into his pocket and gives me a disarming smile. Another false comfort. Another lie.

“Now, if you truly believe that I will never be honest with you, then why ask me questions at all?” He studies my face as his words hit me.

Why do I ask him questions if I know he’s the Prince of

Lies? And yet, has he ever lied to me? He led me to Revna, told me she could help me. That wasn't exactly a lie, she could have, but the goal was to just get me to her. Still, he hadn't lied. He used me to make Luke the leader of the Air Fey with the reason being that there were bigger things in play. Still, not a lie.

He must see the confusion on my face. He sighs, "I've known who you are since the day you were born. I've watched you. When your power showed itself, my initial thought was to kill you. Eliminate any threat. But now," he steps closer and his hand reaches up to caress my cheek.

There's a shock as his skin touches mine. It happens every time he touches me and I never connected the dots. It's the same shock I got when the demon at the club touched me. I refused to see it because I thought he was Michael.

"Now I see the darkness taking a hold of you," His fingertips move down my neck, then down my arm, sending goosebumps across my skin and the butterflies flying again. My breathing becomes heavy and I'm hyper aware of his fingertips on my skin. He grabs my wrist and brings my hand up between us. "And I see the blood on your hands."

My eyes snap to my hand and I see it. The bright red that coats my hand. The warm thickness of *blood*. The lake. The lake of blood that I wanted to swim in. My stomach turns and bile rises in my throat. My knees buckle, and I fall to the ground, turning my head to throw up. I close my eyes but the blood on my hand is a vivid red behind my eyelids. Flashes of that same redness covering Valmont's skin, Andre's lips. I scream and the darkness swallows it.

I feel Lucifer crouch down beside me. "The darkness is not evil, Amarah. Evil comes from what people do in the darkness. The darkness hides many things." He brushes my hair from my face and lifts my chin so I'm forced to look at him. "You and I are the same.

Angels who have fallen. I understand you and I want to help you. I want to help you understand the darkness, control it, master it. I see the darkness in you. I see the blood on your hands, Amarah, and I'm not scared. I'm the only one who will never fear you. I'm the only one who will never recoil from that darkness. Let me help you."

"Why?" I whisper.

His smile is devious, "because together, you and I can do great things, Amarah."

He stands and holds his hand out to me. The offer is more than just to help me stand. He offers to walk with me in the darkness. He offers to see the darkness in me and not run. He offers to teach me not to fear it. Not to fear that part of me. He offers to teach me how to control it. How to master it. The darkness that lurks inside of me terrifies me. The darkness will control me unless I learn how to control it.

I look at his offered hand, at where we're standing in *my* dream. The darkness is real whether I want it to be or not. There's blood on my hands. I *killed* him. I killed Andre. I took an innocent life. I deserve the darkness. But I don't have to be a slave to it.

I look into Lucifer's eyes and I believe him. I believe he will help me master it. He stands there, waiting patiently, with his hand out to me. I close my eyes, take in a deep breath to steady myself, and when I open my eyes, I'm ready.

I reach up and take his hand.

# AUTHOR'S NOTE

Once again, I want to thank you, the reader, for making all of this so enjoyable. Would I be writing if I knew I wouldn't have any readers? Honestly, yes, because this is something that brings me joy, my passion, but happiness is meant to be shared. When I wrote Awaken, I was not in the best place in my life. I was in a very miserable job and Awaken was my escape. I wrote Awaken 100% for ME.

However, Amarah quickly became her own person, and Fey Blood is definitely for you, the reader. As will the remaining two books of the series. I absolutely love to hear your thoughts, reactions and questions so, please do not forget to leave a review where you can! Amazon, Goodreads, YouTube, TikTok, Instagram, Facebook, and/or any other platform that you are a part of. Reviews and spreading the word about us, unknown Indie authors, is one of the biggest things you can do to support us. Other than loving our books of course!

As with Awaken, a year later, I have re-written Fey Blood. Again, I just needed to update everything to be on the same level of where I am currently. Also, I want to be proud of what I put out into the world, and if I'm being honest, looking back on the journey, I AM proud of the growth I've seen. I needed my books to show that too. In addition to the re-write, you can expect to see a new cover for Fey Blood coming in July 2022. Although I love the cover my husband and I made together, I decided that I want more consistency so, all the covers going forward will feature Amarah. So, stay tuned for that!

Hopefully, as I grow and get more experience under my belt, you will see less and less changes being made to my work, but again, THANK YOU to all of you have stuck around through all of these changes and have continued to support my dream.

I see you. I hear you. I appreciate you.

And if I don't, then let me know! My door is always open so, come and find me! Instagram: @harmonya.haun_author

Enjoy a sneak peek into the next book:

# DARK TEMPTATIONS

## An Amarah Rey, Fey Warrior Novel

# Logan: Control The Anger

Stay - JVP Remix by Adelita's Way

I make the hike to the Fire Fey's home in record time. My anger distracting me from my tired limbs, and my Wolf propelling me forward with the need to dominate.

The need to mate.

That last need burns hot in my veins, as I prowl down the long, familiar castle hallways and a frustrated growl escapes my throat. How many times have I made this trip? How many times have I wished that this time would be different? That this time I would *feel* something with my heart and not just with my dick?

I finally reach the large, fire-red door and change back into my human form effortlessly. I don't bother to knock. I storm in, a six-foot, naked, muscled body vibrating with anger. Anger that nothing and no one can damper. Anger that I hide well. Most of the time. She's waiting for me like I knew she would be.

So fucking predictable.

So fucking pathetic.

The Fire Fey Princess is lounging in a sea of black silk pillows and sheets. She attempts to look relaxed, at ease, but everything about her, and this scene, is staged.

Propped and prepped.

A scene for my viewing pleasure. Her long, tan legs are stretched out in front of her. The red lingerie is a vibrant pop of color in all the black, hugging her curves, and presenting them up to me as a gift. A gift I'll certainly accept but not one I necessarily want.

I stand just inside the closed door, chest heaving, fists clenching, and cock stirring. She notices the stirring and slips off the bed. She'll come to me. She always does.

I don't beg.

I don't chase.

I don't have to.

She saunters toward me in her barely-there clothing, swaying her hips excessively. My eyes take all of her in, from her bare feet to the heated look in her eyes. She is stunning, and yet, she does *nothing* for me. Yes, I'm going to fuck her. A man has needs. But it's never more than that, and that truth sends another wave of anger through my body, causing me to shiver.

Hallana smirks, as if my shiver is because of *her*. I don't say shit. I let her think whatever the fuck she wants to think. I never lead her on with pretty words or promises because they would be a lie. I don't need to lie to her. She sees what she wants to see and makes up her own happy fucking story in her head. If she sees the truth, the giant red flags I wave loud and proud, she chooses to ignore them. Why do females fall in love with the *idea* of who men can be? Why do they hang on for dear life to our *potential* and not what's glaringly obvious?

"I've missed you," she says, as she slides her hands up my chest, leaning in to kiss me.

I grab her wrists, to stop the movement, and lead her hands down to my throbbing cock. "Show me how much you've missed me,"

I say through gritted teeth, containing the anger just below the surface. When her hands grip my hard cock, I put pressure on her shoulders, pushing her down. "Show me on your knees, with your mouth."

She kneels in front of me with such heated passion in her eyes. Such need to please me. I watch as she takes my hard cock in her mouth. That first wet, hot touch of her mouth makes my cock twitch and she moans as she slowly works her mouth over me. She's watching me watch her and I know she's trying to be passionate. Trying to be sexy. I don't want, slow and soft. I don't want, *passionate*.

I grip the back of her head and push my cock in her mouth until I feel it hit the back of her throat. Again and again, I fuck her mouth, hard. She's still moaning, still enjoying it so, I push harder, further. I make her swallow my dick until I'm balls deep, down her fucking throat. I hold her head so she can't move until she's gagging and I know she can't breathe. I pull my dick all the way out until just the tip is in her mouth. I hear her take a gasping breath and then I force myself down her throat again. It isn't enough.

"Fuck," I growl in frustration, as I lift her off the floor and carry her to the bed.

The look on her face is clearly one of pride, as if my curse is a declaration of her amazing head skills. It isn't. I set her on her feet and turn her around before she can do or say anything else I don't want to hear. I grab what little fabric there is covering her ass and rip it off her body.

She looks back over her shoulder, "mmmm, I love when you're so eager to be with me."

I push her chest down onto the bed, leaving her standing on the side, her ass and pussy served up as an offering. An offering I'm about to take. I slide the tip inside of her and she starts to moan instantly. I grip both of her wrists, and hold her arms behind her back, as I slam everything I have into her. I'm not exactly small and she isn't ready for all of me in one furious push. She cries out and it isn't a cry of pleasure. I don't fucking care.

I pull almost all the way out before I slam into her again and then again. By the fourth push, her body is open and she's moaning her pleasure into the mattress. Her moans do nothing for me. I don't care if she is enjoying it or in pain. I'm cold and empty inside. Anger is the only emotion driving my body. That and a basic need for release. I just need a damn release. A release I'll get in any way possible.

"Oh my God, Logan, you're going to make me cum," she pants beneath me.

I don't speed up or slow down, I keep the pace I'm doing, knowing this will bring her over the edge. I pump deep inside of her and feel her orgasm, as her pussy squeezes my dick, and soaks it with her pleasure. She cries out again and this time it *is* in pleasure. I still don't give a shit. Her screams just annoy me.

I growl my frustration as I pull out of her, pick her up, and throw her on the bed. I kneel behind her and lift her hips to me while I push her head down into the mattress. I don't want to see her and I don't want to hear her. I just want to fuck her, get my release, and be fucking done with her. I slide my hard cock in her again, and this time, there's no resistance as I move in and out of her in a steady rhythm.

Despite her head being lost in a sea of ridiculous pillows, I still manage to hear her stifled moans. I know she's close to another orgasm so, I let her have it. I'm not that fucked up. I won't touch her, or put my lips on her, but I won't deny her pleasure from my cock. How she can ever think we could be something more than this is beyond me. I've never given her any indication this will ever change.

Yet, she still hopes.

Once she cums, screaming into the mattress, I just want it done. I squeeze her hips and start to pound into her, hard. Pulling almost all the way out in long, hard strokes. I close my eyes and focus on how tight and wet she is.

So eager to please.

So eager to get me to notice her.

To feel *anything* for her.

I growl at the thought and lose myself in the feeling of my cock inside of her. I let out a roar, trying to release the anger, and suddenly I'm sitting up in bed, panting and drenched in sweat.

It takes me a minute to remember I'm at Amarah's house and *not* with Hallana. It had only been a dream. No, a nightmare. A flashback to who I used to be. I can feel some of that anger I've carried with me for centuries starting to rise back up. Anger that was quenched in a *second* the night I found Amarah at that stupid club.

She didn't come back home last night. She left me.

She.

Left.

Me.

Just like my mother abandoned me when I needed her. Just like my pack abandoned me when I needed them. This. This is the catalyst to my anger. Because it's so much easier being angry than it is to be lonely. Last night, Amarah used her power against me. Against *me,* of all people. A growl starts in my chest, but I silence it, as I get out of bed and head into the bathroom.

Turning on the faucet, I splash cold water on my face. I need to get a hold of myself. Amarah isn't acting like the Amarah I know. She just went through a traumatic experience, one she blames herself for, and she's letting the trauma control her. She just needs time and someone to be there for her. I can't be that person if I let my anger start to consume me again. Besides, I'm not really *angry* with her.

No, my feelings are hurt.

My heart feels like it's breaking apart in my chest, and although I haven't felt this type of pain in centuries, it's exactly like I remember it. *Worse*. The spot where our connection usually sits comfortably in my chest is empty. I'm literally missing a piece of myself and I know she's feeling it too. Amarah is exactly where I've been, and where I'm trying desperately not to be again. She's allowing the anger to fill her up.

I won't let her. I won't let her become what I've been for the past three hundred-ish years. I won't let her become an empty vessel where her anger can ride and take over. It's just not an option for her. She is too... *good*. She's a freaking half Angel for fuck's sake. She can conquer this situation, these feelings, and I'm going to be there for her every step of the way, until she's back to being the Amarah I know.

The Amarah that my Wolf chose for life.

The Amarah that I am so in love with, that I don't know who I will become, if I lose her.

No. I won't let her. I *can't* let her. Not only for her sanity but for mine. Does that make me selfish? Perhaps. But my intentions are pure, and coming from a place of experience, love, and caring. It has to be enough. *I* have to be enough. I look at my reflection in the mirror, resolve and determination filling my eyes.

I just have to get through to her. I have to reach her and show her that she's not a bad person. She's not evil. I need to help her realize her truth, and what happened with Andre, is not her fault but a result of war.

I send a message through our bond.

*Amarah, can you hear me? Where are you? I am worried about you.*

Silence.

Deafening silence that sits like an anchor in my chest.

I have no way of knowing if she hears my voice in her mind or not so, I opt for the logical next step. I send her a text message.

Logan: Amarah, where are you? I'm worried about you and I'm going crazy not knowing where you are or if you're even ok. Come home or let me come and get you. I need you here. With me. I need to feel you safe in my arms. Please, Angel, I love you.

Not knowing one single thing is driving me insane. I can't help the crazy thoughts flitting across my mind. Is she cutting our connection off on purpose still or is she just too far away to hear me? Is she unconscious somewhere? Is she hurt? My mind is racing with the worst possible scenarios of Amarah, lying somewhere cold and alone, bleeding out.

I shake my head, "I can't think this way. I just need to find her and talk to her."

I hastily get ready and throw on a pair of dark blue jeans, a red, v-neck t-shirt, and black and red sneakers. I run some styling gel through my hair with my hands, brush my teeth, put on deodorant, and I'm ready to be out the door in less than ten minutes. This intense sense of urgency has me moving faster. I know I have to find her sooner rather than later.

As I walk out into the living room, I notice her dog, Griffin, trailing behind me, and the thought strikes me. I can just wait her out.

She'd *never* leave Griffin without making sure he's taken care of. Knowing this, she'll be back soon, and I can just wait and be here when she comes back. The thought lingers for a second but the anxious pit in my stomach is having no part in it. I can't just sit here and wait. I need to act. I need to go to her. Now.

"Sorry, little buddy," I pick Griffin up and kiss him on his head. I make sure he has water and food before I sit him down on the couch. "I'm gonna go get your momma and we will be back soon."

I merge onto I-40, heading West, and cut across traffic to the far-left lane. I normally drive somewhere between grandpa and reckless, but today, I'm definitely leaning closer to reckless. My nerves are shot. I'm anxious to find Amarah, to get her back home, where I can protect her. Where I can help her. Where she'll be safe.

I park in the first available spot I find, and sprint down the sidewalk towards Headquarters, my heart racing with anticipation. Amarah doesn't have many places she can go. I doubt that she'd go to one of her human friends' houses at a time like this. That would mean she would have to explain what's wrong and everything that's happened. How exactly would she explain The Unseen, Fey power, demons, and war? No, Headquarters has to be where she is. She has a room here available any time she needs it. She's here. She has to be.

I head straight for her room and don't bother knocking as I storm in, bringing my dream, no nightmare, and those same feelings back to the surface. No. This is not the same situation. Not even close. I'm not the same person either. I shake my head and clear those thoughts away as I scan the room. It hasn't been touched. I check the bathroom and walk-in closet just to be sure, but there's no sign that she's been here. There's no trace of her scent either.

I run my hand through my hair in frustration, "Where else can she be?"

Maybe Queen Anaxo has heard from her or seen her. I leave the room behind and go to find the Queen. I find her in the library.

"Ana..."I rush into the library.

"Logan? What's wrong? What happened?"

She's on her feet and heading my way before I can say more. Ana knows me better than anyone else. I watched her grow up and become the Fey Queen. She, unfortunately, witnessed my anguish and anger first-hand. She knows what's at the very heart of me and why. When my pack abandoned me, she took me in, gave me purpose. She gave me a place where I could channel my anger and direct myself towards doing something *good*. She's the closest thing I have to family. Until Amarah.

"Have you seen or heard from Amarah? She left last night and didn't come back. She's not in the right headspace after everything that's happened. I *need* to find her, Ana."

"No, I haven't," she sighs. "I was worried this might happen, but I knew she was with you so, I didn't worry as much as I should have. I should've reached out. What kind of an aunt am I if I don't even check-in?"

I shake my head, "I don't think it would have made a difference. And the fact that she didn't come here, to you, worries me that much more. She's not herself right now, Ana. She's letting the darkness get the best of her and she's acting like *she* is the dangerous one." I start pacing, because I can't stand still for even a second not knowing where Amarah is. “Do you have any idea where she could be?”

“We’ve all been in her shoes, Logan. We’ve all had to overcome our own demons. She’s strong and her heart is *good.* She will get through this.” She puts her hand on my arm, for comfort, stopping my pacing. “Have you checked in with her sister, Iseta?”

“Oh my God, of course, Iseta! How did I not think about reaching out to her first?”

“You’re worried about Amarah and not thinking clearly. That’s normal too, but if you want to be there for her and help her, you’ve got to get a hold of yourself, Logan. I’ve known you for a long time. I know what you struggle with. You have to keep your anger in check if you want to help her.”

“I know! I know. I’m trying.” I say through gritted teeth. “Thank you, Ana. I’m going to call Iseta and keep looking.”

“Let me know when you find her, please. Keep me in the loop and let me know if there’s anything at all I can do to help. She’s my family too, Logan.”

I nod and head back out to my truck. I dial Iseta as I walk. She picks up on the second ring.

“Hey, Logan. Everything ok?”

“I’m not sure. Have you heard from Amarah? Last night she left the house talking about saving me by not being with me and a whole bunch of nonsense about her being evil and dangerous. She didn’t come back and I’m worried about her. I need to find her, Iseta. Please tell me you’ve heard from her?”

She sighs heavily on the other end, “I thought this might happen. She hates hurting people and always puts the blame entirely on herself. She’s always been this way, even when she was younger. She lets her guilt consume her and this is definitely a drastic situation. Someone she cared about lost their life, even though it was *not* her fault, she feels like it is. I'm sorry Logan but I haven't heard from her."

I hold back a burst of curse words, "well, if you haven't heard from her, and she's not with Ana, where else could she be? Do you think she would have gone to one of her friends' houses?"

"No, I don't think she would involve them in anything like this. Especially if she is feeling like *she* is dangerous. She wouldn't put anyone in any kind of danger. There's only one other person I can think of that she might not worry about corrupting or hurting. I'll give you two guesses but you're only gonna need one."

The anger stirs inside of me and a growl escapes my throat, "Valmont."

Made in the USA
Monee, IL
24 October 2022

52a18262-9bd8-4540-896d-5913725d232cR01